A CAST OF VULTURES

Usually sharp-witted editor Sam Clair stumbles through her post-launch-party morning with the hangover to end all hangovers. Before the Nurofen has even kicked in, she finds herself entangled in an elaborate saga of missing neighbours, suspected arson and the odd unidentified body. When the grisly news breaks that the fire has claimed a victim, Sam is already in pursuit. Never has comedy been so deadly as Sam faces down a pair from Thugs 'R' Us, aided by nothing more than a CID boyfriend, a stalwart Goth assistant and a seemingly endless supply of purple-sprouting broccoli.

A CAST OF VULTURES

JUDITH FLANDERS

LARGE
PRINT

First published in Great Britain 2016
by
Allison & Busby Limited

First Isis Edition
published 2018
by arrangement with
Allison & Busby Limited

A catalogue record for this book is available
from the British Library.

ISBN 978–1–78541–607–1 (hb)
ISBN 978–1–78541–613–2 (pb)

Published by
F. A. Thorpe (Publishing)
Anstey, Leicestershire
Set by Words & Graphics Ltd.
Anstey, Leicestershire
Printed and bound in Great Britain by
T. J. International Ltd., Padstow, Cornwall

This book is printed on acid-free paper

For Patrick Hurd

CHAPTER
ONE

There was every possibility that I was dead, and my brain hadn't got the memo. Or maybe it was that I wished I were dead. On reflection, that was more likely.

I opened one eye and took stock. Head, pounding. Brain, fried. Eyes swollen shut, mouth like the bottom of a parrot's cage. Stomach — I decided it was better not to go there. I'm a publisher, and I'm smart, I didn't need to inventory further. I was hungover, and, even worse, for zero enjoyment the night before.

I'd been at the launch party for a new novel. It doesn't matter which novel, because while the books are different, the parties are always the same. We scarcely need to go. Instead, we could just have a drawer full of cut-outs, like those cardboard dolls children used to play with, the ones with the paper dresses with the little tabs at the shoulders to latch them onto the figures. There would be editor dolls in two styles, hipster and librarian. (In both cases, wine glasses would be firmly clutched in their tiny cardboard hands.) There would be a scattering of publicist dolls, all much better dressed. Then a couple of author dolls, one introverted and hating the whole thing, the other thrilled to be out of his or her own head, lapping up the sociability, because being a writer means being alone most of the time, with working lives that make Trappist monks seem chatty. When the sociable ones are let loose on real, live, breathing people, out spill great gushes of uncontrollable talk. The rest of the drawer would hold the rolling cast that moves from launch party to launch party: journalist dolls, book-reviewer dolls, blogger dolls, bookshop-manager dolls, literary-festival-organiser dolls.

These people are, after all, the reason publishing parties are held. We permit authors to think that launch parties are a celebration of their achievement, but that in itself is fiction. The parties are business, a way of persuading the necessary people that the new product is worth their attention. And, like everything else in the world, resources are not fairly distributed. Best-selling authors get glamorous (read, expensive) venues. New authors that publishers have high hopes for get lunch for a dozen in a medium-priced restaurant. Then there are what are known as the mid-list authors, a phrase that strikes fear into the hearts of the accounts department, or it would if the accountants had hearts. These are the authors of books you admire, but never manage to sell in any number, no matter how hard you try. (It is, tragically, still illegal to force people to buy books at gunpoint. I don't know why this kind of restriction is allowed to remain on the statute books.) These authors get anything from a small dinner party at their editor's house, because the editor is too embarrassed to admit that there is no budget for anything else, to, at best, warm white wine and crisps in the private room of a down-at-heels club.

The requirements for a successful publishing party in London are few, and easy to remember. Lots of alcohol and then, really, well, lots more alcohol. That's it. If there's a bowl of peanuts beside the crisps, that's good, but a party doesn't stand or fall by peanuts. Sometimes I imagine a publicist's checklist for these evenings:

Ascertain venue capacity;

Invite three times the number of people, in the expectation that half will not attend;

Of the half that does, remember that at least half of them will bring a friend;

The other half will bring more than one;

Order two bottles of wine per expected attendee;

Don't forget those non-drinkers! Add two bottles of water and one carton of no-brand juice;

Food is essential. One bag of crisps per hundred guests and, if budget permits, half a dozen cocktail sausages;

Relax, proud of a job well done.

The party the previous evening was textbook. It was in one of those Soho backstreets where strip-joints with names like Gentleman's Relish were slowly being replaced by art galleries and noodle bars and "artisanal" pizza places. (Artisanal means that the pizzas are lopsided, and the bottle of olive oil the server, hired for his skinny jeans and attitude, knocks over has a sprig of thyme in it.) The club itself was in a stately, beautifully proportioned eighteenth-century building that had fallen on hard times since its heyday, which was probably when the dinosaurs still roamed the earth. The annual membership fees of their few surviving members barely covered the building's electricity bill. So they made ends meet by renting out space to companies like mine. All you had to do was ignore the peeling strips of paint dangling from the stuccoed ceilings, and the gaps in the intricate parquet floors where cubes of wood had popped out. And that it hadn't been cleaned since before the French Revolution.

Everyone did ignore those details, and the dolls had come out to play. The editor doll was hipster, not frump — he was my colleague Ben, and not only was Ben not a frump, he would never have a frump author, because he would never believe that a frump could write well. And, who knew, frumpitude might be contagious, and he wouldn't risk that. The author doll was therefore a thrilled-to-be-out, rather than a hating-every-minute, type, and she was happily flitting about. Or, she would have flitted, except that there were so many people packed into two rooms that

4

flitting was out of the question. Nothing except determined barging was going to get anyone from point A to point B, so we mostly stayed in the groups we'd arrived with, and drank steadily.

My morning head would suggest it had been too steadily. Jake was already home when I got in the evening before. Being a police detective gave him superskills, and he only looked at me for a moment before he opened the fridge.

"Pasta," he said. "It'll soak up some of the alcohol."

I stared at him severely. "Have you been drinking?"

"No, sweetheart, I haven't. You have."

True. "But I don't need to soak it up. I ate at the party."

"Crisps are not food."

They weren't? I'd have to revise my whole food pyramid. As would the rest of my profession.

Jake clearly felt the conversation was going nowhere. With the water set to boil, he moved to the fridge and began to pull salad-ey things out in silence.

"Where did that come from?" It was Friday, and I did a weekly shop on Saturday mornings. There was rarely much left by Friday night, and never any salad vegetables.

"From Mr Rudiger. He left a postcard on the door to say he had a bag for us." I lived on the ground floor of a Victorian house that had been converted into flats long ago. Above me were Kay and Anthony, and their son Bim. They were actors, with erratic schedules. Not Bim. He's neither an actor, nor does he have an erratic schedule, since kindergarten timetables tend to be fairly fixed. How Kay and Anthony managed their jobs, whether it was night-time stage work, or daytime filming or advertisements or auditions (mostly the latter), and still saw that Bim's life went on as normal, was a mystery to me. But they did.

Mr Rudiger lived above them, on the top floor, and his schedule was even more settled than Bim's, because he never went out. By "never", I don't mean rarely. I mean never. In the nearly twenty years we'd lived in the same house, he'd been past our street door only once that I knew of. He was an architect, a famous one, who had moved to London from Prague sometime after the war. I wasn't sure when, but his career had been entirely in Britain until he retired in his forties, and then, apparently, spent the next three decades living in the flat upstairs. Sometimes he came down for supper, but not very often. Instead, I mostly went up to visit. Mr Rudiger didn't hold with making phone calls to people who live in the same house. In the rare instances he ventured downstairs, he left a postcard on the door if I wasn't in. I never texted him, either, because I doubted he had a mobile phone. He wasn't mobile, so why would he?

But while he wasn't mobile, he was active, and one of his activities was gardening on his roof terrace. He grew more fruit and veg than seemed possible in that tiny space, and we were often the happy recipients of his harvests.

"He also said he had some cuttings for you to take to Viv tomorrow, so will you go up before you set off in the morning?"

That was often the case too. Viv lived five minutes' walk from us. I'd met her when I'd been knocked off my cycle, and she had helped scrape me off the pavement. When I'd gone back to thank her, I'd found her flat was crammed with pots and growbags, filled with every kind of flower imaginable. I hadn't managed to get Viv over to meet Mr Rudiger yet — Viv not only gardened, but nothing happened for a mile or more that she didn't know about, so that took up most of her time. I was, therefore, their go-between, and on my way to and from doing my weekly shop, I ferried cuttings and seeds back and forth as if they were black-market goods: *Oi, mate, I've got some tomato plants in the back o' me van. Throw in a handful of dill seeds, and I'll do them for you for a fiver.* Or perhaps it was more like a Soviet-era spy-drop: *The courgette flowers have blossomed, The fennel flies at midnight.*

I made a non-committal noise, which I hoped covered my response to Mr Rudiger keeping us supplied with food (good), my lack of desire for salad (bad), my wish that Mr Rudiger and Viv could meet so that I could stop being their courier (lazy Sam) and an acknowledgement that Jake was cooking and I was just sitting there watching him (*bad* Sam).

But before I could act on any of those thoughts, Jake had the sauce heated and the pasta boiled and dished up. He put a normal-sized helping at his place, and a much larger one in front of me. "Eat," he said.

Cranky Sam took over. "Why?"

"Because you're cranky when you've been drinking."

This was true. I ate.

* * *

Jake wasn't scheduled to work that weekend, but even so, I wasn't surprised to find he was gone by the time I woke up. I ran, in a half-hearted fashion, a few times a week before work, but Jake liked to hit things, so he went to the gym on Saturday mornings when I was at the farmer's market, and we met up afterwards. He'd come with me to the market a few times, but he drove me crazy, buying all sorts of weird food: blood sausage, or cheese that smelt like it had been dug out of the drains. Then it sat in my fridge for a week, because he was working a particularly difficult case and wasn't home to eat it. Once I'd made him take his purchases back to his own flat, but that was even worse, because when I'd opened his fridge a month later, they were still there, and their mould had got married and had babies. So we had silently agreed a Saturday division of labour: he hit things; I went hunter-gathering.

There was no help for it. I staggered up, and through my morning routine, caffeinating myself liberally as I went. By the time I went upstairs for Mr Rudiger's ferry-load I was as alive as I was going to get. He had a few pots of cuttings and a bag of figs from the tree on his terrace for Viv, and extra figs for me, my fee as courier. I have trouble with deferred gratification, so I ate a fig as I headed downstairs, wiping my sticky hand surreptitiously on the back of my jeans. I doubted that there would be any left by the time Jake got back, but then, I was the courier, not him.

Viv lived halfway between me and the market, so the duty wasn't exactly onerous. We'd got the transfer down

8

to a routine, and I just rested my cycle against the railing when I got to her flat, knocking and calling out, "It's me!" when I heard her footsteps. Viv was barely five feet tall, and so for her the peephole in her front door was a decorative rather than a functional device. We good-morning-ed each other, lovely-day-ed a bit, and I'd handed over Mr Rudiger's consignment before I noticed that she had nothing to give me in exchange. That was unusual, especially as we were in the middle of peak growing season. So was the fact that she was hesitating. Viv went everywhere, knew everything, and you'd have to be a fool to cross her. If I had to guess, I'd say she was seventy, but if someone told me she was a spry and active eighty-eight, I'd believe that too. Or ninety-eight, come to that. What she never was, was hesitant.

So now I waited while she paused for a moment. Finally she said, "Do you have time for a cup of tea?"

I dislike tea, but she wasn't asking me because she thought I was thirsty. I chained up my cycle and went in. Viv's flat was in one of the many council blocks in my neighbourhood that had been built after the war. She'd told me that her parents had been in the first intake of tenants, and she had never left. Nor did it look like she had ever redecorated, apart from a bit of fresh paint now and again. The rooms were a time capsule of 1950s style: black-and-white checked lino, Formica cabinets and all. The rest was plants, plants everywhere, on every surface, on the floor, on top of the small, squat, bulging refrigerator, on the windowsills, hanging from hooks in the ceiling.

There wasn't a moment to look closely, however. Viv moved briskly, thought briskly, and had little patience with people who didn't keep up, physically or mentally. I skipped along to catch up with her as she marched down the hall to the kitchen. That was the only room I'd ever seen for more than a moment, and it was probably the only room she used for anything other than sleeping or a location for more plants.

By the time I reached the doorway, just two steps behind her, she was already carrying the teapot over to the table. Cups and saucers had been laid out, and the biscuit tin was open. Whatever her hesitation earlier, she had planned to ask me in.

I sat and waited while she poured, but I didn't bother to make conversation. She'd get to what she wanted when she was ready. It took longer than I expected. She fussed with the cups, passing me the milk and sugar even after I'd refused both, then the biscuits. Those I didn't refuse: she was a terrific baker. Fresh figs and newly baked biscuits might be the death of me on the morning after a launch party, but it was a hell of a way to go.

Finally she gave a sniff, sat up straight and looked me in the eye for the first time since I'd arrived. This was the Viv I knew and secretly feared. "I don't know what to do. I need some help," she said. No wonder she'd been fidgeting. I doubted those two sentences had ever passed her lips before. Viv always knew what to do, and she gave help, she didn't ask for it, much less "need" it.

"What can I do?" I kept my voice neutral. If she thought I felt sorry for her, she'd probably bite me.

"A friend of mine has gone missing." Once she'd begun, the rest came more easily. "His name is Dennis Harefield. He lives upstairs, has lived there for years. I saw him last week, and he said he'd have supper here on Thursday. Everything was normal. But he didn't come, and there was no one at home when I went up to knock. He hasn't been home since. I've asked, and no one in the block has seen him."

"Since Thursday?"

"Wednesday. It was earlier in the week when I asked him, but one of our neighbours saw him on Wednesday morning. No one has seen him since then."

Only three days, but if he was in his seventies or eighties like Viv, even that short a period was worrying. "His memory is OK?"

Her glare would have shrivelled steel. "He's in his forties." So not dementia, and three days wasn't exactly a big deal. He'd forgotten Viv's supper invitation, and was away for work, or spending a few days with friends or family. Or he'd met someone and supper with Viv had got pushed to the back of his mind.

She saw what I was thinking. "I rang his office — he works for the council — and spoke to a colleague. He hasn't been in since Wednesday, but they were expecting him. He had meetings booked, and hadn't put in for holiday leave. There's something wrong. He didn't stop his newspaper." She looked at me, eyes wide. "He didn't ask me to water his plants."

I could see this was the clincher for her, but, "There could have been a family emergency."

"He doesn't have any family."

"An emergency with a friend, then." I wasn't going to suggest that he'd met someone and was shacked up.

Viv shook her head stubbornly. She looked like a bulldog, small but scrappy, and not ready to give an inch. "I've known him for years. In all that time, he's never forgotten to do something he'd said he'd do. If he said he was coming to supper and he couldn't, he would have phoned or texted. He *never* forgets anything."

Not sex-brain amnesia.

"I thought he might have collapsed, so I asked his next-door neighbours to look in through his windows — you can see his sitting room from the balcony they share." She was speaking more quickly, and I suspected it had been a bit more creative than that.

"What did they see?"

"Nothing. If he's in the flat, he's not in the sitting room. And if he's in the flat, I would have heard him. His flat is directly above this one. I can hear him when he's home, or coming and going. I haven't heard anything since Wednesday night."

"Did you try the hospitals?"

She was scornful. "Of course I did. First thing. No one with his name in any of the hospitals in the phone book." Only Viv would still have a phone book. I tried to remember when I'd last owned one, and so I missed the next part. ". . . the shelters, too, in case he collapsed with no identification, but they don't take people's names."

"You've spoken to the police." This time I was careful not to make it a question, but when Viv looked as though she were sucking lemons, I continued for her. "You did, and they told you there's nothing they can do, a grown man can take off without —" I waved my hand dismissively.

Her lips thinned. "I'm an old woman fussing over nothing."

"The local nick said that? To you?" It wasn't tactful, but I couldn't imagine either that they thought that, or, more especially, that they'd been stupid enough to say it to her face.

She gave a small, tight smile, satisfied that her worth was realised, even as she was annoyed. "No, the locals don't think that, but Missing Persons is centralised. I spoke to someone in a call centre. They've logged it, since it was more than seventy-two hours since he was last seen, but they aren't going to do anything apart from checking the hospitals, which I've done anyway. Which is why —" she gathered herself "— which is why I wanted to speak to you."

"Me?" What could I do? Surreptitiously I looked down at my shirt. Nope. Not my day to wear the Superman "S".

"We need to go and look around his flat. See if he packed a bag, or if there are any messages on his landline."

I wasn't too sure I wanted to be part of snooping on someone I'd never even met. "I don't know about listening to his messages, but when you go up to water his plants while he's away, you can at least see if anything looks odd."

"Oh, I don't have his keys. I've never been into his flat. He may not —" She broke off, unsure if she should say something as unpleasant as the thought she'd just had. I leant forward. "He may not even have any plants."

I hoped my wide eyes would be understood as shock at such an enormity, not an attempt to stifle a hysterical giggle. I concentrated on the main point. "If you don't have his keys, then who does?"

"No one. That's why I need your help. You can easily climb onto his balcony from the neighbours'. His bedroom window is slightly open. If we push a stepladder across from one balcony to the next, you'll be able to climb in with no problem."

She said it in the tone she used to tell me on other weekends that the seedlings she was sending to Mr Rudiger needed to be watered every day.

It is not often, my friends will agree, that I'm rendered completely speechless, but I was then. I tried again, but no, I still had no idea how to respond. Finally, I said, "A stepladder." Don't ask me. I don't know why that was the detail I latched onto. It just was.

Viv looked embarrassed. "I don't think I'm tall enough, even with the ladder." Not, *I'm too old to be climbing over a balcony railing*, you note. Or even, *Maybe, just maybe, I shouldn't be contemplating breaking into someone's flat*. Nope. Her concern was her height.

I nodded as though that made perfect sense. I thought that shrieking, "Holy shit, woman, you want me to *break into someone's flat?*" might tip her off that I disapproved.

She got over her embarrassment at her lack of inches, and continued: "It's the only way to find out where he might have gone, and if he's all right."

I didn't respond, because I still couldn't think of anything to say.

"Someone needs to," she added, as if it were a given. As though it had been handed down to Moses on a tablet of stone. Right after the Ten Commandments, Commandment Eleven said: Thou shalt illegally enter thy neighbour's flat whenever he's been gone longer than you think appropriate.

I began to shake my head, *no*, and found I couldn't stop. *No, no, no.* I pushed myself away from the table. "I can't. It's wrong. I'm sorry. Really sorry. But I can't."

I knew that if I stayed she'd persuade me. So I ran.

I went to the market on automatic pilot. I know I went, and I know I bought things, because when I got home, I had food in my cycle panniers, and it is rare in north London that the food fairy descends, waves a stalk of purple-sprouting broccoli and *poof*, your cupboards are full. But I don't remember any of it, which became evident when I unpacked the bags back at the flat. No milk, no eggs, no bread, but a fine collection of disparate items that looked as if they'd been chosen to illustrate a children's alphabet chart rather than provide a week's supply of suppers: one apple, two bags of beans, three carrots.

I was standing staring accusingly at the food, as though it were its fault, when my phone rang. I looked at the display: Helena.

"Morning, Mother."

"Good morning, darling. I forgot to mention when we last spoke that I'm having a party next Saturday. Drinks and lunch, in the garden if the weather holds."

I made an indeterminate noise. Helena's friends are lovely people — Helena is a lovely person. It's just that she's exhausting to be with, or even sometimes to think about. She's a partner in a commercial law firm and works long hours — she's at her desk every morning by seven, and she rarely puts in less than a twelve-hour day. Yet she still finds time to socialise. She sees friends, she goes to theatre and museums, goes to dinner parties, has dinner parties and, as this call showed, also lunch parties.

By contrast, I'm not much for parties of any sort. Had I not seen photographs of what was indubitably a small, cross, unsocialised baby-me in hospital after Helena had given birth, I would assume I was adopted. While making bright chat to the movers and shakers of the professional world — because those are the people Helena knows, doctors, and lawyers, and Indian chiefs — is pleasant in theory, it's hard work for me in practice. I don't really do groups. Or even two or three people. Sometimes one is a burden. But there was no point in refusing this invitation. Unless I could come up with a good reason — a lunch I'd already agreed to, or theatre tickets I'd already bought, or the Four Horsemen of the Apocalypse scheduled in for an enjoyable afternoon of war, famine, pestilence and death — I wasn't going to get out of it. "I'll check my diary. It's in the other room," I offered feebly, knowing full well that Helena knew full well that I was on my mobile, and could walk the fourteen steps to that faraway "other room" while we were speaking.

She didn't lower herself to point out the obvious. "Splendid. I'll expect you and Jake unless you have a conflict."

Fabulous.

Given my morning, I decided I might as well round it off by letting Mr Rudiger know I didn't have whatever it was Viv had been going to send over, because I'd freaked out when she suggested the odd spot of breaking and entering. As I walked up the stairs, I thought what I'd do if one of my neighbours vanished without warning. Kay and Anthony were in their thirties, and if they disappeared there was no doubt the police would respond the same way they had with Dennis Whoever. Because they lived directly above me, the way Viv's friend did above her, I could tell when they were home too, and which room they were in by their footsteps. If the three of them suddenly weren't there, if they hadn't mentioned they were going away and we'd made plans for dinner? I had never met their families, didn't know what part of the country they came from. Searching for people named Lewis, no location, no first names, wasn't feasible. But I had their keys. Going up to check would be no different from Kay bringing Bim through my flat so he could play in my garden when I was out, or me going up to borrow eggs or milk if I ran out when she wasn't in, both routine occurrences.

If Mr Rudiger went missing, on the other hand, I'd be deeply concerned after three minutes, never mind three days. If he didn't answer his door, I'd worry he'd fallen, or had a stroke, and I'd try and get in touch with his daughter. Petra Rudiger wasn't a common name in London, so I had a fair chance of finding her if the police refused to take it seriously, although I suspected they'd be more concerned about the disappearance of a seventy-something agoraphobe than a forty-something-year-old in full employment. If they did nothing, though? I paused on the stairs. If they did nothing and a window was open at the front, yes, I'd ask our next-door neighbour to give me access to their roof terrace and I'd climb over to Mr Rudiger's. I wouldn't think twice.

I turned around and went downstairs to get my cycle out again.

CHAPTER
TWO

On the way back to Viv, I consoled myself: Viv was a busy woman, rarely at home; it wasn't likely she'd be sitting around waiting for me to come back. But I never had that kind of luck. It was as if she had followed my thought processes, and knew that I would return, and, to the second, when. I had barely knocked before the door opened and Viv came out, already equipped with the stepladder. "The backstairs," was all she said as she set off towards the rear of the building, me scuttling along behind her like a remorseful child.

Viv had been slightly economical when she described the neighbours looking through Harefield's sitting room window from their balcony. They could only have done that by climbing over the railing that separated the single balcony into two. Viv had briefed them today, too, because their door swung open at Viv's knock. She didn't trouble to introduce me to the couple who stood there, just marched through their flat and out to their balcony with nothing more than a "Lovely day" thrown over her shoulder. *For breaking and entering?* I felt like asking, but didn't, being far too cowed. I also didn't ask why, if they were all agreed that this was the right thing to do, the neighbours, both taller than me (and, truthfully, while I was taller than Viv, almost everyone else is taller than me), couldn't have done it. Maybe it was against their tenancy agreement: No pets, no ball games in public areas, no B&E.

Viv was right about one thing. If you had access to the connecting balcony, it wasn't difficult for anyone over five feet tall to reach the next flat. I hit the qualifying height with a few inches to spare, and slid across without a hitch, unfortunately. The neighbours, still silent, passed the ladder over to me, and with that I had no trouble reaching the open bedroom window next to the sitting room, pushing it wide. I left the ladder by the door to the sitting room. I might break and enter to get in, but there was no reason not to leave by the front door.

As I sat on the windowsill, Viv stood on the neighbours' terrace like a staff sergeant giving me my marching orders: "You might not be able to tell if he packed any clothes, but see if his toothbrush is there. And check the fridge. Did he empty it out, or are there any perishables?"

If she was going to play detective, she could be part of the illegal section of the day's activities too. "I'll open the front door. You can come in that way." And I slid inside without waiting for her reply.

I didn't stop to look around, but even walking straight through, by the time I reached the front door, Viv was there already. So were the neighbours, but she wasn't having any of that. This was her moment. "Thank you," she said, regal as the queen, dismissing them without any other words.

And by God, it worked. The man looked like he wanted to protest, but his wife was smart enough not to question Viv. She stepped back right away, towing her husband away behind her before closing their door firmly, leaving us felons on the other side.

"You take the bedroom," said Viv. "I'll look around the sitting room." I didn't know quite what she expected to find — a hand-drawn pirate map with an "x" marking the missing neighbour? But I didn't protest, and meekly headed to the bedroom. I didn't want to be there, and the faster I looked around, the faster I could get out.

I stuck my head into the bathroom first: towels on the floor, toothpaste spit and beard-bristles in the sink. Toothbrush and toothpaste in a glass on the counter. I opened the medicine cabinet. If he'd packed to go away, I couldn't tell. There didn't appear to be gaps where things had been removed. There was a cellophane packet of disposable razors on a shelf, so if he'd taken one, I'd never know. And he might have a travel toothbrush if he went away with any regularity. The towels and the soap were dry, so either he hadn't been back since he was last seen, or he hadn't washed. We could put up a notice: Missing, One slightly smelly council employee.

I returned to the bedroom, which was no tidier. The bed was unmade, piles of clothes were thrown over the single chair, and more spilt onto the floor. I checked his cupboard. More clothes on the floor of it, as well as on hangers. There wasn't a clutch of empty hangers to suggest that some items had been taken for packing, but there was no way of telling for sure. I toed the clothes on the floor to see if there was a suitcase or bag of some sort behind them, but there was nothing. Nor was there anything on the top of the cupboard. Again, he might have taken the bag, or the bag might not exist. I checked the bedside tables. One was empty, the other had a heap of odds and ends on it: dirty tissues, a pair of reading glasses, a part-filled glass. I sniffed at it. Water. Under it was a pile of magazines. I thought that porn had all moved online, but apparently not.

I hastily continued. The drawers beneath were empty, but whether that was because the contents were laid out above, or they'd been packed and taken with him, or whether he just didn't keep anything in them, I had no idea. At any rate, no itineraries, diaries, notes with names of places or hotels or travel plans. I swept my hand across the bottom of the first drawer. Dust, which suggested he didn't put anything in them.

I turned in a circle, but there was nothing else in the room. No chest of drawers, no other furniture. I dropped to my knees and looked under the bed. If there wasn't a bag in the cupboard, he might keep his suitcases there. The blankets and sheets thrown back made a little dark tent underneath, and I reached into my pocket for my phone, which had a handy-dandy torchlight app that my life as an editor had never provided me with an opportunity to use thus far. It gave little more light, but made me feel as if I knew what I was doing. I squinted in the gloom. There was no visible road atlas, no envelope of bus or train tickets, no pad with a list headed "Leave for Acapulco

22

tomorrow" that I could see on the side near me, but the weak torchlight beam barely lit half a metre around. I needed to check the far side to see if there were more than dust bunnies and dirty socks there. I was just disentangling myself from the hanging sheets when a phone rang behind me. In my jittery breaking-and-entering condition I jumped and hit my head on the slats of the bedframe above.

I forgot I was nervous and in a place I wasn't supposed to be. "Shit!" I shouted. That hurt.

The ringing phone was under the pile of clothes on the chair. I started to look through them as Viv bustled through from the sitting room, glaring. "Language!"

I was damned if I was going to apologise. At her urging, I was in a place I didn't want to be, doing something I didn't want to do, in the course of which I'd hurt myself. That was worth a "Shit!", and if she didn't like it she could find someone who didn't swear when they hit their head. I wasn't planning on saying any of that to Viv. I'd hit my head, I hadn't lost my mind.

Instead I said, "There's a phone here, in the pocket of a pair of trousers. I didn't get to it before it stopped ringing, so I didn't see who was calling. They didn't leave a message." Viv took it out of my hand: anything worth looking over was, the gesture said, her job. I left her scrolling through his contacts, and dug around on the floor for my own phone, which I'd dropped when the one on the chair rang.

Once I had it in my hand I gave up. There was nothing to be found in the bedroom. "Did you look in the kitchen?" I asked.

Still scrolling, she shook her head. That "shit" had seriously put me in the doghouse. I didn't care, I just wanted to be out. I checked the fridge, as ordered. There was nothing in it apart from a six-pack of beer. The freezer had a lone bottle of vodka and an ice tray. I opened the two cupboards that were all the tiny galley space contained. Four plates, four bowls, four glasses, four mugs. Cutlery in a drawer. A jar of Nescafé. No food. The bin explained that: at least half a dozen empty silver-foil containers, and a couple of bags with logos of Indian restaurants. The emptiness of the fridge didn't indicate he had gone away, it indicated that he didn't cook.

Viv stood in the doorway. "We're finished here," she said. The words every trespasser wants to hear, so I was right behind her.

Once back in her flat, we went straight to her kitchen, and Viv had the kettle on in an automatic gesture: you were in the kitchen, you made tea. I told her what I'd found, or not found. There was not only no food, there had been no plants anywhere in the flat, so she seemed to be reassessing her friend's character.

"Nothing looked out of place in the sitting room, either," she said. "If he had a computer, it was a laptop, and it wasn't there. I didn't see a case for it, or a charger, so either he took it with him, or maybe he just used his work computer for everything." Viv had missed her calling. The CID should have snapped her up long ago. "There was a phone charger, and it fitted the phone you found." She looked approvingly at me, as if finding a ringing phone a metre away from me was on a par with winning a Nobel Prize.

"Did you find anything on his phone?"

"No messages. The texts were all sent before Wednesday, and none of the ones coming in since indicated they knew where he was, or that the senders thought he'd gone away, apart from one from a work colleague, it looked like, reminding him of a meeting he was missing.

"His contacts are there, but we can't ring each one, can we?" For a moment she looked like she wished we could. "There was one labelled 'Mum', but . . .'"

She trailed off and I picked up, "But you can't ring a strange woman and say her son is missing, and he left his phone behind . . ." *and you got her number by prowling uninvited through his flat*, I added silently.

She acknowledged the spoken part. "There wasn't much in his desk," she went on. "Mostly to do with the boys' club he runs. And his spare keys." She jingled a ring of keys at me.

"His keys." I'd thought we were breaking and entering, but Viv had decided to up the stakes and move on to burglary.

"I'll keep the keys." I must have looked blank, because she became defensive. "It will be easier when one of us goes back for his post."

Goes back? His post? Commandment Twelve: Thou shalt nick and paw through other people's private correspondence.

I made one of those noises again, ones I'd perfected with my mother, and now found I was using on Viv quite a lot too. I don't know what it was about me and bossy older women, but I attracted them like ants to a jam-spill. I was the jam.

I abandoned that analogy, and instead headed home, this time remembering to collect Viv's seedlings for Mr Rudiger before I went.

That was handy, as I could tell Jake that that was why I was late. He hadn't been home when I'd come and gone, but he was waiting when I got back, and had seen the groceries already in the kitchen. "I forgot the sodding cuttings," I mumbled. It wasn't exactly a lie. I had forgotten them. "Viv's neighbour's gone missing, and she was worried. That distracted her, and she didn't hand them over."

Jake just nodded, not interested.

For some insane reason, I felt the need to fill him in. "She called Missing Persons, but they said it was too early for them to do anything. She tried the hospitals, too, but with no results."

"How old is he?"

"Forty-odd." I put my hand out, traffic-cop style. "I know, I know. He's probably away, or visiting friends. She's just worried because he arranged to go over and have a meal with her, and didn't show up and didn't get in touch to cancel." Jake just looked at me. "I agree," I went on, as if he'd said something, "but she's worried all the same."

I left it there, and took the cuttings up to Mr Rudiger. As I walked upstairs, I tried to work out why I hadn't told Jake everything. It wasn't even the breaking and entering, although theoretically Jake would disapprove of that. Cops on the whole don't like it when people break into places. But if I'd told him Mr Rudiger wasn't answering his door, I wouldn't even have to go over his terrace from next door, because Jake would be there before me. He wouldn't think of it as breaking and entering. It was — I stood on the landing and stared at the wall while I thought — it was because we knew Mr Rudiger, and we didn't know Dennis Harefield. That Viv knew Harefield the way we knew Mr Rudiger wouldn't weigh in the balance with Jake. Jake didn't know his neighbours in Hammersmith. He'd lived in his flat there for nearly a decade, but his erratic work hours, and general London life, meant that he rarely saw the people who lived nearby, or, if he did, not enough to recognise them. In the time we'd been together, he'd been surprised by the closeness of people in my street, and he wouldn't move from the more general feeling of distance Londoners have for their neighbours, to the connection we felt to Mr Rudiger, and Viv felt to Harefield.

I left it there for the rest of the day, and through most of Sunday. By evening, however, when Jake settled in front of the television, I found myself telling him that I needed to do what I call desking: sitting at my desk to pay bills, get estimates to renew my household insurance for slightly less than the national debt of a third-world country, check credit card receipts to make sure someone hadn't cloned my card and was living it up at a motocross track in Wisconsin, things like that.

And it wasn't a complete lie. I did desk for myself for a while. And then I pootled about on the computer, doing mainstream online searches — my skills don't go much further than Facebook and Twitter (no accounts for Harefield under any variants of his name I could think of). I googled him too, and to my astonishment got back only a couple of hundred hits. Being named Dennis Harefield was similar to being named Rhododendron Kaufman, or Phylloxera Tradescant: there just weren't that many of them. Not that the scarcity helped. Most of the references were to an Australian officer in World War I, whose house had been used as a field hospital. That was mildly interesting, if you stretched the definition of interesting. There was a Dennis Harefield who was an opera singer. I watched a clip of him singing an aria from *Boris Godunov* on YouTube. No clues there.

And then, finally, well into page three of the Google hits, I found Viv's neighbour. There was a link to the council's website, where he was listed in the environment department, which, as far as I could see, meant he had something to do with street lighting, or maybe parking. It was hard to say, since the website had been designed to ensure that no taxpayers were able to tie any employee to any service they might need. But whatever he did, there he was. I sent an email, merely saying I was a friend of Viv, that she was worried, and would he please get in touch, in case he was on holiday, or had run away with a mail-order bride from Uzbekistan. Or in case, more plausibly, he had simply forgotten to tell Viv he was going away. A man who had no house plants might do anything, after all.

* ★ ★

By Monday, however, Harefield was pushed down the agenda. During the night, I had been woken, first by sirens, then by the noise of a helicopter hovering overhead. Both times I'd thought little of it, and had fallen back asleep immediately. While the streets near me are residential, and very quiet, we're not far from Camden market, and from time to time there is a police crackdown and some mass raids that net them (I presume) a few drug dealers. The problem is no worse around here than anywhere else, but because the market attracts tens of thousands of teenagers, all in urgent need of leather trousers and T-shirts with obscene slogans commenting on their boyfriends' prowess, there is, if not more drug-dealing, then more overt drug dealing, than elsewhere. The pub at the bottom of my street had been a well-known spot to buy weed for years. Recently it had been taken over, poshed up into a gastropub, and it probably now sold the same amount of weed, just behind a more respectable façade.

It was only when Jake and I left for work the next morning that we discovered that the night's activity had been more destructive: at the intersection of the main road we were stopped, blocked by yellow crime-scene tape as far as the eye could see. Jake took this in and headed directly over to a lone PC who was standing, bored, in the road, waiting for some random miscreant with evil in their heart to attempt to cross to the Tube station, so that he could tell them they couldn't.

I knew that the first rule in the PC's Handbook was "Don't tell anyone anything they want to know", so I didn't follow. Instead I found a group of neighbours.

"What's happening?"

As I expected, they knew everything. "A fire," said a woman I recognised but didn't know, adeptly fielding her toddler, who was heading for the crime-scene tape that bounded a now gloriously empty road. "At the corner of Talbot's Road. In the empty house. It started around midnight, and was burning for hours."

I turned behind me, as though I would magically be able to see around the corner to Talbot's Road, so it took me a moment to hear what she said. *The* empty house, not *an* empty house. She wouldn't have said that if she meant a house where the owners were away, or one that was for sale. Everyone in the neighbourhood called the old boarded-up junk shop "the empty house".

This was no longer simply something that was going to delay my trip to work. "Did they all get out OK?" I asked. Because everyone in the neighbourhood also knew that the empty house wasn't empty.

A chorus of "fine" from the group, who were already up to speed. One, a grey-bearded man, volunteered: "I saw Mo half an hour ago. She said they're doing fine."

That was a relief. It meant I could stop being a concerned neighbour and go back to being a commuter whose trip to work was being disrupted. But before I could spend too much mental energy on how I was going to get to the office, Jake was back. "A fire," he said. "In an empty house down —" He gestured down the hill.

"The junk shop," I agreed.

He looked from me to the group surrounding me. "A junk shop?" he asked. "They said it was empty."

"It was a junk shop. Before. Years ago. It hasn't been for a long time." I moved from being a source of information to trying to get some. "What did the PC say? Does he know how it started? And we know everyone got out OK, but did they get all their things out? Do they have somewhere to stay?"

Jake had turned, was about to move away, but now he stopped. Slowly he turned back to our little group. "'Everyone'?" he echoed. "'Somewhere to stay'? The house was empty."

"Yes, technically it was empty."

Jake gave me his police look, flat and guarded, while everyone else remained silent. "How is a house technically empty?" he demanded, as though it were my fault.

I did most of the local shopping, so Jake had little occasion to chat with people who knew what was happening in the area. And he drove to and from work. Maybe the lights behind the boarded-up windows in the empty house weren't as noticeable from a car as they were when you walked past in the dark. "It's technically empty because squatters live — lived — there," I corrected. "I don't know how many, or if they're always the same ones, but there have been people living there for years."

"The same ones for a long time," said the woman with the toddler. "Mo and Dan have a ten-year-old who's been at school with my older boy since

31

kindergarten, so they've been there for at least five years."

"And Mike did my wiring when we moved in," added a woman I'd never seen before. She was dressed like me, office clothes, and had probably been blocked en route as we had been. "That was six years ago. And he'd been recommended to me locally, so he and Steve had probably been there a while by then."

Jake looked at me, toddler-lady and office-lady as though we were suspects in a particularly repellent type of crime. Was knowing your neighbours an arrestable offence? In London it probably was. "How many people were aware that this 'empty' house wasn't empty?"

The others turned to me. *He's yours,* was their unspoken consensus. *You deal with the dummy who doesn't know what goes on on his own doorstep.*

So I did. "Everybody," I said simply.

He was annoyed now. "Everybody, apparently, except the owner." And he grabbed my hand and pulled me in the direction of the crime-scene tape. I looked back over my shoulder, signalling both goodbye and that I'd catch up later with what was going on from the people who knew.

Jake walked us back to the main road, ducking under the crime-scene tape and pulling me with him. "We have some info for your sergeant," he said in passing to the PC, who stood back for us.

The after-effects of the fire became overpowering long before we reached the junction where the house was. There was a smell, not of burning, exactly. I

32

sniffed. It wasn't anything I'd ever smelt before. It smelt, I decided, like wet soot. Not that, previously, I'd have been able to say what dry, much less wet, soot smelt like, but smelling it now, I was sure. It was a leftover kind of smell, not of fire, not of burning, but of once-was-burning, and, overlaid on top, the smell of damp.

There was more crime-scene tape as we got closer, blocking access to the corner plot the house was on. There was also an incident tent covering the small forecourt in the front of the house, the space that, in most residential London streets, was sometimes a small garden patch, but was more often paved over, functioning either as a place to park, or simply as a pressure valve that separated street from home.

When I first moved to the area, before the empty house had been empty, when it had still been a junk shop, there had been an ugly wooden extension in that front space, one step up from being a garden shed, an extension that put the shop's front door right on the street, although I don't know why the owner bothered: the shop was one of those shops you can't figure out how it survived, because it was never open. The chipped vases in the window were never sold, or even moved, but just got dustier and dustier, until you couldn't tell what colour they'd been originally. The window got dirtier too, and gradually it became harder to see that there were any vases there at all. The sole indication that anybody ever came or went was that the post never piled up on the other side of the glass door.

Someone collected it, even though the door was always shut, the sign always turned to "Back in 5 minutes".

I don't know when I noticed the post wasn't being collected, or if I did notice it before the day that the windows were boarded up. The general neighbourhood opinion was that the owner had died, but it was clear no one really knew, and that was a story made up to match the circumstances. I probably also didn't notice when the squatters first moved in — the goal of squatters, after all, is to be unnoticeable. At some point I became aware that at night the rooms were lit up behind the boards. Then the boards over the upper-floor windows came down. The makeshift shed and its door vanished, and the area returned to being a paved yard, before, one day, the paving too vanished and the soil underneath was planted, with a small lean-to at the rear. The house was still known as the empty house, and generically its residents were called the squatters, but the phrase wasn't condemnation, just description, the way the locals you recognise but don't know get tags attached to them: the couple with the yappy dogs, the old man who shouts at children, the people who play the Carpenters' *Greatest Hits* at full volume in their garden on summer weekends. Compared to those last ones, the squatters were model neighbours.

From a distance, the house didn't look too terrible. The white-stuccoed front had black streaks across it, like mascara the morning after the night before. The wooden boards that had covered the ground-floor windows for so many years were gone, presumably ripped away by the fire department, and the windows behind had no glass in them. Then we turned the corner and I sucked in my breath. I realised then that, just as I had never smelt wet soot, so I had never actually seen the after-effects of a fire. Like most people, any fires I'd seen had been on television or film, and in a twisted way my brain had never grasped that it had not experienced the reality. The reality was a wall that was almost entirely a single huge scorch mark. The reality was that you could see the sky through the first-floor windows, since the roof had caved in, and only a few beams were left, broken and jagged and charcoal. The reality was that this was no longer a house, just some walls, and a front door.

Jake kept me moving past it, however, without a chance to take in more, and I was grateful. At the bottom of the hill, a small, shifting group of uniformed and plain-clothes police stood. There was some freemasonry of police that Jake could read, because he walked up to one of the plain-clothes men without needing any of them to be identified. I lagged behind as he took out his warrant card and introduced himself, but he pulled me over and told me to give my information about the residents of the house. I did, including what I knew about the adults who lived there, which wasn't much. Mo worked in the station café. I didn't know what Dan did, or even what he looked like; if I'd seen him around, I didn't know that I had. They had children, but I didn't know how many. I'd used Mike as an electrician too, and Steve did odd jobs around the neighbourhood: he came to me once a year to hack back the ivy growing up the side of our house. At the sergeant's request, I passed over the phone numbers I had for Steve and Mike.

Then I decided to do a little fishing of my own. Being with a CID officer moved me from being a neighbour with information to being someone that they might give driblets of information to in return. "How did it start?"

A uniformed man I'd mentally, but with no certainty, decided was the sergeant shrugged. "Don't know, and we won't until the fire inspectors go through later today." He looked at Jake and continued, "We assumed arson, since the house was empty. If there were squatters living there, it's more likely it was set off by them tapping into the utilities illegally, or leaving a hotplate on. That kind of jerry-rigging is always a danger."

I knew nothing about what squatters did or didn't do, but I noticed that the possible cause had slid from arson to being the fault of the occupants because they were, conveniently, living outside the conventional legal system. But if I pointed that out, whatever information was forthcoming would dry up.

"Who is the owner?" I asked. "I've often wondered why the building's been empty for so long."

The sergeant didn't know, didn't care. "We were just told the house was empty, awaiting redevelopment."

The building was tiny, probably two-up two-down. I wondered how it could be redeveloped into anything. I didn't ask. I'd get better info from the neighbours.

And I did. Jake headed off to his car and I stopped for coffee at the Tube station café on my way to work. Or, rather, I got in line behind everyone who had decided to do the same thing. It was going to be record takings for the café owners that day. Catching up with the news was not just easy: it would have been impossible to have done anything else. Those who lived nearest the empty house told the rest of us that the fire had been put out before dawn, but the police had been there ever since, and more had arrived first thing in the morning. The gossip continued: the café owners had put up Mo and Dan and their kids — they had two — in the flat above the café, which was, happily, between tenants. It was only two rooms, but it was better than nothing, and meant the kids could still walk to school. Mike and Steve were temporarily split up, on the couches of two neighbours, but the word was that they had the promise of a spare room not too far away that they could move into soon.

By the time I reached the head of the queue and ordered, I was caught up: fact, fiction, and everything in between. Mo was running the coffee-machine, and she looked exhausted, but otherwise exactly as she always did, like she was ready to head off to Woodstock in 1969: grey hair in a long plait, dyed Peruvian pullover and — I peered over the counter — yes, buffalo sandals.

"Is there anything I can do?" Even as I asked it, I knew that that was the world's most infuriating, and pointless, question, one that gets asked at births, at weddings, at divorces and deaths, as well as at every intervening crisis point. Mostly there is nothing anyone can do, but asking makes the asker, if not the askee, feel better. I tried to be more practical, concentrating on detail. "Did you get your stuff out? Can I help with that? I don't have much space — I couldn't take furniture — but if you've got boxes or bags I could find a corner to keep them in. Or if —" I didn't want to say, *if all your worldly possessions went up in flames*, so I revised. "If you need to borrow anything, kitchen pots and pans, or bathroom things, or whatever, let me know." I scribbled my name and number on a napkin and passed it across the counter.

Mo took my hand. I'd forgotten how touchy-feely she was, but it went with the plait and the outfits: it's always reassuring when stereotypes hold. "Everyone has been so kind." She brushed her fringe out of her eyes, and in that gesture I could see again how tired she was.

I wasn't being kind. If I had been, I would have offered Steve and Mike the sofa bed in my spare room. But my spare room wasn't a spare room, it was my office, even though I had a real office which — I looked at my watch — I needed to get to. I started to speak and then closed my mouth. If they didn't find a place to stay in a couple of days, I'd offer them the sofa bed, I decided. But God, I hoped that I wouldn't have to. When I first moved to London, I lived in my flat with three friends. Then it had been me and Peter for a long time. And after Peter and I had split up, it had been just me, and I discovered I loved the solitude. Since Jake and I had been together, I had got used to another person being in the flat again, but his strange hours, and the fact that he didn't officially live with me — he still had his own flat across town — meant that for a lot of the time I still felt like I lived alone. I didn't much want to return to flat-sharing, but if I had to, short term, I knew from experience that it was do-able. With luck, Steve and Mike would find somewhere else, and I could make the offer knowing it would be refused. The best of both worlds: I would look like a nice person without having to be a nice person.

And with that rather uncomfortable thought I headed to the Tube. Intermittently through the day, as I worked — I sat in meetings, I emailed back and forth as I negotiated with agents, I had an editorial session with an author, I wrote cover copy for book jackets, did the mathematical juggling on a profit-and-loss sheet to see if I could afford to acquire an impressive, but expensive, book without bankrupting the company — as I worked, I thought about it. I wanted to look like a nice person without having to be one. Was that such a bad thing? Or even unusual? Maybe, I thought hopefully, maybe everyone wanted to appear to be nice without having to act nicely. But I felt itchy, as if a soft, warm layer of self-delusion had been ripped away, and a hard, cold layer of reality had been exposed to the air for the first time.

I didn't like it, and it wasn't helped by a frustrating hour spent dealing with a particularly obtuse agent, who refused to understand you couldn't sell some rights to a book and still keep one hundred per cent of them.

In between my increasingly irritated emails pointing out this harsh fact, I emptied out my in-tray, searching for something to keep me occupied while I waited for the next attempt to make ninety per cent plus twenty per cent still equal one hundred. I needed something mindless. At home, ironing is my occupation of choice for mindless occupation, but ironing boards are rarely to be found in publishing offices. My gaze swept over the piles of paper that snow-drifted across my desk and caught on a half-buried envelope. Exactly what I needed. My passport was about to expire, and the renewal form had been so ridiculously complex I'd shoved it aside for some moment when time, energy and incentive would mesh together in mystic harmony. Or, as was more likely, that moment when I'd run out of time, and I just had to do the damn thing if I ever wanted to leave the country again. Today, I decided, the planets were in alignment. The zodiac had named this passport-renewal day.

I emptied out the mass of paperwork, and put the main form on top. Name. Address. How many years at that address. Previous address. How many years at that address. Mother's maiden name. Name of teachers from kindergarten to degree-level. Teachers' mothers' maiden names. I may not be reporting entirely accurately, but that was the gist. I scratched off question after question, progressing smoothly until I got to the payment section, where I was stumped. Although I've lived in London all my adult life, I'm Canadian both by upbringing and passport. Canadians are amenable, obliging people. Really, we're famous for it. The Canadian passport renewal form, however, must have been outsourced, because it was not amenable, nor obliging. I read the instructions a third time. *Pay by cheque.* I could do that. *Pay in local currency only.* I could do that too. *Make cheque payable to the Canadian government.* I'd make it payable to Attila the Hun and his brother if that would get me a new passport. The problem was — I read the instructions for a fifth time — the problem was that nowhere did it tell me how much to pay. That was insane. A sixth time. The information just wasn't there.

I sighed, and turned to my computer. I'd downloaded the forms, so most likely I had missed one. Just what I needed today, a meander through a government website, looking for a single needle in a haystack of information. Maybe there would be a number to ring, and I could speak to a real live human being. Even government employees can sometimes, in moments of absent-mindedness, be helpful.

Government employees. I stopped my search for the Canadians and googled my local council. There. I rang the main number. And, of course, reached an automated menu. Press 1 if you've lost the will to live. Press 2 if we've got you so worn down you want to cry. I opted for "none of the above" by pressing 0 until I'd driven their phone system into a frenzy and it conceded defeat by transferring me to a person.

"Good afternoon. Dennis Harefield, please." Please, I begged silently, not voicemail and another menu.

And it wasn't. A man's voice. "Planning." Triumph.

"May I speak to Dennis Harefield?"

"He's not in. How may I help?"

"Are you expecting him anytime soon?"

"I don't have his schedule." The voice was getting testy. "What is this concerning?"

There was no use pretending. I hadn't thought up a reason for ringing, and I couldn't see why I should pretend, anyway. "My name is Samantha Clair. I'm calling on behalf of a friend. She can't reach Mr Harefield, and she's worried."

There was a pause. "I don't know anything except he isn't here."

"Did he go on holiday? Was there a family emergency?"

"If there was, he didn't tell anyone. He just didn't show up." The voice was bored.

"I'm sorry to bother you. I know you must be busy." You catch more flies with honey. "Do you know who I can speak to? Who his friends are in the office? If you can pass me along to one of them, that would get me out of your hair."

The voice softened slightly. "I would pass you on if I could, I promise. But Dennis wasn't a friendly type. He didn't socialise with anyone here. When he didn't show up, his boss asked around. There isn't anyone." He'd talked himself back into being fed up. "That's all I know. I have to go. His unscheduled absence has piled a huge amount of work on everyone else."

Damn. "I understand. Thank you for your time, Mr . . ." I let the sentence hang.

He knew what I was doing. "Hunsden. Bill Hunsden. But don't bother to ring back. I don't know anything now, and there's no reason I'll know anything tomorrow, or next week."

"Got it. Thanks again. I appreciate it." I hung up and wrote "Bill Hunsden" on a piece of paper. I looked at it for a moment and added, "Council, planning", and the phone number. I underlined it. Then I looked at the council website and worked out the council's email address style, and sent him an email with my name and contact information, and with Viv's, "in case he heard anything", I wrote. It made me feel as if I'd accomplished something, and it gave me something to tell Viv.

I gathered up my passport application, with the various subsidiary forms that I needed to complete to prove that I was me. Some had to be countersigned by a qualified professional (*a doctor, a veterinarian surgeon, lawyer, or university professor.* What about vets who didn't perform surgery? Wasn't that discrimination? If a university professor was OK, why not a teacher? Weren't violinists trusted members of society? And plumbers? What had plumbers done to make the Canadian government overlook them so scandalously?). Then there were the regulations for the photographs. *Do not smile; head must be in three-quarters profile; left ear must be visible; right hand to be held in the Vulcan salute.* I threw everything into my bag. The day, I decided, was officially over.

The agent and the Canadians between them ensured that I spent the journey home planning out the superpowers I needed to improve the world. My primary one, I decided, would be to kill with a glare everyone who aggravated me: passport officers and the un-mathematical agent obviously, but also the people on the Tube who were having a good time when I wasn't; the tourists huddled around the map on the wall who were blocking the ticket barrier; and mostly myself, for being so cross for so little reason.

If nothing else, it was cool in the tiled station hall. The last month had seen never-ending rain, which had, over the past week, transformed itself into summer. Summer is one of those seasons we are never prepared for in this country. We tell ourselves, and live, as though the British climate were always mild. If you come from Minnesota, or the Sahara, this is true. Otherwise it overlooks the reality that some days, or weeks, will qualify as "cold", and some as "hot". This entire past week had been hot. Maybe even very hot. To be on the un-air-conditioned, barely ventilated Tube in this weather was Method preparation for an audition in one of Dante's circles of hell.

Foreigners think that all social interactions in Britain must legally begin with a discussion of the weather. This is not true. We are only required to talk about the weather in certain, very specific, circumstances. When the temperature rises above 22°. When it drops below 10°. When it rains heavily, or there are showers for more than three days in a row. And when it snows. Or hails. Or it looks like any of these things might happen in the next month. At any of those moments, weather commentary is obligatory.

Fortunately, the evening was well above 22°, and had therefore reached the point where the temperature had become material for discussion for days afterwards, "Isn't it hot?" and "How are you managing in this heat?" morphing imperceptibly into "Wasn't it awful?" and "How did you manage?", which would safely carry us through until the next weather emergency — say a drizzle that continued for more than an hour.

So as I stopped at the newsstand to buy the chocolate I deserved after being so polite to the innumerate agent, "Hey, Azim, nice and cool in here", was my reflexive opening. My credentials established as a respectable member of society, I moved on without waiting for a response. "What's going on?"

Azim had run the newsagent's for years, possibly as long as I'd lived in the neighbourhood, which was getting on for twenty years. If there was anything worth knowing in the area, he was the man to tell you.

He shrugged. "Apart from the fire? The school up near your house was graffitied again."

That was a pity — or a blessing, depending on the quality of the work — but it didn't shake me to the core. "Hmm," I said as I scrabbled in my bag for the change which always collected at the bottom. I hoped that would be ambiguous enough to be taken as a general "tsk-tsk" at the state of the world, or at least engagement with the conversation. Then that seemed rude, so I went on. "Do you have kids there?"

Azim looked astonished. "My children have children."

And so we had a discussion about his grandchildren, their ages, likes, dislikes and general all-round wonderfulness, despite the fact that what I really wanted to do was ask about the empty house, but I couldn't work out how to shift from what his youngest grandchild was expecting for her birthday to the fire. I also realised that using a superpower merely to murder tourists on the Tube, who, it was now abundantly plain, were entirely harmless, was a waste. I was going to develop a time-travel machine that would return me to an era when I hadn't asked someone about his grandchildren.

Finally, however, an influx of passengers off the next train saved me, as a handful appeared in the shop. I waved and slid out, moving quickly up the hill until I reached the corner of Talbot's Road, where I slowed, just as everyone else was doing. The summer warmth had combined with the fire to drive home-loving Brits out onto the street, where they stood in groups, mingling as effortlessly as if they'd been born in Sardinia, and performed a sociable evening *passeggiata* every day of their lives.

In general, apart from superficial chats with shop people, etiquette requires that you wait a decade or two before you do anything as emotionally striptease-ish as nodding to someone you recognise when you pass in the street. Catastrophe, however, was an extenuating circumstance to the otherwise ironclad three-monkey rule — see-speak-and-hear no neighbours. Everyone accepts the rules are in abeyance if there is something really horrible to be chewed over. Fire qualified.

Or this fire did, at any rate. Because whatever we'd been told that morning about the safety of the squatters, once the fire had been contained, and once everything that could be salvaged had been removed, a fireman had found someone who had not been accounted for. And he was dead.

CHAPTER
THREE

As with the line in the café that morning, there was little solid information, and lots of wild speculation. Even the one fact — that a dead man had been found — turned out to be half a fact. There was a body, but he might have been a she, no one was sure. And whoever it was might have had no connection to the house — the body, word on the grapevine said, had been located in the small lean-to.

I stood at the edge of the group, listening for a while, and then pulled out my phone. Jake had said he might be working late, which would mean I didn't expect to see him before I went to sleep. Most evenings he came to my flat, but sometimes he went back to his place instead. It depended on where work had taken him, and how he was feeling. If a case was particularly ugly, he might go back to Hammersmith. Sometimes because he'd gone to the pub with his colleagues, to decompress with people who felt the same, but mostly, I think, because he didn't want to talk.

He knew I didn't expect to hear details of the cases he was working on, but even so, the not-talking was an issue for us, one that, naturally, we didn't talk about. That every job had confidential aspects, I understood. I wouldn't discuss an advance I was offering for a book, either. But more than the not-talking about particular cases, there was the reality that Jake spent his working life dealing with death. He investigated murder; I published books. The people he came into contact with were violent. Or criminal. Or sociopathic. Or, often, all three. However many jokes publishers make about the lunacy of their authors, mostly we like them. In Jake's job, there wasn't much to like. I was, I knew, better off not knowing what he was doing, to whom he was speaking, where he was spending his time and, especially, how dangerous it might be.

This was different, though. It wasn't something that would land on his desk, and so he might be willing to pass on some basic information. I texted: *Can you find update on fire? Word is someone died.*

The first thing I did when I got home was open the windows, in the hope that the temperature inside would drop from "sauna" to merely "tropical" by bedtime. I looked in the fridge, but in the heat dinner seemed like too much effort. Then I reconsidered, and threw some tomatoes, cucumbers and peppers in the blender. *Voilà*, gazpacho. I put it back in the fridge to chill and went upstairs.

Mr Rudiger and I played a formal, if unspoken game whenever I visited, and now I knocked on his door and served my standard opening volley. "Would you like to come down for supper?"

We both knew that this meant, *If you want company, I'm here to provide it.* That evening, he didn't even bother to reply, just stood back and opened the door wider. "The terrace is cool at this hour," was all he said, before leaving me to find my way in while he went to the kitchen, asking, "White or red?" as he went.

"Have you got something non-alcoholic?" The previous night hadn't done any damage, but I didn't need to go looking for trouble.

He reappeared with two glasses of iced coffee. I'd introduced him to this heathenish North American practice, and he pretended to drink it only because I liked it, but — I put my hand on the glass — the coffee had been cold for a while. He'd had it already made, and in the fridge.

I didn't comment, though, and we sat on the terrace and caught up. As always, Mr Rudiger had the news, even if he'd never seen any of the people we were discussing. He knew about the fire, and the body, but as with the group in the street, no more than that.

He'd been an architect, though. He might be able to answer a question that had puzzled me. "What do you suppose the owner meant when he said that the building was going to be redeveloped?"

"Turn it into a proper shop, a modern one?" he suggested.

That was the most likely solution, but even then, "I don't know if you could. It's on a corner, the turn between two rows of terraced houses. And it's tiny — less than half the size of this." I gestured around us, indicating the house we were in. "Maybe not even a quarter the size. I'll take a picture for you tomorrow as I go past."

50

He nodded, as if to acknowledge a subordinate who was doing some research for him. We never talked about why he didn't go out. He just didn't, like some people don't eat meat. If you don't ask vegetarians why they don't want a steak, why would I ask Mr Rudiger why he didn't want to go for a walk?

But that subject got washed aside as I heard my phone. Jake. From the sounds, he was outside. He didn't waste time. "I asked to be notified of news on the fire. They're leaning towards arson, and the man who died was most likely the arsonist, who got trapped as he was setting the fire: there were traces of accelerant on his hands."

I thought of Mo and Dan and their kids, sleeping while someone crept about spilling accelerant.

"In the meantime . . ." Jake hesitated, as if searching for a way to phrase what he wanted to ask. Then, "Did you know there had been a series of fires in your neighbourhood?"

"Really? Where? When? And how many is a series?"

"All within walking distance. One up past the school, the others further east. And all very small until last night. Empty shops a couple of times, otherwise a shed, one was a garage. The one nearest you was a car."

"That was a while ago." I counted back in my head. "In the spring, or maybe even before that."

"So you did know about them?"

"Not that there was a 'them'. I knew about the car because I saw it."

His voice sharpened. "What do you mean, you saw it? You were there?"

"I was on Mr Rudiger's terrace — I'm there now, too, by the way, so you can ask him as well. We saw a huge pillar of black smoke. I rang 999 to report a fire, and they said it had already been called in."

"And then what?"

I pulled the phone away from my ear and stared at it. It had no explanation for that question, so I returned it to my ear and repeated "And then what *what*?"

"And then what did you do?"

I didn't understand what he was asking me. I looked around as though I would find an explanation floating in space. "I don't know, it was months ago." I looked at Mr Rudiger. "Do you know what we did after we saw that car on fire in the spring?" He smiled gently and shook his head, so I returned to Jake. "Neither of us knows. We went on talking, most likely. Or I went downstairs. Or to a movie. I read a book. Played with Bim in the garden. Danced the tango. How the hell do I know what I did one afternoon months ago?"

I could hear him smile. "I meant, did you go and watch the fire?"

I laughed. "Of course not. Why would you even think that?"

"Because you would have if you were a man — not an agoraphobic man." Courteously he excluded Mr Rudiger from his sweeping generalisation. I heard a voice near him, and Jake said, "In a minute." Then he was back. "Got to go. I'll be lateish."

I hung up. If I were a man, I would have gone and watched a car burn? I decided not to share this psychological insight with Mr Rudiger, instead telling him that there had been a series of fires that the police were linking together. He'd heard about a garage burning, as well as seeing the smoke from the car with me, but, like me, he hadn't known that there were more fires to be taken into account, much less that the police were thinking of them as a series.

Mr Rudiger again refused supper, so eventually I went back down. "Lateish" for Jake meant he wouldn't be home in time for dinner, but was likely to be back before I was asleep, so I read a manuscript as I ate, and then sat in the garden for a while. After a time, lateish turned into late, and I decided not to wait up. I was just slipping into sleep when I heard Jake's key in the door. By the time he'd walked the short distance down the hall, I was fully asleep.

In turn, Jake was still asleep when I got up early to go running. I call it running, although people who really do run might question my choice of verb. But that's their problem. The plus of the early morning was that it was cool. I nodded to the various regulars as I passed — the man who ran with two huge Dobermans (did two of them make them Dobermen, I wondered each time I saw them?); the three old men from, I had always assumed, the sheltered accommodation flats near the park, who stood waiting to collect their newspapers from Azim the very second he opened; the woman who looked like she was having a coronary every time she ran — oh wait, no, that was me.

I knew I looked like I was having a coronary every time I ran, there just didn't appear to be anything I could do to change it, so I ignored it, as always. Jake was making coffee by the time I hit the shower, and was reading files at the table when I emerged. He looked up as I filled my cup, but waited to speak until I sat down. Then he began without a preamble. "They ID'd the dead man from the fire last night," he said. "He ran an after-school club, a programme to keep adolescents out of trouble, kids who might be at risk."

"And?"

"And it looks like he didn't keep them out of trouble. It looks like he *was* trouble. Your friends the squatters let him use their shed to store sports equipment for the boys, but the fire investigators found traces of drugs there. And when they searched his flat they found cash. A lot of cash. The kind of cash you have if you're dealing."

"That sounds nasty."

"And nastier if he was the arsonist, which is the working theory."

"Why?"

"Why is it the working theory, or why is it nastier?"

"Neither. You said he had accelerant on his hands; I presume that's why they think he was the arsonist. But why would a youth-worker-slash-drug-dealer *be* an arsonist?"

"Arson's not my area, I don't know much about it, but arsonists tend to fall into two groups — firebugs who set fires for the hell of it, to watch things burn, or people who want to destroy a specific building for a specific reason, usually insurance. Most of the buildings in this series weren't insured, so the latter doesn't hold. In this case, it might be that he wanted to create distractions, to draw attention away from a deal that was going down. And since most firebugs are adolescent boys, or young men, it wouldn't be hard for him to co-opt one of the boys in his group so that he could do whatever deals he was doing while a fire was set elsewhere."

"So he burnt down the house where he was known and stored his club's belongings because . . ." I trailed away.

"It was probably an accident. He might have stored the accelerant there, and it caught when he was moving it, or adding to his stockpile."

Mo and Co. had offered him space to be kind, and had been burnt out of their home. No good deed goes unpunished.

The fire, and the death of a drug dealer/arsonist, would normally have been a distraction at work, but when I got to my desk, with an effort I pushed it to one side. Miranda, my assistant, had recently been quasi-promoted, and I needed to sort out the admin that went with that. "Quasi", because while there was no money to promote her properly, I'd managed to get a holding position carved out for her so she wouldn't leave and find a better job elsewhere. The plan was that she'd work as my assistant three days a week, and two days a week she would be allocated a few books as a junior editor. To start that part of her job, I had asked her to read half a dozen manuscripts that I had on submission. She'd already done some reading for me, writing reports on books she thought were worth pursuing. Now, though, if she liked something, instead of me taking over from there, she'd do what I normally did: run the costings to see what we could afford to pay, then bring the manuscript to the acquisitions meeting to pitch it to our colleagues; if she got the go-ahead, she would make an offer, negotiate with the agent and get a contract finalised, meet and deal with the author, edit the manuscript, brief the art department for the jacket — in short, she would be the editor of the book, not me.

Even if she found a potential acquisition in the pile I'd handed over, however, publishing schedules make frozen treacle look like a speeding bullet, and it would be a year or more before one of those manuscripts turned into a book. In the interim I planned to turn over some of my own books to her. I didn't want her to have to deal with the more difficult agents, or with authors who were known to need lots of hand-holding, or with a manuscript that needed major reconstructive surgery. I wanted to ease her in slowly, although there's no such thing as an edit with training wheels: you have to let go and balance on your own every time. Miranda would ultimately have to cope with all of those things — if she was really lucky, she'd have to cope with them all in one book. For the moment, though, I looked through my list to find half a dozen titles at various stages that she could take responsibility for. So when she called good morning as she breezed by on her way to her desk in the open-plan area outside my door, I called, "When you've got your coffee, will you come in?"

Five minutes later, she was with me. Miranda's coffee cup always made me smile. As far as I know, no one in publishing has ever bought a mug. There were a bunch of mugs in the kitchen of every publishing office, which just materialised over time, everything from mugs advertising books that had long been remaindered, to novelty mugs (World's Best Mum, I Love London/Paris/Some-Other-Damn-Place-I-Don't-Really-Even-Like-Much-Less-Love), to cheap "n" cheerful bog-standard supermarket ranges. The unspoken system was that you grabbed one, and then kept grabbing the same one until one day, magically, it became yours, no matter how ugly it was. Miranda's mug was not only not ugly, it wasn't a mug. Instead she had a cup and saucer, both demurely sprinkled with little pink rosebuds. That it was a cup and saucer was in itself different, the rosebuds even more so. But that it was Miranda's was what made it noteworthy. Miranda might have been the very last Goth in the country, and every single item of clothing she owned was black. Apart from green-and-blue dyed strands of hair, and a series of dayglo feathers in her various piercings, I suspected a coloured item had not touched her skin since primary school. For variety, she layered her black jumpers and tights with more black jumpers, and sometimes a second pair of black tights. Her nail polish was black. As was her eyeliner. Her Doc Martens didn't even have coloured stitching. And she had a pink rosebud cup. I loved Miranda.

This was background affection and admiration. When she sat down I just said, "We need to look at some editorial work for you to take on," and watched her beam before she scudded back to her desk to collect some papers.

When she returned, she said, "I was going to talk to you about that. I had a letter from personnel confirming my job change, but it's not very clear."

She handed it to me and I skimmed through it. It looked clear enough to me, so I just waited for her to go on.

She started and stopped a couple of times, and finally said, as though exasperated, "Are you still my boss? For the new part of the job?"

I looked at the letter again. "I see what you mean. I assumed I was, but it doesn't actually say that, does it?" It didn't. She was, according to the letter of agreement, my assistant for two-thirds of her time; for the rest, she was a junior editor, acquiring new books and authors "under supervision". But who the supervisor was had been left unstated.

"Do you want to do books for someone else?" As long as she had the time, I couldn't see that it mattered.

"Wanting to is over," she said crossly. "I already am. Both David and Ben have told me that they'd like me to take on a couple of their books."

"Have they, by God?" I was sour, and surprised at myself for being sour. Ten seconds before, I had thought that it didn't matter. Now that it had happened, I found that I thought exactly the opposite. "Are they books you want to take on? And how many is a couple? Did they ask you if you have time?" I thought about the two men and revised. "I assume they didn't ask you, they told you."

David Snaith is my boss, and the company's editor-in-chief. He was, therefore, entitled to tell Miranda, not to ask her, and without speaking to me first. It wasn't polite, but he was entitled. Ben, however, was not. He was a colleague on the same rung as I was, and unless Miranda had been made a group junior editor — I looked at the letter from personnel again — she didn't work for him, or at least she didn't without the work being siphoned through me.

She flushed. "Yes, they told me. And yes, they're interesting books. Ben's more so than David's."

"What does Ben want you to do?" I tried to keep the acid out of my voice, but Ben and I were not, shall we say, soulmates, and I think my tone when I mention his name could normally curdle milk. He was twenty-six, and he treated his job like it was the finals of an Olympic 100 metres — only one person could win.

My opinion of him was not a secret, so Miranda looked contrite at the enthusiasm she was so obviously feeling. "It really does sound like fun. It's a memoir, by a guy who was in a gang, then in prison. The manuscript has just been delivered, and Ben wants me to edit it." She looked at me wistfully.

Who was I to say no to a book that interested her, a book its editor wanted to hand on? "Here's what we'll do. I'll talk to personnel, and to David, about lines of reporting. I'm happy for you to take on other editors' books, but I'm going to remind everyone they have to come through me, so that you're not inundated.

Otherwise it will be too easy for everyone to hand over 'just one thing', and then you'll have more work than you can get through in a year. Or" — I scowled ferociously at her — "or it means you won't have time to do my books, and even worse, my admin." I must be one of those bosses everyone is terrified to cross, because she giggled.

After that, the day got away from me. In lots of jobs, you never see an end result, or you never see your contribution to an end result. In mine, you do. Once you've negotiated a contract, or edited a manuscript, or briefed a jacket, you can see you've done something. At least, you can when it goes well. Today was not going to be one of those days. Even lunch, a meeting with an author I had published in the past, and who I liked very much, made me feel like I was chasing my tail. She was having trouble finding a subject for her next book. I had no bright ideas either, so while I think by the time she left she probably felt better for talking it out, I didn't.

On my way back to my desk I paused in the open-plan area. One of the great things about working in a publishing office is that you can ask the strangest questions, and everyone assumes it's to do with a book. I wandered over to the editorial assistants' desks. If they'd been told a car was burning down the road, I asked, would they go and watch? Not only would they not, I discovered, but the very notion made them laugh the way I'd laughed when Jake suggested it. So I asked the people who were standing by the coffee-machine in the kitchen. Two laughed, three said of course they would go and watch. Jake was right, it was a gender split: the laugh-ers were women, the of-course-I'd-watch-ers were men.

Even though I'd just had lunch, I checked out the table where people returning from holiday left a communal treats "ITUP" — in the usual place. One of my colleagues must have been to the eastern Mediterranean. Baklava. The day was improving.

And then it wasn't. When I got back to my desk, brushing away filo crumbs, I found an email to the entire company from Olive, our publishing director. I'm told by friends who work in other fields that "publishing director" sounds like one of those job titles you get when you're middle management, with layers of bosses above you. But in the book world, it's about as high as you can get, unless you work for a conglomerate, when CIA-sounding three-letter acronyms start to appear: CEO, CFO, COO. I'd want to be the last one, because I'd force everyone to pronounce it as a word — Coo! But I'm not the boss, and Timmins & Ross is not a conglomerate. We're owned by a small number of investors, some of whom are the descendants of Mr Timmins and Mrs Ross, and mostly they leave Olive to run the company without a Fortune 500-sounding job title. Which she has done very efficiently since she was appointed nearly ten years ago. Despite this, office gossip had reached a pitch and velocity remarkable even in such a gossipy industry, once it became known that Olive had been having early-morning meetings that were so private she wasn't even telling her secretary whom she was meeting.

Whom she was meeting, and what they had been discussing, were the million-dollar questions. The answer, we feared, was that a takeover was in the offing.

Now an email was asking the entire staff to be in the big meeting room on Thursday morning at ten. I had worked at T&R for half a dozen years, and I couldn't remember a company-wide meeting being called. I would definitely have remembered, because the big meeting room wasn't very big. Our office was three converted eighteenth-century houses rabbit-warrened together by passageways that had steps occurring at random intervals. The big meeting room on the ground floor had probably once been a grand reception room. There was a conference table there, which seated twenty, twenty-five with a push. I assumed our warehouse staff, who were based outside London, wouldn't be coming. Even so, there were eighty-five people in the London office, and eighty-five people in the big meeting room was going to make it worse than the centre of Edinburgh at New Year. Except that we'd be sober. Or was ten in the morning too early to start drinking? A company-wide meeting suggested otherwise.

And on that happy thought, I decided to head home. On the tube I stood, squashed into a corner and without enough space to take out a book. It didn't matter. My thoughts moved between lunch with my author, and how I could have done that better, and forebodings about tomorrow's meeting.

At the station before mine, a passenger kneecapped me with her shopping bag as she fought her way to the door, which made me focus on more mundane matters.

Namely, we barely had anything to eat at home. Jake had said he'd be back at more or less a normal time, and because of my distracted trip to the market on Saturday, I wasn't sure I had enough to put together a meal. There were half a dozen portions of chilli in the freezer, and probably another half-dozen of stew. (What can I say? I grew up in North America, and keeping the freezer stocked is as close as I come to religious observance.) I could stop at the station café and get a couple of salad-ey things to go with one of those. That would cover us.

A station café is not normally a place I'd think of doing food shopping, but about a year ago I noticed a sign in the window: *Daily Specials*. And behind it was always some sort of salad. Once, pressed for time, I'd tried one. It was good, and since I walked past the café every day, I'd got into the habit of picking something up when fresh food ran low.

Mo was behind the counter. She'd been there at seven-thirty when I went in to work; it was after six now.

"Long day," I said.

She looked as if it was just one more in a long line of long days, but she waved it off. "I took a few hours after the lunch rush." She was packing up a green bean and tomato salad neatly, which is easier said than done — green beans are slippy little buggers.

"It looks like I got here just in time." I nodded to the salad dish, which she was scraping to get the last pieces for my order.

"They've done much better than I expected."

"They were your idea? Because I've got to say, they're terrific."

For the first time, her smile spread to her eyes. "Thanks. Yes, they were my idea. They're mine. That is, Steve grows the veg, and I make the salads."

"Grows the veg? Where?"

"That patch out the front of the house, and window boxes. We're on the waiting list for a council allotment, and we thought that next year we might get one, but now, who knows where we'll be living?"

They produced enough veg to feed six people, and still have enough to sell, from window boxes and a front space so small it was barely bigger than a window box itself?

"I need to introduce you to my neighbour. And to Viv, in Chantry Close. They both grow fruit and veg in window boxes too, and on a terrace." Mo nodded in recognition when I mentioned Viv. That wasn't surprising. Knowing everyone, and everything, was the air Viv breathed. And if Steve was a keen gardener, even if he had almost no space, it was a given. "Wait, I've just thought. I have a front garden — not big, but bigger than a window box. Would Steve like to use it? It's planted with bushes, because I don't do anything with it." I know I'm supposed to love gardening, it's the national obsession, but to me it's like making your bed: you do it, then you go to sleep and have to do it again the next day. Except gardening is worse. If it's not watering, it's mulching, or weeding, or pruning, or dead-heading, or any of the other ninety-seven things gardens require. I was always looking for new ways of

64

not-gardening. "We could trade. If he keeps me in salad, or cauliflower, or whatever, he can have the rest."

Mo put her hand to her mouth and her eyes teared.

"Mo? You're supposed to cry when you peel onions. Not when you talk about them."

That brought a smile. "Everyone is being so kind, and it's not like we really live here."

"Of course you live here. And I'd be getting a great deal: someone would look after my garden, and I'd get all the broccoli I could eat."

She pushed the salad box she'd packed over the counter and waved off payment. I wrote down my number again, and told her to get Steve to call. He could come and look at the garden and tell me if he thought the idea would work.

I was buzzing with the brilliance of this scheme when Jake got home, and as we sat down to dinner I began to expand on the possibilities. I'd been building, if not castles in the air, at least an elaborate greenhouse in my front garden, and it took me a while to realise that Jake was not only not contributing, he wasn't eating, either. Instead he was looking at me as if I'd started to speak in tongues.

I stopped abruptly. "What?"

He chose his words carefully, which he did when he was very angry. "Did you miss the part earlier where I told you that your friends the squatters had drug dealing going on in their house?"

I stiffened. "Yes, I think I did miss that part. Because what I heard you say was they'd allowed their shed to be used by a youth worker. A youth worker who, if he

65

was working with minors, had to have passed a criminal records check. So I heard the part where you implicitly told me he'd been approved by the police. I entirely missed the part where there were drug deals being made in the house belonging to 'my' friends." I let my voice make the quotation marks for him and stared him down.

He broke first, pushing his hand through his hair, frustrated. "You don't know these people," he said finally. "You don't even know their last names. A drug dealer and arsonist was operating out of their front garden. And now you plan to give them the run of your house?"

He had a point. Not a good one, but a point, so I tried to match his care in my answer. "I agree, having a drug dealer operate in your front garden is not a good sign. But we don't know that they had any awareness of it — after all, the council who employed him, and the police, thought he was OK. I don't think, therefore, that we can hold the house's residents responsible for his criminal acts. As a separate issue, I agree, I don't know Steve's last name, but I can find it out."

Jake threw up his hands and flung himself back in his seat.

I didn't wait for him to say anything. "I'm not giving Steve the run of my flat. There's a tap outside, and there's no reason for him to come into the house. But I will add, there's never been a problem before."

Jake had loosened up when I said there was no need for Steve to come inside, but I'd blown it to hell with that last sentence. "Before? Why was he here before?"

"I told you, and so did the woman in the street yesterday after the fire. Mike's the local electrician, and he does some plumbing too. He's probably worked for everyone in the neighbourhood. Steve does odd jobs." I gestured outside. "He cuts the ivy back when it needs it."

Jake had his don't-mess-with-me-matey police mask firmly on. "You use a cowboy trader, with no fixed address? Someone whose skills you know nothing about? To do something as dangerous as wiring?"

I was not going to lose my temper. I was not going to lose my temper. I repeated it twice, to make sure I knew. And I was proud I managed to keep my voice level. "He does have a fixed address. He works from that house. And he's not a cowboy. He's qualified. And, what's more, he pays his taxes: he never does work without receipts." I was calm, but I didn't mind playing dirty: Jake's car mechanic of choice insisted on cash payments.

"He's a squatter!" Jake was incandescent.

I stuck to my calm voice, although I suspected my calmness was making Jake angrier. "I understand what you're saying. I understand that from your point of view they are committing criminal trespass, even if what they are doing has only been upgraded from a civil offence in the last few years by a government that I know you think too is doing its very best to criminalise poverty —" I waved off his protest. "I agree. I'm off the point. What the point is that I don't agree with you that squatting is, in and of itself, necessarily wrong. That building had been empty for years before they moved in. Even you —" All expression vanished from Jake's face, and I closed my eyes in regret. I began again. "I know what the law says, but in human terms it is hard to see what harm is being done by six people living in a building no one had used for a decade. Living outside normal property arrangements doesn't make you a criminal, or a vagrant, or a deviant."

He didn't reply, just pulled his plate back and started to eat again, stabbing with his fork as though the meal had made a particularly vicious personal remark.

There was no point trying to get him to see it my way. I went for damage limitation. "Look, how does this sound: he won't have access to the house, because there's no reason for him to; I'll get his last name, and ask for some ID; and I'll arrange for him to come and see the garden while you're here, and make sure he knows you're a cop, and that you live here. And if there's any sign at any point that they knew about the activities of the man in the shed, we'll end the agreement."

"Fine," he said, but without looking up. And went on stabbing at the poor, innocent chilli.

We had silently cleaned up the kitchen, and Jake was pretending to watch television while I pretended to read a manuscript, when Steve texted. I showed it to Jake and said, "In the morning before work?"

"Fine," he said again. Just like "Yeah, right" really means *Not even if you set fire to my hair*, "Fine" always means *How many ways are there to say no in English?*

68

But I had his nominal agreement. I texted Steve a time, and we went to bed, where we pretended to sleep. I hated quarrelling with Jake.

In the morning, I stopped behind him as he was brushing his teeth. "I'm sorry," I said, even if it was more regret that we were at odds than an apology for my actions.

He spat and gave me a small smile in the mirror. "But not sorry enough not to do it." He wasn't asking. He knew I wasn't.

I smiled back into the mirror and shrugged, and he shook his head. And he ruffled my hair as he walked past me into the bedroom. It was a bit the way you pat a small dog, or an overexcited child. But it also signalled his acceptance of my plans, even if he didn't like them. For that I could put up with the odd hair ruffle.

We were drinking our coffee when Steve arrived. I led him into the kitchen and waved him to a seat. "I'm not sure we've ever got as far as last names," I said. "I'm Sam Clair."

"Steve Marshall," he said, sitting.

When he looked towards Jake, I added, "And this is my partner, Jake Field."

"Boyfriend," said Jake, glowering as he put out his hand.

I contemplated banging my head repeatedly against the cupboard I was opening to get Steve a cup, but I managed to refrain. Instead I smiled with saccharine sweetness at Jake. "How about 'the sun around which my world revolves'?" I amended, batting my eyelashes for good measure.

He finally cracked a smile, and poured Steve some coffee, which I took to be a positive sign. "Sit," he said, at least sounding like the good cop, not the bad one, in a good-cop-bad-cop routine.

Steve watched us warily, and I couldn't blame him. Someone wasn't happy, even if Steve wasn't a criminal vagrant deviant. Which he didn't resemble, not any of the elements. He was short, probably only five foot eight or so, and wiry rather than thin. Although I guessed he was in his thirties, with his slightly too-long, mousey-coloured hair, which curled over his forehead and into his eyes, and dressed in his standard uniform of worn jeans and clean white T-shirt, he looked like a college student.

"Have you and Mike found somewhere to stay?" I asked. *Please God, let them have found somewhere to stay.* Whatever I'd originally thought about offering them space, given Jake's response to Steve even working in the garden, anything more was impossible.

"Yeah, we're fine. A bit further away than before, but someone Mike works for has a room in St John's Wood. She's happy for us to stay until we can get sorted out."

That was a relief. "OK. The garden." I looked up. "What do you think?"

His smile could have lit Piccadilly Circus. "I think it's great. It's south-facing, it's bigger than a window box, and it's near most of my jobs. What else could I think?"

"So you're undecided," I teased.

Jake snorted. I thought about accidentally spilling my coffee over him, but decided to hold it in reserve.

Steve looked serious. "Look, it's a wonderful offer, but if you want to change your mind, I entirely understand. Not just now." He grimaced. "Vegetables aren't the most ornamental things. If you decide you can't stand the way it looks, that's fine. Or for any other reason. We can do it, and if you don't like it, I can finish out the season and go. No hard feelings."

I couldn't really ask for more. "Sounds good to me."

He must have spent a while looking at the garden before he rang the bell. "With the space you've got, I can grow what I need for the six of us, if we find somewhere to live together again, and plenty for Mo's salads. I was doing that before, so that'll easily come out of my half of the garden."

"Your half?"

Uncertainty crossed his face. "I thought that was the deal. I do the work for half the produce; you get the other half because it's your garden."

I squeaked. I sounded as if a puppy had had its bum bitten, but the thought of coming home every evening to find a tonne of leeks and a bushel of lettuce on my doorstep was panic-inducing. "Not so fast." I didn't add "Buster", but it was implicit. "There's just the two of us here. If you can feed six, plus make the café's salads on half, the other half is more than I want, or can handle. Way more."

"But that isn't fair," he argued. "You're giving me the space. You should probably get more than half."

"But I don't *want* half, much less more than half." I thought for a moment. "How does this sound? For the first while, until we settle into it, you can let me know once a week or so what's available, and I'll choose what I want, and how much. And I'll let you know in advance which vegetables I detest, so you can allow for that when you plan out what you're going to plant." Visions of baskets of turnips were added to the leeks and onions on my doorstep, and my gorge rose.

"It still doesn't seem right," he said, "but if that's what you want, fine. And if there are weeks when you need extra, you'll let me know."

"That sounds perfect," I said. And it did.

"I can definitely use whatever you don't want. Mo's boss has been after her to supply more — they always run out before the rush hour ends. And I have a friend who has a stall at a farmer's market. She'll take anything I can produce."

It sounded workable to me. "I'd like to keep the big bush at the back. It gives some cover so the window is less overlooked. Otherwise there's nothing I mind losing. You can keep or rip out whatever you like." He nodded. "So. Formalities." I felt my cheeks flush. I wasn't quite sure how to ask him for the information Jake wanted.

Happily, I didn't have to. Steve reached into his pocket. "I thought you'd like references. This is from the council, a contract for planting a couple of the squares as a freelance contractor, plus a letter of completion, approving the work. This is a reference from people in Hampstead I've worked for regularly for a few years now. And I've also put down my personal information — name, phone number and so on. I don't have a permanent address, obviously, at the moment, so I've given you a copy of my driver's licence, and listed my National Insurance number. That way if you come home one day and find some lunatic has bulldozed your front garden and scarpered, you can still track me down."

I peeked over at Jake, who held out the pot to Steve. "More coffee?" he said, and I breathed comfortably for the first time since dinner the night before.

Steve shook his head and pushed himself back from the table. "I need to get over to my first job."

I walked him to the door, running through the usual well-meaning phrases — I hoped he and Mike were settling in their new place, how were Mo and Dan's kids coping? As we stood on the doorstep, Steve turned back to face me. "I — we — really appreciate the help we've had from the neighbours." He stopped my words of protest. "No, I mean it. I've done the odd job for you, but you don't really know us. And now that we've found out that Dennis wasn't just running his boys' club —" He broke off, shaking his head. "I appreciate the sign of good faith."

"Dennis?" It couldn't be, surely.

He frowned. "You know, Dennis, who used our shed for his boys' club. I really can't believe it. He seemed like a terrific bloke."

"Dennis." I said again. "Did he work full-time with the boys' club?" I knew the answer, even as I told myself that I was being ridiculous.

Steve was quizzical — when you discover you've been harbouring a drug-dealing arsonist in your shed, his employment history is probably not most people's first question — but he answered readily enough. "No, the boys' club was just volunteer work in his spare time. He worked for the council."

But he didn't have to tell me that. I already knew. I didn't bother to ask whether he made his bed, or what brand of toothpaste he used, because I knew those things as well.

I don't know what I said to Steve, or the arrangements we made, because I was gearing up to make Jake unhappy again. A regular occurrence.

Jake was putting his files away when I went back inside. I leant against the kitchen door, watching him and trying to work out what to say. Finally, "Viv's missing neighbour."

Jake straightened up and waited.

I closed my eyes and tried again. "I think — no, I know. Viv's missing neighbour is the arsonist."

Nothing. I peeked. Jake was standing staring at me, arms crossed. "Why?"

"The arsonist's name was Dennis, says Steve. He worked for the council. Viv's neighbour Dennis, who works for the council, vanished unexpectedly. What're the odds of two council workers named Dennis, one disappearing and one showing up dead? In the same week, in the same neighbourhood?"

Jake's mouth quirked. "The Office for National Statistics have yet to collect that data." He sighed. "Tell me what you know, I'll pass it on."

74

I did, but apart from the link, I didn't know anything else, and I couldn't see it would interest the police: they'd known his last name, and probably now knew he had been reported missing. The only thing that was odd, and I doubted the police would care, was that Viv liked him. She didn't give out her trust lightly, and she approved of him. Still, I hadn't looked around his flat and thought, *Wow, this looks like a drug dealer lives here*. Drug dealers might well be pleasant socially, and have flats that looked no different from anyone else's. It wasn't my area of expertise.

I finished, "The police probably met Viv when they went to search his flat. She has his keys." I didn't add that she'd acquired them after he'd vanished, not before. Or that we'd been in the flat. There are some things that a girl doesn't have to share.

Jake didn't make much of it. He went back to putting his files together, and I took the cups over to the sink before I began to pack the manuscripts I was working on into my bag. As I did, Jake was reminded. "My 'partner'?" he asked. "Do we run a dental practice?"

I didn't bother to look up. "The way publishing is going, it might be sensible to retrain. I'd be a demon with the floss." I went back to my bag. "I just hate 'boyfriend'. You're not a boy. And that's not what you objected to. You were marking your territory."

He was silent, which meant both that I was right, and that he hadn't known that's what he had been doing. It didn't matter. Things had gone better than I'd hoped. I had a kitchen garden in embryo that I didn't have to work in, a part share in a nascent dental practice, and Jake and I were no longer quarrelling.

It was only when I got home that evening that I remembered I hadn't told Steve what Jake did for a living. Nor could I find the paperwork he had left for me.

CHAPTER
FOUR

Now that I had nothing to occupy me, the questions I'd been blocking out with work during the day came roaring back. I wanted to find out about the house, and about Harefield, if it was in fact him. I texted Jake: *Will you be home for supper?*

Twenty minutes later, there was still no reply, no matter how many times I picked up my phone. I even shook it once, but that didn't dislodge any messages that had got stuck in cyberspace either. I stared at my bag full of manuscripts. It wasn't that I had nothing to keep me busy, but I was antsy, and wanted to be up and doing. I just didn't know what I should be doing. So I searched systematically for Steve's papers. I hadn't absent-mindedly filed them — there wasn't an extra folder on my desk, and I carefully checked the drawers. I hadn't binned them. I went through the recycling box outside to make sure of that. They weren't in the kitchen drawer where I keep my shopping list.

After an hour, I admitted defeat. I looked out the window. It would be daylight for ages. I could go for a walk. I could water the back garden. I needed to do laundry, or I could visit Mr Rudiger. Instead I did what I knew I was going to do from the moment I left the office. I got my cycle out and went to find Viv and hear what she'd managed to dig up on Harefield, and give her my news. I could have rung her, but that seemed less purposeful. Going somewhere made me feel as if I were acting, not just reacting. To what, or about what, was less clear.

The drawback to this brilliant plan, I discovered ten minutes later, was that Viv wasn't home. So instead of hanging about in my sitting room, I was hanging about on her doorstep. I looked at my watch. I'd give it ten minutes. If she wasn't back by then, I'd go home and start supper, and do some work. It was still hot, but the building across the road blocked out the worst glare of the late-afternoon sun. I sat down by her front door and pulled out my phone. There's an app that lets you download free out-of-copyright books, and when I first bought a smartphone I got carried away and loaded up, figuring you never knew when you might need an emergency copy of *Great Expectations*, or *Treasure Island*. So far, *Great Expectations* emergencies had been thin on the ground, but today was apparently the day those advance preparations were going to pay off. I stretched my legs out and began to read.

Miss Havisham had just appeared when the sun was blocked by a cloud. Without my noticing, the day had moved from warm to mild, and I'd definitely been there for longer than ten minutes. I looked up. It wasn't a cloud, it was a person. Sam, my namesake. He was standing less than a metre away from me, and I hadn't heard a thing.

78

Apart from our name, Sam and I have little in common. I'm female, and over forty, and no one ever notices me much. He's eighteen or so, and his south-east Asian dark hair is set off with peroxided blonde tips, his ears are multiply pierced, and his jeans permanently hang down around his arse, which, since he's young and pretty, draws attention. Despite our differences, we like each other.

"You're not texting, and you're not on Facebook," he said. "YouTube without the sound?"

I smiled up at him. "Much worse. I'm reading a book."

He shook his head. He'd already told me what he thought of my bizarre hobby. He looked towards Viv's door. "You waiting for her?"

"Um-hmm. I wanted to hear if she had news of her missing neighbour."

Sam shrugged. He didn't know about missing neighbours. So I moved on. "What's the news on the fire?"

He'd been leaning casually against the wall, but now he pushed himself upright, and his face became blank. "Why?"

"What do you mean, why? A building burnt down two minutes' walk from my house. Of course I'm interested in updates."

He crossed his arms defensively. "Who you asking for?"

"What do you mean? I'm asking for myself, for exactly the reason I said I am — I'm nosy."

No smile. "Not for your boyfriend?" It was an accusation.

"My boyfriend? What's he got to do with it?"

"He's a cop."

"He is. But he's CID. He doesn't do fire investigation. And" — I snorted — "and he definitely wouldn't use me to ask questions. Mostly he tells me to stop asking questions." I waited, but so did Sam, so I tried again. "What's going on?"

Sam leant back against the wall again, but he still didn't look at me. "The cops have been around, 'making enquiries'."

"Talking to you?"

He shrugged. "Me and my mates."

"About the fire? Why?"

He still wouldn't look up. "Because when there's trouble, it's us that's to blame."

I knew this was true. When I first met Sam, I'd been told that he'd been "in trouble" with the police. I didn't know what that meant. It could have been anything from drunk and disorderly to something more serious. I'd never asked, and didn't plan to now, either. Whatever he'd done before, in the time I'd known him he was so clearly a good person.

"They think you know about the fires? One of you?"

He nodded.

"That's nuts."

He smiled, but it was bitter. "Glad you think so, but they don't. They wanted to know where we were Saturday night, and then on Wednesday last week, and a lot of other days, which we think must have been when the other fires were."

"You weren't there." I made sure it wasn't a question.

He was tense, staring at the ground. "I could tell them where I was on Saturday, and last week. Before that, how would I know?" He put on a parody upper-class accent: " 'I'm sorry, officah, but you'll have to ahsk my secretary. She keeps my engagement diary.' I work part-time, when I can get it. I don't know what I was doing three months ago."

"What do you do?" I'd never known. I'd guessed he was seventeen or eighteen, but maybe he was older.

He shrugged. Not a question he liked. "What I can. Building sites, mostly. Sometimes a friend of mine's dad, who's an electrician, gives me a few days' work. I've done the NVQs, but I'm not qualified."

"That's what you want to do? Be an electrician?"

He still wouldn't look at me, his arms crossed defensively.

"How much longer would it take to get qualified?"

"I've got the prelim certificate, but I've got to do an apprenticeship, put in the hours, and getting a place is hard." He glanced over at me, and then away just as quickly. "Why?"

"Just wondering what it took. Look." I went back to the main point. "Would it help if I talked to Jake — my boyfriend? If the police are bothering you? Or would it make it worse?"

He shook his head once, sharply. "It would make it worse."

I'd probably think the same if I were him. "OK. I'm not going to wait any longer for Viv. If you see her, will you say I dropped by to talk to her about Dennis? Tell her —"

"How do you know Dennis?"

"You know him too?" We were both silent, startled. Then I connected the dots. "He ran a youth club. Did you know him from there?"

Sam was back to being mistrustful. "Did your bloke tell you about him?"

"No, Viv did."

"How does she come into this?" He wasn't mistrustful now, he was downright belligerent.

"He lived upstairs here. He went missing last week, and she was worried."

"Last week? Before the fire?"

"Yes." I ploughed on. "What day did you say the police asked you about last week?"

"Wednesday."

"That's it, then. Viv said the neighbours saw him on Wednesday; he was supposed to have dinner with her on Thursday, but he never showed." I added, "She liked him a lot."

Sam swallowed. "We —" he gestured behind him, as though to his absent friends "— we went to the youth group he ran." He paused. "He was a good bloke," he said, as if I had argued the point.

"Was he?" I said neutrally. "I never met him."

"He was, really. The things they're saying about him . . ." He shook his head. "It wasn't Dennis. Just not."

I bent to unchain my cycle. "I'm sure you're right. You knew him, and they didn't."

He eyed me warily, unsure whether my assertion was what I truly believed, or a trap. I decided that repeating myself would make me sound less trustworthy. Finally he said, "I'm not saying he didn't have dodgy friends."

I tried a joke. "Everyone has dodgy friends. Look at me, I live with a cop."

He smiled absent-mindedly, to register he knew it was a joke, but he didn't give it his full attention. It helped him make up his mind, though. "He was a good bloke," he repeated.

I just nodded. He was heading somewhere.

"There were a lot of people like me, who used the club as a place to hang out with our friends."

"Tell me about the club."

"It started off just as a casual group. They were skateboarders."

"And Dennis skateboarded with you?" That sounded implausible.

He laughed, loud and clear. Harefield was seemingly not the type. "No, that wasn't his thing. He was helping us make some dosh, to pay for our kit."

That hadn't been what I imagined when I heard youth-group worker. "How did he do that?"

"A few of the others had been making T-shirts with skateboarding tags, and selling them. Dennis showed us how to do it more professionally. Before, they'd been buying T-shirts from Asda, and with the price of paint, and a market stall, there was barely any profit in it. Dennis explained about buying the materials in bulk, wholesale. That was why we needed the shed, to store everything."

"Sounds like a great idea."

"It was. That was what we mostly did." Sam sobered.

More nodding from me. I could get a job as one of those dogs that go on the rear shelf in the back of cars.

"But there were others." He hesitated, not sure how much to say. Then he went for it. "Some groups are recruiting grounds for gangs. There's a lot of low-level stuff going on —" He left what the "stuff" was unsaid. "Dennis let it happen, not because he was part of it, but because he didn't want to drive off the kids involved." He looked at me directly now for the first time. "He really did want to help. He wanted to keep them out of trouble. Sometimes it worked." He looked away again, and again I remembered how when I first met him he'd been described as having been "in trouble" himself. "Sometimes it didn't. But those kids didn't get thrown out. Dennis kept after them, and then he stayed in touch."

That could be altruism, or it could be an excellent way to set up a network of runners if you were a dealer. Sam wasn't stupid, though, and he didn't think that's what the man had been doing. "If you trusted him, you're probably right," I said, therefore.

We stared at each other. Sam looked as though no one had ever told him that his judgement was probably sound, and didn't know what to do with that. I touched him on the arm and got on my bike.

While we'd been talking, I'd heard my phone ding with a text, so at the next light I checked it. Jake. *Won't be back tonight. Working late, will go to H'smith.* Then a second text. *Inquest on Harefield tomorrow. More then.*

So that was that. I went home and did those very things I'd decided against earlier. Laundry, watering the garden, manuscripts. Who said my life wasn't a roller-coaster ride of thrills?

With Jake sleeping at his flat, I was at the office even earlier than usual in the morning. I always make coffee in the coffee-maker I keep on a filing cabinet as soon as I get in, even before I boot up my computer. Today, however, I picked up my cup to head off to the kitchen, where cheap, nasty coffee sits stewing on a burner. It's a gourmet delight I normally found easy to miss out on, but the kitchen was the gossip nerve-centre, and the place to hear whatever rumours were flying about the morning's group meeting. But before I'd even finished standing up, though, I sat back down, all in one movement. It was too early. Publishing people are, for the most part, vampires, coming to life as daylight ebbs. No one would be in for another hour.

I knew I wouldn't be able to concentrate enough to work on anything that mattered. I pulled over my in-tray to see if there was anything there that I could deal with using half my mind, or perhaps a quarter. The tray was overflowing, which was not a surprise, because these days I barely looked at it. Everything important came by email. Anything that needed to be done on paper was dropped in front of me if I was at my desk, or if I was out of the office, left on my chair so I'd see it when I sat down. Maybe, I thought, staring at the Everest of paper that had piled up without my noticing, maybe I should get rid of the basket altogether. Didn't it just encourage people whose views I wasn't interested in to send me crap I didn't want to know about? Or maybe that sentence was a description of office life.

I started at the top. Meeting minutes, which I tossed unread into my filing basket for Miranda to stick somewhere we would never look at them again. A couple of manuscripts I'd asked her to print out, which I dropped on the floor near my bookbag, to take home to work on. Printouts of jacket roughs, which I'd already looked at and commented on as email attachments: more filing. Printouts of contracts to check and sign. Back in the basket, to be dealt with when I had a functioning brain. I reached the bottom and looked at my watch. It was now 8.35.

I poured some coffee and sipped, staring out the window. 8.37. I sighed and rubbed my face. 8.37 and a quarter. This was going well. I picked up the phone and hit speed dial 1.

"Good morning, darling."

My mother made me, and everyone else, look like a slouch. She was always at her desk by seven. Most days that was annoying, but today it would kill a — I peeked at my watch. 8.38 — a bit of time. But that didn't mean I was going to match her relentless good cheer. I liked being in the office early, but mostly because no one else was, and so I had a space when I didn't have to talk. "Morning," was the most I could manage.

Helena was good, I'll give her that. She didn't speak, just waited. Since she's a corporate lawyer, her area of expertise can best be summarised as "money", and so when the first rumours of Olive's mysterious meetings surfaced, I'd asked her to keep an ear out for any whispers that might indicate a takeover was on the cards. If she'd ever heard anything, she hadn't said, and I'd forgotten to ask. Now was a good time to repeat the question, but to my surprise, when I opened my mouth, what came out was, "Mother, do you know how — or if — you can find out about drug dealers, and distribution? Local networks, I mean?"

Helena knows about everything. "The Home Office compiles figures for arrests, and it's likely it's broken down geographically," she said, almost absently, as if this were the type of question a mother expected from her child. *Mummy, why is the sky blue? Mummy, where did Fido go when he died? Mummy, how do you find out about drug dealers?* "That is, if you mean in Britain." As if I might be interested in drug dealing in Pretoria, or Novosibirsk.

"Yes, here. In my neighbourhood."

One of the blessings of Helena is that, while she knows everything, and everyone, she rarely displays any curiosity. If she had asked me why I wanted to know, I would have said vaguely that I needed it for a manuscript I was working on. In the face of her lack of follow-up, though, I found myself explaining. "A house on Talbot's Road burnt down at the weekend. They found a man dead in a shed outside, and the assumption from the circumstances is that he was an arsonist, using fires to cover his drug dealing. He worked with a youth group, mentoring boys, and they seem to think that was suspicious too. That he was using the boys as part of his distribution network. So I wanted to know more about the link between the youth groups and gangs, and how drug-distribution systems operated — how he would have been using the boys, if he could have been doing it without some of the other boys knowing." Sam believed Harefield was clean, after all.

"What does the group do?" asked Helena. "Was it a sports group? Did they travel to play matches, perhaps?"

"No, I could see how that would work. But this sounds much more harmless: they just made T-shirts with skateboard logos on them."

Helena sounded engaged now. "To sell them?"

I had no idea, so I said, smartly, "I have no idea."

"There's a starting point, then. Selling is already a distribution network. Who they sold to, and where, might tell you more. However, it's not my area." I'd never heard Helena say she didn't know something before. If I kept a diary, I'd pull it out now and paste a gold star on the page in commemoration. "The police are the people to ask, but you know that." By which she meant, if I wasn't asking Jake, she presumed there was a reason. "Otherwise an academic who works in the field? Criminology? I'll see who I can find."

And she was gone. One more task in Helena Clair's ever-expanding, ever-achievable To-Do list: Find my daughter a criminologist.

I was still shaking my head at the phone when I heard voices in the open-plan area outside my office. I leant back to look around the door. Yep, the seething masses had seethed. I picked up my cup and headed to the kitchen.

As had everyone else. There was a group of four inside, which meant the little galley space was at capacity, and then in the hall around it was what looked like an early-morning drinks party, except that everyone was clutching a mug, and the conversation was not superficial. Instead it was "Did you hear?" and "What if?" I joined in. I knew it was pointless, that everyone else knew it was pointless, but it was our livelihood, and no one was going to get any work done before the mystery meeting we'd been summoned to.

We quickly ran through the possible rumours, and moved on to the impossible ones, before settling into more ordinary conversation, some work-related, some social, and even more falling into that fuzzy in-between area. Publishing is relentlessly social, and so a conversation about authors, or agents, or acquisitions can, in the blink of an eye, shift from work — Did you know that XXX agent had sold YYY's new novel to ZZZ? — to gossip — Did you know that XXX was sleeping with YYY, and that was why the novel wasn't offered to QQQ, because QQQ had had a relationship with YYY, and it had ended messily?

All good things must come to an end, however, and as it got closer to ten, conversations grew quieter, and then ceased, and we headed down to the meeting.

Our group sidled in as though we'd been caught smoking behind the bike shed, and had been sent to the headmaster's office, shuffling silently to the back of the room instead of sitting at the table. Only swots sat at the front, so they could wave their hands in the air, calling, "Oh, please, Miss, I know the answer, I know," while the cool kids sneered balefully behind them.

And, in a fine example of how school life never leaves you, I stood halfway between the two groups. I knew — I'd always known — that I was a swot, not a cool kid, but I'd so longed to be the latter and evade the former that I'd always ended up on the edges of both. I told myself I wasn't in between, that I was just standing at the front of the group by the wall because I was short, but I knew in my heart I belonged with the nerds. Screw it. I pushed back into the wall crowd, and watched Olive, who was standing at the end of the room away from the door talking to three people.

One was Evie, her secretary. The other two were strangers, I was pretty sure. I leant towards Miranda, who was behind me — there had never been any doubt she was cool. "Do we know them?"

"Never seen them before. None of us has."

What the assistants didn't know wasn't worth knowing. If no one in the room recognised them, they weren't publishing people.

As we waited for the rest of the company to arrive, I watched the two strangers. They were both in their twenties, he probably a handful of years older than she. He looked like he thought he was good-looking, and he was, in that he was young, with lots of well-cut brown

90

hair, matched by a well-cut dark suit. Those three things — youth, good hair and good clothes — get you a long way in your twenties. In a few years he'd be pudgy, but now he was just a little, well, soft was probably the best word. His features were a little too small for his face, and they would grow smaller as he grew bigger. His colleague was the opposite. She was not naturally attractive, having forceful, masculine features that were greatly oversized for her tiny frame: heavy, blue-veined eyelids, big horsey teeth. But while the man assumed his natural advantages would carry him through, she had taken her disadvantages and turned herself into something spectacular. Her hair was blonde and done in an elaborate 1930s style. She wore no make-up, and a pair of thick, black-framed spectacles ensured its lack was noticeable. The push-pull continued with her suit, which was entirely office-appropriate, neither too low-cut nor too short, but so fitted you could count every clavicle on her whip-thin body. She was, basically, every man's fantasy dominatrix librarian.

I was pulled out of my girly fan-clubbing when Olive cleared her throat. She didn't have to do more, because no one had been talking since we'd arrived. "Thank you for coming." She looked up from her notes and grinned. "Not that you had a choice."

That was why we liked Olive.

"As you know, we've had a hard year." Smiles vanished. "Our investors, however, are behind us. Profits, while they have dropped, are carrying us through. We have plans for new markets" — she looked over at the digital media team, who, I noted unkindly, were sitting with the nerds — "and we have some very promising projects in the pipeline."

We began to relax, even as we knew that we shouldn't. If everything was so perfect, why were we there, and who were these people?

"However." There it was. "However, it has been a hard year. To try and forestall more hard years, we have been looking at our structural organisation."

I looked around the room and nearly laughed. Everyone over the age of thirty-five had clenched their teeth. It is impossible to work in publishing for more than five years without the company that employs you undertaking a restructure. It's one of those things you just live through, like chickenpox. Or maybe something a little more serious, like shingles. It's not as bad as the Black Death: it only kills a few. But when times are hard, managers decide to reorganise how the company is run, and who reports to whom.

Normally, within each company, there are a bunch of mini-publishers, called imprints. Timmins & Ross published about half its books with T&R on the spine. For the rest, ten years ago they'd bought out a publisher of craft books that was going bust, and so our craft books were still published under the old name. Then there were our sports books, our literary fiction, our business list — each of them was published under a different imprint. Each imprint had it own editors, its own reporting structures and bosses. Apart from editorial, where an in-depth knowledge of the subject was essential — it doesn't take a genius to understand that the sports editor shouldn't acquire books on economics — other departments, like design, marketing and publicity, were pooled. Most companies are organised like this, and departments and reporting lines are, for the most part, a mixture of history, organic development, company takeovers, and changes in structure to give people you wanted to hire a job they were suited for. And then there was that other ingredient, the pragmatic "it works better this way".

But because it was hard to give one reason why any imprint or department was structured the way it was, it was also the standard jumping-off point for anyone who wanted to "fix" things. If Bob didn't, or did, report to Accounting, or sales didn't have oversight of promotional material, all would be well, and we'd make a billion pounds a minute. That was always the standard explanation, and it was the reason, too, that we were clenching our teeth. Another restructure, with the expense, time, energy and upheaval that that entailed, and then in a few months we'd end up just where we'd been before. I'm not being cynical. Before I worked at T&R, after a restructuring at my old company that took months, and cost tens, if not hundreds of thousands of pounds, my boss was shocked when I pointed out that the shiny new job he was offering me covered half of what I was already doing, and it came with a higher salary. That was a fun day.

Except that it hadn't been, and this wasn't going to be either. I refocused on Olive. She was introducing the two strangers who were — oh joy — management consultants. They would, she assured us brightly, be working their way through the company over the next few weeks, meeting staff, individually and in groups, to discuss what we did, and come up with new and thrilling ways of doing it in half the time for a tenth of the money.

A few people stopped pretending, and as Olive painted this rosy image of our gloriously efficient and financially prosperous future, sighs could be heard. By the time she'd finished, the gloves were off, and arms were crossing across bodies around the room. Not happy.

Olive knew it. Her smile, normally so sunny, grew tight. "I know you'll welcome Adam Rossiter," she said, her tone warning, *You'd better*. He stood and the woman beside him sat back. He smiled at us with flagrantly bored insincerity, and read out a paragraph from a sheet he held. His company (name unintelligible) was so excited to be working with a publisher as well known as — he checked the paper again — as Timmins & Ross. He was looking forward to learning from us as much as we learnt from them, and it was a great opportunity.

So great that he couldn't be bothered to memorise the four sentences he'd just read. Or the name of the company that was paying his bill. Or look at anyone. Or introduce his colleague.

My arms were folded too. It was either that, or I'd throw something. Once. Just once. Just one sodding time, I wanted to be in a meeting where, if the people doing a presentation were a man and a woman, the woman got to speak. Not even lead. Just speak.

94

Today was not going to be that day, but at least I was not alone. As we walked out, Sandra, from publicity, said in a whisper intended to be heard in the next county, "Since she's got two X-chromosomes, no one needs to know her name."

Olive and her little management buddies retreated to a huddle by the window, and the rest of us just retreated.

Miranda trailed me into my office. "What's going to happen?"

I waved my hand in dismissal. "A bunch of bullshit. They'll piss around for a few months, send in a bill for a few hundred thousand pounds, and after they've gone we'll reorganise their reorganisation so that we can get the same work done we were already doing, after we've hired new people to replace the ones they made redundant."

She stiffened. "Redundant?"

I was careless. "Management consultants never think they've done a good job if everyone is happy when they leave." Then I looked at her, wide-eyed and terrified. I'd forgotten she was only twenty-two and hadn't been through this before. And she'd told me a few weeks before that she and a friend had made an offer on their first flat. "Try not to worry. I know that sounds impossible, but you're essential. Your job is essential."

She didn't look convinced. And she looked less convinced by late afternoon. I'd come back after our weekly cover meeting, which is when the art department shows the potential designs for the jackets of the upcoming books, to be approved by the editors, marketing, sales and publicity people. Everyone was on edge, and discussions that would normally have been calm, even pleasant, degenerated into playgroup-like squabbling about who had delivered work late, and whose fault it was. Finding a memo from the consultants to the senior editors on my desk was the icing on the cake. They were, they wrote, setting up meetings with each division "to map out and explore our journey in the creative enterprise that is Timmins & Ross". After that group hug, a stark order: block out three hours on Tuesday — that is, in less than three working days, we needed to clear our calendars, whatever we had scheduled. They had written "please", but it was an order. If our journeys in the creative enterprise were meant to involve doing any work, that was just too damn bad. Then the sign-off: "We look forward to learning from you!" and a smiley face.

Miranda must have heard me reading, because she called through the wall: "After the morning with the editors, they've summoned the assistants for the afternoon. So no one will do any work the entire day. Isn't that great?" I ditched my earlier plan to become a dentist and decided I'd run away and join the circus. I could be a clown. I already had lots of badly fitting clothes.

CHAPTER
FIVE

The general feeling of irritability that pervaded the building was not helped by the weather. It had already been hot on the commute in. It quickly worked its way past that, to hotter, and then to Oh-dear-lord-this-is-unbearable. I frowned at the sky as I headed home. When it was my turn to run the universe, things were going to be very different. But it wasn't my turn yet, and I waded to the Tube through the lowering, clammy air, air that felt as if a thunderstorm were due. And, until it arrived, the Tube itself was going to be worse. Fancy-pants cities like Paris and New York have air-conditioning on their undergrounds. We Brits pretend we're too tough to need it, butching it out summer after summer. Today the temperatures underground would have seen you prosecuted for cruelty to animals, had you been transporting cattle.

No cattle in my tube carriage, just lots of smelly, sweaty people. When I was above ground again, I made a quick stop and then headed out of the station. As I walked past the café, Mo knocked on the window and gestured me in. She was always there: her hours seemed to be "From opening until she fell over from tiredness".

"Steve hasn't talked about anything else," she began. "At least, that's when he hasn't been drawing plans of what he can grow with so much extra space." As she spoke, she was boxing up a salad. "He asked me to say, if I saw you, that he'd like to start clearing the ground as soon as possible. He wanted to check it was OK with you."

I shrugged. "Sure. Whenever he likes."

She passed me the box, again refusing payment. Between my future harvest from Steve, Mr Rudiger's contributions, and now salads from Mo, I might end up like Dennis Harefield, never having to cook at all. The thought of Harefield made me say, as I balanced the salad on the top of my bookbag, "Can you sit for a few minutes? Do you have time for a cup of tea?"

I don't know what possessed me. I'd never said more than three sentences to the woman before. I don't like strangers. I don't like bland chat. And I don't like tea.

Mo was as startled as I was, and then she smiled. "Thanks. It would be good to have a break."

She made herself a cup of tea, and me some coffee — she paid attention to her customers. We sat.

I couldn't exactly say, *So, tell me, why were you giving space to a drug dealer?* I went for, "Is it always so quiet in here in the evenings? Why do you stay open if it is?" instead.

"We used to close after the school run was finished, but once I began the prepared food, even though we still don't get customers who sit, the rush-hour takings went up and the owner extended our hours. So it's really my own fault." She slumped, and then straightened. I got the feeling that Mo was used to fighting her own battles, and everyone else's. "On the other hand, it's because I found him another revenue stream that he's letting us stay in the flat upstairs while we're . . . until we're . . ."

She might be used to fighting, but she couldn't bring herself to say the word "homeless", and the "until" made it worse. Until what? Even if the house was rebuilt and made habitable again, there was no guarantee that they'd be allowed to move back into what had been their home for years. If anything, now it was forcibly going to be renovated, it was almost a certainty the owner would make sure they didn't move back. If he hadn't known about them before, he did now.

Her voice trembled. "We're still on the council waiting list for housing, but who knows how long that will take? And that was home. We'd been there ten years; there was every chance we'd have been able to stay. Dennis was helping us with that —" She cut herself off.

This had to be horribly painful: Dennis had deceived them, and used their generosity against them. "Had you known him a long time?"

"Three, maybe four years? More?" She waved her hand vaguely. "He was a regular at the Neighbourhood Association, and we knew him from there. Once the boys began their T-shirt thing —" She paused, checking I was up to date with "the T-shirt thing". I was. "After that, he needed a place for their equipment. The shed was convenient for him, and he was helpful to us —

he . . ." She took a deep breath and finished off her tea before she went on, her voice steadier. "He was also helping the boys with the council, which was planning to sell off the railway arches where they skated. Dennis was helping them work with the Neighbourhood Association to protect the space. That's what he was good at. He was . . ." Her lip trembled again. Then she pulled her shoulders back. This was the Mo who looked after her family, the café, her customers. She was a carer, not someone who was cared for. She stood, pushing her cup and emotion aside. "Speaking of which, will you be coming to the Neighbourhood Association meeting this evening?" She gave me a stern look.

Which I deserved. I had never once, in the twenty-odd years I'd lived there, gone to a Neighbourhood Association meeting. I'm not terrific with groups, I don't play well with others. In truth, if I could find an anti-joiner club to join, I would. We'd have badges that read "Home Alone", and we would wear them proudly at the hour dedicated to our meetings, as we each sat quietly by ourselves in our own houses.

"I'll try," I said. That was a translation of, *I will, right after hell freezes over.*

Unfortunately, Mo appeared to be bilingual, and her stare responded to the meaning, not the words. "I'll see you there, then," she said, dismissing me with a flick of her grey plait. "St Thomas's church hall. Seven o'clock."

"Sir, yes, sir!" I replied, snapping out a spiffy salute. But only in my head. Out loud, I just repeated, "I'll try." Even to myself I sounded meek, not evasive, this time.

Another bossy older woman. Maybe it was like ducklings. I'd imprinted on Helena at birth, and now I automatically followed the instructions of any imperious-sounding woman a set number of years older than me. Blaming it on biological determinism made me feel a bit better, because otherwise I was just a wimp.

Refusing to entertain that as a possibility, when I got home I dropped my bag by the door and took my purchases upstairs to Mr Rudiger. I knocked, and when he opened the door I didn't even bother going through the routine of inviting him downstairs so that he could refuse and invite me in.

Instead, I just waved the plastic bag in the air. "Pimm's!" I carolled, in the tone of a day-care assistant whipping out the SpongeBob SquarePants jigsaw. Only then did I hesitate. When I'd tried out iced coffee on Mr Rudiger, he'd gone all Central European on me. Maybe six decades in Britain wasn't long enough to appreciate Pimm's either? But it wasn't like Marmite, where your mother's mother's mother had to have been born here before you didn't gag when you smelt it. Pimm's was cool, delicious, and 99.9 per cent gin. What's not to like?

And Mr Rudiger was smiling, and it wasn't that rictus smile he'd given me with my iced coffee. "We're on the terrace," he said.

We? This was the first time I'd just barged in, and he had company. "I didn't mean to interrupt." I began to edge backwards, but he took the bag in one hand, and my elbow in the other. As usual, he looked benevolently amused by me.

Once out on the terrace, I saw the joke too. Helena. Not that she was a joke, of course, just that I hadn't expected her. I wasn't aware she was on visiting terms with Mr Rudiger, and she rarely left her office before six, mostly much later. I looked at my watch: not quite six now, and from the empty glass in front of her, she'd been there for a while. I kissed her, but raised my eyebrows. *What time do you call this, Missy?* the eyebrows said sternly.

Before she had time to reply to them, Mr Rudiger had reappeared with a tray. Glasses, lots of ice, a jug of Pimm's and a pair of scissors, which he quickly used in his window boxes to cut some mint and — I sniffed — lovage, maybe? I wasn't certain I knew what lovage smelt, or even looked, like, but it sounded right for Pimm's. Like most things in life, I'd read about it rather than experienced it.

I had my mind on higher things, like gin, so it took me a moment to notice that Helena was making a space for the tray on the small table, which was otherwise covered with files and documents.

"Are you two going into business together?" I asked, sitting down.

Helena laughed. "Perhaps we should. There must be money in children's playgrounds?" she suggested speculatively to Mr Rudiger.

He didn't reply, merely looking amused again.

My nose was out of joint. *My* mother, and *my* friend and neighbour, discussing things *I* knew nothing about.

I pretended to myself I was rising above it, and took the glass Mr Rudiger handed me. I couldn't decide what I wanted to do more, take a healthy swallow, or hold the iced glass to my face and neck. So I alternated the two, and felt much better.

Helena took a daintier sip, and deigned to fill me in. "Pavel is acting as an unofficial consultant to my women's shelter," she said, gesturing to the files she had now neatly piled on one corner of the table.

I hadn't known Helena was involved with a women's shelter, but it didn't surprise me. In addition to her full-time career as partner in a law firm, and her busy social life, Helena sat on what I conservatively estimated to be 197 committees and charities. I often wondered if she was secretly two people, or possibly even three, because I had no idea how she had time to do half of what she accomplished daily. And if she hadn't been so damn nice, that would have been aggravating.

But she was nice. And she might be three people, so a new charity wasn't a surprise. What Mr Rudiger had to do with a women's shelter, however, I couldn't imagine, so I put on my best do-go-on face, and waited.

Mr Rudiger waved away the title of consultant. "Helena asked me to look at the plans for the building. It's a terraced house, so it's not ideal."

Helena was blunter. "It's hopeless. We need to provide security for women and children who have left abusive homes, and the building just isn't designed for that. Pavel has been suggesting low-cost ways of adapting the entrances so that visitors can be screened."

Helena would co-opt the devil himself if his skill set was a good fit for one of her charities — central heating in the devil's case, or barbecuing. She also disapproved of people who didn't work. Mr Rudiger was past retirement age, but that wouldn't slow Helena down. This was a win-win for her: she'd get the help her charity needed, and he'd be working. Now I thought about it, I couldn't understand why she hadn't been around before.

I sat back, half-listening to the conversation about safety grilles and keys that couldn't be duplicated, but mostly drifting, letting my gaze move gently from the plants — the tomatoes were nearly ripe, I noticed — to the houses and trees beyond. I was happy with my drink, and with company that only required my presence, not my participation.

More than happy. I was nearly asleep when Helena stood up and gathered her papers. I pulled myself back to the present and hastily ran through the contents of my fridge. "Would you like to stay for supper?" I asked. "And would you like to come down too?" I added to Mr Rudiger. While his refusal to go outside was almost absolute, he occasionally made forays down to my flat.

Helena had plans, as she always did, while Mr Rudiger simply shook his head: not tonight.

Which meant that by seven I had no real excuse. Jake had texted that the case he was working would keep him out "lateish". Even if he'd had time to find out what had happened at the inquest, I wouldn't get any information for hours, if then, while someone, or everyone, at the meeting would most likely have the most up-to-the-minute information. And since Jake was a policeman, even if he'd had time to get the facts, he wouldn't have heard half the rumours and speculation. Local gossip would be far more extensive, and probably more accurate. I googled the church hall, and found it was two streets away from me. So I went.

I kept my head, though, aiming to arrive just after eight. With luck, I'd miss most of the main business, pick up the gossip and still get points for having attended. I thanked my cynical stars as I slid into a seat at the rear, because an hour after the start time, the meeting was still going strong, the participants showing no sign of flagging. A group of about thirty sat on folding chairs. I suspected that most had come for the same reason I had. Five people sat facing the rest of us, the committee, or organisers, or whatever they called themselves. Viv was one of the five, and so was Mo.

Meetings are meetings, whatever the subject. This one, too, had a passive-aggressive minute-taker, and they were therefore fighting battles that had already been fought. Instead of being about cover copy, or illustrations, or marketing budgets, however, there was a skirmish about parking zones, a recapitulation of what sounded like a long-running saga of planning permits for change of use from residential to commercial zoning for some houses near the station, and an even longer-running tussle over the little neighbourhood park, which the committee wanted to have legally declared a common, so the council would be unable to sell it. I tranced out. Rather than attempting to follow the intricacies of zoning laws, I havered over whether I should offer a smaller advance for a book I had on submission, and leave the serial rights with the agent, or whether to wade in with a big-money offer and hope that we could sell serial for enough to cover my arse.

By the time I mentally rejoined the meeting I was in, rather than the one I'd be in the following day, things were winding down. It wouldn't be much longer before I could hear about the inquest, as well as tell Viv what I'd learnt about Harefield, although now I'd seen that she and Mo were on a committee together, I suspected she already knew.

The committee members finally stood, but even then they continued talking, clustered in a little group at the front. I stayed in my seat. Sooner or later they'd have to pass me on their way out, and I'd nab Viv when they did. I looked down the row to see if anyone wanted to get past me. The man next to me was the only one left. He had paid little more attention to the meeting than I had, texting or emailing the entire time. He didn't look up now, either — he may possibly not even have noticed that the meeting was over. He wasn't the sort I expected to see there. He was probably in his thirties, and was wearing a suit, while I'd imagined the meeting would be attended entirely by retirees, and — I looked at the people heading to the door — I wasn't wrong, either. Over half were sixty-plus. Of the rest — I tried to categorise them as I waited — there was a heavy sprinkling of Mo-types, concerned, middle-aged women. The retirees had a few men among them, but the younger group was almost entirely female. Most of these were women who would grow up to be Mo, and then later to be Viv. From the contributions I had listened to, they were parents, teachers or social workers. Of the few younger men who had spoken, one had identified himself as a social worker, another was the local councillor. The man on my right on his phone appeared to be none of these things, and had his age and gender not made him stand out, his lack of interest, and his suit, would have.

As I was checking out the said suit, stylish and expensive, he looked up from his phone and caught me. So, I smiled briefly and said, as if I longed to initiate a conversation with a stranger, "I've never been to one of these before."

He returned to his phone. "My father can't get to them anymore, and he misses the local news, so I come."

That would have been sweet, if he hadn't been texting as he said it. Unless he was texting his father. Then it was still sweet.

I didn't really care, though. I nodded and smiled, to indicate that I'd heard, but had no interest in following up. He looked relieved.

I tuned in instead to the conversation in the row in front of us, where the fire had now taken over as the main topic. A woman who looked as if she should be running empires, but I knew worked behind the counter at the chemist on the high street, had been to the inquest, which was interesting enough that even Mr Suit slowed his thumbs and listened, although he never once looked up from his screen. The identification of Dennis Harefield had been confirmed, she reported, and the cause of death, which was smoke inhalation. He had also had a skull fracture, probably from where a beam had fallen in. I shivered, and hoped that at least it had been quick, and the man hadn't had to lie there, knowing he was trapped.

As she was speaking, her group was enlarged by others who wanted to hear the news: the social worker from the front row, and also Azim, whom I hadn't spotted earlier, but was not at all surprised to see.

He and the chemist-shop woman, whose name appeared to be Sarah, had both been at the inquest, and they competed to dole out the details, which were, in reality, almost nil, since the inquest had been adjourned without the police reporting more than that they were making ongoing enquiries. There was nothing about Harefield's drug dealing, nor his youth group, nor what the police had found in his flat that had made them certain he was a dealer. I hadn't noticed anything, but then, I wasn't looking for drug-dealer paraphernalia, and now I thought about it, I didn't think I knew what drug-dealer paraphernalia looked like — scales and baggies, I was guessing from my extensive knowledge of drug dealing in films. And the money. I hadn't noticed scales and baggies, and I probably would have, given the skeletal provision of his kitchen equipment. I hadn't spotted large wodges of cash either, but I hadn't checked the sitting room. I also hadn't gone through the piles of his clothes, either, so it was more than possible that I'd been blind to anything worth seeing.

Sarah reluctantly ceded her place as chief know-all to Azim, who took over as the information exchange when it came to the fires. They had started nearly a year ago, he reported, his eyes gleaming, and there had been one or two a month, more in the summer, fewer in the winter, which according to Azim, who was either quoting information he'd learnt at the inquest, or he was an aficionado of *CSI*, was the standard pattern. Except for this last fire, they'd been quickly extinguished, without spreading or even causing much damage. He said that the fire inspector had suggested it was the age of the wiring in the empty house that had blown that fire up into something larger, and more dangerous.

Sarah muscled her way back in. "The police didn't even know the building was occupied," she reminded us, to head shakes all round at the police's ignorance. "Why would the wiring be old when Mike lived there?" Head shakes turned into nods, and there followed a free-for-all on the many failings of the police. Sarah led the charge, but to my surprise, Azim wasn't far behind on their general uselessness. I'd never had long chats with him, but I'd have expected him to be a law-and-order type. Another stereotype bit the dust.

Out of the corner of my eye, I saw Viv heading to the door, so I leant across the suit, who wasn't paying Azim's monologue any mind, and had long ago returned to his phone. I intercepted her and we swapped information. The news that her upstairs neighbour was the man in the empty house's shed was, naturally, now no longer news, so I tacked on my abortive phone call to Harefield's colleague at the council.

"You may well be able to get more out of him than I could," I said, buttering Viv up shamelessly to cover up my lack of information. "His name is Bill Hunsden, and he works in planning. I'll send you his number."

Azim abandoned the inadequacies of the police and joined our conversation. "You have been investigating Mr Harefield?" he asked me.

His intervention was not taken well by Viv. I'd never seen the two of them together before, but, from the way they faced each other, they frequently met, and vied for supremacy.

"'Investigating' is hardly the word, Azim," she said loftily.

He annoyed her further by not responding verbally, merely looking knowing.

She ploughed on. "Dennis was a good man, and Sam has been helping me look for him this past week, not just since the fire." Her tone dismissed the johnny-come-latelies that were the police, finally whipping into action when they had a body stuck under their nose.

I tried to smooth the friction between the two. "Dennis was a good friend of Viv's, Azim," I said, my eyes silently adding, *So will you shut the hell up?*

I'm not sure if Azim was trying to be helpful, or if he was deliberately being provocative, but his deep bass voice soothingly saying, "We can all be fooled by people", was the match that set off the entire box of fireworks.

110

Viv was all of five foot tall. And standing in the church hall aisle, she positively loomed over the six feet of Azim. Harefield was, she made clear, a man of unimpeachable integrity. There was no question that the police had made a grotesque error, and she shared this view, loudly, forthrightly, and at length, to anyone within, at my conservative estimate, a five-kilometre radius. Azim switched sides, and argued briefly that the police must know what they were talking about, that they wouldn't say a man was a drug dealer without cause, but Viv, half his size and possibly a third of his weight, pinned him with a glare, and he quickly subsided.

This wasn't a discussion I felt I needed to be part of, but Viv wasn't having any of it. "She can back me up," she said, holding onto my forearm with a death grip, and presenting me to the group as Exhibit A. "There was nothing in Dennis's flat, was there? She can tell you."

Put on the spot I stammered and umm-ed and err-ed. Finally, "I didn't see anything, but then, I wouldn't have known —"

Happily, I didn't have to finish that thought, because Viv was in full flow, itemising exactly what we had seen in Harefield's flat, and how all of it indicated the spotless incorruptibility of his character. The lack of food in his kitchen was highlighted to prove that he spent his entire time working, either at the council or with the boys, and so didn't have time to cook, while the unmade bed and the towels on the floor and the piles of dirty clothes only added to this view: "He took so little time for himself that Sam had to positively crawl under the bed to look for his suitcases — bedclothes everywhere," she announced dramatically, as if the floodwaters had washed over a city, and the sole surviving resident — me — had heroically staggered through the mud plains to rescue its sole surviving kitten. I attempted to look modest, but suspected it looked more like I'd swallowed a frog.

Finally, "And he didn't even have his phone with him! What kind of drug dealer doesn't use a phone?" she demanded, proving to me, at any rate, that her expertise came from bulk consumption of *Breaking Bad*. She pinned me with a glare as I attempted to back away. "Sam can tell you. She saw it. Although her language when it rang. I know she was startled, and hit her head on the bed frame, but that's no excuse, now is it?" And she was off again, although this time it was young-people-today and when-I-was-a-girl. It was charming that she thought I was young, but I couldn't see the coroner accepting my youth, or even my bad language, as evidence that Harefield was not a dealer.

To get the spotlight off my linguistic turpitude, I returned to my single contribution, his colleague at the council. Flustered, I now couldn't remember his name, and was reduced weakly to suggesting that "that nice man in planning" would vouch for his character. Since he hadn't been a nice man, and the lie showed on my face, no one paid me much attention. I was done. I switched to platitudes on the loss of a friend for lack of anything better, and stealthily began to move backwards until I had walked myself entirely out of the

112

group, and made a break for it. I'd been to my first Neighbourhood Association meeting, and I'd survived. I might even go again, in another twenty years or so. Or longer. I was sure I could fit longer into my diary.

I was reading in bed when Jake got home: it was well past lateish, and heading towards late by then. He sat down on the side of the bed and rubbed his face.

"Bad day?"

"Bad case. There are children involved." I didn't know whether that meant they were the victims, or the perpetrators, or just innocent bystanders, but that he didn't tell me was matched by my not wanting to know. I moved my feet down to where he was sitting, circling them gently against his leg in what I hoped would be understood as a sign of wordless solidarity. Unless he thought I was just trying to warm them up. One or the other.

"I left you some supper in the fridge. It just needs heating."

He leant over and kissed me hello. "I ate."

I licked my lips exaggeratedly. "Only if beer is one of the food groups."

He smiled. "You should be a detective."

"I could inaugurate a new field, forensic culinary mapping. I'd identify any pub in a ten-mile radius, and separate the craft-beer crazies from the Guinness gang."

"You know I was in a pub?"

I didn't need to be a forensic culinary mapper for that. "A PC walking the beat would know you were in a pub: you taste of beer and you smell of cigarettes. Unless Scotland Yard is organised on entirely different principles than I'd imagined, you've been in a pub, as well as standing outside with the smokers."

"With my DS and the team." He got up and started to undress. "It was post-work work."

My job also involved a lot of what looked like socialising, but was in reality work. I returned half my attention to my book.

"I'm meeting up with a few of them on Sunday, and that will be social. Do you want to come?" He had his back to me and his voice was casual.

"Sure, if you want."

He looked over his shoulder. Not casual at all, said his body language.

I put my book down. "You thought I'd say no?"

He gave that little head shuffle that means it was fifty-fifty. "I thought you might not want to. You don't like pubs, you don't like socialising, and you don't like strangers."

"What better way to spend a Sunday, then, than socialising with strangers in a pub?" My voice was light, but I was shocked that he thought I wouldn't be willing to spend time with his friends. I thought about our life. He'd met some of my friends, although his work schedule meant that I saw them more often on my own. It was only recently that Jake had told his superiors that I — someone he'd met in an official CID capacity — was in his life. Before that, he couldn't have introduced me to any of his work friends even if he'd wanted to, and afterwards we'd kept to the same pattern, probably mostly driven by inertia, but also, I now recognised, driven by my dislike, as Jake had so neatly put it, of pubs, socialising and strangers. That wasn't good. I didn't want my introversion to keep him from his friends.

"Sunday, then," I said. "It's a date."

CHAPTER
SIX

I was in the pub, socialising with strangers, when the fire alarm went off. We continued to talk, assuming it was a false alarm, but the volume increased, the endless woop-woop making conversation impossible. I said to the group around me, "I guess I shouldn't have had that sneaky cigarette while I was standing under the smoke detector," and they laughed. I did too, because I don't smoke. But the fire alarm didn't give up — woop-woop, it went, getting louder and louder.

It wasn't my cigarette that had set it off, I decided. It was a stronger smell than that. I was trying to work out why someone would be burning toast in a pub when the dream broke. No pub, no sneaky cigarettes, not even any toast. The woop-woop was my alarm clock, and it was morning. I reached out and grappled on the bedside table. Still in a deep sleep haze, I had hit several buttons on the clock before I was awake enough to remember that not only did I not smoke, my radio just switched on in the morning — I didn't have an alarm that went woop-woop. I opened my eyes. It was too dark to be morning. The woop-woop was coming from the street.

I sat up and turned on the light. Half past two, and Jake's side of the bed was empty, the sheets tossed back.

The sitting room was lit up like a stage set when I walked in. It wasn't half past two there, it was high noon. Still no Jake. I peered out the front window. What looked like every resident on the street was outside, standing around in dressing gowns or a mix "n" match of clothes dragged on in the dark. As I watched, a policeman headed up the road, his arms spread wide, gesturing the bystanders back as though they were a Jumbo coming in to land.

I found some shoes and went out to join the dressing-gown contingent. As soon as I opened the front door, I could see, and smell, everything. The pub on the corner was on fire, and the woop-woop was more engines arriving.

I'd laughed when Jake had suggested I might have gone to watch a car burn, but standing there, I realised why people did. In Canada, when I was a child, I'd once gone whale-watching on the St Lawrence. There's one area in the river where a specific type of algae, or seaweed, or plankton, or whatever it is, is plentiful, and the whales migrate there for a seasonal all-you-can-eat buffet. Or those were the jokes we made onshore. Once we were in the boat, it was a different story. The organisers apologised: we would only see minke whales that day, the "only" because minke whales are the smallest of the whales found there, and we wouldn't get the full experience. Then a pod surfaced. Each of those small whales was the size of a city block, the height of

117

an apartment building. It wasn't that they were beautiful, although they were, or that viewing them was interesting, although it was. It was that there, suddenly, on a perfectly ordinary day, were creatures on a scale so far outside our experience that we barely knew how to respond.

The fire was like that. If you'd asked me beforehand, I would have guessed that it would have been a visual experience. Instead, the heat pushed at us like a living thing, while the noise, the hissing and crackling, was even more aggressively alive. And it was an emotional experience, fiercer, and more beautiful, than I could have imagined. Like the whales, here, suddenly, on a perfectly ordinary day, in a perfectly ordinary street, was a sight so far outside my experience I barely knew how to respond. The term "force of nature" is a cliché, and a particularly colourless one. Until I was faced by an animal the size of a row of houses, or a fire that was devouring a building alive, and then I understood it. This was why people stood and stared, or ran to watch. Not because they were ghouls, hoping for something nasty, but because what they were seeing was almost incomprehensible in scale.

So I stood and stared, like everyone else. I don't know for how long, but when an arm went around my shoulders, I was so absorbed in that crazed, destructive beauty that I jumped and gave a yelp. Jake was amused. "Promise me you'll tell everyone here that that's not how you usually react when I touch you."

I shook my head sorrowfully. "Too late. They've seen it now. They'll never believe all those lies I tell to cover this tragic reality."

He laughed and let go. "I came to tell you to get dressed. They want to move everyone further down the street. I'll go for Mr Rudiger. And have you seen the Lewises? Are they out here?" He looked around. He was dressed already, which didn't surprise me. I knew from experience with late-night work calls that he could move from deep sleep to being out the door in less time than it took him to say "I'm on my way".

"I saw Kay and Anthony, but not Bim. I'll tell them they need to wake him." Then I processed what he'd said. "Moving us? Why? Is the fire spreading?"

His voice was professionally soothing. "No, no. But it's a dead-end street, and the route out is past the pub: they want a controlled exit until the fire has been contained. It's nothing more than that." Some uniformed police appeared behind him, and they were saying the same thing, in the same professionally soothing tone. There must have been a class in it at cop school: Soothing 101.

It worked, though. I turned to go, professionally soothed and merely asking, "How long do you think we'll be out? Should I get my bag and office clothes?"

"Whatever's quickest." He looked at his watch. "They want everyone out in the next ten minutes, so hop it."

I hopped it. I was dressed and heading back out as Jake came down the stairs with Mr Rudiger in front of him. He looked as if he were off to sit in a café and watch the world go by.

"Good morning," he said. Mr Rudiger might not go out, but nothing ruffled his calm.

I snorted a small laugh. "Good morning to you, too. Have you got" — I wasn't sure what it was he should have, because I didn't know how long we'd be out of the house. So I handed Jake his wallet and phone, which I'd collected along with my things, and ended with a vague — "whatever you need? Where's Bim?" I looked around the hallway, as though he might be lurking under the doormat.

"Outside already, and having a wonderful time." Jake had designated himself hall monitor for our building.

As we walked down the front path we were met by a clipboard-carrying woman in a high-vis jacket. We confirmed that everyone was out of our house, and I added that the neighbours to the left were on holiday, and had no pets. She checked us and them off, and handed us over to another high-vis-er, to be escorted in groups past the pub. It was like being back in kindergarten, although with more dramatic lighting. I was surprised we weren't made to hold hands with a responsible adult.

We were permitted to stop a few hundred metres down the road. Jake had already disappeared again. Mr Rudiger took up a perch on a neighbour's garden wall and nodded back towards the fire. "Over there, on the right."

I looked. Jake was standing with a woman who was pointing to the rear of the pub. Then part of the fire crew moved between us, and I couldn't see him anymore.

"He'll let us know what he's found out when he's back." I rethought that. "Or some of it." The flames that had been visible through the upstairs window of the pub were gone now. The noise, which had been almost overpowering, had altered. The whoosh of the flames, their hiss and splatter, had lessened, and instead the sound of water being pumped out predominated, a steady, even stream of sound that soothed, rather than the erratic crackle and roar of the fire that had exhilarated, but also threatened. Another sense took over. The smell, of smoke and soot, had worked its way into my dream, but after a few minutes outside I'd become accustomed to it, and had stopped noticing it. Now a heavy blanket of smell predominated, no longer the smell of burning, but the smell of wet wood, wet charcoal, wet plaster. As with the empty house, but stronger, just the smell of burnt wet.

We sat watching, mesmerised, barely speaking. There must have been over a hundred people on the street — the fifty or so from our road, who had been forced to leave their houses, and then more from the houses and flats nearby, people who had come out to see what was happening, and had stayed, captured by the fire. As it got later, more kept arriving from nearby streets, having woken up and heard the news. Further down the road was a group of teenagers. I waved to Sam, who was on the edge of the group. He waved back, but furtively. I understood. Being on waving terms with a middle-aged woman wasn't going to do his street-cred any good.

It was more than an hour later, when the fire was no longer visible, and the fire crew were no longer moving at a frantic pace, when I looked at my watch: nearly five. I turned to Mr Rudiger. "What are you going to do? Do you want to use my phone to ring your daughter?"

He thought for a moment. "Not yet. If they don't let us go back inside in the next hour or two, I'll call then."

I considered my options. I could go to the café and get coffee, and then go to work. If I went to Jake's, I could have the coffee and also a shower. I sniffed at myself, not that that told me anything, since the fire smell was everywhere. Even with a shower, my clothes were going to reek, and I didn't have any office clothes at his place. I could go to Helena's, which was closer, and have the coffee and shower there too, but I'd be no better off in the clothes department. We were the same height, but there the physical resemblance ended. She looked like Tinkerbell's smarter sister; I was closer to a baroque putto, but with more chest. And without the trumpet.

Decision made. "I'm going down to the café. It must be open by now. Are you ready for coffee?" I asked Mr Rudiger. A redundant question. He was always as ready for coffee as I was.

Kay, on his other side, reached into her bag. "I'm in. And maybe some juice for Bim? Let me give you some money. I'd come to help, but . . ." She had one finger firmly hooked into the collar of Bim's T-shirt as he strained against it, his body yearning towards the fire engines like a mini Leaning Tower of Pisa, his eyes as bright as the flames had been. This was, by far, the best day of his entire life.

I was pleased she wasn't going to come with me, although I didn't say so. Kay is one of the most elegant-looking people I know, and if there's anything she can drop, or knock over, or bump into, in a five-kilometre radius, she'll drop, or knock over or bump into it. Then she'll knock into the person helping her up. And then drop whatever it is again. It's better to keep her away from hot liquids whenever possible. So I waved away her cash and headed down the road. At the corner, a figure peeled off from the group there. Sam. Either he thought his friends wouldn't notice, or food and drink overrode the need for cool. I gave him a "Hey", and he shambled along behind me without speaking.

Mo and another server had the café open, and were loading up trays with cups of tea and coffee. She gave me a smile as we came in, but didn't pause in her pouring. When one tray was ready, she filled a bag with rolls, put it on top and handed it to Sam. "For the fire crew and the police. *Not* for you and your friends. If you send a couple of them down here, and if they do some carrying for the oldies, I'll make up another tray for you."

Sam grinned. "Free food? They'll help."

Mo handed me a matching tray and spoke to me as sternly as she had to Sam: "Are you going to be able to keep this to the people who are on the street because they have to be, not the ones who are sightseeing?"

"I'll do my best." I lied every time I spoke to Mo. I had no idea how I could accomplish what she was asking — check IDs? Demand to see utility bills, to prove where they lived before handing over an Americano? I'd aim for the older people and children.

The ones in the middle could either take themselves down to the café or do without.

As we headed back up the hill, Sam shouted out to a few of his friends, sending them down the way we'd come, and we continued on towards the crowd. But before we'd gone far, Sam's tray clattered, the hot liquid slopping around.

I balanced mine carefully and turned, to see him staring back at his friends.

"What's wrong?"

He shook his head without replying. He wasn't looking at the boys, I realised, but at a man standing slightly apart from them. The man felt his eyes on him, and looked up. He looked at Sam, no expression on his face, before turning and walking away.

"Who was that?"

"No one," said Sam shortly, turning and starting to walk again.

"Didn't look like no one. Looked like someone," I prodded.

He scowled at me. Then, reluctantly, "A friend of Dennis," he said.

I raised my eyebrows and waited.

"One of those people I told you about. The ones that Dennis stayed friends with, even though . . ."

"Who is he?"

Sam stopped dead and looked at me sternly. "Don't you go near him. Just don't." If he hadn't been carrying a tray, he would have crossed his arms, and possibly called me "young lady".

"I'm just asking about him."

He didn't change his tone. "His name's Kevin. I don't know what his last name is, so that's good. Because you don't need to know."

He strode away, jaw fixed, and I followed. I reached Mr Rudiger without dropping anything, and rested the tray on the wall beside him.

"I'll help," said a confident bass voice.

I turned. Azim. I looked around quickly. Seeing him, it now occurred to me that there'd been no sign of Viv. Given the last interaction she'd had with Azim, I was grateful, or we'd have the battle of the coffee cups, but it was unlike her to miss out on a big event. And it was just as unlikely to see Azim. He ran the newsagent, but that didn't mean he lived nearby. He was standing in front of me, however, so it appeared that he did.

I just nodded to him, and said, "Oldies first?" as I began to pass out the cups. When the tray was empty, he picked it up and asked, "The station café?" and was off for refills before I'd replied. Then he did the trip twice more, stopping and chatting to everyone, effortlessly separating the forcibly-out-of-their-houses-and-therefore-eligible-for-coffee sheep from the having-a-wonderful-time-sightseeing goats as he handed out cups.

We continued to pass out and collect, and the crowd continued to grow as the news spread. Azim was now surrounded by a little pack of Neighbourhood Watch people — Sarah, I saw, was in her element, as was the social worker from the audience. Dan was there with his children, and even the suit from the church hall stood on the edge of the group, drawn, no doubt, by the crowd on his way to work.

Jake wandered by at some point, with a "Don't quote me, but you'll probably be able to go home in the next hour or so", so I decided it was worth waiting it out. I emailed Miranda to say I'd be in late, and then sat on the wall with Mr Rudiger. He was enjoying himself, I think, exchanging banalities with anyone who approached, in between looking on as if the events of the night had been laid on for his entertainment.

Just before eight we were officially told we'd shortly be allowed back home. Kay had vanished briefly, and I had a sleeping Bim on my lap. Azim and his helpers came and thunked down the last of the trays on the wall beside me, which had become, by unspoken agreement, the collection point for empty cups.

"By the way," he said, "I'm Azim, from the newsagent's at the station." He reached around me to shake hands with Mr Rudiger. The past few hours had produced a formula for meeting neighbours with acute bed-hair for the first time. The name-rank-serial-number introduction was: which street you lived in, how you had heard about the fire, a brief segue into opinions about the pub itself, and what you thought was likely to happen to it.

Sarah overshared: she lived with her sister in a flat not far from our street; they'd been woken by the fire engines and were both there in the thick of it, although her sister didn't attend the Neighbourhood Association meetings with any regularity. (Head shaking all round.) Dan we knew about. Mr Rudiger and Kay were both

126

succinct, sticking to names and addresses. The suit didn't give his name, just said his father lived nearby and he'd come over to make sure he was safe, staying afterwards, as he put it, "to gawp".

What a good son. Which reminded me. I fished out my phone and texted Helena. *Just in case you hear, fire in my street during the night. We're fine, damage to pub only.* What a good daughter.

By the time I looked up, one of the high-vis-ers was walking along the street, calling out that we could go back home.

Kay moved to lift Bim off my lap, but the suit was faster. "Let me. He's heavy." And he was walking with him towards our street before any of us had time to protest. His "This way?" made up our minds, and we trailed along behind him, with Azim bringing up the rear.

Jake met us just as we reached the pub, leaving behind a little cluster of police and fire investigators. Azim peeled off there too, his motivation in joining the residents becoming clear as he dawdled, waiting to get the scoop from the authorities.

I tilted my head to the pub. "Are you done here?" I asked Jake, before leaning against him and confiding, "I'm shattered. Almost as tired as if I'd had to abandon my warm bed in the middle of the night because of a fire."

"How strange. And yes, I'm done. It's not my business, anyway." He was telling himself that as much as me.

"What's the consensus?" Azim might head for the professionals, but I had better contacts.

"The pub burnt down."

"No!" I widened my eyes. "Thank God we pay taxes so we can have a police force that knows what it's doing." I clutched my invisible pearls for good measure.

Jake looked a little abashed. "They don't know much more than that. The investigators are just beginning their walk-through, and it'll be a few days before there's more than a preliminary report. All they have at the moment is that no one was inside, and that the ignition point was probably in the backyard. If that's the case, and there's no traces of accelerant, or electrical failure, it might have been nothing more than a cigarette."

"But there have been other fires."

"That's the concern. The earlier ones were, they thought, kids, or distractions set up by Harefield. The empty house then looked like the finish, Harefield caught in a fire of his own making. This changes things. It couldn't have been Harefield. So either it's a coincidence, which is possible — places do burn down — or someone is using the earlier series, although why they would want to isn't at all clear."

I didn't have anything to say to that, so for once I didn't say anything. Maybe I should try that more often. I stopped and looked back at the pub. Water and charcoal, doors and windows destroyed, it had gone from being a viable business to being a pile of bricks in just hours. I shivered, and watched the fire crew preparing to leave. As the first engine pulled away, two men were revealed standing at the end of the pool of light cast by the street lamp: Azim and Dennis's friend Kevin, heads bent, eyes on the pavement, they were talking intently.

Jake's arm went around me and pulled, and I turned and walked away. As we reached the front door to my house, our new friend was coming down the stairs, having presumably dropped Bim off. "Lovely to meet you," he said without stopping as I got out my keys. I mechanically said goodbye, but my attention was on the flat door. It took me several futile turns of the key to realise that I hadn't locked up when we'd been told to leave, just left it on the latch. That I wasn't the sparkliest pixie in the forest at three in the morning was not really news.

"Who was that?" Jake asked once the door was closed behind him.

"A neighbour. His father lives nearby, and he came over to check on him. He goes to Neighbourhood Association meetings. Now you know everything I know."

"That's unlikely. I don't know what the Neighbourhood Association is, for starters." And with that the bastard had stripped off and beaten me to the shower before I'd even walked down the hall.

An hour later I was ready to leave. I'd finally managed to get my turn in the shower by the simple expedient of standing on the bath mat and snapping, "You! Out!" Once I took his place, I understood why I had to force him out. Under the running water, the smell of burning lifted. The moment I put my head out, it returned. I smelt of it, even after washing myself over

129

and over. My clothes smelt of it, even the clean ones in the cupboard. The whole house stank of it. There was no point opening the windows, because outside was even worse. It was everywhere, a thick, sour, heavy smell.

Now that it was over, the exhilaration that watching the fire had produced had worn off, and the stench, the brute reality that someone may have burnt down a building with no concern for the lives of those nearby, combined with lack of sleep to produce a queasy feeling, a mixture of fear and anxiety that sat low in my stomach. I tried to ignore it, and went upstairs. I wanted to check on both sets of neighbours, to let us reassure each other that we were all right, and then head to the office, so that I could pretend that nothing bad was happening. Denial was a wonderful place to be: lovely scenery, great beaches.

I stood listening for a moment outside Mr Rudiger's door. I didn't want to wake him if he'd gone back to bed. I should have known better. My neighbour has hearing that makes bats feel so inadequate they're on waiting lists for bat-sized cochlear implants, and he had the door open before I lifted my hand to knock.

Mr Rudiger's age, and lack of mobility, should have meant the night had taken a toll. Instead he looked exactly as he always did, nattily dressed in a white shirt and dark trousers, his shoes shined, his face freshly shaved. I was three decades younger, and looked exhausted, my hair already escaping from its clip, my clothes clean but unpressed, my shoes not having seen polish since the accession of Queen Elizabeth. Elizabeth I.

So much for my planned offer of help. "Just checking in," I said instead. "I stopped by Kay and Anthony's too." I shrugged, not sure how to explain why I felt the need to do so. "We seem to have become family since last night."

Mr Rudiger looked at me the way he does when I'm being particularly dense, fond but under no misapprehensions: "We always were," he said.

By the time I reached the office, it was lunchtime, and the building was deserted. I sat at my desk and gazed around vaguely, as if the room belonged to someone else, someone I was only mildly interested in knowing. I was dizzy from lack of sleep, being a hard-core eight-hour-a-night woman by preference. My brain refused to let go of the smell of burning, which clung to me like an aura, even though objectively I knew I had washed it off hours before. I stared at the wall, seeing the flames still burning.

"Sam. Sam!" A voice was calling, and I turned. Miranda was at the door. "Are you all right?"

I returned to the present. A bad-tempered present. "Of course I am. Why shouldn't I be?"

She put her finger to her chin in pantomime puzzlement. "Maybe because I've been calling your name for the last five minutes? Or because you're not answering your phone?"

I wasn't? "I didn't hear you. Or it."

"Exactly."

Oh. "I was thinking." I tried a smile. "Always a major undertaking."

"I could smell the burning rubber from my desk."

Burning. I flinched, and scrubbed at my face, trying to wipe away the tiredness. "It's just that I'm operating on very little sleep. There was a fire down the road from me last night, and they made us leave. We didn't get back home until this morning."

"Why are you here? Go home, get some sleep." She didn't add "Duh" to the end of the sentence, but with the tone of voice she was using, it wasn't necessary.

It would have been the sensible thing to do, but I didn't want to smell that wet burning smell again. I brushed off her concern. "Soon." I gathered myself. "Has Kath been in touch?" I was bidding on a book, and the agent, Kath Strong, was a demon for squeezing out final-final offers long after you thought you'd made a final offer.

Miranda looked stern. "That's why I came in. She's emailed and she's rung. She couldn't get hold of you, so she phoned me."

Oops. I checked my email, and there it was. Or, rather, there they were: three emails from Kath. "Thanks. I'll take care of it." Luckily this would take neither time nor brainpower. The auction had reached the upper limit of what I could offer. I tapped out a quick reply, dropping out. It was a damn good novel, but I could barely make the figures work at the level we'd agreed. We'd be shooting ourselves in the foot financially if I went any higher. If I hadn't been so tired, I would have been disappointed. I'd loved the book. I reminded myself of the saying my first publishing boss always recited in these circumstances: "Never be afraid to walk away." He was right, but it still felt like failure most times.

I had no energy for that emotion today, however. That was the only benefit I could see coming out of the fire. I told myself that with a good night's sleep I'd be fine. Not perky, but fine. I don't really perk. It's hard to perk when your natural state is that an unknown something dreadful will shortly happen to an unknown someone in an unexpected somewhere. With eight hours' sleep I manage not to expect that the something dreadful will occur in the next twenty minutes. That's as positive as I get. Without the sleep, there was no hope of positivity. And my un-perky worldview was once more proved the correct one when Miranda returned just as I hit "send" on my email to Kath. She had her cup and saucer in one hand, but put it down on the filing cabinet to pour me a cup from my pot. This was not good.

"I'm guessing you need to talk to me, and I'm also guessing I'm not going to like it."

She shut the door, which, even if I hadn't picked up on her butter-her-up-with-coffee clue, would have told me that whatever it was was going to be serious. "Since you're not going home . . ."

"What's up?" seemed a suitably innocuous lead-in, so I went for it.

"It's Ben's book."

I resisted the temptation to put my head down on my desk and whimper. Ben runs our literary fiction list, and he despises the kind of commercial women's fiction I publish. He also despises anyone over the age of thirty-two. And, I've always suspected, he despises women more generally, although that might be my rationalisation for why he doesn't like me. But, cut to the chase, I'm three for three: a woman over thirty-two who publishes commercial women's fiction, so yes, he doesn't like me, although, to be fair, I don't like him either. This was not one of those carefully guarded secrets. Everyone in the office knew. Possibly everyone within Greater London. He may have taken out ads in *The Times*.

Given our mutual hostility, therefore, if Miranda had run-of-the-mill editorial queries on the book she was working on for him, she wouldn't bring them to me.

I pretended to smile. "What's the problem?"

She turned her big, pretty eyes towards me and blinked slowly. "The book's good, you know? Really good."

That couldn't be the problem, so I nodded and sipped my coffee. When nothing more was forthcoming, I prodded. "Remind me what it's about. It's a memoir, isn't it?"

That unstuck her logjam. "Yes, a memoir, by someone who was in a gang. He tells the story of how he got into the gang, and what life was like, the drug dealing, violence . . ." She trailed off, allowing me to assume the etceteras. "Then there's his arrest and time in prison."

"And?"

"And it's wonderfully written, it's exciting, and —" she spoke in a rush now "— and I don't believe a word of it. I think he made most of it up."

"Oh."

She laughed, the Miranda I knew returning. "I was hoping for a little more guidance than 'Oh'."

"How about 'Oh, flaming Nora'?" I looked at my empty mug. "If you were going to dump this on my lap, you could have spiked my coffee with brandy." I got up and poured us both more. "Let's break this down. Tell me about the author first. Have you been in touch with him? What did Ben tell you about him?"

She shook her head. "It's one of those he's-writing-under-a-pseudonym-so-no-one-kills-him deals. No one gets to meet him, or be in touch with him at all."

"Who's the agent?"

"No agent. I checked the file. A lawyer negotiated the contract, and everything goes through him."

If the author wasn't a professional writer, it wasn't unheard of that he didn't have an agent, and while lawyers generally represented big-name authors, the situation wasn't unknown.

I tried to approach it from another angle. "What set your alarm bells ringing?"

"It's not one thing, it's a lot of little things." She wiggled her fingers, those little things creeping about. "He says at the beginning that he's changed names and places — he's describing criminal acts among people who have not been arrested, so it makes sense that he's protecting himself from blowback, as well as protecting others from police attention."

"And himself from libel actions, if the people he's writing about haven't been accused of the crimes he's saying they committed."

"Exactly. And that's fine, I expect that information to have been altered. It's that there are details that aren't right when there's no reason for him to have changed them."

"Like what?"

"He uses current slang, but says it was in use ten years ago, when the events happened."

"That doesn't necessarily mean anything except he isn't very attuned to language. And if he's not a writer by trade, he might well not be." If that was the worst of it, there wasn't a problem.

She shook her head vehemently, curly hair flying. "He is very attuned to language. He may not have written before, I don't know, but he's good. Really good. That's a minor example. There are more concrete concerns. For example, my grandmother lives a couple of streets away from the school he says he went to, so I know the area, and the school wasn't there then. Once I spotted that, I began to check other details. He was prosecuted for possession of cannabis, which he says was a class C drug. It has been since 2005, but by then, according to his own chronology, he'd already been convicted. And then there's his imprisonment: at one stage he says he was a Category C prisoner, at another that he was in a young offenders' institution." She gave a wintry little smile. "My extensive research on Wikipedia tells me that only adult prisoners are categorised, and he was a minor. He should know this, and yet, somehow, he doesn't."

I put my hands up, palms outward, to stop the avalanche of detail. "Short version. You think the book is bogus."

Miranda isn't quiet, and she isn't hesitant, but now she was both. "I think it must be," she finally said in a very small voice.

I wanted to tell her there wouldn't be a problem, but that wasn't the case. "Have you got a copy of the contract?" I asked it as a question, even as I held out my hand for it. Miranda was insanely efficient. There was no question she had the contract. She pulled it out and doodled glumly on her manuscript while I went over it. Ben had spent what in technical publishing jargon was known as a shitload of money on this book. I flicked through to the warranty clause, praying it wasn't standard. God did not have publishers on his answered-prayers rota that week: the clause was entirely standard, with the author guaranteeing that the book contained nothing that was "materially inaccurate". To outsiders, that was our get-out-of-jail-free card. If we could show the author had fabricated parts of his story, he would have to pay back his advance. But insiders knew it was more than likely that the advance had long been spent. Best case scenario? We would find ourselves legally in the right, but with no way of recouping the huge chunk of cash we'd spent, and with legal bills on top of that.

I flipped the pages back together. "You have to tell Ben." Miranda flinched. "I know you don't want to. He isn't going to be happy, but if the queries you raise don't have an explanation, if the author can't tell us what these inconsistencies mean, we can't publish the book as it stands. If the author has a reason for the inconsistencies, you can go ahead. If he doesn't, and the writing is as good as you say, maybe we can publish it as a novel."

Miranda didn't answer, just stared at the cup in her lap, turning it round and round in its saucer.

I summoned a positive tone and mapped out a plan of action for her. "Write it down, list out the details that don't fit, then do a covering memo, outlining what you've just told me. But don't just dump it on Ben's desk and run. Talk him through it. If you're right, Ben should be grateful it's been caught early on. It would be much worse if we'd published it, and then found out. That would be a public humiliation for him, and a very expensive situation for the company." The operative word was "should". I didn't think Ben would be grateful at all, and it would still be a humiliation. Not a public one, but the whole company, and most of the rest of the industry, would know that he'd fallen for a hoax. But it would still be better than the story coming out in the newspapers.

Miranda stood up. "If I were your full-time assistant still, you'd have to do this, not me," she said mutinously.

"And that's why you're being paid the big bucks now." We snorted in tandem. The salary increase that went with her new job could be seen only through the most powerful of microscopes. "If you want me to look

138

at the memo before you hand it to Ben, shoot a draft over to me." I'd make sure the tone was disengaged, as though it were nobody's fault. "Use the passive voice a lot."

She cocked her head to the side. *Hunh?*

"It's a way of not allocating blame. When I said before 'Ben should be grateful it's been caught early on', *it's been caught* is better than *I caught it*. The latter says *I caught it, so why didn't you?* while the former just says *the universe is conspiring against us*."

She laughed, but shook her head at the same time. "If you think that's going to make it OK with Ben, smoke inhalation has made you delusional."

More than likely.

CHAPTER
SEVEN

I could have used a little more delusion that evening. Dazed with lack of sleep, all I wanted was a quiet night in. I'd planned to potter around, make supper and then head to bed. But as I walked home from the Tube, the smell turned thoughts of food into a rancid lump in my gut. I decided I might never eat again, and briefly wondered whether we could get a book out of it. Lord knows, diet books that were realistic — eat less, exercise more, yadda-yadda — never sold. *Lose Weight the Arson Way* might have a future. By the time I reached the corner, the jokes dried up. There was crime-scene tape outside the pub, just as there had been outside the empty house. The smell and the signs of police investigation combined together to make me even queasier.

My thoughts grew more positive when I saw Steve in my front garden. Half of the area had already been cleared, and he was wrestling with a rosemary bush, his back to me. I coughed gently and he spun around.

"Wow," I said, looking at what must have been hours of work.

"You don't mind?"

"Mind what?" I hopscotched over the tools and dug-up greenery that littered the path.

"That I made a start." He was standing, rosemary bush in one hand, shovel in the other. "I didn't want to rush you, but if I move now, I can get one late summer crop turned around before I begin to sow for winter."

"I told you, *mi* garden *es su* garden. Do what you like." I waved a hand at an untold world of doing-what-he-liked-ness, and continued up the stairs. At the front door, I hesitated. I didn't want to set a pattern so that every time he was there I felt I needed to play hostess, but that good-girl training dies hard. Or, in reality, is alive and kicking, because I heard myself saying, "Do you want anything? A cup of tea? Water?" *Please say no, please say no.*

"No, thanks. I've got everything I need." He dangled the rosemary bush in the direction of my recycling boxes, where I now saw he had a water bottle and a thermos set out.

What a great guy.

"Before you go, though, have you thought any more about what you'd like me to plant, apart from the basics? Do you want me to transfer any of the herbs you have in pots in the back? Otherwise I'll just put in some quick-return crops: lettuces, radishes, things like that."

It seemed rude to say that I'd forgotten his question about what he should grow the moment after he'd asked it, so I promised to text him a list of what I liked and didn't like first thing in the morning.

Inside, I dropped my things by the front door. Without bothering to put anything away, I headed to the kitchen first, and then settled into my reading position against the arm of the sitting-room sofa. I had coffee, I had manuscripts on submission that needed to be read, I had — I scrabbled through my bag — a manuscript I needed to edit before the author went away the following week. In a word, I was set: there was no reason for me to move from my little work cocoon in the cushions for the rest of the day. Maybe forever.

So naturally I immediately reached down for my phone, which was somewhere in the pile of papers I'd just spilt across the floor. As always, Helena answered on the first ring. Helena rarely troubled with "hello". If she could have answered every ringing phone with "Tell me quickly what it is you want, I'm a busy woman", and not be regarded as odd, she would have.

"Just checking in after last night," I said.

"Mmm," she replied. This meant: a) about time you rang; b) tell me everything; and c) while you're doing that, I'm going to get through another three tasks simultaneously. Most importantly, it also meant, d) but don't for a moment imagine that I'm not paying attention, because in ten years I'll still be able to cite this conversation verbatim if I need to.

So I told her about the fire, and the adjourned inquest. Which moved me straight along to the Neighbourhood Association meeting, and Viv's views on Harefield's double life, and Sam's information about the boys' club, and that the police had questioned them.

Helena, of course, was way ahead of me. "I asked a friend to see where the police investigation had got to, and why they were so sure he was a drug dealer."

"You did? When?"

Helena was tart. "After we spoke and you asked about drug dealers."

I thought back to that conversation. "Did I even mention a name?" I didn't think I had.

"No, but you said a house had burnt down in Talbot's Road, and someone had died. It wasn't very hard to find out who you were talking about."

Mostly when I talk to Helena I feel like one of those small dogs with short legs, a cocker spaniel maybe, which needs to race along frantically behind its owner just to keep pace. She was used to my puffing along in her wake, and so she continued without pause. "Did you know they found £25,000 in cash in his flat?"

Jake had said it was a lot. The amount couldn't have been mentioned at the inquest, or it would have been the main topic for discussion at the Neighbourhood Association meeting. But if Helena said that the police had found £25,000 in Harefield's flat, then they had found £25,000. "No wonder they thought he was a drug dealer." Then I thought about it. "Wait a minute. Where did they find it?" That was a lot of cash. It wasn't something you could stuff away in an envelope.

"Why?"

I was confused. "Why what?"

Helena was at her most patient, which meant that she thought I was being slow. "Why do you want to know where the cash was found?"

That wasn't something I particularly wanted to discuss with my mother. There was no help for it, however. "Viv took me with her when she went to check out Harefield's flat after he disappeared. She was worried that he might have been taken ill, and was lying there. And if not, she thought he might have been called away and forgotten to tell her. So she went to see if he'd taken his suitcases, or a bunch of clothes had obviously been packed up or his toothbrush was gone."

"I see."

I suspected she did see, right down to my climbing over the balcony. But I wasn't going to confess to that unless I was forced to. Instead I returned to the cash. "Wouldn't that much money take up a lot of space?" I'd never seen £25,000 in cash, but even a few hundred pounds was bulky. I couldn't believe that both Viv and I would have missed it.

"Does that question mean you didn't see it when you were there?" I heard Helena shuffling some papers. "It was in a satchel, under his bed."

"Viv did the sitting room, I took the bedroom. And I don't think I saw anything like that." I closed my eyes and tried to visualise Harefield's bedroom. "I looked under his bed. I know I did. I used the light from my phone, because the bedclothes were thrown back, and I could barely see without it. But I didn't see a bag."

Helena's voice was sharp now. "Are you saying you didn't see a bag, or there wasn't a bag?"

I understood the difference, and I sagged, defeated. "I think I have to say that I didn't see one. It was dark under there, so I was about to move to check the other side when Harefield's phone rang. I jumped, and dropped my own phone. I went over to search for his, and I think I picked mine up and Viv came in to ask about the call. I forgot what I'd been doing, and left the room. So no, I can't swear there was nothing under the bed."

She was silent. So I repeated, "I can't."

Her voice was neutral, no judgement. "That's that, then. It was there when the police searched. And you're not sure."

I wasn't sure. But all the same, I didn't think it was there.

"You might want to mention it to Jake," she said.

"Want" was probably not the verb I would have chosen, but I knew what she meant. After we hung up, I focused on practicalities, texting Jake: *Will you be home for supper?* Then I dropped the manuscript I'd been holding in my lap and picked up my laptop. Google was my friend. "Kevin", "skateboard", "T-shirts", and "Camden market" together led me straight to a map of the market, with a stall marked as run by one Kevin Munroe, who sold skateboard-motif clothing.

Then I sat staring for a while, thinking not about skateboards, nor T-shirts, nor even Dennis Harefield. Instead I wondered how Steve had known I had herb pots in my back garden. And about Azim, a man who in twenty years I'd never once seen outside of his newsagent's, who was, suddenly, everywhere.

I was in the kitchen making supper when the front door opened. As it did, I heard a ping, and checked my phone. *Yes,* said a text from Jake. And then he was in the kitchen. I waved my phone at him. "Cute," I said.

He washed his hands and face at the sink, then turned to get a bottle of wine out of the fridge. "I was in meetings all afternoon with my phone switched off; then I was driving. I saw your message as I walked up the street."

"Lucky for you I made enough dinner to feed two."

He rolled his eyes. "You always make enough for ten."

I resented the implication that I was a complete idiot. I was only part idiot. "Six."

"Six hungry people."

This was true. I changed the subject. "Still the same bad case?"

He took a swig of his wine, as if washing out his mouth, too, before handing me a glass and making a non-committal noise. Then, "We made some arrests. That's why I wasn't checking my texts. Interviews."

"That sounds like a step forward." Since I had no idea what the case was about, nor was I prepared to ask if the interviews had given the results he wanted, encouraging banalities was all I was good for. Even if Encouraging Banalities sounded like it was a Seattle indie rock band. I decided that that thought probably didn't need to be shared.

Jake did better on no sleep than I did — he was called out often enough at night — but he still had to be tired. I'd been up since 2.30, and he'd been out of the house before that. "It's early, but do you want to eat soon, and try and catch up on some sleep?"

"Unless you're hungry, shall we sit and have a drink first?" That was British for "no": always state your preference by phrasing it as a question was the rule.

I wasn't hungry, just tired, so we moved into the sitting room. I looked out the window and saw Steve was gone. Jake saw me looking. "He was packing up as I left. He'd said he planned to get the soil turned and fertilised tomorrow, and planted by the end of the week."

"Quick work."

Jake no longer seemed disturbed that he was working out front. Progress. I moved to sit down, putting my feet up on the coffee table where I'd piled my manuscripts, none of which I'd given so much as a look at, with my laptop open on top. I wasn't going to mention my googling to Jake, but, "I spoke to Sam the other day. Boy Sam," I clarified, in case Jake thought I'd taken to referring to myself in the third person. "He says he and his friends have been questioned by the police about the fires." Sam had said not to mention it to Jake, but if I told Jake this was unofficial, not something to be passed on to his colleagues, I was sure he wouldn't. It wasn't his case, or even his division.

Jake didn't look surprised, just giving a what-were-you-expecting shrug.

"Why would they know anything? Or, rather, why would the police assume they knew something?"

He sighed at the question. Truth be told, he was probably sighing at my hostile tone, but I chose to ignore that. "It's the profile. Boys. Teens."

I was snippy. "Could you elaborate, for us slow folk who don't make snap assumptions about people we don't know?" I turned to face him on the sofa, hackles up.

Jake held up a hand: stop. "The police aren't concentrating on the boys because boys generally are a problem," he said. "They're concentrating on them because they knew Harefield, they spent time with him, and in addition they fit the age and gender profile of the majority of arsonists. Arson for insurance doesn't have the same profile, but this series isn't about insurance: several of the buildings were uninsured. When it's not an insurance matter, arson is most often a form of vandalism, and the perpetrators are almost always teenagers — teenaged boys, more specifically. These boys also live in the area where the fires were set, another factor." He poured himself another drink and held the bottle up to me in an unspoken question. I shook my head and rolled my hand in a keep-going gesture. "There's nothing more to say. That's why the police questioned them. Imagine your entire street had been graffitied one night. Would you expect the police to interview you and Mr Rudiger, or would they interview teenaged boys? Who is more likely to have been involved?" He raised his hands, a poster boy for outraged patience. "If eighty per cent of one type of crime is committed by one type of person — age, gender, location, known acquaintance — we tend to focus on that type. Profiling is rough, but it's not baseless."

I decided not to discuss what happened when you only questioned one group of people — hey presto, you caught the perpetrators in that group, but the perpetrators who didn't fit the profile meantime merrily went on perpetrating. Mr Rudiger and I might be the King and Queen of Graffiti, and they'd never find out, because they'd never think to interview us. But I wasn't going to change the way the police operated. I wasn't even going to change the way Jake operated.

I shrugged ungraciously by way of reply, so he continued: "My guess is that there were CCTV cameras near several of the incidents. The tapes would have been checked and it may be that some of Harefield's boys could be identified at more than one fire. Firebugs — people who set fires for the hell of it — like to watch. It's likely some of Sam's friends were seen on the tapes."

Maybe I *was* going to attempt to change the way the police operated. "Why would that mean anything other than that they'd gone to watch a fire in the neighbourhood? According to you, *I* might have gone to watch the car burn." I stabbed at my chest to emphasise who "I" was. "If I had, I'd be on that CCTV footage. Would you expect your colleagues to question me?"

"If you'd been there, and were then seen on the tapes at another couple of the fires in the same series, then yes, probably."

I hated when Jake was rational, and he expected me to be rational too. But I wasn't ready to concede entirely. "Maybe. But you said last night that the pub and the empty house were different. Neither fits into your 'essentially vandalism' category, so why should the boys be hauled in in connection with the empty house?"

"It's not my category," he said absently. "And it's true, the two incidents do appear to be different. They thought that the fire in Talbot's Road might have been an accident, one where the arsonist himself was killed. But if the pub fire is another in the series, that's no longer a consideration: Harefield couldn't have set the pub on fire, so the question is, was Harefield the arsonist, or was he simply the ideas man, and someone else set the fires for him, and then caught him in his own trap?"

"Why can't it be two lots of people?"

He stared at me as if he were trying to work out how to say something. Finally he found a diplomatic form of words. "Because two arsonists in one small geographic area, in one short period of time, is a coincidence too far, wouldn't you say?" He was good. I barely heard the unspoken "dummy" at the end of the sentence.

I would normally agree with him, but not when I'd just presented it as a reason for the police not to harass Sam. And Sam didn't believe that Harefield was either the arsonist or the "ideas man". I decided not to mention that again, at least, not right away. "Dinner?" seemed like a more tactful response.

By unspoken agreement, we stayed away from the subject while we ate, but I couldn't postpone it forever. I waited until we were cleaning up, and I had my hands in the sink, carefully scrubbing a pot so that I didn't

150

have to look at Jake. "Helena says I have to talk to you about something."

Jake picked up the clean glasses from the dish drainer. "Two of your favourite things," he said. "Doing what Helena tells you, and talking." He nudged me gently. "Get it over with."

"You know I said Viv had the keys to Harefield's flat?" I began. Jake nodded, drying the glasses and putting them away, making I'm-listening noises. "When she was worried about him, when Missing Persons were telling her there was nothing they could do, I sort of — well, we went to check out his flat together. We had a look round, to see if he'd packed up and gone off somewhere. I looked in his bedroom."

Jake pulled the clean pan I'd been scrubbing over and over out of my hands and turned off the tap. I stayed facing the sink. "Helena said the police found a satchel full of cash under his bed. I looked there, to see if there was a suitcase or something. I didn't see a satchel." I turned to him. "I can't swear it wasn't there, but I can, and do, say that I don't think it was."

He handed me a tea towel. "You do find trouble, don't you?" But he wasn't annoyed. "I'll pass it on, but officially this will carry no weight: if you're not sure, you're not sure." He leant back against the counter and stared at me for a moment. "But between us, how sure are you?"

I stared back hopelessly. "I don't know. The room was messy, sheets and towels all over the place, so I keep thinking I might have overlooked it. It was dark under the bed, too. But I've got a good memory, and an

151

even better visual memory. And my mind sort of works in categories . . ." Jake raised his eyebrows. "I don't know how to explain it. I'm tidy." I waved my arm around the kitchen. "I'm tidy because things that go together in my head get put together."

I could see he still didn't understand, so I used the examples in front of us. "There are different kinds of belonging. My spice rack is alphabetised because cumin doesn't belong next to turmeric, it belongs after cinnamon and before dill seeds. The scissors are kept beside the knife rack, even though there's no place for them there, and it would be tidier if I kept them in a drawer. But scissors and knives both cut things, so they belong together. It makes me —" I knew how weird it was, and it wasn't something I'd normally admit to, but there was no help for it now "— It makes me actively unhappy if the scissors are in the drawer with writing things, not on the counter with the cutting things."

Jake stared at me for a moment, then silently walked over to the shelf where I kept the spice jars. He bent and looked at them, moving his head left to right, working his way along the alphabet. Still silent, he sat back down, started to speak, then closed his mouth. Then he shook his head.

I kept going. "Don't forget baking supplies: flour, buckwheat; flour, rye; flour, spelt. Self-raising flour is a problem. It's wheat, so does it go after the spelt, or does it go before, because it's self-raising? Sometimes it's labelled all-purpose flour — maybe it goes at the front of the shelf, with the 'a's? I don't know what to do with it, which is why it's on a different shelf altogether." I

152

tried to get back on track. "What I'm trying to say is, I was looking under the bed for a suitcase, so it's likely I would have noticed a satchel, because a satchel is the same family as a suitcase, just as knives are in the same family as scissors." Jake was still speechless. "I realise that this isn't anything the police can use . . ."

At that, Jake burst out laughing. Then he didn't stop. Finally he put his head down on the table. He didn't quite hold his ribs, but it looked like he was thinking about it. I waited. He didn't lift his head off the table, but he looked up. "The police can't use 'a satchel is first cousin to a suitcase'?"

I was sure that there was a witty comeback to that, one that would at one and the same time make clear my certainty while defusing my peculiar thought processes. But I was too tired to come up with it. I was too tired to care. I finished wiping down the counters and flicked on the dishwasher. "Helena said to tell you, so I followed orders: I told you. Now, I know it's not even nine, but I'm done. Finished. I'm going to bed."

In the morning, when I woke up, Jake was gone and had left a note, "At the gym", as he did most Saturdays. It also added, somewhat mysteriously, "Don't worry, I'll be back in plenty of time."

Don't worry? Time? Then I remembered. It was the day of Helena's party. I pulled the pillow over my head and whined into it for a while. When I lifted it off, nothing had changed. I still had to go to Helena's party.

Steve and Mike were both in the garden when I collected my cycle from under the stairs, but I waved and said, "Don't stop on my account", which they appeared to understand was code for "Hey, guys, how about we don't talk." There's only so much sociability a person can take in any twenty-four-hour period, and with Helena's knees-up looming, my sociability levels were going to be stretched to their limits.

I'd slept in, and I was a good hour late when I got to Viv's. She always had a packed schedule — you don't get to be the eyes and ears of a densely populated neighbourhood by sitting at home and knitting. She wasn't sitting at home, much less knitting, when I got there. I rang and waited, but there was no "What do you want?", Viv's greeting of choice. I set Mr Rudiger's offerings on her doorstep, only then noticing a plastic bag on the mat. I peered in. Yes, seedlings, and a note. "Mr R." it said. Nothing for the messenger. I was just a small cog in the wheel that was the Great Garden Swap.

I was almost at the turn-off for the market when I spotted Viv standing outside the train station. I was stopped at the lights, so I had hopped off and was walking towards her before I realised that one of the three people she was talking to — or, if I was reading the situation correctly, one of the three people she was haranguing — was a policeman. I stood back and waited as she jabbed her finger in his direction and he replied, rabbit-in-the-headlights, by nodding frantically. When she had him suitably cowed, she gestured behind her. My turn.

"Good morning," I said, dividing it up among the three of them.

Viv kept an iron grip on the conversation. "This is PC Neill. And his colleagues. Community police officers." As such, they didn't rate highly enough to have names, said her tone. "I've been trying to find out how many times the police are going to traipse in and out of Dennis's flat. They've been keeping me up nights. I can't afford to be short on sleep." She said this with the grave importance of the keeper of the nuclear detonator, the free world at risk from a finger shaky with lack of eight hours' solid rest.

It was a challenge, but I didn't smile. "I'm sure PC Neill isn't responsible for that. It'll be either the arson people, or detectives from the drugs division, I imagine, who have been investigating."

I wasn't sure of the proper names of the various departments, but I doubted Viv knew either, and the poor constable in front of us had been so terrorised by Viv that he was agreeing with everything — if I'd said the Prime Minister of New Zealand, aided by a team of crack haka dancers, had stepped in to take charge, he would have backed me up on that too.

Viv folded her arms and looked me up and down. I was no better than the police. "And then what?"

I was silent.

She snorted: she'd thought as much. "Apart from morrising above my head at midnight, what are the police doing?" She looked over at the poor PC, who couldn't have been much older than Sam. "He won't tell me anything."

I thought he might cry, which would embarrass all of us, so I interrupted. "Look, they're there, they're doing something, that's what you wanted last week, when they weren't doing anything, isn't it?"

The community officers had used my appearance as a cover to back away, pretending that they'd made entirely different career choices — poultry farming, perhaps, or oil-rig construction — and were now in the vicinity merely by chance. The PC's radio squawked. It was probably his mother, reminding him to be home by ten, but he too now used the interruption as an opportunity to retreat.

I wheeled my cycle beside Viv as she marched to the crossing. She was ignoring me, payment for siding with the PC. I should have been grateful, and headed off to the market, but to my horror I heard myself saying, "I was told Harefield had a friend who worked at Camden market. I thought I'd go down this morning and see if he'd talk to me."

I'd thought this would pacify her, since she'd been complaining that no one was doing anything, but instead I got a glare. "How long have you known about him? Why didn't you tell me his name, and I could have gone to see him while you were at work?"

I thought quickly. "I found out about him on the night of the fire; I couldn't have told you until yesterday. And since the market is half-operational during the week, we'd have had to wait until today anyway, to make sure he was there."

I got a grudging nod. Excuse accepted.

Since we were pooling information, she handed over her share. "I've been trying to find his family. I rang his colleague at the council. The one whose name you gave me." This merited another sniff. Whatever he'd said, it was my fault.

I tried to be optimistic. "What did he say?"

"He said he didn't know, and passed me on to personnel, or manpower, or human resources, or whatever they call themselves. They weren't any help, either. They wouldn't tell me who they had down as his next-of-kin." She stiffened her spine. "So I've given it to someone else." Now she was a police divisional inspector, allocating assignments. "One of my friends has a grandson who is good at computers. He's promised to do a search for me."

"That's an excellent idea." I added, hopefully, "The police may be more active now that the pub burnt down, since they can't think Harefield was the arsonist for that."

Viv was scornful. "They'll just bother the boys more."

"Have they come back to question them again?"

Viv made an exasperated "tuh" noise, which I took to be her view on the reappearance of the police.

I was concerned. "They should have someone to look out for them. My mother is a solicitor. I can ask her to recommend someone."

"Who is going to pay for that?"

"No one. That is, they won't need to pay. She'll find them someone who works with —" I hadn't thought of a diplomatic form of words, and I stumbled. "Someone who works with boys who have been in trouble." There. That sounded all right. "They do it without a fee," I added quickly.

She was suspicious. "Since when?"

"Plenty of lawyers take on extra cases for people they think need help, or are about things they're interested in, and they don't charge."

She didn't reply, just marched along, arms swinging. She just didn't believe me.

"They do, really. The good guys, at least. My mum is one of them, and her friends too. I think I should ask her to find someone for Sam and the other boys."

Decision made. "They need it," she said.

CHAPTER
EIGHT

At the market, I bought flowers for Helena, and then, as an afterthought, texted her: *Anything you want from the market for your party? Ice cream from the place that does bizarre flavours: basil, ginger beer, liquorice?* Helena was fanatically organised. She made storm troopers look like they'd majored in interpretative dance. She'd already have everything she needed, so something she didn't need would be more useful. And if she said no, I could go back to bed later with ginger beer ice cream.

I whizzed through my shopping as quickly as I could and then, stocked up for the week ahead, I headed down to Camden market. The contrast between the two markets could not have been more extreme. The farmers' market I went to consisted of twenty produce stalls that were erected every Saturday in a school car park, and was attended by several hundred mostly middle-aged people, intermixed with a sprinkling of young marrieds pushing their progeny, and oldsters dragging shopping trolleys. Camden market, on the other hand, had possibly a thousand or so vendors selling to an average of fifteen thousand mostly teenaged customers, who wouldn't be seen dead with either a pushchair or a pull-bag. And instead of organic rye bread, or courgette flowers, these customers were getting their eyebrows pierced, or were looking for Doc Martens.

Fifteen thousand is a lot of people, so in the years I'd lived less than a kilometre away, I'd devised numerous routes especially to avoid the main drag where the stalls were concentrated. It felt strange now to be searching out the most congested area, but that was what my map had assured me I needed to do. After a few minutes, I realised I'd do better on foot, so I dumped my cycle, chaining it to a lamp post.

Then I headed in, feeling like one of those soldiers going over the top in World War I movies. They knew it wasn't going to be pretty, but stiff upper lip and all that. And it wasn't pretty, if you were over twenty-seven and had few occasions for lava lamps, skull rings or more Celtic jewellery than there had ever been Celts. I kept moving forward, putting me at odds with everyone else, none of whom had any firm destination, but were simply drifting from stall to stall.

I tried to keep on a straight path to where I estimated the stall was, shaking my head "no" to the dozens of people thrusting out ads for merchandise, for shops and for concerts at the passers-by, shaking it "no" again as stallholders promoted their goods, which were, they promised, cheap, beautiful, cheap, original, and did I mention cheap?

The online map had put Kevin Munroe's stall next to a row of takeaway food places, and a pub. In taking evasive action around various groups of teens, I'd got myself turned around, and had lost any sense of where I was. I swayed in a circle, trying to get my bearings. A heavily tattooed man stood by the doorway to a shop. "Which way is the Hawley Arms?" I asked.

He looked at his watch ostentatiously. "A little early for a pint, girl?"

I gave a polite, if forced, smile, the kind women have been giving men who get in their face for centuries. "I'm looking for a stall that's right next to it."

"A tattoo before you head off there?" he offered.

I didn't need to force that smile. I laughed out loud. "Because I'm the type, right?"

He smiled back, honestly this time. "There's no type. I could do you something small." He gestured to my cleavage. "A rosebud would look good there."

"It would." I was serious. "And then over the years, as gravity takes over, my partner and I can watch it turn into a long-stemmed beauty rose. It would be so romantic."

He raised his hands. "I surrender. A woman with an eye on the future isn't my customer base." Wasn't that the truth. "The Hawley Arms is that way: head for the railway cutting and you'll see it in front of you."

I grinned and gave him a mock salute before I set off. I might have an eye on the future, but you never knew when you'll need an emergency rosebud.

Once I located the pub, finding Kevin Munroe's stall wasn't difficult. It was large, evidently very popular, and therefore surrounded by what looked like hundreds of teenaged boys, all turning over piles of T-shirts covered with graffiti designs. Sam had said that some of

161

the boys had made T-shirts before Harefield had helped them set up a more professional sales system. I wondered if Munroe was that system.

The man behind the stall was the man I'd seen with Azim on the night of the fire. He was tall and very thin, so thin he probably looked even taller, and he was a decade or so older than Sam and his friends. I stood in the shadow of the next row of stalls and watched as he bantered with his customers, selling his stock almost without pause. I didn't approach. At first I told myself I would "in a few minutes", minutes that, however, were never up. Then I admitted I wasn't moving for two reasons. First, Munroe was more than a little frightening. He was dealing avuncularly with the teens shopping for shirts, but he had an air of menace. I had planned to be a customer, and fall into casual chat with him. Looking at him, I changed my mind.

And that brought up the second reason: What could I ask him? *Was Harefield dealing drugs, and were you his distribution conduit? Want to tell me about it? — Yes, just speak into the microphone.* And anyway, I had been hoping that Harefield had been the good guy Viv thought him. If this more-than-slightly frightening man was his friend, that seemed increasingly unlikely, and I didn't know how to proceed.

Or was Munroe the prime mover? What if Harefield had been on the level, and the drugs in the shed had nothing to do with him? What if one of his boys was working with Munroe, and they had cached the drugs in the shed, and Harefield had found them? Then what? I was no longer watching Munroe, just staring blankly into space, trying to sort out where that might lead me. If Harefield had found the drugs, he might not have gone straight to the police. I considered. If it were me, I would want to know which of my boys had been involved. So perhaps Harefield had asked questions, or maybe he'd found the boy — and Munroe — with the drugs. They'd knocked him out and set fire to the shed to destroy the evidence and stop Harefield from going to the police.

I ran through that scenario a few times. It would explain Harefield's death, and also explain why everyone who knew Harefield thought he was a straight arrow, but he was nevertheless a straight arrow found in a shed with drugs, and with — I stopped. With drug-dealer sums of cash in his flat. Damn. That didn't work.

I refocused on Munroe's stall, and blinked. A short, bald man wearing the same graffiti-style shirt that Munroe had been wearing was standing in his place. Munroe was nowhere to be seen. I stepped away from the stalls and looked around crossly. My, hadn't that gone well.

A voice came from directly behind me. "Looking for me, doll?"

No one had ever called me "doll", and until that moment, I would have been willing to bet that no one ever would, but all the same I knew it was me who was being addressed. I swung around. And there was Munroe, leaning against the street railing and smiling mockingly at me.

I took an unconscious step back. "Why would you think that?" Jesus, I was pathetic.

"Because you've been standing watching me for the past twenty minutes? Or maybe it's because you were also staring at me two nights ago when the pub burnt down?" His questions came in a sneering sing-song. "Or do you just like looking at me? You're a bit long in the tooth for me, but . . ."

He'd looked frightening when I saw him at the fire, and that was nothing to the chill coming off him now. But since he was right, I had been watching him, there was no point in pretending. I ignored his last sentence and blurted out the question I had already decided I couldn't ask. "I'm trying to find out about Dennis Harefield," I said. "What I'm hearing is so at odds — he was a great guy, he was a drug dealer, he helped out people who found themselves in trouble, he was an arsonist. They can't all be true."

"Why not? And why the hell should I talk to some silly moo who comes nosing around asking questions?"

From "girl" to "doll" to "silly moo": the day was definitely going downhill. I ignored the name-calling. "Because I think he was a good guy, and I'd like to find out more. Can I buy you a drink?" I gestured towards the Hawley Arms even as I knew the verdict was in: I was officially certifiable.

Munroe stared blankly at me. He should have been handsome: tall, long blonde hair, surfer-dude body. But the blankness was pervasive, and it was frightening. He shook his head once, sharply. "I don't have time," he said, but before I could ask when he would have time,

164

he added, "and I won't have time later, either. There's nothing I can tell you. Nothing I will tell you. Harefield was a good bloke. He worked with kids, and he did his best. Not all of the kids ended up in a good place." I presumed he was talking about himself. "I know nothing about arson, and I don't believe Harefield did, either. That's it. No more, so piss off, you hear?"

He turned and started to walk away.

"Did you work with him and his boys' club?" I called after him.

He stopped. "No," he said finally, "I didn't." He moved so quickly I wouldn't have had time to step back again even if I'd had the smarts to. He grabbed my upper arms and squeezed hard, shaking me sharply. "Just fuck off out of it. Harefield knew nothing. Nothing. And you need to keep your nose out of it before you make people angry." He shook me again, pushed me backwards and strode away.

I stared at where his retreating back had been long after the crowd had closed around it. That was one terrifying man, and I wouldn't put anything past him, not arson, not drug dealing, not failing to separate his plastics from his glass when he put his recycling out. If someone told me that he'd once saved seventeen schoolchildren from drowning, that would be time enough to revise my view. But if it turned out it had only been sixteen schoolchildren, that wasn't going to tip the scales in his favour. I shivered.

Jake was back from the gym by the time I got home, and I allowed him to assume I'd come straight from the market. It wasn't a lie, and besides, there were probably lots of things he didn't tell me, I consoled myself as I went to change for Helena's lunch. It was still achingly hot, so my wardrobe choices were limited, as in, I had one possible item, so there was no choice at all. I pulled on the single dress I owned that was light enough, slapped on some lippie and glared at the mirror: that was as good as it was going to get.

Then I looked at myself again. Specifically, at my arms where Munroe had grabbed me and two reddish handprints had emerged. I turned and looked behind. You could even see the individual fingermarks where he'd gripped tight. By evening, they'd be purple. I didn't want to have to explain it — I couldn't see how I could explain it — so I dug around and found a cardigan. I double-checked. If you weren't too picky, my shoes matched the dress. My bruises were covered. By my standards, the outfit was a success.

"Ready," I said, reporting for duty.

Jake was diplomatic. "A cardigan?" he said. "It's sweltering."

"The neckline is more low-cut than I realised when I tried it on," I improvised, but it was also the truth. It was just that normally I didn't care. Maybe I should go back to the market and get that tattoo. "If you look at the dress from my eye level, it's fine."

"But no one over the age of fourteen is your eye level." Jake was stating the obvious. Everyone is taller than I am. "Wouldn't it have been easier to take the dress back and buy another one?"

166

"Easy" isn't a word I associate with shopping. Nor is "pleasant", nor "enjoyable", nor "fun". "Waste of time and energy" are words I associate with shopping. The only thing more boring than shopping for clothes was discussing clothes. "Let's go," was therefore my response.

On the way out, we met Kay and Anthony and Bim on their way in, and we did neighbourly chit-chat on the front steps. Bim had no interest in we-must-have-a-drink-soon, so he wandered back to the newly turned front garden and crouched, nose to the ground, bottom swaying as he investigated. That led us, naturally, to the work Steve was doing, and reminded me of the question I'd had the day before. "Did you let Steve into my flat?"

Kay looked startled at the abrupt question. "You mean recently? No."

"Are you sure?"

She checked my expression. "How sure do I have to be?"

I shifted uncomfortably, avoiding her stare by watching Bim, who had found buried treasure, and was excavating for more. "Steve said something about the back garden, but I can't remember him ever being out there. I thought if he'd told you I'd asked him to do some work, you might have let him in because — well, because I probably would have if he'd said that about your flat. I'd just assume you'd forgotten to tell me."

Kay was disappointed in me. "I wouldn't let anyone in if you hadn't told me they were coming. And Steve wouldn't try to get in without your knowledge."

167

I flushed. "Put like that, no, I don't think you would, or he would. I just can't figure out how he knew what was growing out there." And it frightened me. Which in turn made me feel stupid, because nothing very frightening had happened. So Steve knew I grew chives by the back door: not really *Silence of the Lambs* territory.

Kay pressed her lips tightly together and called to Bim. He bounded up, eager to show off his booty. When none of us displayed enthusiasm, he stepped back, his eyes moving from face to face. Kay continued to stare at me reproachfully, I was both apologetic and defiant, Jake had his there-will-be-questions-about-this-later face on, and Anthony was pretending he was a visitor from another country who didn't speak the language. I must have looked the unhappiest, because Bim reached a decision. "Here," he said kindly. "For you." And he handed me half a worm, still wiggling madly.

As we walked into Helena's, I thought that half a worm might prove to be the highlight of my day. Jake and I had had a terse conversation on the way over that ran: Him: *If you thought Steve had blagged his way in, why didn't you say something to me?* Me: *I forgot.* Him: *You* FORGOT? Me: Silence that continued right up to Helena's front door.

Once inside, I took a deep breath. Helena's parties were always lovely — between her social life, her professional life, and the charities she was involved with, she knew more people, from more varied backgrounds, than anyone I'd ever come across. And all

168

of them were interesting, bright, funny, clever — everything that makes for good company. I looked around at these terrific people scattered across her kitchen and out into the garden, and wondered if anyone would notice if I locked myself in the loo and read a book.

Jake had left me at the kitchen door, and now returned with two glasses. "Don't even think about it," he warned.

Damn. I took a sip of my drink. Lemon and something. I looked over at his glass. Beer. "Are you supervising my alcohol intake?"

"Until you've had something to eat."

He was right, but I don't like being told what to do, and I dislike it even more when the teller is right and I'm wrong. So I walked away. Let him fend for himself, even if that meant I'd have to interact with other people, which was low down on my list of Fun Things to Do. I wandered over to the table where the food was laid out. Helena has no interest in cooking, so for parties she puts out salads and cold meat and cheese. Today there were also a couple of lasagnes, which I recognised had come from the Italian deli halfway between her house and mine. Normally I would have leapt right in. Today, Jake telling me to eat had put my back up. I broke off a chunk of bread.

"That's not going to get you very far," a voice behind me said.

I turned. A tall, stooped man, probably in his sixties, blonde hair turning to straw, and little round specs like John Lennon used to wear. Lennon's were a style statement. This man wore his because his mum had bought him a pair like it when he was twelve, and it had never occurred to him that he might choose differently now.

It was likely that we had met before, but I never remembered anyone's face, much less their names. As he looked like the type of person who wouldn't remember either, I took a punt, smiled, and held out my hand. "I'm Sam Clair. And I'm not hungry yet."

"If you keep eating bread, you never will be." He stared, waiting for me to move on to wiser food choices.

"I'll bear it in mind. And you are . . ."

". . . having lasagne. It's mushroom. Good for you."

It probably was, but, "No. I say, *I'm Sam Clair*, and then you tell me who you are."

He smiled widely. "I'm not very good at small talk. I'm Victor Walker."

He was even worse at small talk than I was, which cheered me up. "After that, Victor-not-very-good-at-small-talk, since my last name tells you I'm probably related to Helena, you tell me how you know her, and what it is you do. Then it will be my turn again, and I'll tell you that yes, I'm Helena's daughter, and that I work in publishing. From that exchange, we'll have gathered enough information that we can decide if we're interested enough to continue to talk to each other. If we're not, you say, *I see a friend I must speak to before they leave*, or, *I'm just going to refill my glass*, and then you move on to the next person, where you do it over again — although you can leave out the side-light on the need to eat one's vegetables if you

170

want. Then you keep doing it until you finally find someone you want to talk to, or it's time to leave, whichever comes first."

He looked interested. "If only someone had handed me that on an index card years ago. Let me see. Point 1: I know Helena because we're neighbours." He lifted his chin towards the garden, to indicate the direction of his house. "Point 2: I'm a historian. Subsection 2a, which you should add to your outline of *Small-talk for Dummies* when you have time to revise it: I teach local history and research method."

He stared at me, thinking he'd delivered the killer line that made sane people flee. I'm such a nerd, I found it fascinating, so I took another piece of bread, and under his disapproving stare added some cheese, and prodded him out into the garden to talk. Jake found us there half an hour later, and I introduced the two men. "Victor has been telling me about the research he's doing into this area — all about post-war rebuilding."

Jake handed over another glass, and leant against the wall behind me, saying absently, "You need to drink, it's hot out." If I didn't reach the National Institute for Health's optimum nutritional intake that weekend, it wasn't going to be for lack of supervision from my friends. He left a hand on my shoulder and turned to the older man. "Was there a lot of rebuilding around here?" One of the nicest things about Jake is that he's interested in everything.

Victor was happy to return to what was evidently the passion of his life. "An enormous amount. Because the railway lines into central London run through the

171

district, it was a prime target for the Luftwaffe, and was heavily bombed, which meant, in turn, that there was a lot of rebuilding, especially social housing, in the following decade."

"I have a friend who has lived in a tower block near the Heath since her parents moved in when it was first built," I offered it like car keys dangled in front of a fractious baby. "I'd guess that was the 1950s. Her lino has definitely been there since then."

Victor dove straight for the shiny objects. "How extraordinary. Would you introduce me? I've been recording interviews with anyone who has been living in the area over the last half-century, but a continuous tenancy from the 1950s is extremely rare." Now he was a botanist who had stumbled across a jungle orchid the world had mourned as extinct.

"Then she's a prime candidate. She's not only been living there the whole time, she knows everyone. She can put you on to other long-termers. Give me your phone number." Victor, bless him, pulled out a tiny pocket diary and turned to the flyleaf, where he had his number written out. I texted Viv with it, knowing she'd adore the chance to tell an academic everything she knew, and that she was certain he didn't.

After that, the lunch party ran on, as lunch parties often do, into supper. I was enjoying myself, which was what I usually found happened once I forced myself out. I remembered to mention Sam's problem to Helena, and she introduced me to a colleague who worked with youth groups. Even with Helena's standard Superwoman Service, that was impressive. I outlined the situation, and Connie agreed that Sam and his friends needed legal assistance. She told me to get Sam to ring her on Monday to discuss it, and she would either take it on herself, or find the right person to do it. I could see why she and Helena were friends. They had the same modus operandi: see a problem, solve the problem, move on to the next problem. Beside us, Jake was involved in a heated discussion about parole with a bunch of Helena's lawyer friends, so he was happy too.

I was sitting in a deckchair, listening to him and his new friends, who had now moved on to limited licence, whatever that was, when Victor bounded up again.

I smiled up at him. "I thought you'd gone home." We'd said goodbye several hours before.

He waved that off as unimportant. "I had. But I got a text from your friend. She says she's meeting a friend at his flat this evening, and that he's also been living in the same house since the end of the war. She says I can come round and have a preliminary chat with both of them if I like, and I thought since you'd introduced me you'd like to come too." He extended this invitation as if it were a matter of unimaginable good fortune that I'd be able to join him, the way a millionaire would say "I thought you might like to see my yacht". Which made it hard to say no.

Victor was oblivious. "From what your friend tells me, this man is a find. He's eighty, and he was a rag-and-bone man right up until the 1960s, when he got rid of his horse and cart and began to sell the same sort of goods from a shop."

"I have a very faint memory of a man with a horse and cart coming round when I was very small," I said, "but even though I know it's a real memory, it's still hard to make myself believe that it happened in my lifetime." If it had appeared in Miranda's gang memoir, I would have thought the chronology was impossible, and it was another indication it was all made up.

Victor nodded. "I tell my students that people their grandparents' age saw cattle being driven down the high street, but they don't believe me. That's what these interviews are for, to show how even someone not very old" — how tactful — "can remember a rag-and-bone man's cart. And then I want to show the continuity: how the son of the rag-and-bone man goes into retail, how the dairy the cattle were driven to becomes a pizza place, but still keeps the dairy tiles on the walls." I knew exactly the restaurant he meant. "It's all change, but it's a progression, not a break. Everything overlaps, from a horse and cart or a dairy to a restaurant or a shopping centre."

Behind Victor's back, I made bug-eyes at Jake. *Help!* they shrieked. Without obvious haste he disentangled himself from his group and wandered over. "Ready to go?" he asked blandly.

Victor, previously the most polite of men, in his excitement at the thought of two new interviewees spoke right over my Yes-I'm-exhausted-and-ready-for-bed: "We're going to see Sam's friend Viv, and" — he consulted his phone — "and her friend Arthur."

Jake was every bit as enthusiastic. "Good plan." I wondered if murder was one of those things that, if

174

other people witnessed it they had to report it, or if there was some leeway. Had Helena perhaps left the big bread knife out on the table? Then he continued, "We've got a car. Why don't we meet you there? I'll park and do email while Sam introduces you, and then once you're set, I'll take her home."

I decided to leave the bread knife where it was.

Viv's friend Arthur lived in Talbot's Road, not far from the empty house. As we drove over, I traced out the long route we had to take by road, because the street layout wound around the railway line, just as Victor had said. The railway, and its network, took precedence in laying out the district, which I supposed historically had been the reality: the railways had been the prime commercial network, the houses were built afterwards, supply following demand.

Then I sat up. The rail network distributed goods across the country. I thought back to my trip to the market that morning, and the thousands of customers getting their retail fixes for the week.

I stared out the window. "If Harefield —" I hated saying this. "If Harefield was a drug dealer — That is, apart from finding the drug residue, and the cash, do the police know where Harefield was dealing, or how?"

Jake was succinct. "No."

"No? Just 'no'?"

"I know you. I know you can't leave things alone, so I asked a favour and had a look at the file."

It made me sound like the local nosy parker, but on the other hand, he wasn't wrong, and I hadn't been able to leave it alone, so I ignored that part. "Go on."

He drove for a dozen metres in silence. Then, "Harefield had a juvenile record, but that was nearly twenty years ago. He'd straightened up, finished university, got a job at the council, worked with local boys, had a good track record. Everything we knew about him said he was on the level. There was nothing to link him to any dealing. He didn't have any connections Specialist Crime could find to any known distribution networks. He had some dodgy friends, but they had been boys he'd worked with." He shrugged. "If you work with at-risk boys and young offenders, they're not all going to stay clean. Some didn't, and Harefield didn't necessarily lose touch with them. But until we found the drug residue, and the cash, it looked like he'd kept in touch as a mentor, hoping to change their situations. Afterwards, of course . . ." He let the sentence drift.

I felt like I'd fallen through the rabbit hole. Viv had been saying from the start that Harefield was one of the good guys, and the police had been telling her right back that she was straightforwardly wrong. Now, according to Jake, the police had thought he'd been clean, just at the moment I — "I've worked out how he might have been distributing."

This time the silence was longer, and tenser. "All right," he said. "How?"

"Harefield had been helping the boys in his group make T-shirts, helping them buy what they needed wholesale."

Jake nodded. "We know that. The materials were in the shed — or at least, the paints they used were what had accelerated the fire."

"He had a friend. His name is Kevin Munroe. I saw him on the street at the pub fire. He was watching with everyone else."

"And . . .?"

"And he sells T-shirts with skateboarding designs in Camden market. And he was talking to Azim at the fire."

Jake was not in the CID for no reason. "And you think they were using the market as a distribution point. And Azim — he's the local newsagent? What are you suggesting, that the boys who deliver papers are being used too?"

I shrugged uncomfortably. "It would work, wouldn't it?"

Jake tipped his head. "It would. It might. I'll pass it on." He looked over at me. "And then you don't have to concern yourself with it anymore."

I'd like that. I'd gone from Harefield being Viv's friend, and a good guy, to pointing out how he might have used as drug couriers the boys I'd also been defending and had just found legal counsel for. I felt nauseous, and it wasn't the mushroom lasagne.

Even if it meant having to go through yet another social interaction — I was so far past my daily quota I didn't blink — I was glad when we reached Talbot's Road, so I could stop thinking about Harefield. We didn't need to look for the street number. Victor was standing outside in the dusk, and as I opened the car door, an elderly voice croaked out accusingly, "You're the polite runner."

A man was standing beside Victor, and he was talking to me. I recognised him at once. If you run or walk your dog regularly first thing in the morning, you tend to see the same people over and over. I have always given them names. One of the runners is Marge, because the first time I saw her she had tied her hair up in a purple scarf, and in the dawn light she looked like Marge Simpson's twin. Another is The Greek, because I think she looks Greek, even if I couldn't tell you what looking Greek looks like. And Victor's rag-and-bone man, it now appeared, was one of the Old Paper Guys, the three elderly men I saw most mornings as they waited outside the station for Azim to open his newsagent's. Where they were made them the Paper Guys, and Arthur was the oldest, which did the rest. As I always said "Good morning" to them as I ran past, that apparently in turn made me polite, as well as a runner, to them.

I was amazed to learn Arthur was eighty. My conservative estimate would have been 180. He had some sort of spinal condition that kept him bent over, only able to look up by turning his head at an angle. And he barely walked, shuffling along with a stick at a snail's pace. Despite that, I regularly saw him a good half-mile from what I now learnt was his house, so he was much more mobile than appearances would suggest. And younger.

He was also in charge of this encounter. Victor introduced him more formally as Arthur Winslow, and he waved his stick at me in greeting, and then again to gesture me towards the entrance of his basement flat. "Come in," he said. "Viv's already here."

With a final cautionary *If I don't make it out, send in the troops* glance at Jake, I followed.

Viv was at the door, and she took over as we hit the threshold, hustling the three of us into the front room. It should have been a pleasant space. The houses on Talbot's Road were well proportioned, much wider than mine, and Arthur's faced south, so it would get a lot of light. But the brown corduroy curtains were drawn, and it felt as if they always were. Add in a brown corduroy armchair, beige-turning-brown walls, and a single overhead light fixture with one weak bulb, and it was plain that this was not a house that saw many visitors. The brown armchair was the only upholstered furniture in the room, the two wooden kitchen chairs facing it most likely having been brought in for the interview. The room was clean, and cared for, but not welcoming.

Arthur waved his stick at me again, pointing to the chairs. I was the youngest in the room by a couple of decades, and also had no plans to stay. I waved back, feeling more than a little redundant. "I just came in to say hello, then I'll leave you to get on."

Even though it had been he who had insisted I come, Victor looked relieved that his interview wasn't going to be turned into a neighbourhood tea party. Viv had other notions. "You took photos of my flat. I want you to show them to Victor."

I had taken photos of her flat? I stared, puzzled. "When I had that jasmine flowering," she prodded, as you would to a slow and slightly recalcitrant pupil.

Viv was as proud of growing her jasmine from a root cutting as Zeus must have been to see Athena springing fully formed from his forehead — "This little trick?" they both shrugged modestly. Victor would have to wade through endless photos of cuttings to see her kitchen, but that wasn't my problem. He was the one who'd got me here.

"Absolutely!" I enthused. I found my phone and pulled up my photos, scrolling through until I found the flower images. "There," I said, handing the phone over to Victor. "Just go through them and email the ones you want to yourself."

"And me," Arthur chipped in. "I don't get far these days," he said, waving his stick meaningfully. "I haven't been in Viv's block since I was on the cart. I'd like to see it again."

Whatever floated his boat. Victor fumbled with the unfamiliar phone, but when they both recited their email addresses, he seemed to know what he was doing, so I kept out of it. Then I said my goodbyes and started to edge back to the door. Viv nodded at me and flicked her eyes to the hall, following hard behind me as though we had state secrets we needed to discuss in private.

I had no plans to share my new thoughts about her friend Dennis, or my conversation with his friend Kevin. But, "Did you ever manage to find out if Dennis had any family?" I presumed at some point there would be a funeral, and she'd want to go.

She shook her head sharply, but with an expression of satisfaction that surprised me, until she said, "I've been collecting his post in the meantime."

"His post?" I echoed. "Wouldn't the police want that?"

Her self-congratulation nearly filled the room. "They came to me for the key, and I went up with them. There was nothing on the mat."

"Because you'd already collected it?" I wasn't sure why, or what purpose it served, but she was so pleased with herself I couldn't help smiling at her.

Viv wasn't of the generation that said *You betcha*, but her face said it for her. "I've got it here. I've had a look at it, but I can't see anything that leads us back to his family. I thought you might look too." The original let's-break-into-my-missing-neighbour's-flat episode had shown that Viv hadn't much use for personal boundaries. Now she reached out and casually lifted my handbag off my shoulder, tucking a manila envelope into the front pocket, before turning back to the men hovering by the sitting-room door. "My neighbour died. And Sam takes plant cuttings to one of her neighbours," she said, as though this were an explanation, and as though the two things were linked. In a way, they were. If we hadn't instituted the cuttings swap, she wouldn't have known me well enough to share her worries about Harefield.

Nevertheless, it sounded odd, so I elaborated, explaining that Viv's neighbour had no connection to my neighbour with the green thumb. "Viv's on my way to the market on the weekend, so it's no trouble." I looked at the Old Paper Guy. "If you ever need me to pick up anything for you at the market, you're on my route too. And anyway, you may be doomed. I'll

181

probably soon have gluts to get rid of, without ever having to go shopping again." I told them about Steve using my front garden. "If he grew enough for six people in the empty house, I'm terrified of how much he'll produce in a ten-square-metre patch."

Arthur waved his stick, which I now understood was his reply to most things. "Mo gives me salads when I go past the café to get my paper. And Mike fixed my lights for me a while back." It must have been quite a while back. Maybe 1947, if the single bulb was anything to go by, but Arthur seemed happy enough with it. He turned to Victor. "People say the area has changed, that no one knows the people they live next to anymore. But it's still the same. We're still a community." He pointed his stick at me. "My son does my heavy shopping. It's what children are for."

Like Mr Rudiger's daughter did his. I liked the idea that every neighbourhood was filled with Arthurs and Mr Rudigers, independent with a little bit of help. Although Arthur was less benevolently amused by the world than Mr Rudiger: "He's not good for much else," he added matter-of-factly. "I was a rent collector, and he is too, just like I followed my dad into the rag-and-bone trade. You buy junk, you sell junk, you're a junk seller. You own a building, you collect the rent, you're a rent collector." He was talking to himself, not us.

Victor made soothing noises, a lot of children-todays, intermixed with a few what-can-you-dos.

I took that as my cue, and drifted down the hall to the front door.

182

When we got home, I thought if I had to talk to another person that day, even Jake, I might just stand up on a chair and start to howl like a werewolf. To avoid that very real peril, I went straight to bed. Jake was texting as I walked down the hall, and then he detoured by the sitting room for the football round-up, but he followed me not long after. So it wasn't until the morning that I went into the kitchen and found the footprint by the back door. A footprint, and a chip of wood which, when I looked more closely, had been gouged out of the back door frame, next to the lock.

CHAPTER
NINE

I had already made coffee, and was about to take a sip. I didn't realise my hand was shaking until I saw the brown splashes land on the floor next to the footprint. I didn't call out to Jake. I didn't do anything. I just stood there, staring at the floor, mutely holding my quickly emptying cup. Then it was gone from my hand, and Jake was turning me to face him.

"What is it? What's happened?"

It wasn't my hand that was shaking, it was all of me. I was shivering, as though I had a fever. Jake nabbed his sweatshirt, which was hanging on the back of a chair, and pulled it over my head. He put his hand on my forehead, and when he found I wasn't ill, he said again, "What's happened?"

I pointed behind me, without turning to look at it, as though the print might erase itself if I didn't look at it. "There. A footprint. Or, at least, dirt from someone's shoe. And bits of wood. Someone jimmied the lock."

Jake moved around me, keeping me turned away, but never taking his hand off my arm. I felt it tense when he saw what I had seen. But, "Come," he said, as he pulled me out of the kitchen. He stopped me in the doorway and went back for coffee, dumping some sugar in it quickly, then he led me to the sitting room, pushing me gently onto the sofa before handing me the cup. "Here. Drink."

At some point I hoped that people would stop telling me what to eat and drink. But I was glad it wasn't today. I drank. The sugar was vile, but I knew he'd added it to counteract the shock. He kept his hand on me as he took out his phone and spoke briefly, then said, "Someone will be here soon. When they've checked it out, we'll get the locks changed. Don't worry, it will be all right."

It wouldn't, but there was no point in saying that. So, "It was the shock. I'm fine now," I said instead.

We both knew that was as much of a lie as "It will be all right". And we both pretended it wasn't, and sat silently, waiting.

It wasn't more than ten minutes before the bell rang. Jake opened the door to two men, one in uniform. He was sent to the kitchen, while Jake introduced the other: "DS Richards," he said. "Tell him what you know. I'll be in the kitchen."

What I knew? I didn't know anything. That was why I was so frightened. I decided I'd keep on pretending everything was fine. "Where do I start?"

The sergeant was a short, square man, probably a few years younger than me, plain-faced, with the sort of snub nose you normally see on children. He hadn't grown out of his, and it made him unthreatening, endearing even. I doubted that was the case, but I allowed myself to be reassured when he replied, "Start with when your friend went missing."

So I did. Or, rather, I explained that he wasn't my friend, that I'd never met him, before telling him about going with Viv to Harefield's flat, and about the fires. About Kevin Munroe, although I might have skimped a little on my trip down to the market. I told him about Steve and his missing documents, as well as Steve's unexplained knowledge of my back garden. With this new incident, also involving my garden, the missing documents took on a more sinister light. At least, they did in my mind. I couldn't make Richards feel it, no matter how hard I tried. Indeed, the harder I tried, the less interested he became, almost visibly classing me as unstable. When he said, "You probably just put them somewhere and forgot" for the third time, I gave up. I knew I hadn't done that. My alphabetised spice rack was just the tip of an obsessive iceberg. My office doesn't resemble an editor's office in the movies, where the stage directions read something like, *Piles of manuscripts spill off the desk and onto the floor, where further piles of paper are to be found mixed with books, ashtrays and dozens of red pencils.* Apart from anything else, editors in England don't use red pencils. Red pencils are for American publishers. Here we use ordinary lead pencils, and these days we mostly work on screen. My desk has a jar of pencils and an in-tray for things to be dealt with: bills, shopping lists, a lightbulb to remind me to buy more. There is an open diary, and two piles of manuscripts. Neatly piled manuscripts, corners aligned. That's it. But even seeing the evidence of insane tidiness all around him wasn't going to change Richards' view: people misplaced papers every day, therefore I'd misplaced Steve's papers.

I gave up and returned to today's garden incursion, and as I was finishing up, "I am sure that the mud and wood were not on the floor yesterday morning," Jake came back.

"Agreed," he said. "We were both in the kitchen yesterday, and the door to the garden was open. I closed and locked it before we went out, and I would have noticed it then."

Richards nodded acknowledgement of Jake's contribution, but kept his attention on me. "After that?"

"I didn't go into the kitchen again until this morning. We were out yesterday from just after noon until —" I looked over at Jake "— until about nine?"

"Later. It was ten minutes or so before *Match of the Day* when we got in."

"Ten hours," said Richards, his voice slightly accusing as he put his notebook in his pocket. Note to self: leave smaller window of opportunity for future break-ins, to make creation of alibis more difficult.

The bell rang again. "That'll be the locksmith," said Jake, and moved back to the door. "Work out how many keys you need made for the new locks. He'll have two and we'll get any extras cut this afternoon. For now, give Richards a rundown on who has keys now."

Richards agreed, if not enthusiastically. If it hadn't been for Jake, this wouldn't have rated a visit even from the local plods. He pulled out his notebook again, using it as an opportunity to sneak a glance at his watch. He wanted to be gone.

Jake wandered in and out as I ran down a list of keyholders, dividing his attention between the crime-scene technician in the kitchen, the locksmith working on the front door, and loading me up with more sugar. I tried to tell him I was no longer shivering, nor suffering from shock, and that if he persisted I would be as cranky as a four-year-old on a birthday-cake high. He appeared to feel it was worth the risk.

"My cleaning lady, who has come to me once a week for nearly ten years," I continued, reaching for my phone to get her number for Richards. "My two sets of neighbours upstairs. My mother. That's it. Oh, and Jake." I tilted my head in the direction of the hall, to make sure Richards knew who I was talking about.

He knew. "I'll put him at the top of the list to take to the basement at Scotland Yard for the third degree," he said, which was the first human remark he'd made.

"Sensible." I was suddenly exhausted. I'd forgotten how tiring being afraid was.

Jake came back and sat on the arm of the sofa next to me. I leant in towards him and stage-whispered, "You're heading the suspects list."

"Mm-hmm," he agreed. "That's the first lesson we learn in police college: when someone's tried to gouge out a lock, look for a person with a key."

I frowned. "You're right. Why did they damage the door if they had a key? And they did have a key, because the damage is inside, not out, and that door opens from the inside without one. Whoever it was came in through the front door."

Jake and Richards nodded in tandem. They'd known that all along, and Richards' expression added that that was why he wasn't taking the whole episode very seriously. I wasn't ready to accept where his line of reasoning was going, so I made it a question: "Are you saying no one broke in?"

Richards left it to Jake to explain things to the village idiot. He said gently, "No one physically broke in, because the two front doors — the door to the street, and the door to your flat — show no signs of damage. But someone *was* here. It's still breaking and entering, and that's why we want to know who had access to keys."

Richards had that list. I wasn't going to be sidetracked by going over it again. "If no one broke in, why is my back door damaged?"

"It's a good question." So good that no one had an answer.

Finally the technician packed up, and Richards went upstairs to talk to the Lewises and Mr Rudiger. I paid the locksmith and took the duplicate keys for the three doors. Jake watched in silence until he was gone, and then said mildly, "Are you going to give everyone keys again?"

My chin went out. The hell with what biologists say about fight-or-flight responses to fear. This was fight-or-fight. "Who do you suggest I omit? Which of my friends and family should I not trust?" Just as I had remembered how tiring fear was, I also now remembered that fear made me bad-tempered. Most people who know me will point out that many things make me bad-tempered, but fear *really* does it for me. I went on, my voice rising. "Mr Rudiger? My cleaning lady, who has worked for me for *ten bloody years*? Or maybe my mother. Let's put Helena at the top of the list, shall we?" Maybe not bad-tempered. Maybe completely, force-ten-gale furious.

Jake knew it was fear, and was sympathetic, which kicked my fury up a notch, straight to undiluted rage. "Sweetheart —" he was beginning when my phone rang. Number withheld, said the screen.

I didn't want his sympathy, and I never want to listen to sentences that begin "Sweetheart" in that tone of voice, so I answered. Even a double-glazing hard sell would be an improvement on "Sweetheart".

Or not. "Sam?" asked a quavering, young-sounding voice.

"This is Sam. Who is this?"

"It's Sam." I would never have recognised that high-pitched voice. He sounded like he hadn't reached puberty yet.

"What is it, Sam? Tell me." I tried to sound soothing.

"I'm in the nick. We've been arrested." He swallowed. "I probably shouldn't have rung you, but Viv told me yesterday that you said . . ." He trailed away, and then started again. "I didn't know what to do. My mum's not around, and —"

I broke in. "Of course you should have called me, Sam. That was exactly the right thing to do. I spoke to a solicitor yesterday, and she's expecting to hear from you, so don't worry."

He was silent.

190

"It will be OK," I said, just the way Jake had said it to me an hour earlier. "It will, I promise. Tell me where you are, and I'll phone the lawyer and she'll sort it out. Her name is Connie, and she's nice. You'll like her." I sounded as if I was promising him a turn with the Fuzzy Felt if he drank his milk, but it was the best equivalent I could manage of Jake's sugary coffee. I had started to scrabble for paper when Jake's notebook and pen landed on the coffee table. I looked up to see him standing over me, eyes concerned. I turned my attention back to Sam and jotted down the information Connie would need. "Don't worry," I repeated. "Someone will be there soon." My God, I'd replicated the entire conversation I'd had with Jake an hour before. Any second Sam would tell me how many spare keys he needed.

I shook away the thought, and just before I hung up I remembered. "Sam!"

"Yeah?" His voice was still wobbly.

"What's your last name?"

In all the time I'd known him, I'd never thought to ask. At least the question got a watery laugh from him.

"Malik." He spelt it.

"Gotcha. Connie will deal with this. Promise."

I disconnected and dug Connie's card out of my bag. There was a mobile number, so I rang that first, and when it went to voicemail, left a message, watching Jake take in the news out of the corner of my eye. Then I rang the office number on the card. As I hoped, an out-of-hours duty solicitor answered. I explained that I'd met Connie the day before, and then once again outlined what had happened to Sam, and where he was being held. She said she'd find Connie and ring me back with an update. I didn't want to wait, though, so after I disconnected I hit speed dial 1: Helena.

Today I was grateful when she picked up on the first ring. I didn't waste time. "Sam's been arrested."

"When? Where is he? Have you let Connie know?" She doesn't waste time either. It's genetic.

"I've left a message on her mobile, and spoken to the duty solicitor at her office. What else should I be doing?" I demanded.

"Nothing at the moment. Leave it with me, and keep your phone where you can hear it." She hung up.

I stared accusingly at Jake. "Arrested," I said. I didn't say anything else. He knew I was holding him responsible.

He didn't try to claim innocence. Just, "Helena on one side, the entire Met on the other?" He made weighing motions with his hands. "I know which one I'd back."

Me too. But, "That poor boy. He was terrified. And I don't think there's anyone at home who looks after him."

Jake shrugged lightly. "He's not a boy. He's nearly eighteen."

"That's a boy." Then I did a double take. "How do you know how old he is?"

"I told you, I looked into it. The police questioned him. You're right, though, he doesn't have anyone. His father's long gone, his mother moves on from boyfriend to boyfriend, some better, some . . ." He didn't finish,

192

but it was plain that the some who were better were few and far between. "It's good that he's got you and Helena."

Jake can be very law-and-order-ey, so it was a relief to know there wouldn't be any resistance to my helping Sam. And I was ridiculously pleased that he equated my help with Helena's. If only.

He hesitated. "The solicitor Helena found . . ."

"What about her?" Was he suggesting that someone better could be found? Someone better than Helena's recommendation? Was the man mad?

He wasn't. "Is she working pro bono?"

"I don't know. The plan was, once she talked to Sam, she'd see if it was something she'd take on. Given today's news, my guess is that she'll do the immediate work without charge, as a favour to Helena, and then if the case needs more time than she has, she'll find someone else who can do it." I looked away.

But Jake knew. "You mean, you and Helena will cover her bill."

I hoped it wouldn't come to that. I earned well for publishing, but not the kind of well that made solicitors' fees negligible. But if it did come to that, I earned a hell of a lot more than a boy trying to train as an electrician, and between me, Helena, and whatever pro-bono hours she could cajole out of her friends, it would be manageable. "Yep."

He stood. "It's been a slightly more exciting Sunday than usual. Do you want to cancel the pub?"

Bugger. I'd forgotten we were supposed to meet his friends for a drink and lunch. "Absolutely not," I lied shamelessly. I looked down at my clothes. If I were a better person, I'd change, to give the illusion that I was looking forward to this outing, and I cared what these strangers thought of me. I wasn't a better person, I wasn't looking forward to it, and I would care what they thought, but only in retrospect, when it was too late. "Just let me put on a nicer shirt, and I'll be ready. Where are we meeting? What time is kick-off?"

Jake looked at his phone. "In an hour, in Richmond, so we need to get a move on. If there's traffic, we'll be late."

An hour there, probably more stuck in the Sunday-return-to-London congestion on the way home. Or — "Or we could take the overground. It will be slightly faster, and on the way back we could walk along the river, or go to Kew." I don't know what made me think of Kew Gardens. If I lived in south London I'd probably go there a lot, but as I've always been a resolute north-sider, I doubt I've been there three times in my whole life. "It'll help to walk the jitters out." I was surprised to find I'd said that out loud.

So was Jake, but he smiled sweetly. "Jitters from the break-in, or jitters from socialising?"

"I was thinking about this morning, but now you mention it . . ." I smiled to show I was joking, but we both knew I wasn't. So we went by overground.

The pub where Jake and his friends met looked like a Hollywood designer had received a stock request for a setting in Ye Olde Englishe Pubbe. Richmond raises the bar high, by already resembling a stage set, filled with big houses set back behind gardens primped within an

194

inch of their lives. Even the wildflower, cottage-style gardens were regimented wildernesses. The pub faced the village green (first tick in any Olde Worlde Checkliste), a small, whitewashed, eighteenth-century building (second tick). Inside, it had wood-panelled walls and, even in this heat, an open fire (ticks three and four). The customers ranged from a few tourists to families who came to the same pub for a drink before lunch every Sunday of their lives.

Which made Jake's friends noticeable. There were five of them around a table at the back when we arrived. Jake and I aren't much for PDAs, but he put his arm around me as we stood in the doorway, waiting for our eyes to adjust to the low light coming in the diamond-paned casement windows (yes, another tick). I suspect he did it because I'd unconsciously moved closer as five faces swung towards us. They weren't unfriendly faces, but they weren't friendly, either. Assessing cop faces, even the ones who weren't cops.

I straightened my shoulders as we walked over and Jake made introductions. His friend and colleague Chris, whom I'd met once before, and his wife Jan. Paula, the DS from their team, and her boyfriend Joe, with, behind them in a carrycot, their baby, asleep. And a man named Andrew Reilly, whose job was not specified. I smiled around vaguely, and then gave myself an immediate breather by following Jake when he went to get a round.

When we returned, I took the chair next to Paula. I could do baby-convo more easily than I could do police talk. So I did that for a while: the baby was eight weeks

195

old, Paula was still on maternity leave, she wasn't sure how much more leave she was going to take, dee-dah, dee-dah. If you worked in publishing, which was ninety per cent female, and ninety per cent of that female was *young* female, you learnt very quickly how the chorus went. But Paula's mind wasn't on what we were discussing. More than half her attention was on the conversation Chris and Jake were having about a case. As she made no pretence of being interested in talking to me, I let it die away and turned to Joe, on my other side. I remembered the cheat-sheet bullet points I'd listed for Victor. I didn't have to ask Joe how he knew these people, so I moved on to Item 2. "What do you do?" I asked. "Are you a detective too?"

"God, no." He looked conspiratorial. "I'm the enemy. I'm a social worker."

"Social workers are the enemy?"

"Definitely. We're the ones who tell the police why they shouldn't arrest the people they want to arrest. I mostly work with boys who have been in gangs, so the police are particularly interested in arresting my boys."

I liked that he thought of the boys he worked with as "his". And the gang thing was interesting.

He looked at me mistrustfully. "What?" he demanded.

"What what?"

"When I said 'gangs', you got a calculating look on your face."

I didn't know what a calculating look looked like, but I attempted to replace it with an apologetic one. I wasn't going to talk to him about Sam, though. "It's

196

true," I said instead. "I was calculating, because your job suddenly intersects with mine. I work for a publisher, and we're doing a memoir, supposedly by an ex-gang member. Some of it seems implausible, but I can't say my gang experience is extensive."

He was interested. "What sounds odd to you?"

I tried to remember Miranda's points. The only one that came to mind was that someone in a young offenders unit had been denoted a category C prisoner. "Could that happen?"

Joe shook his head once, firmly. "Never. Next?"

I laughed. "This is fun. Like a vending machine. I put the coin in, out pops a reply. No choices, no substitutions." Then I was forced to admit, "I can't remember any of the other details that were worrying the editor. But maybe —" I hesitated, trying to ensure that my face didn't look calculating again. "Maybe you, or one of your colleagues, could look at the manuscript? See what you think?"

I didn't have to worry about looking calculating. Instead I blushed. I'd just asked a man who I'd known for five minutes, a man with an eight-week-old baby and a demanding job, to put in several hours' work for a friend of his partner's colleague. Classy move, Clair. "Or not. It was a silly idea. Sorry."

"Where is the book set?"

"At least partly in East London. Hackney."

He looked relieved. "It's not my district, and the circumstances would be different. But I mentor a few students who are doing practical work as part of their degrees. They always need —" He didn't blush, but he looked embarrassed too.

I leapt in. "They need cash? I have to warn you, we don't pay a lot — it's publishing, and the money is always crap." It was. I paid outside readers a measly £75 for up to 400 pages. I was ashamed even to mention that sum, and I heard myself saying, "I could pay about £150." I couldn't, not only because that was double the going rate, but because it wasn't my book. But I'd got myself into this mess, I'd work out how to fiddle the money if he found me a reader. I handed Joe my card. "If one of them has the time, great; if not, no pressure."

I looked up to find Jake shaking his head at me across the table. *Hypocrite*, I telegraphed back. He used social opportunities to question people, and he couldn't deny it, because I'd been there when he was doing it. But I also knew that it would be more appropriate if I now made small talk rather than trying to hire his friends to vet T&R's manuscripts. Paula was still deep in conversation with Chris, having both turned her back on me and plonked her elbow on the table so that I was cut out entirely. *Not interested in your input, Sunshine*, the elbow said.

I looked past Joe, where Andrew Reilly was sitting, and smiled. "Hello again," I said. Not hugely original, and it probably deserved no more than the tight little smile he sent back. No teeth. He appeared to be as thrilled to see me as Paula had been. Was this how all outsiders got treated? Or maybe I'd forgotten to put on deodorant. Whatever, I wasn't feeling the love. I tried again. "Have you known Jake long?"

"A while."

Big fake smile. "That clears that up."

Joe snorted. Someone was on my side, and wasn't it lovely that I was sitting having a drink with people who were taking sides for a reason no one had shared with me.

Reilly finally, grudgingly, threw me a conversational bone. "Do you do a lot of gang-related books?" He'd been listening, if not speaking.

"None." I was crisp. "This isn't my book, it's a colleague's."

"You're just mixing in, then?"

I remained civil, but by the skin of my teeth. "Not mixing in. Asking for advice from an expert." No smile now, fake or otherwise, at least from me. Joe grinned widely at my reply.

Reilly matched my lack. "So you weren't mixing in with Harefield, either?"

I blinked. "How do you know about him?"

He was tight-lipped. "I've seen the file."

"Are you an arson specialist?"

He looked disgusted. Perhaps being an arson specialist was the lowest form of police life. "Drugs. And I hear your expert opinion is that we don't know what we're doing."

"I'm sorry?" I looked from him to Jake, who was sitting silently now, but, from his tense posture, wasn't going to stay silent for long.

"Field tells me you think Harefield was a saint, and we've fitted him up."

I purposely didn't look at Jake again, and I kept my voice level. "I'm sure that's not what 'Field' told you, because 'Field' knows I don't think anything of the kind. I do wonder that Harefield's neighbours, his colleagues, his boys, all of whom have known him for years, have been so thoroughly hoodwinked, while the people who came across him after his death have uncovered the unsavoury reality so easily, but that's another story."

"Like I said, you think we've fitted him up." I don't think even he believed that. He was trying to provoke me, so there was only one response. "Another round?" I asked brightly. No one was ready for their next one, and since Jake had got the last one, it wasn't our turn, but I had a choice: buy another round of drinks, or beat Andrew Reilly's nasty, self-satisfied face in with the fireplace poker. And I wasn't sure Martha Stewart had directions on how to get bloodstains out of eighteenth-century wall panelling.

Jake started to stand, but Chris put his hand on his shoulder. "It's my round. Sam, will you help me carry?"

By the time we got back to the table, the small groups that had been talking one-to-one had broken up and everyone was discussing holiday plans. I contributed a few sentences, mostly so Jake wouldn't feel worse than he already did, but I wasn't exactly pulled away from the world's most gripping conversation when my phone rang. Another "number withheld".

200

I answered, and when I heard the voice, excused myself, mouthing "Connie" at Jake as I walked to the door. It didn't take long. She and Helena between them had moved mountains. Sam had been arrested, but not charged. He'd be released by the end of the day.

"He's a minor, isn't he?" I asked.

"Officially he lives with his mother; she's the adult on record for the paperwork. But since he'll be eighteen in a few months, they're not making her come down to collect him. Which is fortunate, because no one has been able to find her."

Poor Sam.

"Was it just him? He said 'we've' been arrested, but I didn't think to ask who, or how many."

Connie snorted. "It was five of them. I did them as a job lot — it's more paperwork, but it doesn't take much more time."

"Apart from being unable to say where they were on specific dates a few months back, was there any reason for the arrest?"

She hesitated. "That's why I'm ringing you, rather than just texting to say it's done and they'll be home soon. Sam trusts you, and you might be able to get something out of him. None of them will say where they were, and their neighbours have told the police the five of them are routinely out at nights."

"They're boys," I said. "They were probably out drinking, or spraying graffiti, or groping girls, whatever it is that adolescent hormones make you think is fun."

"Probably. But since they won't say, it's a problem. So far we've had no indication why these five in particular have been connected to the fires, but at this stage the police have no obligation to tell us what information they've received. It might be that they have good reasons, although if they did, they would most likely have charged the boys." She became brisk. "I've told the boys I'll continue to represent them, and they have my number if there's a problem. Meanwhile, if you can get anything out of them, it would be wise to try."

"Understood." I did understand, I just wasn't sure Sam would.

I didn't think Sam's arrest was something Jake's friends and I would see eye to eye on, so when I rejoined the group I just said, "Connie's sorted it out for the moment," to Jake as I passed behind him. He stopped me, snagging a chair from the table behind us and setting it down between him and Chris. "Sit," he said. The chair was half in the walkway between our booth and the crowd propping up the bar, but if it kept me away from Reilly, it was worth getting knocked about by people heading to the loo.

Jake gave Chris enough to be included: "This is the arsonist. The dead drug dealer." Chris nodded in recognition. Jake turned back to me. "Were the boys charged?" I shook my head. "Good."

"Good? Scheming lawyer snatches profiled suspects out of the hands of the stalwart coppers is 'good'? I've corrupted you beyond all hope of redemption."

Given I was sitting surrounded by a handful of his colleagues, this was not the brightest thing I've ever said. Jake must have thought the same, because he dropped the subject and joined in the group discussion, which had moved on to schools. I knew from experience that house prices would be next. It was like going to the hairdresser.

Soon there was a general murmur of is-that-the-times and must-get-ons. We said goodbye on the pavement outside the pub, and then began to walk towards Kew. At least, I did. Jake stayed where he was, so when I'd reached an arm's length away, I rebounded like an elastic band.

"Are you hungry?" he said, pulling me close.

As I said, we're not demonstrative in public. Something was up. "I'm not, but it's long past lunchtime. Do you want to eat? We could have something here." I pulled back. "Come to that, why didn't we? Didn't you say you usually have lunch at these get-togethers?"

His eyebrows drew together. "I didn't realise Paula was going to be there, since she's officially on leave. Or that Reilly was going to be such a bastard — it's not even his case. When you went to get drinks I had a go at him, and we decided it would be better if we just left."

I was horrified. "That was my fault? They were pissed off because I was there?"

"It was *not* your fault." He was vehement. "Reilly was nasty because he thinks the same way you do, and he doesn't like someone else pointing it out."

That was Reilly. "Why was Pau —" Oh. "Paula is your ex?" Jake looked like Billy Bunter, caught with his hand in the biscuit tin. Except that Billy's biscuit consumption before he met me was his own business, not mine. "It's fine. She's ex. Why would I care? Hell, why does she? She's got a partner and a child. She's not languishing for you." I made what I liked to believe was a languishing expression, although I think it probably looked more like a cow with indigestion in at least three of its four stomachs.

"It's not that. It's —" He stopped, and started again. "Apart from Paula, the team is entirely men. She had to fight to get where she is. She has trouble when another woman comes along. It's territorial."

"Fair enough. Dickish of her to take it out on me, but fair enough." The whole morning had me too rattled to give this any importance. "We'll try again when she's not there, or she can get used to me. Whatever you think will work best. In the meantime, let's get something to eat so that you don't faint at Kew. But not back in there, or I'll start correcting the apostrophes on their blackboard menu." It's my version of community service, providing a good spelling environment for all, but some people just don't appreciate it.

CHAPTER
TEN

By the time we'd finished eating, the afternoon was winding down, but I'd said I wanted to go to Kew, and by God, after the debacle of the pub, Jake was determined that I would get my visit. We scrapped the river walk, and headed for the nearest entrance.

It had been spring the last time I'd been to the gardens, and I'd aimed for the acres of crocuses and bluebells and flowering cherry trees and magnolias, none of which was now in season. We started with a map consultation, and agreed to head to the water-lily house, but we quickly went off track, literally, diverted by pretty views, then veering to avoid school groups, and then simply wandering without paying much attention to our destination.

My main purpose, walking my jitters out, was as well served by being aimless, and for an hour or so, Jake left the decisions to me. When we saw the pagoda from a distance, however, he began to nudge me in its direction. In all the time he and I had been together, we had never done anything sightseeing-like, and now I wondered if our approaches might not be compatible. I'm more of a once-over-lightly type — I like art, for example, but after an hour in a museum I'm *That was fun, now where's the cake?* Just as Jake liked hitting things in a gym rather than "going round in circles", as he dubbed my early-morning runs, so now it seemed that he liked excursions with a purpose.

From a distance, the Chinese-style building was a charming landmark, a way of locating yourself in the botanical garden's huge grounds. When we reached it, however, it became clear that those eighteenth-century builders put their hearts into it: the pagoda was still sweetly silly plonked down in south London, but it was also ludicrously, disproportionately tall. Two hundred and fifty-three steps, the sign announced: ten storeys. I drew Jake's attention to this with a small cough.

"It'll be an amazing view."

Yes it would, if my lungs, and my legs, didn't abandon my body for the body of someone more sensible, someone who didn't decide to walk up ten flights of stairs for fun. On the one hand, I didn't want to be a killjoy. On the other, maybe I wouldn't have to be, because there was a second sign, warning that admission was strictly limited, owing to the narrowness of the spiral staircase. But, "No problem," said the cheery man at the door. "It's late, and almost everyone is on their way out." Fantastic.

And then, when we came out at the top, it *was* fantastic. The standard thing to say when you see a view like that is that it looks like a picture, or a postcard, or, if you're old-fashioned, a picture postcard. But those comparisons suggest that what you're looking at is something familiar. From the middle of this enormous park, the distance, the light and the angle

206

combined to make the city that sprawled in front of us seem entirely strange: not a picture, not a postcard, but something new, something that had been carefully designed to be seen only from this one vantage point. An embroidery, perhaps, as the late-afternoon sun bounced off the details. The roads were made of black silk, the glass skyscrapers were little pieces of mirrored sequins sewn onto the fabric next to the rough, dirty-brown wool of the river.

We were alone on the viewing platform, and the solitude intensified the feeling that all of London had been created just so it could be seen from this one place, at this one time, by us two, from above. Thinking the word "above" had me drawing back from the balustrade. While I don't exactly have vertigo, heights are not my friends. So as we moved around the full circuit of the pagoda, I lurked slightly behind Jake, peeping around his shoulders, keeping his body between me and the great out-there.

Because I was hanging back, I heard a slight scuff of shoes. Someone else was with us at the top.

There was no reason why there shouldn't be. There had been a steady trickle of people descending as we'd climbed up. It would have been more surprising to find ourselves alone. It was just that, while the gardens below had been filled with people, up above they had vanished from my mind as the sampler-like perfection of the view, and the silence, gave the illusion of complete isolation. The thin shuffle of feet was therefore oddly jarring, a reminder that we were in a public space.

It was one person — there were no voices — and whoever it was must have been enjoying the solitude as much as we were, because they stayed resolutely on the other side of the platform, walking at the same pace, keeping the turret housing the central staircase between us to preserve the illusion of privacy.

It was Jake, not the unseen tourist, who destroyed the pagoda's sense of being set apart from the world, or, at least, his phone did.

He looked at the screen and sighed as he tapped it. "Field."

I stared out to the north, but he didn't take long. "I need to go in," he said apologetically.

I'd worked that out. "I'm going to stay a bit longer, but I'll walk over to the entrance with you." If I got to Kew only once every five years, it was silly to cut the visit short.

He looked at me curiously. "You're being very good-humoured about this."

"I am? I'll have to up my game."

He smiled and tugged at my earlobe. "I forget how self-sufficient you are."

I don't think of myself as self-sufficient. I read for a living, and reading isn't something you need other people around to do. But that didn't mean I wasn't going to ham it up. I put my hand to my forehead in tragedy mode. "You're right, I don't need you. Go, and never darken my pagoda again." I stopped play-acting. "Are you going to the office?"

He shook his head. "On-site."

That meant a crime scene, but Kew was peaceful and pastoral and I didn't want to hear about dead people.

We had reached the head of the stairs, but Jake lingered. "You don't have to come down if you're not leaving. You probably won't want to climb 253 stairs again anytime soon."

I hadn't wanted to do it the first time. I looked back at the view. Mind made up. "I'll stay up here for a bit, and see you back at the ranch." Jake's footsteps lightly running down the stairs quickly faded, and without a body to block me from the reality of how high I was, I stayed back against the wall that surrounded the staircase, keeping one of the upright supports in my peripheral vision. That quieted my vertigo, and I just let my eyes roam, thinking of nothing in particular.

The silence was complete, and I stood enjoying it before I began to move around the platform again, shifting carefully to keep the supports between me and emptiness. As I did so, I heard the feet on the other side. Once again I'd forgotten I wasn't alone. I stopped. So did the feet. I rolled my eyes. That was, surely, taking a desire for privacy to an extreme. I moved more swiftly, the hell with keeping my eyes on the uprights. Vertigo could be cured, I found, by being irritated by someone so ostentatiously staying away from me.

Whatever, the mood had been broken, and I headed back to the stairs. The invisible tourist had the same plan: the feet moved swiftly again. I slowed. If we ended up going down together, I might have to make inane wasn't-that-lovely chat for ten storeys, a special sort of hell. I feigned renewed interest in the view, which I was no longer seeing. Let him leave, and I'd follow after a few minutes.

But no one did leave. *Why the hell not?* I mentally shouted. What was the lunatic doing, apart from driving me mad? I wondered if it was Andrew Reilly. As soon as the thought appeared, I knew how absurd it was, but I couldn't shake the idea that it was someone I knew, and they were hiding from me. Who, or why, anyone would want to do that was beyond comprehension, but there it was.

I had just made up my mind to head down when I heard the steps again, even though I hadn't moved. And now I realised that it wasn't one person. At least two people were coming around to my side of the viewing platform, although they hadn't said a word to each other the entire time we'd been up there. And they were picking up speed.

I turned my back, standing nearer the balustrade despite my vertigo, determined to let them pass behind me as I pretended not to be aware of them. But before they rounded the corner, an explosion of sound boomed out of the staircase. Well, not an explosion, just two children shrieking, "Last one up is a rotten egg!" over and over, while adult voices below carried on another conversation. And then they tumbled out the door and sprinted round and round the platform, both of them shouting that they were the winner.

I took the opportunity and slid past first the children, and then their parents puffing along a few corkscrew turns below. Even if the other visitors followed me, they would be a couple of dozen stairs behind, and I could pretend not to know they were there. Or so I told myself. In fact, I was ashamed to admit, even to myself, that the fact that two people had been at the top for half an hour without saying a word to each other had brought back my jitters. So I didn't admit it. I just decided that I wanted to be somewhere else, somewhere with lots of people nearby.

I walked over to a map. The Palm House wasn't far, but it was too hot to head for an environment temperature-controlled for tropical plants. I was also near the treetop walk. That sounded cooler, even if it meant more sodding stairs. My legs already hated me for the pagoda, so I might as well introduce them to another few flights and make today masochism central. With luck, when I got there the queue would be too long, and I could call it quits without having to admit it was because I was out of shape.

Naturally, the queue was not only not too long, it was entirely non-existent. Most visitors were heading home, and I was moving against the flow. I began to climb once more. After the fifth flight of stairs I was pausing to breathe heavily at each landing. If Jake had been there I would have pointed strategically to interesting sights, even though he would have known, and I would have known that he would have known, that it was really so I could do important things like inhale. I never knew who I was trying to fool, him or me.

By the eighth landing, there was no one at all going up, and instead of pretend-admiring the view, I switched over to pretending to stand aside so the crowds going down could pass. I looked at the city in the distance. I was just reaching the height where we were above the trees. Because the walk was in a small wooded close, London looked paradoxically much further away than it had when I'd been at twice the height at the top of the pagoda. I was trying to work out why that was when a body slammed into me, knocking me flat against the railings. If I'd been tall, or even average height, it might have been scary. For most people the railing was waist high, but for short-stuffs like me, it was closer to chest level, and I'd more or less bounced off the top bar. As it was, I was more annoyed than hurt. By the time I turned, all I could see were the backs of a school group. One of the kids must have thought push-the-lady was funny. Or maybe it had been one of the teachers, infected by extended exposure to adolescents. Ho ho, I enunciated. But silently. I didn't want to be taken for a madwoman.

I continued on up, and in another five minutes had reached the top. The staircase was in a sort of nodule, a round outcropping of the walkway, which was a wooden path like one of those rope bridges in a 1950s' movies set in Africa, usually starring Deborah Kerr, where the hero escapes across the bridge while the rascally villains hack away at the support ropes. I took a giant step back onto the staircase, then shook my head. This wasn't a rope bridge in a film; it was a tourist site in a botanical garden. And the "ropes" — I flicked a nervous glance behind me — were steel beams. But even if it wasn't a rope bridge, part of my

212

not-quite-vertigo is that I don't like it when the floor moves. I bounced lightly on my feet. Like this one was doing.

I gave myself a pep talk. It was a lovely piece of design, I silently encouraged me. I looked again. The sign below had said the walkway was two hundred metres long, but as it wove in and out of the trees growing beneath, the circuit looked longer. More nodules like the staircase outcropping were set along the path at intervals, except that they weren't stairs, they were viewing platforms. If I kept to the centre of the walkway, I'd be fine, and I could leave admiring the view, or the vegetation, or whatever the hell I was supposed to be admiring, till I reached the platforms, which were wider, and had concrete floors.

I started off, only to hear a tannoy announcement: the attraction would close in another ten minutes. I considered. Ten minutes was enough time either to walk fast around the whole walkway, or to admire the views, but not both. I decided I'd do the circuit, and I stopped clutching at the railing as I set off just as someone was leaving one of the adjacent platforms. We crashed into each other like Laurel and Hardy at their most tiresome.

I stumbled, pushed into the railings once more, apologising as I went. I didn't think it had been my fault, but if English manners require you to apologise to a person in the street when they step on your foot, then the logic behind it requires you also to apologise if someone bumps into you twenty metres in the air. I expected to hear the same sort of apology back, but instead, "My ankle." The man dropped to one knee and wrapped his hands around the other leg, his head down. Really? I'd done that much damage?

I stood silent. "Are you all right?" was redundant, since he plainly wasn't. But walking away wasn't an option, and I wasn't sure what else to do. The man was maybe in his late twenties, and dark. Dark, close-cropped hair, dark colouring, dark stubble. Dark T-shirt and jeans. Altogether, not a look I associate with Kew, but my head is filled with so many stereotypes, sometimes I think there can't be space for anything else. Silently I held out my hand. He took it, and I helped him to stand. He was less than average height, and slight, but the arm I was holding was muscled. This was no lightweight I'd brought down. He shifted his weight, testing his ankle, which made him hiss with pain.

"Sprained," he said in an accusing tone, the subtext of which was *You brute*. I resisted flexing my muscles strong-man-at-the-circus style, and merely bent to pick up my handbag, which I'd dropped when we clashed. "I'll go and find someone to help you down."

He didn't let go of my arm. "There are lifts over there."

Now they tell me. I could have taken a lift up. Or I could have left with Jake. Or I could have stayed at home, found a packet of chocolate digestives and had a pleasant day reading on the sofa.

Life is filled with roads not taken. "Lean on me."

He lifted his arm to put it round my shoulder. And the lights went out.

★ ★ ★

214

I was curled in a ball, my knees pressed tight against my chest, my hands tucked under my chin. It wasn't comfortable. I had the headache from hell, and I was — I tried to straighten my legs — I was jammed in somehow, and couldn't move. I opened my eyes, although my head was begging me not to do that. A pair of legs was in front of me, dressed in black jeans. The feet were facing away from me. I lifted my head and a starburst of pain exploded behind my ear. I closed my eyes again and concentrated on not vomiting. If I couldn't move, vomiting wouldn't be pretty. When the bile receded, I looked up again. The legs were attached to the man with the sprained ankle. His head was down. He was — listening? I heard voices, and footsteps. Sprained Ankle moved back towards me as they went past.

By the time my half-functioning brain had worked out he was hiding from whoever the voices were, they had passed. It was probably better to figure out what was happening before I drew attention to myself, anyway. Sprained Ankle didn't move, so I looked around as much as I could without lifting my head. I was in an enforced foetal curl, with my bum and feet pressed against the railings I'd looked over earlier: we were still on the treetop walkway. At the other end, my head and shoulders were propped up against a wall of some sort. I couldn't move my hands or my head to check it out without Sprained Ankle discovering I was awake. Working out as much as I could while he thought I was unconscious felt like the way to go.

I reconstructed what I could remember, and was forced to conclude that the man had coshed me. Even if I had sprained his ankle by knocking into him, that seemed an overreaction. Furthermore, most people don't carry coshes — they are not part of the dress code at Kew — so it was unlikely he had been a passing victim of my clumsiness and had responded in a fit of pique.

I had got that far when he moved. I could feel it coming — the tenseness left his body — which gave me time to close my eyes. I heard him walk a few steps away. And then I could more than hear his nearness as he turned and his foot thudded into my ribs. "Stupid bitch," he said. Sprained ankle my arse, I thought. Indignation at being fooled kept both my mouth and my eyes shut. I grunted, but didn't move. I don't know if unconscious people grunt when they're kicked. Either they do, or he didn't know either. At any rate, it didn't faze him. He kicked me again, then I felt my handbag pulled out from underneath me. If I'd realised it was there, I might have risked moving to get at my phone. Too late.

"Stupid bitch," he repeated. *If we're discussing stupidity,* I thought, *can we begin with yours? All this, to steal a handbag with only twenty quid in it?* He didn't have to knock me out. I would have given it to him. I carry a lot of stuff in my bag — a phone, an iPad, a book, as well as wallet, credit cards, make-up and odds and ends that sift down to the bottom and get forgotten. Even good electronics and an almost new lipstick, which I rarely remembered to wear but which I loved because the colour was called "Venom", couldn't make my bag a worthwhile haul. Besides, he didn't look like a Venom type of guy. Then again, he hadn't asked my views.

I heard a thump, and allowed my eyes to slit open. I could see him through the railings. He was standing, back to me, going through my bag. He dropped my phone and my iPad onto the walkway and casually stamped on them. Then he bent, shovelling the pieces of electronics back into the bag, before leaning out and tossing the whole thing over the railing. He never looked in my wallet, didn't check anything else. Not a mugging. I thought back to the footsteps I'd heard on the pagoda viewing platform, and they took on a more ominous cast.

He sank down against the railing. He checked his watch, then put his head back and just sat. And sat. He was waiting. For someone, or to make sure everyone had left the grounds? Neither felt like it was going to have a happy ending for me. I stared at him, trying to memorise everything I could, but there wasn't much to remember. He looked like any twenty-something you'd see in the pub or on the Tube.

I looked around as far as I could without making a sound by moving my body. He was too close for that. The layout said we were in one of the nodules off the walkway, while the wall I was propped up against told me it wasn't a viewing platform. Maybe it was the staircase, although I didn't remember them having solid walls. We'd been heading to the lifts. They might have a similar layout: a circular nodule with lifts in the centre instead of stairs.

I slid a glance over to Sprained Ankle again. His head was leaning against the railing, and if he wasn't asleep, he also wasn't paying attention to me. I risked lifting my head a few inches. I could see a viewing platform a few metres away. It was held up by a single support that rose from the ground and then, under the platform, split into three struts designed to look like tree branches that arced out around the railings. Apart from the platform's single entrance onto the walkway, there was no way down. If I was right, and I was wedged in beside the lift shaft, my platform had another exit, but I didn't imagine that Sprained Ankle would hang about peacefully while I pressed the call button and waited for a lift to come. If, of course, it even ran after visitor hours.

I turned my wrist and looked down. Just after six o'clock. I wasn't sure what time it had been when I'd heard the announcement that the walkway would close in ten minutes. Kew itself closed at six, so it had probably been about five-thirtyish. Which would mean I'd been unconscious for fifteen minutes or so. I tried to work out how knowing this helped me. I couldn't see that it did.

I attempted to flex my legs. I was in two minds. I could get up and run and scream. If I was going to do that, I needed to do it now. The later it got, the less likely there would be anyone in the grounds to hear me. Or I could keep playing possum, and hope that whenever whatever it was that was going to happen,

218

happened, I could come up with something other than screaming and shouting.

The strangest thing was how calm I was. I'd been attacked, and my attacker was waiting, either for someone to help him do something nasty to me, or for dark, when he would do something nasty to me. Neither was going to be good. And yet I was lying there with no sense of panic. Maybe I needed to be hit over the head more often.

I do have some advice now for would-be attackers. If you are waiting for reinforcements who will arrive in a lift, don't prop your attackee up against said lift-shaft wall. If you do, she will know before you do that they are on their way. This important life lesson was borne home when I felt the wall behind me vibrate. The lift was on the move.

The first, and most hopeful, possibility was that it was someone who worked for Kew, coming to check that all the visitors had left. Then I remembered the voices I'd heard when Sprained Ankle had been standing beside me, and I realised that that check had already been made, and Sprained Ankle had been hiding from the staff. It was therefore more likely that the lift was transporting Sprained Ankle's friends. The stairs and the lift were now both blocked by people who were not happy with me, one of whom had already demonstrated his unhappiness by hitting me on the head.

Before I had reached the end of this thought, I was on the move. I would like to be able to say that I had a plan, that I'd gone over my situation, and was responding to the circumstances in a logical and premeditated fashion. Perhaps sometime soon that is the way I'll tell this story. In reality, however, everything that followed was driven by adrenaline and instinct, and more than a drop or two of panic.

Sprained Ankle had heard the lift and was getting up, his head bent over his phone, texting as he did. Before he was fully upright, I was on my feet. One of my legs slid out from under me. It was dead from having been bent for so long. It didn't matter, though, because I wasn't running. There was nowhere to run to. I went in the only direction I could. Over the railing.

It took me longer than it should have — the railing was designed specifically to prevent people doing what I was doing — and Sprained Ankle's hand was on my own ankle as I finally slid over. But he was that fraction of a second too late. I grabbed at the supporting strut below that mirrored the one I had seen on the next viewing platform, and let my body fall.

I'm female, and not a very athletic female at that. I have no upper-body strength. I make Jake lift anything that weighs more than a teacup. So I didn't have much hope that I'd be able to hang on, much less be able to move and hide. But I didn't have any hope at all if I'd stayed where I was.

The fall was — terrifying is the only word. I wrapped both my arms around the metal strut and kicked at Sprained Ankle's hand even as my brain was screaming that if I kicked him away, I would fall to my death. But my mind and my body paid no more attention to each other than they usually did. I kicked and kicked, and momentum, and my body weight, carried me away from him, and from the railing. It took a second, two at the most, but as I arced out into the air, it felt like it lasted a year.

And then I hung, that same body weight that had taken me away from the immediate threat now pulling me down into a void. I'd wrapped both arms around the strut as I dived over the railing, but I had a minute or so at most. I wouldn't be able to hold on for longer. Every second increased the chances that my arms would weaken, slip. I was going to have to use my non-existent stomach muscles to pull myself up and get my legs on the strut too. I pressed my face closer to my hands and lifted my body. My legs came nowhere near the strut. I tried again. And again. This time, when my body fell back, my grip loosened. I tensed up, pulling my face in closer to the strut, scraping it along the metal. I welcomed the abrasion against my skin. It meant I was still hanging on.

The adrenaline surged with the slip. I rocked my body, and this time my left leg hooked briefly over the strut. Not enough, and I fell back. Again. I was getting weaker. Again. And I was there. One leg hooked over the support was enough to give me the purchase I needed, at least until I could catch my breath. Then I could try and get the other leg around too. I gave a count of five, and there I was, wrapped around the strut, arms and legs grasping tight like a baby koala around a eucalyptus.

I risked a quick look around. The viewing platform I had seen from above had three struts branching off from the upright support. This one had only two, because of the lift shaft in the centre, beside the upright. If I slid down to the point where the two struts met the support, I'd be able to lean against the wall of the lift too. First I would have to turn over and get on top of the strut I was hanging onto from underneath. Inch by inch I manoeuvred, until finally I lay on top, panting. I don't know how long I stayed like that, trying to quell the hysteria that was bubbling up now that I was thinking rather than reacting.

I hadn't panicked in those first minutes. I hadn't had time. Now black spots appeared in front of my eyes, and one hand slipped, slick with sweat. That brought me back. I counted breaths, in and out, in and out. The spots receded, and the rushing noise in my ears quietened.

In that quiet, I could hear the two men. I'd almost forgotten about them. I'd been so focused on keeping my grip, on not falling to my death, that the reason I was there, the reason I was acting like a female Indiana Jones — if Indiana Jones had ever had an adventure in a botanical garden — had been pushed to the back of my mind.

Their voices brought it back to the forefront. My dive over the side had taken seconds, not the years it had felt like. The two men were almost directly above me. I could see their shadows on the ground, two heads bobbing above the railing. I risked a look up. The wooden floorboards showed me nothing. I couldn't see them, or what they were doing. With luck, that meant they couldn't see me either.

Then I heard the lift. One, or both, was going down. I had planned to move down to the top of the main support pole carefully, but like my header over the rails, I moved instead on instinct, sliding down in seconds until my feet reached the place where the two struts met the lift. I withdrew into the shadows of the wall as the light spilt out below when the lift door opened. A man emerged.

He was bald, or had a shaven head, and was heavier, stockier, than Sprained Ankle. I only saw him for a moment before he moved away from the light of the lift, and into the shadow cast by the walkway, and then he was an outline. He could see better: he had a torch, which he began to use. He was searching the ground, looking for me down there, quartering the area under the platform systematically.

My stomach churned. He was right. That was where logic said I should have been, under the platform, mangled, probably dead. When he didn't find me, he was going to look up. Directly under the walkway, in this densely wooded part of the gardens, it was dark. But the sun hadn't set, it would be light for hours still, and even without a torch it wouldn't be that difficult to spot me. With the torch I might as well have a sparkler lit on top of my head, topped by a flashing neon arrow: *Here she is!*

I looked around. The strut I'd slid down led up to the viewing platform, and nowhere else. The second strut also led up to the viewing platform, and nowhere else. Even if I crawled back to where I'd been, I wouldn't be able to return to the viewing platform.

Momentum and gravity had taken me down; it would need far more strength than I possessed to take me back in the opposite direction, even if my attackers were to give me the time, and it seemed like a good idea. I was sure they wouldn't, and it didn't.

The torch beam broke into this entirely futile train of thought. Baldy had given up on the ground and was waving it in the air to get Sprained Ankle's attention.

"She's not here." He wasn't whispering, but he pitched his voice low.

"If she fell, she wouldn't have been able to run. Try the railings," came the reply I didn't want to hear.

The light began to play along the underside of the walkway. It wouldn't take long. It didn't. The beam of light found me. Pinned me.

"She's there. No way up for her. No way down." No shit. I heard Sprained Ankle move above me, and then his shadow on the grass returned as he leant out to look down. The lift-door light flashed out and Baldy got back in. I felt the vibration behind me as he returned to the top, and then the two voices arguing. If I could get over the railings and onto the support pole, so could Sprained Ankle, said Baldy. He was in charge, but Sprained Ankle was putting up a good fight. He might fall and break his neck, was his main complaint. A girl can always dream, but I had to agree with Baldy. If I could do it, so could someone else, and Sprained Ankle was in much better shape than me.

I looked up at the struts again. The second one, the one I hadn't been on, was hidden at its far end by branches from the surrounding trees. Branches

224

wouldn't keep me hidden for long, but even that amount of cover might make me feel less like a sitting duck. If Sprained Ankle came down the strut I'd been on, he'd be able to kick at me from above. If I was at the far end of the second strut, I'd be somewhat hidden, and above him I could be the kicker rather than the kicked. On the other hand, if I crawled up there, I would lose the support of the lift-shaft wall. I'd be back to koala-clinging mode, which was not one I had planned to repeat.

Not planned to repeat until I heard Sprained Ankle say, "Fuck it, just go down and shoot the bitch."

Plans change.

CHAPTER
ELEVEN

As with my abrupt descent down the first strut, my ascent up its neighbour was done without conscious thought or volition. In case this ever comes in handy, I can tell you that "Shoot the bitch" is a phrase that makes hazardous physical activity seem like a catnap in the sun. I'd shinned my way up and was pulling the branches around me before I was even aware I was on the move.

And also before I heard Baldy's reply, which, once I was in place, my brain processed for me: "It's supposed to look like an accident, you fuckwit."

"So shoot around her. Scare her into falling."

I scrabbled with my feet, pushing myself higher up the strut, further into the branches of the tree. I wasn't sure if that was smart or not — if they couldn't see me, they might shoot me even if they weren't aiming at me — but just as closing your eyes when something frightening happens is a natural response, so, I found, is hiding in trees when men argue the merits of shooting you, or shooting at you.

I pressed my mouth closed, determined not to make a sound. And then, if I'd had a hand that wasn't clinging onto metal and branches for dear life, I would have slapped it against my forehead. Not make a sound? That had been the right thing to do when they didn't know where I was, but there was no advantage to it now. Now I needed someone to hear me. So I screamed. And screamed. And then, for a change of pace, I screamed some more.

Two things happened. Screaming released my tamped-down fear, and I became hysterical. And it gave me a sore throat. Nothing else. No one appeared astride a white charger, looking for a stray damsel in distress to fill their monthly rescue quota. Even so, I went on screaming long after it became clear that it wasn't going to help, just because I couldn't stop.

And then, suddenly, I did. I stopped, and listened, and heard — nothing. If the two men were still there, they were being entirely silent. I waited. Still nothing. It had become dark enough that, in the shade of the tree, I could no longer see my watch, so I counted off what I thought was about five minutes in my head. I did it again. Still nothing.

I tried shouting some more, telling myself that this was shouting now, not screaming, that this wasn't panic, that it was part of my plan. My plan was — I scrabbled around — my plan was to shout intermittently for a while, and listen out for the men for the rest of the time. It wasn't the best plan I'd ever heard of. It didn't seem to have much purpose, but it was the only one that I could come up with. After a while, I decided to try and count out an hour. If the men were waiting at the base of the pole, I'd hear them sooner or later: they didn't strike me as being very good at their jobs, more like they'd been rented from the Thugs "R" Us bargain basement. I didn't believe that they could wait in silence for an hour.

I had barely counted out a minute before I heard them, first back on the walkway, then on the ground. My shouting had had the single result of letting them know that no one was in earshot. Their voices raised, they continued their argument about getting onto the strut from above. Baldy finally conceded that it was only possible for those in a state of blind panic, or possibly just those who were totally nuts. The need to have my death — they discussed my death as if it had no more importance than getting caught in rush-hour traffic — the need to have it look accidental was apparently paramount, and now they could no longer see me, Sprained Ankle agreed that they couldn't risk shooting around me, for fear of hitting me. Instead, they tried climbing the pole (a failure), and then the tree among whose branches I was hiding (also a failure, although a longer, slower, less absolute, and therefore on my part a more nerve-racking failure). They debated the location of ladders, and vanished, presumably to search for one.

I kept watch for the torch that would mark their return. Because they might come from a direction behind the tree, where I wouldn't be able to see the light, I kept a hand on the largest branch, hoping that I would feel the vibrations as they set a ladder against the trunk, or started to climb. I didn't know what I would do if that happened, but I wanted to have a head start on whatever it was going to be.

228

I pushed myself more firmly into the crook of the strut, jamming my feet against the metal. I thanked the good lord that I hadn't been a better person, and had been too lazy to change my clothes and put on a dress to meet Jake's friends. If I'd been wearing a dress, I'd have been wearing shoes with a heel, instead of the rubber-soled flats I had on. Next time Helena bemoaned my lack of interest in fashion, I'd explain that I was keeping things pared down to maximise emergency tree-and-strut-climbing needs.

I had time to think that through. Hell, I had time to recite the entire *Encyclopaedia Britannica*, had it still existed in this age of Wikipedia. I couldn't tell how much time had passed. Had they given up and left? Were they going elsewhere for a ladder, and they'd be back? If I knew that an hour had passed, or two, or three, then I could have made guesses. But I couldn't see my watch, and I'd long lost count in my attempt to measure out an hour. Perhaps it just felt like an hour, and they had been gone less than a quarter of an hour? It was possible. The whole episode, from the moment I'd bumped into Sprained Ankle, seemed to have flashed by in seconds, and yet also to have taken hours to unfold.

I began to count again, but kept getting sidetracked by thoughts of ladders, or guns, and losing my place. I started to shiver. Excess adrenaline, I informed myself, based on extensive first-hand knowledge of crime fiction. But it wasn't just internal. My clothes were clammy with sweat from the climb, and were clinging damply to my cooling body as I sat unmoving.

No one returned, as far as I could tell: no lights, no voices. There were no vibrations to suggest climbing. I sat and shivered and clung to my perch. I didn't really have any choice. The two men had failed to climb the tree because it had no branches for the first five metres or so from the ground. I had been pleased when I heard them say that, as it prevented them from getting up. It also now prevented me from getting down. The pole by the lift was worse, a full eight metres without a handhold.

Small sounds filled the air. Night birds. Rustling in the grass, which at various points I attributed to the wind, to animals, and to my two attackers. I sat some more. I was hidden, I was fairly well supported, and if I could hang on until the gardens reopened, I would most likely be fine. I repeated this out loud. I tried it again, replacing "most likely", which was beginning to sound sarcastic, with "will": I will be fine, I will be fine.

Gradually the adrenaline crash caught up with me. Fear should have kept me awake, but instead I was so tired I could barely hold my head up. I decided to make lists. Things I needed to do at home: the plant in the front hall needed watering; I still hadn't completed my passport application; a button had come off a skirt long enough ago that the safety pin I'd been using as a temporary fix was itself in danger of falling off. I moved from there to thinking about Ben, and the conversation that we needed to have about his author. The management consultants kept me going for some time. Then for a while I sang to stay awake. I can't carry a tune, but I didn't think the Kew animals were in a position to complain, and if the men were nearby, they deserved to hear a ferociously off-key rendition of "Don't You Feel My Leg" (the Dirty Dozen Brass Band version).

I moved on to worrying about Sam. With Connie representing him, and Helena prodding her along, I was sure he'd be fine, but it would have been good to have spoken to him, or at least have received confirmation that he'd been released. I thought about that prick Andrew Reilly, and Jake's assertion that he was so nasty because he agreed with me about Harefield.

That brought me back in a circle. Once I knew that this wasn't a random mugging, it was impossible to think that the two thugs after me had nothing to do with Harefield's death, or at least the fact that I'd been asking questions about the man. It might have been because I'd rejected a string of jacket roughs produced by the art department's latest wunderkind, but somehow I doubted it. I mean, it was more than likely that the designer had said he wanted to kill me. Agents too had most likely said the same. And while I liked to think that every one of my authors loved me dearly, it might be that some of them wouldn't have been broken-hearted to hear I was dead. But kill me? Kill me as in dead, not as in that-woman-is-such-a-pain-in-the-arse kill me?

The last time someone had tried to kill me — I spent a few minutes distracted by the fact that my life had reached a place where I could formulate a sentence beginning "The last time someone had tried to kill me"

231

— the last time it had happened, a friend had been murdered. This time, no one I knew had been murdered. Dennis Harefield was dead, it was true, but I didn't know him. And according to the police, he was a drug dealer who had died accidentally in the place he stored his drugs.

But today, with Reilly, Jake had let slip that the police agreed with my view of the situation: that Harefield's friends and colleagues thought the notion of him dealing was absurd. If that were the case, then perhaps my idea that the drugs that had been found in the shed were not his was not so far from the truth. But that didn't explain how I came into the story, much less why someone wanted me dead. I tried to remember everyone I'd discussed Harefield with. I'd left a message with his colleague at the council, saying I was trying to locate him for a friend. I'd talked to Sam and Viv, but neither of them wanted to stop me: I was Viv's garden seedlings connection, and she valued that too much to lose me. I couldn't even think frivolously about Sam. Sam wouldn't do anything to hurt me. Victor? Arthur? I briefly toyed with the image of Arthur haring through Kew Gardens, bent over and waving his stick, but while that was entertaining, it didn't get any closer to answering the question. The only person I'd spoken to who seemed dangerous was Kevin Munroe. He knew I was asking questions. But he should know, too, that I didn't know anything, and, from my cack-handed attempt to interview him, it was unlikely I ever would.

And how would he know who I was, much less where I was? I hadn't looked behind me after I'd left the market. It was possible that he'd followed me home, and then had sicced these two men onto me. But for what? Just asking questions? If he'd followed me and investigated me enough to find out who I was, he'd also have learnt I lived with a CID detective. Surely me dying, even accidentally, would cast more suspicion on those people I'd spoken to. Much as I'd have liked to pin this on Kevin, I couldn't work out why he'd have done something so counterproductive.

I thought about Azim, who was popping up everywhere, but that sounded even more far-fetched. Even if he was using his delivery boys to distribute drugs — and while the method was theoretically possible, there was no evidence that this was the case — and even if he thought I was suspicious of him, as with Kevin he had no way of knowing I was going to Kew, and even more reason than Kevin to make sure I didn't die in suspicious circumstances. That was a dead end too.

I tried from another angle. The men had said my death had to look accidental. What I knew was important enough that someone wanted me dead, but in addition, that no one should know that I had known it. I ran back through the idea, and it didn't make much sense. But neither did someone trying to accident me to death. The word "accident" took me back to the top of the pagoda. Someone had been there, and had carefully kept out of sight until Jake had left. Then they had begun moving towards me. If the children hadn't appeared, what might have happened? Someone else, or possibly the same someone, had knocked into me on the stairs going up to the treetop walk. If I'd been a few inches taller I wouldn't have bounced off the railing, I would have gone over it. I mentally apologised to the children I'd blamed. Soz, kids.

All the while, I tried very hard not to think about Jake. He'd been called out to a crime scene, and when that happened, he often didn't come back to the flat, which meant no one would know I wasn't at home. Mr Rudiger would, because he had super-hearing and kept track of the people in the house. But I hadn't promised to go up and see him, so as far as he knew I might be at Jake's, or out at a party. There was no reason for him to do anything, call anyone. I couldn't see if my handbag was still on the ground where it had been tossed from the walkway, but it was likely it was there: if my death was to look like an accident, they'd want it found near me. Jake might have texted to say he wasn't coming home, but he wouldn't expect a reply. If he'd gone back to his own flat, I was on my own.

I didn't know what time Kew opened. I prayed it might be early, for pre-work joggers and dog-walkers, but imagining a British institution might set its hours for the convenience of its paying customers was delusional, a sign I'd been sitting in a tree for far too long. My head snapped against the strut: I had nearly dozed off again. I gripped more tightly, and began to sing once more. If, at some future point in time, the lyrics to "Waterloo Sunset" are needed to save civilisation as we know it, or for a pub quiz tiebreak, I expect to be in heavy demand.

I was running through "Always Look on the Bright Side of Life" for a second time when I heard voices. And they weren't just talking. They were calling. It had to be Sprained Ankle and his friend, because the staff wouldn't arrive before dawn, and even when they did start work, why would they shout? Maybe the men had lost track of which support I'd climbed? I pushed back more firmly into the leaves.

The voices faded, and then came nearer once more. I could see a torch bobbing, then more than one. There were five, no six, torch beams swinging back and forth in measured arcs. Had Baldy got some colleagues to help? And did thugs call their fellow thugs "colleagues"? I thunked my head on the strut. This was not the moment for editorial nit-picking. I refocused on the lights, and then thunked my head again, even if I was going to give myself concussion if I stayed there much longer. They couldn't be Baldy's friends, because Baldy knew where I was: up. The people holding these torches didn't. They were searching the ground.

I heard a crackle and fizz. Static. A radio. This wasn't Baldy & Co. And they weren't Kew employees either. They were the police.

I knew that I should slide down to the main post again, where they would be able to see me, but when I tried to, neither my muscles nor my brain would allow me to move. The muscles were cramped from hours of hanging on, and stiff from the able-to-leap-tall-buildings-in-a-single-bound antics I'd put them through. My brain wasn't cramped, or stiff, it was just frozen. Earlier, fear had moved me from implausible plan to impossible action with nothing in between. With what looked like a rescue team below me, my brain was telling me what any sane brain would have said all those hours ago: *If you climb down there you will die.*

I attempted a shout, but my voice had frozen along with my muscles. I had to clear my throat several times before even I could hear myself. And then it took a few more tries before it was loud enough for anyone on the ground to hear. "Hello? Hello? Up here." Even to myself the words were feeble, but past experience had failed to give me any indication of what to say when perched in a tree before dawn in a botanical garden. A gap in my education.

Finally I broke off a small branch and threw it down. That, together with a peeved "Hey!" made two of the torches shift sharply upwards. I shook the branches and shouted again. Voices came nearer, and a torch beam traced out a path along the strut to the trees. Then a man called, "Are you Samantha Clair?"

What, there were two women up trees in Kew Gardens in the middle of the night? It was a more exciting place than I'd thought.

That was not, however, a sensible response, so I settled on a croaked "Yes". It sounded like a tree frog was speaking.

The torches gathered around, and I could see the shouter in their light, his hand cupped around his mouth as though I were a steamboat he was hailing in a dense fog. "Hang tight," he called.

236

Ya think? One of the beams found me among the branches. I ducked to get the light out of my eyes. "Stop that. It's dangerous," I snapped, as though sitting in treetops was a recommended activity when performed torch-free.

The light moved away from my face. "Are you hurt?"

"Yes. No. I don't know." I'd kept relatively calm all night. Now the cavalry had arrived, I was going to pieces.

The person on the ground came to the same conclusion. "They're coming," he said in the tone people use on frightened children and kittens. "They'll only be a few minutes." Nice kitty.

I heard an engine, but it was on the other side of the tree, and I couldn't see anything until it pulled up under the walkway. The light of the torches showed it was one of those open carts, a cross between a golf cart and those things that take oldies to their gate at airports. Even before it came to a halt, a shadow in the front seat was out and jogging over, to pull up short under the pole with hands on hips.

"Jesus fucking Christ, Sam!"

Jake.

Just as one day I will be able to pretend I had a plan when I dived over the railings, so too I would like to believe that one day I will be able to pretend that everything went smoothly after that, that I was helped down in a dignified manner, that I gave an orderly, maybe even bullet-pointed statement to the police, and then went home, still dignified, to rest quietly. I would like to believe that I will be able to tell the story this way one day, because the reality swung from embarrassing to outright humiliating.

After twenty minutes or so of people hanging about on the ground and staring up at me, a cherry-picker drove up and parked beside the golf cart under the walkway. Its arm was raised until a platform nestled next to me. Standing in it was a middle-aged man in Kew overalls. He opened a gate in the side and said, in broad Glaswegian, "In you get, hen."

The pretend me smiled a polite-middle-class-female smile, thanked him graciously for his help while apologising for putting him to so much trouble, before stepping daintily onto the platform that was now firmly beneath me. The real me, however, clung ever more tightly to the metal strut, burst into tears and shook my head wildly from side to side. It wasn't even that I was scared, or thought I might fall. It wasn't anything rational.

You would think the man in the cherry-picker had been plucking wailing women out of trees for years. "I'm Walter," he said, "and I know you're Samantha." And after that he didn't say anything that could be accurately transcribed, just a litany of *All right now, hens*, and *Shhhs*. He didn't try to make me let go of the strut, or lift me away, just petted me like a small animal. I don't know what they teach them at horticultural college, but Walter must have gone for an advanced degree.

After a few minutes he pulled back and looked at me. "Ready to try?"

I nodded, and he slowly unwound one of my arms from the strut, wrapping it around his shoulder before moving to the other arm. Then my legs followed, and I was clinging to Walter instead of the support, with my face mashed into his neck. We descended like that, and even when we reached the ground he kept holding on to me, his murmurs as soothing as a mother cat's rough licks.

I felt another hand on my back, also petting the shuddery kitten, and I turned my head. When Walter saw I recognised Jake, he transferred me across, never letting my feet touch the ground.

"Can you stand?" Jake asked. "Do you want to?"

I shook my head and wiped my nose on his shirt before I looked up. "But I really need to pee."

I said it wasn't dignified.

Jake gave a bark of a laugh and smoothed my hair back. "If you've been up there all this time, you probably do. Let's get you cleaned up." And he carried me over to the golf cart, saying to someone as he passed, "Back at the offices."

We drew up to a building that looked like an elementary school, but I barely saw it as Jake carried me straight through to what must have been the staff loo. He put me down once the door swung shut behind us, and said, "A paramedic is on the way."

I waved it off with one hand, but clutched the sink hard with the other for support. "Don't need one. It's just scrapes."

"Humour me."

I looked in the mirror and worked at not shrieking. My hair looked like the big reveal on a programme starring David Attenborough. My face had a great raw patch on one side, where I'd scraped it on the metal strut. My hands were ripped to shreds. He was right. "And a tetanus jab."

Back in someone's office, I sat on a desk and had my face and hands disinfected and bandaged. The scrapes ran down my neck, and I removed what was left of my shirt so that they could be cleaned too.

"What's that?"

Jake was glaring at the side of my ribs. I craned my neck round to see. Bruising. "That must be where he kicked me."

He closed his eyes. I recognised that look. I'd been the cause of it before, but I couldn't see how this was my fault. I tried to distract him. "Do you think the gift shop has a T-shirt I could wear?"

He took a deep breath, then opened the door and spoke to someone outside. By the time the paramedics had finished, a T-shirt had materialised, illustrated front and back with the wildflowers of Kew. It wouldn't have been my first choice, but then, spending the night hanging onto a metal pole wasn't on my first-choice list either. I put the shirt on and the paramedic wrapped a shiny metallic blanket around me. It was only then I realised I was shivering.

Tea followed, with the paramedic adding four spoons of sugar. My dentist was going to have a heart attack at my next check-up. I tried to take the cup, but the shaking was too strong. Jake held it to my lips. "Sip," he said. I did. "Again." I did.

We kept on that way until I'd had half. Then, "You need to tell us what happened. It can't wait."

I knew it couldn't. "Of course."

Four uniforms filed in, a woman and three men. The woman and one of the men were introduced, but I didn't listen to their names. Jake moved closer to me and looked over at the woman. "OK if I begin?"

She gestured: *Be my guest.*

"Start from where I left you," said Jake. "What did you do right after?"

That was easier than trying to work out what was important and what order to put it in. "I stayed up on the top of the pagoda. There were footsteps." And slowly, with a lot of I-forgot-to-says and doubling back to fill in, I told them everything.

As I knew from experience, the police never feel you've had the full benefit of the giving-a-statement experience until you've repeated a story a minimum of three times, although they prefer to aim for double figures. The woman took me through everything again, and her colleagues joined in, asking me to go over what the men had said in particular, then their appearance. I described Sprained Ankle at least five times. Baldy got less attention: I'd only glimpsed him briefly from above.

After they pressed me on Sprained Ankle's appearance a sixth time, I asked, trying to tamp down any sign of exasperation, "Don't I get to go somewhere and look at mugshots, or is that just on television?"

The woman smirked. "We're technologically advanced. I'll email you a link, and you can look online."

The miracles of modern life: on the one hand, you no longer had to sit in a police station drinking instant coffee, on the other, you develop carpal tunnel.

Then one of the men who had not been introduced said, "Do you think they actually had a weapon?"

I blinked. "They discussed shooting me. What else would they have meant?"

Jake's expression said he thought it was a sensible question. "They might have been trying to frighten you, so that you'd come down if you thought they'd shoot."

I considered that. "I believed them, but whether that's because I'm not up on thugs, or because they really had a gun, I can't tell you. Does it matter?"

"If they were armed, it points towards professional criminals rather than violent amateurs."

Was I supposed to be miffed that whoever wanted me dead hadn't been willing to spring for top-of-the-line thugs, or relieved that they'd cheaped out on entry-level brawn?

No one said anything for a few minutes. Finally Jake moved on. "Where were they from?"

I stared at him. "I only request photo ID before an assault: I never thought to ask for proof of address. And as luck would have it, we didn't have time for them to show me photos of their seaside cottage before it got dark."

One of the uniforms turned a laugh into a pretend cough. Jake knew me well enough that he just continued as though I'd said something rational. "Did they have accents? Were they Londoners?"

I played it back in my head. "Yes. Probably. I don't know." I leant against him. "Maybe estuary?" I never claimed to be a good witness.

He pushed the tea towards me again. By my count I was on my third cup, but I knew he was right, and I needed it, and at least I'd reached the stage where I could hold it without spilling. I drank. Then, "Please can I go home? I know you need more, but later? Tomorrow? Please." I closed my eyes. I was going to cry again.

I was still leaning against Jake, and I could feel him turn towards the woman. She must have agreed, because the others stood, and Jake pulled away. "Come on, tiger. Can you walk?"

I slid off the desk and found that yes, I could. And we went home.

In books, after the heroine is rescued, it says "And we went home". The authors omit that the heroine is wrapped in a silver blanket and wearing a Wildflowers of Kew T-shirt. Or that, even though she's filthy, the bandages on her hand are bulky and have to be kept dry, so her partner has to brush her teeth and wash her and help her in the loo. Which is why books are so much better than life.

But even in real life I was eventually clean and dry, and I headed straight for bed. Jake piled the spare duvet, which I keep for when someone is sleeping on the sofa bed, on top of ours. Then he vanished, returning with a hot-water bottle — from Mr Rudiger,

243

I learnt later. I was vaguely aware when he tucked it in by my feet. I felt his hand on my head, and nodded into it when he said, "I've left a message with Miranda to say you're ill, and I've let Helena know you're home in one piece," but I was asleep before he'd reached the end of the sentence.

It was early afternoon when I woke up, and the flat was silent. I shuffled down the hall to the kitchen, and there was Mr Rudiger, stirring a pot on the stove. "Ready for lunch?" he asked, as if he frequently dropped by my flat to cook while I slept. "It's minestrone." What I love most about Mr Rudiger is that he never bothers with the superfluous — no "How are you feeling?" when the answer was plainly "Like death on toast" — and he never talks for the sake of talking.

Instead he dished up the soup and cut me some bread from a baguette, both of which he must have brought downstairs with him, because neither had been in my kitchen when I went out the previous day. We sat in silence and ate. With a little effort, I managed to lift both the spoon and my glass without spilling. When I'd had enough, Mr Rudiger washed the dishes. I was too — not even tired — I was too apathetic to move. Initiating anything was too much effort, so I sat and watched him, and when he finished I let him lead me to the sitting room and guide me to the sofa. He covered me with a blanket, and then sat in an armchair across the room, picked up his book, found his place and started to read. He was, said his withdrawal, there if I needed him, but I didn't have to interact. So I didn't.

244

I stared at nothing for a while, and then I slept some more.

It was dark when I woke, and Mr Rudiger was no longer in his chair, although the book was open, face down, which suggested he hadn't gone far. I heard voices down the hall, but staring into space still seemed like enough activity for the moment, so I did that again. Eventually the voices drew nearer: Mr Rudiger and Jake.

When he saw I was awake, Jake switched on a lamp behind me. Mr Rudiger collected his book silently. I sat up, and Jake came over to sit next to me. After a few minutes he said quietly, "You know I need to ask you more, don't you?"

I did, but first it was my turn. "What happened last night?"

Jake blew out a breath. He didn't enjoy remembering the previous night. *Join the club, buddy.* "I got home at eleven, and you weren't there." He crossed his arms against the memory. "I tried to ring you, but got the recording saying your number was unavailable. I assumed you'd forgotten to charge your phone. I rang Helena, and the Lewises and Mr Rudiger. Mr Rudiger said he hadn't heard you come in. Helena and I worked through a list of your friends. By midnight I'd had a colleague run your Oyster card through the system: you hadn't been on the overground, or any public transport, after you'd used your card for our trip to Richmond. So I got onto the Richmond force and asked them to make enquiries." He shrugged. "It was too early to do anything officially, but I called in a few favours and some off-duty friends helped. We got Kew's security to let us in and began a search. We'd been there an hour before we found you, because we started at the pagoda." Dear lord, he thought I'd fallen ten storeys from the top of the pagoda. "You and I had discussed walking along the Thames towpath. Dragging the river would have been next." It was a miracle he was as calm as he was when they'd found me.

I didn't say anything, because I didn't know what to say, so after a minute he went on. "We spent this afternoon shifting the case from Richmond to us." I looked up at that and he shook his head. "Not me. Chris is heading up the team. I'm not on it, for obvious reasons." He slid his eyes over to me. I wasn't going to like whatever was coming next. "Paula is his DS."

Oh yay.

It was early, but Jake hadn't slept at all the night before, and I was incapable of doing anything. He showed me the link the Richmond force had emailed before the transfer, to try and identify my attackers. I pushed it away. "Tomorrow," I said, and he nodded.

Then I remembered. "What's the news on Sam?"

He smiled. "Helena and her friend between them put the fear of God into someone. They're back home. They won't be questioned again without one of Helena's heavy-hitters sitting beside them." He shook his head, and I wasn't certain if it was admiration for Helena, or rueful recognition that his colleagues had better find someone else to question. I decided not to ask.

We went to bed, and within minutes Jake's breathing had evened out. He was asleep. I stared at the ceiling for hours. Now I'd stopped being afraid, and was no longer in a tree, I was angry. Enough. I needed to find out who wanted to kill me, and why.

CHAPTER
TWELVE

Jake and I had been together long enough that we could have a lot of our arguments silently, mentally leaping ahead to the end without having to go through the rigmarole of fighting it out. When I woke the next morning, I said, "I'm going to work," and stood braced for the list of reasons why that wasn't going to happen. Jake braced too, but then he let it go, merely saying, "I'm taking you."

So that was that. Not the "that" I'd been expecting, but that was that all the same.

I was stiff and sore, but the cuts on my hands had scabbed over, and I decided that meant I could do without most of the bandages. Being able to wash and dress myself did wonders for my morale.

When I got to the kitchen, Jake handed me my coffee and I sat looking out into the garden. It was another hot, still day. The garden needed watering. Maybe I could use my injured hands as an excuse, and make Jake do it. Then I remembered that he'd been called out on his day off, and right after that he'd spent the night looking for me. Maybe I'd have the garden declared a site of scientific interest. It could be an example of Darwinian theory, where we watched survival of the fittest in action.

Jake sat down with his breakfast, bringing me back to more practical matters. "Will I have to talk to your colleagues again?"

"I'm afraid so. But they'll want you to have looked through the photos first, see if you can identify the men."

That would postpone another interview, and the further away, the better. A problem postponed is a problem I can pretend doesn't exist. But I couldn't really. Instead I told Jake what I'd been thinking about in the tree. Not about knowing the lyrics to "Waterloo Sunset". I'd dazzle him with that another time. But that the whole thing had to be connected to Harefield, and that the only people I could think of who might be involved in that way were Azim and Kevin Munroe.

Jake nodded. "I've already spoken to Chris."

I felt horrible for putting Azim forward like that — he'd done nothing except go to a Neighbourhood Association meeting and watch a fire. I'd done the same, and I didn't think I was suspicious. "I'll text Viv to see if anyone has been asking her about Harefield. She knew him, after all, and she's also been asking questions, and if no one has been bothering her . . ." I trailed off.

"Who have you spoken to about Harefield? Anyone, no matter how briefly."

I was going to ace the next pub quiz. "You, Viv, Helena. Sam. The man who answered Harefield's phone at his office. I can't remember his name, and anyway, I only asked if he knew where Harefield was. It was before we knew he was dead, so it was really a non-conversation. That's it." I reconsidered. "The cops from the local nick knew Viv and I had been asking about him, because I was there when she was telling one of them off, but unless they asked her later, they don't know my name." I tried to remember what they looked like, and failed. No surprise. I often don't recognise people who work in my building. "There were a couple of community police officers there too, and they could have been Sprained Ankle and his friend, but why would they be?"

Jake appeared to think the same. "What are your plans today?"

"I need to talk to Ben about —" I pulled myself together. Jake wanted to know where I was going to be when, not the minutiae of office politics. I started over. "I'll be at the office all day. I don't have any outside meetings scheduled. And Helena texted yesterday to say she'd be at home this evening. I ought to go over so she can see I'm alive." I headed him off before he could interrupt. "I'll take a taxi booked on the company account, not public transport. Promise." I held up my hand: Boy Scout's oath.

Then I remembered. "But I need to borrow some cash. I have no phone, no cards, no nothing." The police had found my bag under the walkway, but when I told them Sprained Ankle had pawed his way through it, they'd handed it over to their technicians.

I should have had more faith in Jake. He tipped his chin towards the hall. "It's by the front door.

Everything will need cleaning — it was dusted for prints — and you should have a quick look before we leave and let me know if anything is missing."

Jake was right: the interior almost glowed in the dark from the phosphorescent powder that had been scattered wholesale. I dumped everything onto the floor and ran through it, wiping as I went.

"All there, apart from my phone and iPad," I grumbled. "Unless Sprained Ankle had a runny nose and nicked a tissue."

"We'll stop on the way and pick up new ones for you. Electronics, not tissues. And if you email Chris, he'll give you a crime number — you can claim it on your insurance, because you were mugged."

That made me feel better. "Why did he do it, though?" I asked. "Sprained Ankle, I mean? Why smash up my toys?"

"So that you couldn't be located by the phone signal. If you'd gone over the railings, it's not that far down. A person might survive a twenty-metre fall, but if their location couldn't be pinpointed, and they lay there all night, the outlook would be less good."

I noticed that he'd switched halfway from "you" to "they". I didn't think he'd done it consciously, but I agreed with the choice: I didn't want to think about it happening to me, either. I dropped the subject, and on the way to work, by unspoken agreement, we talked about anything not related to violent death — a film we wanted to see, when Jake might put in for leave, and what we would do with the free time.

We stopped and did the phone thing, Jake's warrant card helping speed the process along when I realised I had no proof of address when it came time to transfer my old number to the new phone. I hurried through it. I had a lot to do. First on my list was deflecting questions about my injured face and hands at the office, so I stopped for a few minutes to talk to Bernie at reception, meeting her gasp as she took in the glory that was my scraped face with a shrug.

"I was doored." Dooring is a standard cycling hazard, when someone in a parked car opens their door into a cyclist's path. I've never been doored, but it's common enough, and it wouldn't be questioned.

It wasn't. We had a quick run-through of Cycling Accidents of People We Know, finishing with a rousing chorus of Evil Smidsys, which is what cyclists call drivers who don't pay attention and then attempt to absolve themselves of responsibility by saying "Sorry, mate, I didn't see you". That would ensure a prosaic explanation for my scabbed and bruised face would be telegraphed through the building, necessitating nothing further from me than a sympathetic hearing of the circumstances of other people's accidents.

Miranda wasn't under any illusions. She'd seen me bruised and bashed about too often. She stood now, checking me over as I walked down the hall. She didn't speak for a moment, letting her eyes slowly take it in. Then she shook her head. "Maybe it's time for a safer hobby. Crochet might work for you."

I didn't stop. "You know I'd just put my eye out with the hook."

She nodded regretfully. No argument there.

I made coffee and began to weed out my emails from the weekend and the day I'd missed. I hadn't had the energy to check in yesterday, so there was a backlog. I dealt with anything that needed yes/no responses, forwarded more to Miranda with instructions, and deleted or parked another batch. That left a dozen or so that required that I pay attention when I replied. And of those, just one was urgent. It was an email from the management consultants, reminding the editors that our session with them was booked for — I looked at my watch and managed not to scream — for five minutes ago.

I disconnected my new iPad, which had just finished syncing from my computer, and ran. By the time I arrived, T&R's other seven editors, plus David, our editor-in-chief, were gathered around the table in the big meeting room. I slid into a seat, trying out my I've-been-here-all-along-what-are-you-looking-at face. It wasn't very good, since I'm excessively punctual, so I don't have to practise it very often.

I dumped my tablet, reached for some coffee and looked around. Two of the management consultants were the pair who had been at the initial meeting: Adam Rossiter and the woman he hadn't troubled to introduce. The other woman was as dark as the dominatrix librarian was blonde, as flouncy-girlie-curvy as the librarian was severe. Now that senior management was represented only by David, Rossiter took a back seat as the two women set up their PowerPoint presentation. (Of course there was

PowerPoint. Management consultants would wither away and die if they couldn't show slides printed with the exact same words that were being spoken, mashed between old *New Yorker* cartoons. But I digress.)

The two women, who introduced themselves as Annie and Jessie, tag-teamed their introduction while Rossiter scrolled through his phone. The women, they told us, were thrilled to be yadda-yadda, excited to be something-or-othered, and in general, they were as enthusiastic as a basket of puppies to be working on this restructuring, which was, they promised, the start of "a journey we will take together as we learn to feedback our thoughts to produce new ways of growing an enriched product". I tried to suspend judgement — all right, no I didn't, I was as judgemental as hell, but I tried not to grimace. At least, I tried not to until I saw the first slide. Which was, they informed us, "a schematic of their plan for the new editorial department's un-silo-ed way of working, mapped out as an organigram".

I decided I could either return to childhood and make vomiting noises, or I could zone out for a while. So I zoned. I flicked through the calendars and the contacts on my new phone and tablet, to make sure both had synced. I checked my email. Sadly, nothing had appeared in my in-box that couldn't wait. I opened the tablet's book reader, to double-check that it had loaded the manuscripts I had on submission. And after the work side of things was taken care of, I began to play. The tablet had come preloaded with more apps

254

than the old one, most of which I had no use for, and spent a few minutes deleting.

The tablet had far more capacity than my old one. When I had time, I'd download more music. I flicked over to my photos. On the old tablet I'd kept them pared down, but now I no longer had to. Having decided that, I further decided that New Tablet equalled New Sam, and I'd organise them. There were a bunch that were of people I could barely remember at events I'd rather forget. The photos of Viv's jasmine that Victor, Viv and even Arthur now had. They were followed by a photo that must have been snapped by accident. I peered at it: dust bunnies and dirty socks. Photos of paintings: I take them in museums, then I forget who painted then, and where they were.

I was about to move on to the app store when I realised that no one in the meeting was speaking. I looked up. The diagram of our bright, shiny future editorial department was still up and had rendered our gabby group mute. Finally Jessie, the dark-haired, bouncier of the two women, spoke. "Initial thoughts?"

I'd lost track of where we were, so I had no thoughts, initial or otherwise. After an embarrassingly long pause, Roger cleared his throat. Rog runs our sports list, and if you had asked me before this meeting, I would have said it was impossible to rile him. He was so laid back that sometimes I worried he's wasn't merely horizontal, but dead. Now he did something I'd never seen him do before: he sat up straight. Then he carefully folded his hands and stared at little Jessie like a vicar about to pounce on a choirboy who'd been caught sneaking sweets during the organ voluntary. She managed to hold onto her bounce until he said what was, clearly, the last thing she'd expected. "Would you spell that, please?" Roger asked.

"Spell?" The bounce was leaking away, a slow puncture.

"An" — he held the word out with metaphorical tongs — "an organigram?"

The puncture was patched. She was *so* happy to elaborate. This was her favourite part. "Yes!" she cried. "It's an *organisational diagram*, so it's an organigram." She stressed the relevant syllables of each word for us slowpokes, and beamed. A little ray of organigrammatic sunshine.

Silence. Rossiter briefly looked up from his phone, but decided not to become involved and dropped his eyes again. Annie, the dominatrix librarian, leapt in to salvage the wreckage by moving us on from terminology to detail. How, she asked brightly, did we enrich our product? This appeared to mean, what did we do to make our books more valuable in the time between their acquisition and publication, and what indicators did we use to measure that increase in value?

We stared at the women. Then we stared at each other. They wanted benchmarks, things that could be checked off on a list. They didn't want to know how, or even if, we made the books we acquired better. They wanted objective criteria that could be applied to every book in an identical way to indicate that these books were more valuable after they had been through the editorial process.

Silently, we came to a collective agreement: banging our heads on the table was not going to help. So for the next hour we attempted to explain what editing was, how it was done, and why. The more we talked, the less they understood. Roger, finally, in exasperation said, "If anyone except the author and the editor can tell that a book has been edited after it's done, then the editor has done a lousy job."

Now it was Annie and Jessie's turn to stare blankly at us. I could see that they were managing not to whirl their fingers by their temples in the universal sign for "nuts" with effort. I tried an analogy to back Rog up. "Being an editor is like finding a station on the radio. You tune and fiddle until you get rid of the static. Once you've homed in on the station, the listeners don't need to know about the fiddling you had to do to get there." I added, to kill off their benchmark fixation: "And you don't leave the station just at the edge of the reception band, so the listeners will know how bad the static was before."

I thought that was a nifty way of putting it, but the Three Musketeers weren't buying any. At least, Rossiter wasn't listening, while Annie and Jessie simply didn't understand, and, furthermore, didn't want to. A job where the height of excellence was to be invisible was incomprehensible to them. Worse, a job that left no trace was a job the output of which could not be measured. If the output couldn't be measured, then it couldn't be increased to make more money, or decreased to make savings. More terrifying to them, why would anyone hire management consultants if that were the case? We went round and round, chasing our tails. I decided it would be better not to share my own view of the publishing business: that manuscripts are acquired on instinct, and the rest of the job is spent creating a rationale to justify that gut response.

It was Ben who cracked. "I have a request." He raised his hand, the good schoolboy. Annie and Jessie bounced happily. Someone was finally engaging with them. "As a courtesy," he said, even more politely, "as a courtesy, do you think you could perhaps stop referring to books as 'product'?"

The women went back to giving each other little side glances. Even Rossiter looked up, puzzled by the strangeness of the request. What was wrong with "product"?

"'Product'," Ben responded to the unspoken question, his voice still level, "is a word that suggests that each item — or, to use the technical term, each 'book' — is interchangeable. This is not the case, and if you are under the impression that it is, that any one can be substituted for any other, then you have failed to understand the business you are so gleefully restructuring — excuse me, re-silo-ing. And, if you have failed to understand the business, then not only is our company wasting money on your fees, but you are wasting our time, when we could be back at our desks, busily enriching our product in our old-fashioned, un-siloed way." Then he very carefully picked up his papers, stood, and, just as carefully, pushed his chair neatly under the table. "Ladies and gentlemen?" said the twenty-six-year-old, looking around. And, somehow, it wasn't pompous, or silly. The eight of us, excluding David, gathered our belongings as one, and silently filed out of the room.

It wasn't going to solve anything, but by God it was satisfying. The downside was that it looked like I might have to revise my opinion that Ben was a poisonous little runt. I hated doing that: the mental paperwork was exhausting. By the time I got back to my office, however, I realised that that wasn't going to be a problem. Even if I had been planning to try and like Ben, Ben wasn't going to try and like me in return, because there on my desk, lying foursquare in the centre, where I couldn't even pretend not to see it, was Miranda's draft memo about the bogus gangbanger book.

She left no doubts about it. Her memo was a total demolition job, persuasive, thorough, and completely irrefutable. In three concise pages, Miranda had proved beyond doubt that she deserved her promotion, and also made it a certainty that Ben was going to hate me to the end of time. There was no way we could publish this book; Miranda was my assistant, ergo, its non-publication was going to be my fault.

Unless. I stared out the window. Unless I could persuade Ben to use the problems Miranda had uncovered as a weapon in our battle against the product-enrichers. In this situation, Miranda hadn't fine-tuned a radio station. I brought that metaphor to a screaming halt. It was more like looking at a piece of fabric, I decided. Ben was a retailer who wanted to buy a range of cashmere jumpers. To an amateur, the jumpers had a pretty design and sleek finish, and so the jumpers should fetch a high price. But to a knitting expert — Miranda — the shoddy manufacturing process behind them was apparent. The moment these pretty jumpers were subjected to wear and tear, they would unravel, customers would demand their money back, and in addition would swear never to buy a T&R jumper again. This wasn't about product enrichment; it was about having the expertise to know when a product was of inferior quality, to prevent financial losses and a public-relations disaster down the road.

Maybe I could swing it. I messaged Ben: *Things to discuss. Are you free for lunch/drink at some point?* That would confuse the hell out of him. The last civil thing we'd said to each other in the past half-year had been — I thought for a moment. I wasn't sure we had said a civil word to each other in the past half-year.

There's a first time for everything.

Ben messaged back almost immediately. "On holiday from Thurs, so Weds?" Which was worse, I wondered, having men try to kill me in a botanical garden, or telling Ben his book was bogus? I stared hopelessly at the screen. Both. Both in forty-eight hours was definitely worse. "Great!" I typed. "Tomorrow first thing?" I wanted to add an emoji, but I couldn't find the one for sarcasm.

What I did find, however, were sixteen messages from the other editors, the gist of which was "Pub. At six." I texted an "I'm in", and then also shot off a quick text to Sam, asking him if there was any news. After that the day got swallowed in catching up on what I'd missed the day before, plus various "secret" pre-pub meetings (you could tell they were secret, because we closed the door) and, mostly, fighting off intermittent waves of fear. From my schooldays onwards, I had always worked with my desk facing a wall, to cut down on distractions. That layout, however, put my back to the door, which now felt like a very bad decision. Had my cut-up hands permitted, I would have rearranged my office furniture. As they didn't, I just looked over my shoulder a lot, which was neither an efficient use of my time, nor conducive to getting any work done. I spent the day on high alert, ready for a madman to rush in and — what? Assault me with a proof copy of *A Tour of the Tour de France*, picked up from the pulp shelf outside my door? Whatever it was that a madman might do in a publishing house, I was on the alert for it, and it was exhausting, and stupid, and more exhausting for recognising how stupid it was.

It was also, apparently, highly visible to others. Or at least it was to Miranda. She came in as I was on the phone to an agent about an author I admired but who was notoriously resistant to having her work edited, who always hated her jacket designs, and who adamantly refused to do any publicity, a publisher's triple whammy. On a good day, that would have been a tense conversation, even without factoring in that I disliked the agent because she never listened to anyone except herself. Today that was mostly a blessing, because I was listening to neither of us.

Miranda was. Her eyebrows rose and her lips pursed as she leant against the door jamb, waiting for me to finish. When I finally got the agent to pause long enough so that I could say goodbye in publishing-ese — "We must have lunch" — Miranda just gathered up my handbag and my bookbag and asked, "Did you have anything else?" I shook my head silently, and she handed the bags over. "See you tomorrow," she said firmly.

I was now being bossed around by younger women as well as older. I refused to think of the implications, and said instead, "I can't go. The editors are meeting at six."

She knew that. The assistants knew everything. "If you leave for the pub now, you'll be ten minutes early, but tomorrow you won't have to ring back all the people you're ringing now, when you can't remember what you talked about."

Ouch. "I'm going to quit," I announced. "Pack it in and become a hermit. The only thing is, I don't know where you find job openings for hermits."

"The classifieds in the back of the *London Review of Books*," she said, hustling me out the door. The assistants really did know everything.

As I walked past reception a text pinged in. Steve. *Just to say I'll be working late in your garden a few nights this week, so don't worry if you hear noises outside.*

That was thoughtful of him. And it would make a great horror film: a woman alone at home hears ominous sounds in the night. She investigates, and her screams carry for miles as she discovers . . . tomatoes being planted.

I shared this with Rog, who was also leaving early for our local, and we planned out the schedule for a gardening-cum-horror-film festival. *The Nightmare on Elm Street* was about a neighbourhood terrorised by Dutch elm disease, while the villain of the *Jeepers Creepers* series made his bid for world domination through an infestation of Japanese knotweed.

Once at the pub, the others joined in the game, and it took a while to settle down to our more immediate problems. That was partly because we had no control, no way of stopping what was happening, and so our meeting could do little except entrench us in our positions. The conversation was contentious, circular and filled with implausible scenarios, ranging from the entire department quitting en masse to staging a publishing version of a hunger strike, where we'd refuse to take agents out to lunch. The only unexpected aspect was that Ben, the youngest and newest member of the department, continued in the role he'd slipped into that morning, and became our de facto leader. I had had nothing but miserable interactions with him, and even I had to admit he was impressive. He kept us on topic, he made people feel that they'd been heard even as he neatly headed off their rambling digressions — in short, he was in charge not because he'd decided he would be, but because the rest of us decided he should be.

I knew from experience that the meeting would swiftly move from discussion of the management consultants to discussion of our colleagues, and from there it was anybody's guess — it could be who was sleeping with whom, or it could be the situation in

Syria. Whatever it was, we never stayed on point for long, so on my way out of the building I had asked Bernie to order me a cab for six-thirty, to give me an excuse for cutting out as soon as I could.

It was too early for Helena to be home, but I had a key, and Helena's house felt like a refuge, unlike mine, where I'd had a break-in by an unknown person, and where Steve also seemed to have gained access with no trouble. I moved straight to her welcoming yellow kitchen and poured myself a glass of iced coffee and then just waited. I didn't try to work out what was going on, or make any other use of my time, productive or recreational. I just let go of everything.

Helena tippy-tapped in about half an hour later. Really, it's a wonder anyone is intimidated by her, much less everyone. She's not even five foot two (she claims five foot three, but she lies), and from her neat little curly head down to her neat little high-heeled feet, she could be a picture-book definition of "demure", if picture books took to defining words like "demure". And yet grown men quailed when she glanced their way. She's a mystery.

She kissed me hello with no more visible emotion than any other day, but looked carefully at my face and said, "You handled that well." My throat tightened. Praise from Helena was both sparing, and sincere. I thought I'd been an idiot, treed like a cat in the dark. Now I felt six feet tall.

"Thanks," I said. We're undemonstrative, what can I tell you? If you were expecting an out-take from one of those Neapolitan realist films where everyone screams at each other all the time, you've got the wrong address.

I gave her the *Reader's Digest* version of what had happened at Kew. It wasn't something I wanted to linger on, and she must have agreed that she didn't need to hear it. Either that or she'd spoken to Jake, which was more likely. In any case, she allowed the conversation to move on to more soothing topics. We performed the ritual scandalised discussion of the guests at her party, which as far as I'm concerned is the only reason ever to have a party; she checked to see if I'd be free for dinner on my birthday, which was coming up; and we discussed a case of hers that was about to go to court. Her assistant was on maternity leave and, "The paperwork is out of control without her there," Helena moaned.

Out of control to Helena most likely meant that two memos had been left unfiled for twenty minutes. But the word paperwork reminded me. I'd had my passport application in my bag all week, as if the act of carrying it around would substitute for dealing with it. I dragged the envelope out now and dumped the contents on the table. "Will you please sign to prove to the passport people that I am me?"

Helena paged slowly through the forms. God bless her, I've been her daughter for my entire life, but she still wasn't going to sign something without reading it first.

Rightly, as it proved. She pushed it back to me. "I can't."

I snatched it back petulantly. "Why? You're a solicitor. It says that's one of the professions they accept." I jabbed at the paragraph.

She gave me one of those fond looks that mothers give their children when they're being particularly dense. But all she said was, "I'm also your mother. The person who vouches for you can't be related to you."

"But I don't know any vets," I whined.

The fond look turned into a pull-yourself-together one. "Leave it with me."

Happily. I loved people who said "Leave it with me". I thought of Steve, and his I'll-grow-it-you-eat-it plan. Maybe it wasn't bossy women I attracted, maybe I just let everyone run my life.

Helena had returned to telling me about her case, and was in the middle of telling me about the young but shark-like barrister who was leading it, and I dutifully tuned back in. ". . . and so he said, 'You can't fight city hall', but I *like* fighting city hall." Helena's shark-like barrister could be no sharkier than Helena when she smelt blood in the water, and if she wanted to fight city hall, then — My mind stuttered and a series of sentences echoed in my head: the Neighbourhood Association trying to turn a local park into a legally protected space, so it couldn't be built on; the planning issues about re-zoning properties for commercial use; Mo telling me Dennis had helped the skateboarders fight off developers who wanted the land where they skated.

I said abruptly, "Mother, how do you find out who owns a building?"

266

She raised an eyebrow at the interruption. "The Land Registry, dear." As always, she asked no follow-up question, just clarified: "The register is online, but if a property is owned by a company, you won't get much information." And she returned to the wonders of her barrister, and we ate dinner, and all the while I turned an idea over in my head.

When I got home, I googled the Land Registry. Helena was right, not that I'd had any doubts. There it was, at the top of the homepage: "Find out who owns a property or piece of land." For three quid, it assured me, as long as I had those two essentials of modern life, a credit card and Adobe Acrobat, the information could be mine, with the caveat that the website would not be able to supply information on tunnels, pipelines, mines and minerals or airspace leases. Although the thought of leasing the airspace over my flat had never previously occurred to me, the Land Registry's refusal to let me know if it were possible now seemed wilfully obstructive. Then I remembered the £3 fee. Finding out if I could lease airspace would probably cost at least a fiver, and I wasn't sure I was willing to spend so recklessly.

I began to fill in an application, and then I realised I didn't know the address of the empty house. I could wait and ask Steve when I next saw him, although I couldn't think how I could explain why I was nosing around searching for the owner. I googled "Talbot's Road", and "fire", to see if there were any reports that might have mentioned the address. The local newspaper had a small article, and a couple of blogs

267

had mentioned it, but all they said was "a fire on Talbot's Road", which got me no further forward. I tried the Post Office website to see if there was a way of searching for addresses, but if there was, I didn't have the skills to find it.

This reminder of my limited computer skills moved me naturally to Viv, and her friend whose grandson was good at computers. That might mean anything from him helping his gran post pictures on her Facebook page to him being a hacker wanted by Interpol for denial of service attacks that had brought the Pentagon to its knees. There was one way to find out. I shot Viv a quick text: *Could I speak to your friend's grandson? Need help with a computer search.* Then I went back to the Land Registry and in default of getting any of my questions answered, clicked on "Check average property prices and sales in my area". That was fun, if a little terrifying. The half-dozen sales in my street over the past decade showed the almost hallucinatory price-rise in property that I knew about from the newspapers. Here, when it was about my own street, it stopped being a political story and became real. A flat that had been (sort of, and thank you Mr Mortgage Lender) affordable when I'd bought it as a sitting tenant nearly twenty years before might now be just about affordable to a two-salaried couple both working in law, or investment banking, or something like that, but if I were starting out today, I'd be living an hour's journey out of the centre, and grateful every day that it was only an hour.

268

I was dragged out of this nasty little reality check by the phone. I jumped and scrabbled for it — no one rang me at ten at night. The number was blocked, but I was worried about Sam, even though objectively I knew he was being guarded by Helena and her watchdogs.

"What?" demanded a voice I didn't recognise.

What what? At least no one was asking me if I wanted to win some luggage by completing a marketing survey. So, "Is this the Miss Congeniality hotline?" I snapped. I didn't, really. Instead I went for, "What do you mean, 'What?' You rang me."

"Huh."

Twenty seconds, I mentally warned the voice. *That's all you're getting, because it's only Tuesday, and already this has not been a good week.* "Who is this?" I didn't bother trying not to snarl.

"Viv told me to call."

It was Viv's friend's grandson, responding to my text, and he wasn't being unpleasant, he was most likely a teenager, and he just lacked social skills. Since I did too, I empathised. "Thanks for ringing so quickly. This may be a very quick question. I've been trying to find an address for a building. That is, um — what is your name?"

"Why?"

Yes, he was a teenager. "Because I don't want to call you 'um'. And because, if you don't tell me, I'll tell Viv, who will tell your grandmother, who will give you a hard time. It doesn't even have to be your real name. Just something better than 'um'."

He snorted. "Stinger."

Naturally. "OK, Stinger, thank you for that. Now, my question. I was trying to find out the address for a building, but that was so that I could get some information on it from a government website." I got the snorting sound again. It was excellently done, and I hoped his computer skills matched up. "Yes, exactly. That's why I called on you." Flattery will get me everywhere, or at least I hoped it would. "Can you find out who owns a building for me? And if it's a company, who the directors are?" I explained where the building was, and what had happened to it.

I got an aggrieved silence, and I didn't blame him, so I doubled down on the flattery. "I'm sure you can find it in twenty seconds, while I couldn't manage it in twenty years." I left unspoken that I'd tattle on him to his grandma if he didn't shape up, and instead finished with, "Let me give you my email address."

That was snort-worthy too. "You think I couldn't find it?"

"Not for a minute, Stinger. I think you have it already."

He recited it to me, smug.

"You're scary." He wasn't, but if you call yourself Stinger, you probably want to be.

CHAPTER
THIRTEEN

I need a couple of cups of coffee in the morning before I'm human. When Jake is there, we have coffee together, but if he isn't staying over, I don't bother and wait until I get to the office. He'd texted after Stinger and I had our meeting of souls the previous evening, to say he was working out west past the airport, and so would go back to his own flat when he was done. All of which is to explain why, when Ben put his head around my door at eight the following morning, I was at least three cups shy of being ready for him.

"Come in," I said warmly, pretending to him, and to me, that I was fully caffeinated and happy to see him. "Or shall we go across the road? I could use a croissant." I could think of nothing I wanted less, but it would move our discussion onto neutral ground, and give me an extra five minutes to rally. Ben probably thought the same, so we walked silently to the café the office staff used as our regular pit stop. I'm sure it had a name, but I'd never heard it called anything except "across the road".

When we arrived, the takeaway queue was long, but there weren't many sitting at the tables, so we headed to a booth in the back, ordering coffee and croissants as we passed the counter. Which was a pity, as it gave us no reason to delay our discussion. Apart from the single sentence he'd used to order, Ben hadn't said anything since we'd left my office. I couldn't predict how the conversation would go, but the needle was swinging somewhere between "badly" and "downright awful".

I began with a bit of smarm. "First, I wanted to say how grateful I was that you took the lead with the management consultants. I couldn't have done that." He nodded, but didn't look any friendlier. Not a surprise. We'd never been friendly. But while it was smarm, it was honest smarm: I truly couldn't have done it. I ploughed on. "So." I stopped. Then began again. "So, Miranda was telling me about the gang memoir she's editing for you." The temperature dropped from cool to frosty. "And I was thinking, while she's produced some queries that are difficult, it might be excellent ammunition for this reorganisation chaos."

"Queries." Ben's voice was, shall we say, not welcoming. About as not-welcoming as a haemophiliac would be when introduced to a vampire in a dark alley.

"She thinks the author might have —" I had given a lot of thought to the next word "— might have embellished his text. There are some points where the details don't quite ring true, she says." There were points where an entire bell tower was ringing a carillon of false notes, but that could come later. I waved my hand in grand dismissal. "Nothing that she wouldn't normally sort out with you. But it seemed an awfully opportune weapon ..." I trailed off, I hoped tantalisingly.

The Ice Age that had descended at the first part of my speech thawed slightly. A Little Ice Age, at least. "A weapon?"

I nodded vigorously. "Absolutely. They made it plain the other day that they want to get rid of the in-house editing and farm everything out to freelancers because they don't know what editing is, and so if it vanishes they think it won't matter. We can use this manuscript as a perfect example of why editors are not only essential, they're cost-efficient. If Miranda is right, and there are problems she's isolated, she's saved the company a lot of money, and also a public-relations situation. If the manuscript had gone to a freelance who was paid by the hour, they would have put the commas in the right places, but they would have felt it was their job not to dig deeper because asking questions would rack up costs. But you didn't farm it out, you gave it to Miranda, who is bright enough to spot the problems that were worrying you." I was going to go to hell for the number of lies I was telling. "It's ammunition, isn't it — proving why in-house resources are essential." I sat back and stirred my coffee to give Ben time to think.

"Will you give me a quick rundown of what she spotted? I imagine it will confirm my concerns, but it's sensible to compare notes." He was good. If it weren't that he'd torn his croissant into ever-tinier pieces, until there wasn't one larger than a dust mite, I might almost have believed him.

I pushed across Miranda's line-by-line breakdown and he read as I sipped my coffee and watched him out of the corner of my eye. If Ben and I ever got onto boys'-night card-playing terms, I'd insist that croissants be served as part of the deal. Each time he hit something nasty on Miranda's list, his hand went back to the pastry.

It took him forever to read the two pages through. Then he went back to the top of the first page and began again. Finally he laid the memo face down on the table, carefully squaring it up, then folding his hands on top, as if that would physically suppress the information it contained. "I'd spotted a few red flags, of course." *Liar.* "But I must admit, nothing like this." All right, that was more generous than I'd expected. "If she's right — and based on this memo, I don't see how she can be wrong — the book is unpublishable. I should have seen it, and I didn't." *Much* more generous. "And I like your idea of using it as management-consultant fodder. Let's do it." Damn. He'd acknowledged he'd made a mistake, acknowledged that someone had caught what he'd missed, and further acknowledged that someone else had found a solution. Did that mean I was going to have to learn to like him?

"How do you want to proceed? On the manuscript front, I met a social worker this weekend who works with boys in gangs. He might be able to put us on to someone who will look at it for you."

"That sounds good: we're definitely going to need an expert report if we're going to cancel the contract. Do you want to get in touch with him, or does Miranda have time?" He was doing everything right, now not even automatically assuming Miranda's hours were his

274

to apportion, as he had when he'd first handed her the book.

"It'll be good experience for her to do it."

He considered. "As for the management consultants, I could map out a plan before I go, and perhaps get Rog and some of the others to read it and see what they think. Shall we email some times, see if we can fit in a quick meeting later today?"

I ticked it off in my head. Miranda no longer had to confront Ben; we might have a way of winning the Great Reorganisation Battle; and if any redundancies were going to be made, Miranda had put herself in a position where it was impossible she would be among them. A worthwhile twenty minutes. I smiled.

For the rest of the day, the editorial department looked like one of those French farces, where there are six characters and seven doors, and everyone rushes in and out, madly slamming them open and shut. We talked and talked — one of publishing's best skills — and finally got a memo written just before it was time for us to head off for yet another talk-fest, a dinner where one of the big fiction prizes was due to be announced.

I arrived a few minutes after the start time on the invitation. While publishing meetings always begin late, it is impossible to be too early for a publishing party. If editorial meetings had a bar, we'd be on time for them, too. This prize was sponsored by a City property firm, and so it was held in the recently renovated private rooms at the Royal Academy where — I looked around as I walked in — five hundred publishers, authors, journalists and corporate sponsors and their guests were being served champagne. The crowd was starkly divided, like a wedding with his and her sides of the church. The sponsors and their guests were encased in dark suits, accessorised by expensive haircuts and watches, or in short, tight cocktail dresses, accessorised by blonde highlights and serious holy-moley jewellery, depending on gender. The publishing contingent had grey suits, haircuts that were several weeks past their cut-by dates and checked the time on their phones, or floaty dresses that the kindly would call "arty", less-good blonde highlights, and chunky silver or amber jewellery.

I jumped right in, determined to put aside for a while all things connected with thugs, botanical gardens and management consultants, chatting, with the help of a couple of glasses of champagne, with strangers. Because it was, as Jake had called it, post-work work, and part of my job. We moved next door for dinner and I found my table. One of my authors had reached the prize's longlist, although she'd fallen at that hurdle. She and her husband, her agent and his wife, the publicist who had looked after her book, a couple of her friends and I were seated together. As Magda said when she arrived, the bonus of not being shortlisted was that she didn't have to stay sober for four hours, only to find out at the end she might as well have been plastered, because she hadn't won and so wouldn't have to give a speech.

We sat and I took stock. Magda was directly across from me, between her publicist and her agent, who had represented her for longer than I'd been her editor.

276

That was good, she'd be well looked after. Charlie, her husband, was on my left. I knew he wasn't a writer, so my task for the evening would be to make sure he didn't feel left out. We introduced ourselves and made chit-chat about Magda's book not making the shortlist, after which I gave him a rundown on the other people at the table. Charlie looked at the place card in front of the still-empty seat on my right. "George Hammond," he read. "Who is he? Do you know him?"

I waggled my head: maybe yes, maybe no. "It depends on whether you ask him or me. If you ask me, then yes, I've known him for years. He was an editor, then he moved into journalism, and then PR — branding, that sort of thing."

Charlie was puzzled. "And if I asked him?"

"We probably haven't met more than twenty or thirty times — twenty or thirty if you don't count the year we worked for the same company — but I'll give you excellent odds that George will sit down, hold out his hand to me and say, 'I'm George Hammond'. He never recognises me."

As I was finishing the sentence, the chair beside me was pulled out, but before I could turn, Charlie leant in and whispered, "Course officials have declared the race will be abandoned and bets are void. He just squinted at your place card. Although, if it's any consolation, he looked at you first, and then the card, so you were right, he doesn't recognise you. Technically, you should have won."

Dinner was going to be fine: I didn't have a vested interest in the award; my author was surrounded by her friends and supported by her agent, so didn't need me; George was an OK person, he just lived in his head, which I entirely understood; and Charlie was going to be fun to talk to. Only a tiny proportion of my job involves editing or manuscript acquisition. On a bad day, I estimated it at ten per cent, while the other ninety per cent could best be described as hand-holding, making sure people were happy, or at least comfortable. Maybe we should recategorise the industry as one of the caring professions, and put in for government grants. We could suggest the management consultants add that to their revenue-optimisation plans. Thinking of them and their jargon was a bad idea, so I turned back to Charlie and did my tell-me-all-about-yourself routine. He was a solicitor, and, I found to my relief, knew more people than I did at the party. He was sitting with the book people because of Magda, but he did commercial property and corporate law, so he knew most of the sponsors and their guests. "Although," he carefully added, "I do pro-bono work too, so that Magda will still speak to me."

"My mother is a solicitor; she's explained that you don't always eat live babies for breakfast."

He looked over the top of his spectacles. "If you believe that, I own a bridge in Brooklyn you might be interested in buying."

"Tempting. But before I take you up on it, tell me about your pro-bono work. What does that mean for someone who works in commercial property? Do you wander the streets offering free conveyancing?"

278

He laughed. "What a splendid idea. I could set up a stand outside Waitrose, to catch the impoverished middle classes: 'Granny flats a speciality'. No, I work with people who have been unfairly evicted, or whose leases have been raised extortionately, or wrongfully terminated. Since squatting became a criminal offence, I've started taking cases there too. The law is recent, which means that until a few dozen cases go through the courts, we won't really understand it. For now, no one knows what the parameters are, especially on time limitations, which are new, and —" He stopped short. "I'm sorry, I can bore for Britain on precedent and case law."

He was Victor, just with more money and a better suit: another geek who loved his subject. I was one too, but publishing attracts geeks who love *every* subject. Editors know a little bit about lots of arcane areas. "I did a book on that once," was the standard phrase for being able to name the seven hills of Rome, or knowing that bees have a positive electric charge and flowers a negative one when they're full of nectar. So I was happy to learn more about wrongful terminations of leases. Maybe I'd send him pictures of Viv's flat — a happy lease story to match his nasty ones. Victor, at any rate, had thought a fifty-year tenancy was worth celebrating. I smiled sunnily. "Is this where I'm supposed to say, 'No, it's fascinating, please go on', in a high-pitched little-girl voice?"

Charlie picked up the menu and examined it. "Yes, you're right on cue: that's after the potatoes, and before dessert."

Before I could come up with more witty dinner-table repartee, the CEO of the sponsoring property firm stood up, and the speeches began. I listened for at least a nanosecond while he told us how very important culture was to society, in case a bunch of people at a literary prize hadn't already been aware of that. As he spoke, Charlie gave me a whispered parallel commentary, telling me how the man had been expelled from his golf club for cheating on his wife. "Although adultery," he was careful to explain, "isn't technically a matter for the committee, in this case they made an exception, as the adultery took place on the ninth green."

I could understand that. "I've heard that that's terrible for the grass."

Magda glared at us as we laughed a little too loudly, and we ducked our heads and pretended to be ashamed. I opened my handbag and rootled around in it, not looking for anything in particular, just so that I didn't catch Charlie's eye and start snickering again.

He whispered, "It was worse than that. Everybody's tee-off times were delayed."

I laughed out loud, and dropped my bag on the floor so that I could hide under the table for a minute, picking everything up while I put my at-work face back on, piling everything back in topsy-turvy. My phone had come to rest by George's foot. I gestured to him to kick it towards me. George being George, it took several whispered instructions before light dawned and he reached down to get it. I was just relieved he hadn't stepped on it too. Losing two in a week would be embarrassing.

By the time I had pulled myself together, the CEO had turned the microphone over to the publicist for the prize. Across the room, publishers began to whisper and chat, or read email and tweet. It looked like we'd choreographed it, and Charlie looked at me questioningly. I risked Magda's wrath and leant in. The woman was notorious. She had given the identical speech at the longlist announcement. And then again at the shortlist announcement. And although I hadn't been there, apparently at last year's shortlist, longlist and prize announcements too. I condensed it for Charlie: "Her childhood influence was an aunt who was a librarian for MI5. Then it's a fifteen-minute rundown on her childhood reading, the lowlight being an extract from a book report she wrote for her aunt when she was ten."

Charlie had an incisive legal mind. "Why didn't they invite the aunt?"

Since they hadn't, I filled in the time by swapping Charlie's adultery-on-the-ninth-green story for the entirely unverified, but believed gleefully by everyone, rumour concerning the chairman of the judging panel, an architectural historian who had received his knighthood, so the story went, because his name was identical to that of the chairman of the national water board, who had gone to school with the Attorney General, which therefore made him a natural candidate for the honours system.

By the time I'd wound down, so had MI5's niece, and we were on to the prize announcement. The winner

281

was a book not published by T&R, written by an author I didn't know, whose book I hadn't read. The author immediately won my admiration, however, by making the shortest speech in the history of literary-prize-givings, and its end signalled that we could leave.

The noise levels peaked as we all made a move, so it was a moment before I realised my handbag was playing Ella Fitzgerald. I examined my new phone. The timer was flashing: George must have hit the app by accident when he handed it back to me. Thank God it hadn't happened five minutes earlier. By this stage it was barely audible over the noise of publishers mingling: after pre-dinner drinks, dinner drinks and after-dinner drinks, publishers were a noisy lot, so no one noticed.

I circled the table saying my goodbyes, stopping longer for a chat with Magda and her agent. By the time we'd agreed that Magda's new book was far enough along that she wanted to discuss it, and that we'd email to set up a date for lunch, most of the others at our table had wandered off, either to go home, or to talk to their friends seated elsewhere. I bent to give Charlie the publishing double-kiss that is a legal requirement for anyone who has spent more than ninety seconds together. As I turned my cheek to him, I saw a man across the room nod and raise a hand at me in a token wave.

I had nodded and smiled in return before I saw that Charlie, too, was waving. "That serves me right for being snotty about George," I admitted. "I'm no better than he is. I don't recognise half the people I'm supposed to, and then I think I know people I've never met." I tilted my head towards the man who had been waving to Charlie. "I thought he was waving to me, and that I therefore must know him. If he'd come over, I would have acted as if we were old pals and I was thrilled to see him."

"Be grateful he didn't. He's a developer. Not my client, but my firm acts for him. Not a pleasant chap." Charlie looked at me very seriously. "As your dinner-party solicitor, I am obliged to recommend that if he invites you to the ninth green, you insist on a formal letter of non-engagement."

I stared back just as gravely. "Only a fool disregards counsel's opinion."

I had promised Jake I wouldn't take public transport, but the theatres were letting out as I started home, and I knew I'd never find a taxi. I decided, with the cheeriness that four glasses of champagne can bring, that it didn't matter, because I was with a large group of my colleagues, and so we set off for the Tube together.

Which was fine and dandy until we got to the station. None of the others lived in my direction, and they peeled off for different lines. Still, the West End was heaving with people and I'd just stay well back from the platform edge until the train had pulled in. Not a problem I assured myself, no longer cheerful. I looked back over my shoulder a lot, but no one was paying any attention to me. I pushed into the middle of a group as they waited for the tube door to open. That left my station and the walk home.

But someone, or something, was looking out for me, because two stops before mine, who should get on but Kay. I greeted her from the other end of the carriage like she was Livingstone, and I was a slightly drunken Stanley: "Kay!" I called, semaphoring with my arms above my head.

She headed towards me, but I wasn't done shouting. "Of all the tube carriages, in all the world, you had to walk into mine," I carolled.

She laughed. "I've spent a week doing a walk-on part in a pub-theatre production of a Japanese play translated by someone who doesn't speak Japanese. It's really bad, so I'm thrilled to hear someone thinks I'm Ingrid Bergman."

"I thought Bogie said that to *Ingmar* Bergman."

She hesitated. "Are you drunk, or is that a joke?"

"It was a joke, but if you had to ask, let's just pretend I'm drunk." I smiled at her affectionately. We looked like the finalists in a Least Likely to be Friends competition. I was wearing my best dress, because of the dinner: a navy shift, with a beige scarf over it. Kay had on one of her twinkly-elf outfits, this time a little yellow sundress with ducks embroidered around the hem, accessorised with pink-glitter jelly shoes. I don't know how anyone over the age of six can wear pink-glitter shoes and still look authoritative, but Kay did. Maybe it went with being tall and blonde and beautiful. Never having been any of those things, I

284

wouldn't know. On the plus side, I don't own a ducky dress. So it's swings and roundabouts.

We walked out of the station, and I shot a quick look around, and then breathed a sigh of relief. I didn't want to walk alone, but it wasn't fair to walk with Kay without warning her that I was — it sounded so melodramatic I was embarrassed even to think the words — I was in danger. I didn't have to, though, I was relieved to see. The road between the station and Talbot's Road was blocked by roadworks, with half a dozen workers hard at it, probably racing to get the job finished before the morning rush hour. With so many people around, everything would be fine, although I might have been the only person to consider men with pneumatic drills a welcome addition to the neighbourhood. Under normal circumstances I'd be enraged that the council had issued permits for heavy-duty road-breaking at nearly midnight. In the daytime the noise would have been bad; at night, it was a big up-yours to the residents. Amazing what a little bit of palm-greasing will buy you, I thought cynically.

We were almost at the turn-off for our street when I saw, down the road, the door to Arthur's flat open. I looked at my watch. I felt like Arthur's mother: was this any hour for him to be going out?

It wasn't Arthur, though, because the man who came out wasn't bent over. It was Kay who recognised him. "Hey!" she called from a hundred metres away. I shushed her — it was nearly midnight on a weeknight. Even with pneumatic drills around the corner, we'd get no brownie points for shouting in the street. She was undeterred. "That's the man who brought Bim home on the night of the fire."

I looked again. If it was the same man, he didn't recognise Kay, because he made no acknowledgement. Maybe he didn't see her, maybe he didn't recognise her, or maybe he was used to strange women waving to him in the street at midnight. Maybe all three.

Kay had walked on before she realised I hadn't moved. "Sam?" she asked.

I stopped staring at the man, who was getting into a parked car. "It's just . . ." I shook myself. "Nothing."

But it wasn't nothing. It was a whole bunch of nothings, which somehow were adding up to something. A big, rather nasty something.

CHAPTER
FOURTEEN

Jake had texted to say he'd be "very late", which was even later than "late", which was in turn later than "lateish". I went out into the garden. It was still warm, and I unfolded one of the chairs we use on the two days a year it's neither too hot nor too cold to sit outside. Sitting in the dark has advantages. There are no expectations. I didn't have to be clever, or productive, or useful in the dark.

In the dark, I could brood. And what I was brooding on was the man outside Arthur Winslow's flat. Arthur had said he had a son who did his shopping for him and looked after him more generally. This man we'd seen had been leaving Arthur's flat at midnight. It seemed safe to conclude that he was Arthur's son. And, as Kay said, he was also the man we had met at the fire. The same man I had sat next to at the Neighbourhood Association meeting, when he'd told me he was there to pick up news for his father. Which took us back to Arthur, and made a nice, neat circular package of reasons why it wasn't strange to see this particular man outside that flat at this hour.

But I was putting other things into the package, and it was no longer so neat. Arthur had told us he had been a rent collector. If I'd thought about that comment at all, which I hadn't, I'd have assumed it meant that he owned the house he lived in, renting out the upstairs to give him an income, which enabled him to live in the basement flat. But maybe he meant more, that he owned several, or even lots, of houses. He had also said his son was a rent collector. No one under the age of eighty used that word: it reeked of World War Two and pea-soup fogs. People who owned rental properties were landlords, or, if they owned lots, they were "in property". I matched up the suit the man at the Neighbourhood Association meeting had been wearing with the suits of the property firm sponsors at the prize dinner. I thought of Charlie telling me that some of them were not nice men. That some were men who were so not-nice that he would warn a woman he had just met to stay away from them, and I didn't think Charlie said that sort of thing lightly.

I thought about that for a while. Viv and Mo both thought Dennis Harefield was a good man, and both of them were pragmatic, sensible women. The only people who didn't think Harefield was on the up and up were people who didn't know him. Wouldn't it make more sense to believe the people who had at least met him?

I thought of something else Charlie had said, and then I went inside and booted up my computer. I was just beginning to find the information I needed when an email pinged in. It was from Stinger, and it was brief: "Here you go," it said.

The attachment proved the brief message was right: here I went indeed. Stinger had attached a Land

Registry certificate showing that the empty house was owned by a company called AJW & Son. And even before I turned to the next document, a scanned page from a register of company directors, I knew what I would find. And I did. The director of AJW & Son was one Arthur James Winslow, and its chief financial officer was Frederick Winslow, presumably the son of "& Son".

I emailed Stinger back. *Thanks. Can you find out what other properties AJW & Son own? And maybe if Frederick Winslow has other directorships?*

Five mins.

I stared at my email, willing it to disgorge the answer. When it didn't, I distracted myself by returning to a website that was explaining the ramifications of Sections 29 and 30 of the Limitation Act of 1980 — which if I were in government, I would have made sure had a snappier title. I was still struggling with the legalese when my email pinged again.

He might be short on social graces, or even phone skills, but Stinger knew his stuff. The first attachment was a compilation of Land Registry reports. Aside from the empty house, AJW & Son owned three houses by the station, two more on the high street, another four near the school, and a handful at addresses I didn't recognise, but the postcodes indicated were spread across north London.

The second attachment, which Stinger had labelled "Your Frederick Winslow bloke", listed his director-ships: the AJW & Son financial directorship, and one which said he was managing director and chairman of a company called R&B Property. And there was a third attachment. Stinger either loved the chase, or he just wanted to stop me emailing him. More Land Registry certificates, this time for R&B's properties. I clicked through them, one by one. Seventeen, no eighteen houses on Talbot's Road, another six on the street adjacent. The rest were commercial properties, all in outer London suburbs.

I was an editor. I worked better on paper. I pulled a pad towards me and began to write, jotting down events in chronological order, adding in the information I'd found online, which was easy to locate once I knew what I was looking for.

I looked up to text Jake. *Will you be home soon? If yes, I'll wait up.*

The phone rang before I'd even returned to the screen. "What's wrong?"

I hadn't meant to worry him, but I'd been attacked three days ago, and now I was texting him at — I looked at my watch — at past one in the morning.

"Nothing's wrong. It's just . . ." I rubbed my eyes. "Where are you?"

"I'm on my way home. About twenty minutes away. Tell me what's wrong."

"*Nothing.*"

I could hear him smile. "You're such a liar. You texted me at one in the morning, which you've never done. You're up at one in the morning, even though the last time you saw one in the morning was when you were at university." Probably not even then. I'm not really a party girl.

290

"All right, all right, we know you're a detective, you don't have to show off."

He didn't reply, just let me stew. As he knew I would, I went on, "It would be easier to tell you face to face."

I could also hear him stop smiling. "Sam, you're worrying me. What is it?"

I hated this. "I know why the empty house burnt down. I know why Dennis Harefield was there. I know why I was attacked, and who wants me dead."

Jake didn't say anything. He wanted to come home at night to someone who didn't know about dead men, or assaults on his girlfriend, or arson. Finally he gave in. "Go for it."

So I did. "This isn't about drugs, and it's only tangentially about arson. They were there to lead you astray." I didn't add, *and they did*. "It starts with the empty house. It was a junk shop when I first moved here, nearly twenty years ago. Then the shop closed, and after a while squatters moved in." Jake knew this, but he let me tell it in order, so I could get the story, and my head, straight. I checked my notes before I began again. "I got this off a government website. For a long time, if you took someone else's land, and lived on it continuously, it just became yours. That's how the Grosvenor family ended up owning most of Belgravia."

"You rang me at one in the morning to tell my why the Grosvenors own the West End?"

I stopped rambling. "The law has changed, but what's important is that after squatters have lived in a property for ten years, they can apply to have ownership of where they're living legally transferred over to them. There's a process: they file an application, after which the owners have sixty-five days to object; if they don't respond within that time, the squatters become the registered proprietors. The owners then have another two years to evict them. If they don't do that either, ownership of the property is formally handed to the squatters." I gestured all that aside, as though Jake could see me. "That's background. Now, I don't know when Mo and Dan and Steve and Mike moved in, but last week Mo said something along the lines of 'we'd been in the house for ten years; there was every chance we'd have been able to stay'. She said Dennis was helping them with 'that', meaning helping them with the possibility of staying." That might mean they'd filed the notification, and were in the sixty-five-day waiting period, or it might mean there had been no objection, and unless they were evicted, they were waiting out the two-year period.

"Waiting it out until the fire. I was talking tonight to the husband of one of my authors. He's a solicitor, and he mentioned unfair evictions, and used the phrase 'time limitations', which made me think of what Mo had said. I've just emailed him to ask if being burnt out of your house would count as eviction. When he answers, I'll let you know, but I bet anything that gets them physically out of the property fits the legal definition of eviction."

Jake didn't speak, and I could hear his car indicator as he mentally evaluated what I'd told him. It was a few seconds before he said slowly, "You think the owner might have missed the date for objecting, and arranged to have the building burnt down? Why wouldn't he just have them evicted in that two-year period?" He was trying to tell me politely he thought my idea was absurd.

Which was fine, because that idea was absurd, and it wasn't what I thought at all. "No. I think the owner missed the date for objecting because he didn't plan to object. I don't think it was the owner who burnt the place down, because I know who the owner is."

I knew the next bit without notes, but I pretended I was reading. I don't know why I thought it would make me look more official to Jake, who couldn't see me. "The house is owned by a company called AJW & Son, and the company director is a man named Arthur Winslow. The man Victor interviewed in that flat on Talbot's Road is named Arthur Winslow. He was a rag-and-bone man, and then he had a shop. That Arthur Winslow also knows Mo, who gives him free salads, and Mike, who does electrical repairs for him. I think it's safe to conclude that the Arthur Winslow we know in Talbot's Road is the director of AJW & Son, which owns the empty house."

"That sounds unarguable, and anyway it can easily be checked in the morning. But it's a big leap from him knowing Mo and Mike to deciding that he'll let them take legal possession of his property. People in the property business tend not to give up assets like that." Jake's voice was carefully neutral. "And it makes arson even less likely."

"I'm not done." He waited. "When the empty house burnt down, the police said they'd been told it was empty because it was 'awaiting redevelopment'. I wondered then how a tiny house like that could be 'redeveloped', and I remembered that again tonight, when I saw that AJW & Son's finance director was a man named Frederick Winslow. AJW doesn't own any other properties on Talbot's Road, but Frederick Winslow is the director of a company that owns more than a dozen houses along the street.

"So I checked the council's website for planning permission, and found there is a project pending approval, one which will see that whole stretch of Talbot's Road, together with the next street, re-zoned for commercial usage, knocking down the houses and replacing them with shops and office space. And the company name on the plans is R&B Property."

Jake was trying to be patient. "Sam, I'm not sure where you're going with this. Arthur Winslow owns property. So does Frederick, who is somehow related to him. Frederick Winslow's company, also a property business, is planning a redevelopment. How does that get us to burning down a house his relative — maybe his father — owns? And more, how does that get us to drugs, and to you?"

"Here's the thing. R&B's plans for redevelopment of the site include the empty house on their schematics. There is no contingency for the redevelopment to go ahead without that corner plot, no alternate plans, no nothing. They just show it as though R&B owns the property, even though it doesn't, and even though AJW & Son didn't contest the squatters' claim, so it looks like they never will."

294

I rushed on, in case Jake had some killer rebuttal I hadn't thought of. "That's the property side. The drugs side is that — well, the drugs side is that there isn't a drugs side." Jake began to interrupt. "Wait," I said, with all the authority of a lollipop-lady eyeing down a teenager hustling along late to school. He waited. "Mo said Dennis Harefield was helping them to stay in their house. If they'd filed a claim, therefore, he would have known about it — he may even have filed it for them. That means he knew who owned the house, and that it wasn't R&B. On top of that, he worked in the council's planning office, and so it seems likely that he would also know that plans had been filed to redevelop the street."

Jake was sharp now. "How do you know he worked in the planning office?"

"Because when he went missing, before anyone knew he was dead, when Viv had me looking for him, I rang his office and the man who answered the phone said 'Planning'." I ventured a small smile. "Sherlock Holmes would be so proud." Jake didn't respond. "His name was Bill Hunsden," I offered. "The man who answered."

Jake was now taking me seriously, so I went on. "As I was coming home this evening, I saw the roadworks by the station, and I was thinking that the contractors must have paid off someone at the council to get a permit to drill at midnight." He waited for me to tell him what that had to do with anything. "Thinking of paying people off made me think that it wouldn't be unheard of for a planning officer to be paid off, perhaps to take a pay-off to not notice that one of the buildings on a redevelopment plan has no Land Registry certificate that matches all of the other properties on the proposal."

"And you think that was Harefield?"

"No, I think the opposite. I think Harefield found out that the ownership of the properties involved in this plan did not tally, that one of his colleagues had approved the paperwork anyway, and he was going to notify his superiors."

"And he was killed?" Jake was sceptical, and I couldn't blame him.

"Possibly accidentally. According to the inquest, Harefield died of smoke inhalation, but he had also been hit on the head, it was presumed by falling masonry or a beam. But maybe he confronted the developer, or even the person in planning who had authorised the application. There was a fight, he was hit on the head, and after that someone had the bright idea of putting him in the shed by the empty house, and torching it. That would have the advantage of getting the squatters out of the property as well as getting rid of Harefield. People would think — people *did* think — that this was just one more fire in a series of fires. Add in some drugs and lots of cash, and *voilà*, Harefield was a drug dealer, so . . ." I didn't want to say, so a trail of breadcrumbs had led everyone astray, especially as the police had only been too happy to scamper after the tasty little morsels.

I heard the indicator again. "The chronology doesn't work. Harefield didn't turn up at his office on

296

Thursday, but he was alive and breathing enough to inhale smoke on Saturday night when the house burnt down. Where was he in between? And why?" Jake was thinking aloud, and continued on. "Let's summarise. You think Frederick Winslow expected to buy a property his father owned, or at least be permitted to incorporate it into his plans. Instead he discovered that his father was ceding legal possession of it to the squatters. It's a corner property, and without it his development is in jeopardy. He then learns from his contact in the council's planning department that a colleague is aware both of his father's plans to cede ownership of the house, and that R&B's plans can't proceed without it. He meets Harefield, somehow keeps him out of circulation for a few days and during those days he sets up a scenario to make it look like Harefield was a drug dealer who had been caught in, or had caused, a fire, the fire serving the dual purpose of eliminating both Harefield and the squatter problem."

"Yes. But now you say it, the money he left in Harefield's flat — the £25,000. It's an awful lot, isn't it? He'd never see it again."

Jake made a dismissive sound. "How many houses did you say were going to be torn down to create this retail area?"

"About two dozen."

"And property prices, even for residential, would rate that at what — twenty, twenty-five million if they were just sold as houses?"

I knew that from Land Registry site. "At least."

He was bland. "So he's protecting a deal where the land value is twenty-five million. Once the properties were turned into shops, the rental value would double, or treble. So no, spending a thousandth of that initial sum to ensure his deal goes through doesn't seem excessive. If he was paying off planners, he'd be spending that already."

Put like that, no, it didn't. I mentally copied Jake's dismissive sound: Pffft.

Then there was a thump, a car door, and Jake's voice came through more plainly. "I'm at Talbot's Road. I've parked and I'm going to have a look around. I'll be home in twenty minutes or so. Will you write everything out for me, make notes?"

"What are you doing?" I demanded. I always stayed out of Jake's work, but this wasn't his work.

"Just having a look around." It didn't sound any more concrete by virtue of being said twice. "Give me the house numbers. Which ones are part of the redevelopment scheme?"

I read them out and he repeated them, writing them down. Then he said, "Twenty minutes," and hung up.

I opened my mouth and closed it again. I hadn't told him any of the important parts. Important parts like why someone wanted me dead.

CHAPTER
FIFTEEN

The phrase "why someone wanted me dead" echoed in my head. I looked at my laptop, still open to the squatting websites I'd been researching. While I'd been figuring out the details, it was as though it had happened to someone else. Now I was back to reality: people I knew had been burnt out of their house, their friend had been murdered, and someone wanted me dead. I decided I didn't want to think about it anymore, so I shut everything down.

I undressed and got into bed. I pretended to myself that I was going to read until Jake got home, even though I knew that there was too much rattling through my head. And then I was out like a light, asleep even before I finished the thought: "I'll never manage to rea —" If my life had been a cartoon, the remainder of the panels would have been filled with Zs.

I'm not a heavy sleeper, though, and I was vaguely aware of the front door opening and footsteps coming down the hall. But while I was used to Jake coming in late, I wasn't used to him sliding into the room in the dark and putting his hand over my mouth. A low voice in my ear, so low it was almost a vibration rather than a sound, said, "Don't make any noise."

I didn't. I bit the hand.

"Fuck," said the voice. Then, "It's Sam. Stop that."

Sam? The hand loosened enough that I could turn my head. It was Sam all right, kneeling beside the bed. He put his mouth to my ear again. "Your man's been knocked out," he breathed. "There were two of them, so I came here. Where's your phone? We'll call the cops but we have to get out first. One of the men is in the next room. Do you understand?"

He waited until I nodded.

"Can we get out the window?"

I nodded again. It opened on a light well, and we could jump down into the garden from there. I wasn't sure what we'd do after that — there was no street access from the garden — but I'd burn that bridge when we came to it. Sam took his hand away and stood and I got out of bed, snatching my phone from its charger as he gently eased the window up. I joined him, and we were both out, and Sam had the window closed, before I even knew I'd moved.

The tar-paper surface of the light well was gritty under my bare feet. Sam pushed me back against the wall between my bedroom window and that of the spare room, putting his finger to his lips and then pointing to the room I used as an office. He was right. A light danced inside. A torch? I gripped my phone tighter.

I nodded, an acknowledgement that I'd seen it and understood. I was ready to move, but again Sam pulled me back. This time he didn't gesture. He unbuttoned his overalls. I'd never seen him in anything but homeboy jeans, but by the ambient light he was wearing what looked like a uniform. He shrugged out of the top and pulled off the T-shirt he wore underneath, holding it out to me as he looked in the other direction. Christ, I was naked. I'd been too startled, first, and then too scared, to notice, but here I was, standing with an adolescent boy in a light well at two in the morning, with only a phone to cover myself with. And phone coverage, as we all know, is never very reliable.

I'd have to be embarrassed some other time. I put the shirt on and, still silent, we moved to the open end of the light well. Sam looked over the edge and then jumped the few feet, gesturing to me to follow. He seemed to know what he was doing, so I did as I was told.

There was nowhere to hide in the garden. We stayed pressed to the wall of the house, but if anyone looked out of the kitchen door, they'd see us. Sam breathed in my ear again: "Is there any way to the street from here?"

I shook my head and moved my mouth to his ear. "That house" — I pointed to the left — "that's the end of the terrace." I'd never been in their garden, and didn't know if it had street access, but I knew for sure the garden on the other side had none. And if we could get over the fence, then at least we'd be hidden from the person in my house, and I could call the police without being heard.

I saw Sam work it out too, and then he nudged me towards the fence. I looked up. It had to be two and a half metres high. And I'm — well, I'm not. More like one and a half. And despite zapping around the treetops at Kew, I'm not athletic. Sheer terror had made me agile then. I wasn't terrified now, just afraid.

Sam gave me no chance to think. He patted his thigh. "One foot here. Next on my shoulder, and you're at the top."

I looked at him. He was less than half my age, he'd barely left school, and had none of the education that I'd been taught to think was what mattered. I stood on my tiptoes and kissed his cheek. "Thanks." And then I was up and at the top of the fence before I knew I'd even started. And, happily, before I remembered I wasn't wearing underwear. Instead of that I focused on how I was going to get down the other side without Sam as my climbing frame. That resolved itself quickly when I overbalanced, and half-slid, half-fell. Sam dropped lightly down beside me a moment later.

Without speaking, we crossed the neighbours' garden. Once we were around the side of their house I clicked at my phone to give us some light. A second outing for the torchlight app. I'd have to write an online recommendation: "Handy for fleeing household invasion!" But that could wait. The light showed a gate closed with a deadbolt. We were out, and on the street.

Even so, I live on a dead-end street, and we would have to pass my house to get to the main road. I pulled Sam back into the shadow of the neighbours' front steps. Voices carry at night, so I kept mine low. "I'll ring the police from here." I had begun to hit 999 when I saw his head go up.

"Not cops. Fire."

Everything became simpler. Now we didn't need to be quiet, unseen, we needed to make as much noise as possible, to get everyone up and out of their houses. "I'll take this side, you do that one," I shouted to Sam, and even as I reported the fire with my phone to my ear, I was already ringing bells and banging on doors. I sprinted to my house first. There was no doubt where the fire was — the light I'd seen in my office hadn't been anything nearly as anodyne as a torch — and we had to get the Lewises and Mr Rudiger out fast.

The 999 operator was calm, promising an engine was minutes away. I didn't need calm, I needed the police. I disconnected and scrolled down to Jake's work number as I ran. I didn't know if anyone would answer at that hour of the morning, but at the very least, I hoped the call would be forwarded. A voice replied on the second ring, "CID," so I was already ahead of the game.

"I have to speak to Chris," I blurted, still banging on doors as I worked my way down the street. I must have heard Chris' last name several times, but it had never stuck. Then I backtracked. "Inspector Jacob Field has been assaulted, and a house has been set on fire. Chris is in charge of the case. Please locate him."

This voice was calm. "Where was the assault? Where is the inspector now?"

"I don't know. I —" I looked around. Sam had deputed several neighbours to check that everyone was out, and was back beside me. "Where is Jake?"

"Talbot's Road. By the roadworks at the junction of the high street."

I relayed the information as the fire engines arrived, my voice rising to be heard over the sirens. I began to run towards Talbot's Road, Sam moving alongside me at a jog.

"Officers are on their way. Do *not* approach the scene," said the voice on the phone, but I had no plans to pay any attention to it. It was a matter of minutes from my house to the roadworks, but when I reached the crossing, there was no one there. I stood, staring at the empty road: cars parked, houses dark, no Jake.

I was both winded and frantic. "Where?" I shook at Sam's arm. "Where did you see him?"

He pointed to a spot on the pavement, and I described it over the phone. "There are dark marks on the pavement where the assault took place." I wasn't ready to say "blood". "But there's no one here."

And I was off and running again, the answer obvious. "He's in the flat," I called. I don't know if I was telling Sam or the man on the phone. "They've put him in the flat and they're going to burn it down. *Again.*"

My bare feet slapped along the pavement. Neighbours were spilling out along the adjacent street, drawn by the sirens, just as they had for the pub fire. I kept running as I turned into my street, running until I was stopped by a fireman who was moving everyone away from my house.

"He's in the flat," I said again, this time to anyone who would listen.

Wearing nothing more than a T-shirt has advantages. I slipped out of the man's grasp and ran up to the house, only to be blocked by another fireman on the front steps. "There's someone still in there," I gasped.

He gave me that Crazy Lady look that men reserve for any women over the age of twenty-four who behave in ways they don't think appropriate. "Everyone's out," he said.

I was leaning over, hands on knees, panting, but I had enough breath for this. "No, he's unconscious. He wouldn't have heard anything." I stood up straight, to explain both to him and the man on the phone, who I suddenly realised was still there. "They've taken him from Talbot's Road where he was knocked out, and carried him to the flat. It'll burn down, and he'll be dead. It'll be like the last fire." I was shrieking at them both, even though I knew it gave them more reason to think I was a Crazy Lady.

I grabbed Sam, who had stayed beside me the whole time. "Sam, explain it to him." I pushed him towards the fireman on the path, distracting him enough to give me the seconds I needed to run up the stairs and into my flat.

The fire had barely had a chance to take hold. If Sam hadn't woken me, if we hadn't called the fire in, it would have been a different story, but this was the story that we were reading now. The place was filled with smoke, and there were firemen everywhere, but there was no urgency in their movements.

"There's an unconscious man —" I said again, leaning against the wall.

"There's no one here. We've been right the way through."

I just nodded. *Yes, there is.* "Boiler cupboard. Behind the kitchen door, on the left." If they'd checked all the rooms, it was the only place he could be, and unless they'd looked behind the door, they wouldn't notice the cupboard.

The fireman stared at me for a moment, then turned and walked down the hall, pulling his mask back on. I knew what he would find, because the last I had heard from Jake he was on Talbot's Road, Sam had seen him knocked out on Talbot's Road, and he wasn't on Talbot's Road now. It took no imagination to work out what had happened. One man took Jake's keys and went to my house to set a fire, the other called in help and carried Jake to the flat, dumping him there while Sam and I were climbing over the garden fence. It would have been the empty house all over again: an unconscious man assumed to have died in a fire, this time with a dead woman too. Me.

I was pulled away from the door by the fireman I'd slipped past. He'd morphed from humouring the Crazy Lady to full-blown fury with a member of the public who wasn't doing what she was told, but it didn't matter now. Someone had gone to look for Jake. I realised I was still holding the phone, and I lifted it to my ear to see if the CID person was still there, waving a "Shush!" to the angry fireman, and, when that had no effect, snapping, "I'm on the phone!" as if I were a

306

housewife interrupted by a particularly persistent Jehovah's Witness with a pile of *Watchtowers* to get shot of.

I attempted to calm myself enough to decide what the police needed to know, but he didn't wait, which was probably a good thing. "Where are you?" he said.

I gave my address, adding, "The fire department is already here. There's a fire." I admit, the first sentence probably meant I didn't need the second, but this was life, not editorial decisions. "I went to Talbot's Road, to where Inspector Field was assaulted. He wasn't there. I think he was carried back and left here, and then the house was set on fire." I didn't really expect him to believe me. Without the back-story, it sounded ridiculous. "Look, his colleague Chris, whose last name I don't remember, knows about this. It's part of a case he's working. I was assaulted a couple of days ago, and —"

For the first time, the voice stopped sounding like a speak-your-weight machine. "Are you Sam?"

I pulled the phone away from my ear and stared at it. This person knew me? "Yes, I'm Sam."

"Hold on." His voice was sharp now, and then faded as he turned from the phone. I couldn't hear the words, but the tone sounded like he was giving instructions. Then I stopped listening, because the front door of the house opened, and out came a fireman. And he was carrying Jake.

Time went elastic after that. The previous hour, from talking to Jake, through Sam appearing in my bedroom, and running to Talbot's Road and back, had felt like it had taken seconds. Now the seconds it took for the fireman to bring Jake down the stairs lasted for hours. The you-got-past-me-once angry fireman wouldn't let me go to him, so I had to stand for all those hours, waiting.

An ambulance nosed its way around the fire engines, and Jake was finally out of the house. I walked behind with my hand on his back. Everyone felt such a sense of triumph that I was no longer trying to force my way into a burning building that they didn't try to stop me, and by the time we reached the ambulance, Jake was conscious and coughing.

He was set down and, with a little help, he stood briefly before the ambulance's rear doors opened, and they sat him gently on the step. I kept a hand on him, in case someone tried to snatch him away and return him to the burning flat. And when the paramedic slipped an oxygen mask over his face and tried to move me to one side, Jake's hand shot out and clasped my wrist, pulling me down to sit on the step with him. I patted his arm. *Don't worry*, the pat said, *Crazy Lady isn't going anywhere.* Sam appeared at some point and stood on my other side. His posture radiated *Not moving either*, and nobody tried to argue.

We sat there until Chris and Paula and what felt like a thousand more policemen arrived. The paramedics wanted Jake to go to hospital, but he shook them off, claiming he was fine. He'd been in a cupboard, and so had been fairly well protected from the smoke. His head wound worried me more. Once they'd cleaned away the blood, it was surprisingly small, but still, he'd been unconscious. That couldn't be good, but when the paramedics didn't argue with him, I decided I wouldn't either.

Instead, I agreed when they suggested that they clean and bandage my feet. I hadn't noticed, but there must have been glass, or at least sharp grit, somewhere on Talbot's Road. That was being done when Mr Rudiger came over to tell me his daughter had come to take him home with her; the Lewises, he added, were on their way to Kay's parents. The police co-opted a room in one of my neighbours' houses, and once the fire department had given the all-clear, we were taken there. Helena appeared at some point. I don't know who had phoned her. Probably Mr Rudiger. To my surprise, Connie was with her. She moved to talk to Sam, and I didn't ask questions. I felt like I was watching television: it was mildly interesting, but I was merely an observer.

Finally Chris came over, with Paula pretending to smile at me beside him. "Jake gave me an outline on the phone earlier, but I'd like to hear it myself." I pulled myself together and repeated everything that I had pieced together about the Winslows, father and son. Like Jake, the gap between Harefield disappearing and Harefield turning up dead in the empty house worried him, but this time I got to explain.

"Yes, Harefield vanished on a Wednesday, and wasn't seen until he was found dead days later. And yes, I don't know where he was in between, but I do know why, and it's why I was attacked, too." This was the part

309

I was sure of. "When he disappeared, his friend Viv was worried." I filled in quickly the details of who Viv was, how I knew her, and that she and Harefield lived in the same building. "Viv and I went up to Dennis's flat on Saturday afternoon, before the fire. She wanted to make sure he hadn't collapsed, or at least to see if we could work out if he'd planned to be away." I looked at Jake, and then back at Chris. "I looked under his bed, to see if there were suitcases. I told Jake that I couldn't be sure, but I didn't think I had seen a satchel with money. The satchel that was found after the fire."

Paula joined in. "You're not sure?" She gave me a look-at-me-I'm-smiling-at-you smile, but her tone was patronising.

I ignored both tone and smile. "No, I'm not sure. That is, I am sure I didn't see it, but I can't be sure it wasn't there — that I hadn't missed it."

Her face said she found me lacking as a witness, and I would have agreed with her, except, "I can't be sure, but my phone can." I was still clutching it in my hand, had been clutching it ever since Sam and I had slid out my bedroom window, and now I held it out to Chris. "When I was looking under the bed at Harefield's flat, the bed where the police found the satchel, I was using a torch app on my phone. Then Harefield's phone rang. I jumped, and hit my head, and dropped the phone. This evening I also dropped my phone. The person who handed it back to me must have touched the screen when he picked it up, because an app had been opened: you know how easy it is to do that accidentally. It made me think, and so when I got home, I looked through my photos and found one which, according to the tag, was taken on Saturday. It's a picture of dust bunnies and socks, with some bedding in the background. No bag, no money, no nothing."

Chris and Jake, both of whom had been sitting slumped, now straightened. Chris took the phone out of my hand and said, "You can swear that you took this photo?"

"No, I had no idea I had taken that photo. But I can swear that at the time the tag says the photo was taken, I was in Dennis Harefield's flat, and I can swear that I was using my phone as a torch under his bed at that time, and that I was startled and dropped it."

He looked carefully at the photo, checked the tag and, after looking at his watch, jotted down something in his notebook.

Jake pulled my attention back. "What I don't understand is how anyone knows you're involved, much less why anyone would know that you have this photo, especially since you didn't even know you had it until tonight."

I ticked off the steps on my fingers. "One: on my way home this evening I saw a man coming out of Arthur's flat. He was the man who had been sitting beside me at the Neighbourhood Association meeting when Viv told everyone within earshot that she and I had been in Harefield's flat, and that I'd searched under his bed.

"Two: on Saturday evening I showed Victor photos I had on my phone of Viv's flat, and he emailed them to himself, to Viv and to Arthur. He doesn't strike me as the world's most technologically able person, and if he emailed my entire photo cache, it wouldn't surprise me.

The under-the-bed photo follows the last of Viv's pictures, and so anyone flicking through them would see it. Assume for the moment that the man I saw coming out of Arthur's flat, the man who knew from the Neighbourhood Watch meeting that I'd searched Harefield's bedroom, is Arthur's son. Arthur had very possibly just received a group of photos he had said he was interested in looking at. If he was flicking through them on a phone, then he would almost certainly see the photo of the underneath of Harefield's bed.

"Three: the person who set up Harefield's death to look like the death of a drug dealer, by placing drugs in the shed where he died and dumping a bag of cash in his flat, had a vested interest in making sure that I couldn't tell anyone that there had been nothing under the bed, and that no one ever found the photo of that nothingness on my phone.

"Which takes us to four: the day after the dust-bunny photo was emailed, I was assaulted, and my phone was smashed." I lifted my hands, palms up.

Chris didn't seem to need a five. "You think Frederick Winslow was shown the photograph by his father."

It wasn't a question, but I answered it anyway. "Not in a Wow-look-at-the-sock-"n"-dust-bunny-photo-some-loony-tune-sent-me way. Arthur said his son visited regularly; Frederick Winslow told me his father was interested in local goings-on. So son visits father, says 'What's up, Dad?', father tells son he's been interviewed about local history, tells his son about the academic interviewing him, about Viv and me, and shows him the photographs of a flat from the good old

312

days. The final image, as they're flicking through, is of the bed. The son knows from the Neighbourhood Association meeting who Viv is, and that I searched under Harefield's bed. Now he knows I have a photo of that, too."

I gestured to the phone still in Chris's hand. "He didn't know that I didn't know I had this photo. If I wasn't able to talk, and my phone had been smashed, no one was going to check a Cloud backup to see if, by chance, I happened to have any incriminating photos of a non-drug dealer's under-the-bed dust bunnies."

Jake had been silent, but now joined in. "Then the pub fire afterwards was to reinforce the idea that the empty house was just one fire in a series. Winslow didn't even have to be involved with the earlier ones — they could easily have been the work of vandals."

I'd forgotten about that fire. "And Winslow would know about the fires, because they were discussed at the Neighbourhood Association meetings, and he went to those regularly."

Paula put in again, "You keep saying Winslow, but you don't know even that the man coming out of Arthur Winslow's flat was his son."

This was true. "I don't. All I can say is he was the man who overheard the discussion about my searching under Harefield's bed."

She looked sour, as though that proved, or didn't prove, something, but didn't comment further.

Chris called to one of the uniforms to find us some photos of Frederick Winslow for me to ID, before turning to Sam. "Tell me your side."

Sam didn't like being around the police, and when we had moved inside, he'd become even more uncomfortable, fidgeting every time a uniformed officer walked past. But uncomfortable or not, he had stayed within touching distance since my mad run to Talbot's Road. Now he looked at Connie. She lifted her chin. *I'm watching out for you*, she silently reassured him.

He turned back to Chris. "You know we were arrested."

"For arson."

"We had no alibis. We weren't where we said we were. We —" He checked with Connie again, and she repeated her chin lift. "We've been working on the black." He shrugged, as though it should have been obvious to everyone.

On the black? I didn't ask, but he looked at me to explain. "I couldn't get work, except with a road crew who paid me under the table. Even if I'd told the police where I'd been, the company would have denied it, because they don't pay tax for us. And after that they would have sacked me." He turned back to Chris and gestured towards Talbot's Road. "I was working up the road tonight. I saw Sam and her friend go past just before midnight. Sam's friend called out to someone who came out of one of the houses. He didn't answer, got into a parked car, but he didn't drive away, just sat there. I forgot about him. An hour or so after that, we'd finished for the night and I was packing up when I saw Sam's bloke."

Paula interrupted. "You know him?"

"Nah, but I seen him about with her. Knew who he was. He was looking at the houses at the other end of the street, where the fire was. I was the last of our crew to leave, and I heard a thump. I looked back, and saw him lying on the pavement and someone going through his pockets." Sam looked his age for the first time. "He was a big geezer, so I waited behind the compressor." He was apologising for not confronting a man who had just assaulted a police officer. "He made a call, and then another bloke arrived a few minutes later." He looked uncertain. "He could have been the bloke in the car, I wasn't looking that way anymore."

Paula was intimidating. "Are you saying the man who joined him was the man Sam and her friend had waved to?"

He nodded, but it was now even less committed. "Maybe. I don't know."

Her sniff said what she thought of that.

After a minute, Connie nodded at Sam, and he continued. "They went through Ja — the inspector's pockets." I squeezed his hand. He'd saved both Jake's and my life. He could call Jake by his first name. "The second bloke, the one who arrived after, headed off towards Sam's house, and I followed."

Paula interrupted, still aggressive. "How did he know who the inspector was, or where he lived, where she" — charmingly, she gestured to me instead of using my name — "where she lived?"

I knew the answer to the last part, so I interrupted. "He was at the pub fire, and carried my upstairs neighbours' child home. Jake and I passed him in the hallway as he was leaving."

When Paula asked the question, Jake had begun to empty his pockets. "There's nothing missing except my keys, and —" he turned his notebook over in his hand. "My notebook was in my hand when I was knocked out. It's here in my pocket now, but the page where I'd written down the numbers of the houses in Talbot's Road has been torn out."

Sam continued with his story. "When the bloke got to Sam's house he left the door open, so I went in too, to make sure Sam was OK. She wasn't, so we left. That's all." He said it as though thugs in the night, fires and rescuing sleeping editors were part of the daily grind.

I joined in. "The fire had to be spur of the moment, after Winslow realised I knew Arthur, and now I'd seen him coming out of Arthur's house, as well as having the photo that proved Harefield was set up. Jake was looking at the houses he owned in Talbot's Road. It was a good bet I knew about the planning application. If Jake and I had —" I cleared my throat and started again. "If Jake and I had died in the fire, it would have been just one more fire in the series. There would have been no reason to connect it to Winslow."

One of the men by the door moved towards us, and Chris stood. "A moment."

While he was talking to them, I looked at Paula. "What happens now with the boys who were arrested?" I asked. "Does their arrest get voided, or expunged, or whatever it's called? So they don't have it on their record?"

Jake's hand tightened in mine. We hadn't been together for that long, so we hadn't developed that communication system some couples have, where they speak without saying anything. But if we'd been together for ten minutes, I would still have understood that death grip. It said, *Shut up.*

Too late. Paula was beyond frosty. "Procedure will be followed." Which I believe is police-speak for *Bugger off.* The tone added: *I'm only being this polite because you're sitting beside my ex. Don't push your luck.*

I don't like being told what to do, even silently, but before I could push my luck, Chris was back with a handful of photos. "Do you recognise any of these men?"

I took them, and Sam looked over my shoulder. All of them dark, handsome men in their thirties. We pointed to the same image at the same moment. "Him," we chorused, as if we were gold medallists in the Olympic synchronised photo-identifying team relay.

Chris double-checked for the record: "That's the man from the Neighbourhood Association meeting?"

"Yes. And he's also the man I saw coming out of Arthur Winslow's flat on Talbot's Road tonight."

"Sam?"

Sam was sure too. "I don't know if he's the man who came out of the flat and sat in the parked car, but he's the man I followed to Sam's flat tonight."

Chris was silent, moving back to the group at the door, but I was damned if I was going to be left hanging. "Is it Frederick Winslow?"

Paula looked more sour than ever, but Chris wasn't worried. "It is." He gave instructions to the uniforms, and then came back, looking at Sam. "Can you describe the other man? Would you be able to recognise him again?"

Sam's description of the "big geezer" who had knocked Jake out sounded like the man at Kew, but then again lots of people were big, bald geezers.

I knew objectively that the police didn't need to know, or even want to know, the same things I wanted to know. They didn't need to find out why things had happened, just that they *had* happened. I rested my head on the back of the sofa and closed my eyes. Jake sat beside me, listening to his colleagues but mostly staying out of the conversation — whether because he was suffering from concussion and smoke inhalation, or because he was personally involved, I didn't know. Sam sat on my other side, my teenaged protector. And I fell asleep, feeling safe for the first time in weeks.

Epilogue

The summer weather was holding, but the heat was no longer stifling, merely pleasant. It was the type of late-summer warmth that in my Canadian childhood had been called an Indian summer, but in Britain, Indians are from south-east Asia, and their climate is different. And in Canada these days it's probably called a First Nations summer. So we can strike the metaphor. Delete. All I'm really saying is, it was still warm.

Which was welcome, because it was Bim's birthday. He and ten six-year-olds would shortly be screaming through my garden, the traditional venue for his parties. Kay had suggested that perhaps, as Bim was getting older, they ought to think of moving it somewhere the children could play organised games. But in reality she was just being tactful. She suggested moving it because she was worried about me.

The fire damage to our building had been minimal, and the Lewises and Mr Rudiger had moved home within days. I stayed at Jake's for a couple of weeks. I told everyone it was because the damage to my flat was worse, and to a point that was true. The sitting room and hall had had to be repainted, and the carpet was so water-damaged it had to be replaced. The sofa was reupholstered, and industrial cleaners hired to get the stink of smoke out. But really, I stayed at Jake's because I was afraid. I'd been afraid even before the fire, but afterwards it ratcheted up several levels, moving me from fear to terror every time I found myself home alone.

No one was taken in by my housekeeping excuses. I arrived at the flat one day to check on the repainting and found Jake watching a man install an alarm, so he had known.

It was even harder to pretend after Sam and I went through thousands of photos of "big bald geezers", and I went through thousands more of twentyish dark-haired men who didn't have sprained ankles. We both saw a bunch of "maybes", but nothing we could be sure of until I asked, "Do property developers have their own construction crews? Or at least use the same ones regularly?" Quite quickly after that Sam identified a foreman who worked for a construction company affiliated with R&B Property as the bald geezer, and I agreed that he could be the man at Kew, although I couldn't say for sure, since I'd only glimpsed him. However the foreman's phone records revealed who he'd rung after Jake had been knocked out, and two more men from the construction crew were brought in for questioning, one of whom was a slight, dark-haired man. I easily identified him as my Kew attacker, and the fingerprints taken from my handbag confirmed it.

But I became more, not less, frightened after they were arrested. Jake came home from work two days after they were charged with assaulting me at Kew, and Jake on Talbot's Road. He didn't even take his jacket off, just stood in the middle of his sitting room, hands at his side, as though giving evidence in court.

"You were right," he bit out.

"About?" I was right a lot, or at least I thought I was, but it didn't seem like a time to make jokes.

"They've pulled the CCTV footage for the street outside the flats where Harefield lived, and the fires." He was tight-jawed with rage. Then he exploded. "*Bloody* Reilly. And *bloody, bloody* Paula. Between the two of them, we were fucked. We should have had it all before the fire in your flat."

He was so angry he barely knew I was there. He paced up and down the small room, three steps to the window, three back to the door, three to the window again. "Reilly had the footage from the CCTV cameras on the street outside Harefield's flat, and footage from the fires. He was supposed to get it checked. If he had, he would have seen your two attackers coming and going from Harefield's flat, plain as day, in and out. And if he'd had that compared to the fire cameras, he'd have seen both those faces at the empty house fire *and* at the pub fire."

He stopped pacing but wasn't any less angry. "Checking CCTV footage is time-consuming. He should have found a couple of juniors and had them go through it, and he didn't because he's a lazy bastard — a nasty, lazy bastard. Paula — who isn't lazy, and isn't

321

nasty — decided to be both, because she took a scunner to you. After Kew, after Chris took the case, and it became her job, she never chased Reilly up, which meant he sat on his fat arse and did fuck all."

That was bad. Not Reilly, he didn't matter. Paula did. Jake wasn't angry, he was betrayed. Paula was his ex and his team's DS. But anything I said would make him feel worse. I moved towards the kitchen to start dinner, briefly touching him on the shoulder as I passed.

I was sorting through his cupboards looking for condiments when he finally moved. "Reilly's been given a formal warning," he said from the doorway behind me.

I changed the subject, making it less personal. "Are they any closer to charging Winslow?" He'd been charged with corrupting a public official — bribing Harefield's colleague in the planning office to fiddle applications for him — but he'd been bailed immediately. I hated that I might see him on the street: another reason I was still at Jake's.

Jake knew I wasn't talking about bribery. "They're still putting a case together."

Winslow had hired thugs to try and kill me, and Jake; they had either killed Harefield, or left him to die in a fire; and had arranged for at least three fires, possibly more. But the thugs weren't talking, and so far the police were having trouble proving any link between them and Winslow. They'd worked for him, but no one could be found who had seen them together, and no payments outside their salaries had been found.

"He'll go down for the bribery, at least."

That didn't sound like enough.

Jake moved behind me and reached up to the top shelf and pulled down the jar of mustard I was looking for. What an excellent place to keep it. He kissed the top of my head. "I know you only keep me around to reach the high shelves."

I looked lofty. "Don't flatter yourself. I know everything there is to know about stepladders."

I also knew I needed to move back home. There was no place for me to work at Jake's, the condiments were stored on the top shelves, and I hated the commute: it was a long walk to the Tube station, and after dark that creeped me out. If I was going to be creeped out, I figured, I might as well be creeped out in familiar surroundings.

So I moved back into my flat the evening before Bim's birthday. Kay and I had been emailing, and I knew she'd have everything set up and ready — we'd been doing this for years. I was therefore unsurprised, as I sat in the kitchen drinking my first cup of coffee of the day, the sun making the kitchen gleam, to see boxes in the garden. It was a larger pile than usual, but Bim was getting bigger, so maybe the party games were too.

The doorbell rang, making me jump. Who came round before nine on a Sunday morning? Jake answered it, and then I heard the familiar tap-tap. Helena did. I had a cup out for her and was brewing a second pot of coffee by the time she'd reached the kitchen door.

"Happy birthday, darling."

Bim and I share a birthday. It took him a while to get his head around the reality that two people could be born on the same day and not be the same age, but he's dealt with that trauma now. He's not sure why I don't ask my friends over for cake and jelly in the garden too, but he accepts that different people like different things, even if it goes without saying that everyone likes cake and jelly.

Helena put an envelope on the counter. Not cake and jelly, but still, a birthday card was always good. As I moved to pick it up, she pulled it back again. "Not yet," she said.

Not yet?

"It's your present, but not only from me, and not only for you. You have to wait."

I didn't mind waiting, and I liked presents as much as cake and jelly and cards, but even before people had taken to breaking into my flat at regular intervals, I hadn't been keen on uninvited guests.

I was less keen now. "Other people are coming? Before nine, on a weekend?" I looked past Helena to Jake, who had followed behind her. If you can shrug without moving your shoulders, he shrugged. *Don't look at me, lady.* So I didn't. I just poured more coffee and waited.

Not for long. A tap at the flat door came even before I had sat down again. I stiffened. How had someone got past the front door to the house? Jake saw my response and headed down the hall. What if he hadn't been home? Seventeen impossible scenarios, and a few possible ones, had scudded through my mind before I heard the two voices coming back towards the kitchen and I relaxed. No one could mistake Mr Rudiger's voice, deep and resonant and with a lilt surviving from his Central European youth.

I moved back to the stove. More coffee. Before I had even poured in the water, there was another bang on the door. This one didn't frighten me. It was a fusillade of knocks, accompanied by a shrill little voice shouting, "Use your key!" The Lewises, probably with more supplies.

By the time Jake had let them in too, and Bim had careened ahead and barrelled into the garden to investigate the party preparations, Mr Rudiger had set out a plate of croissants, with the envelope Helena had smacked my hands away from sitting on top. Even without a present, croissants made the early morning visitor-flood bearable. I stood on tiptoe to kiss him. "Thank you."

He pushed the envelope towards me. "You don't know what it is yet."

"The present is from you and Helena?"

He nodded, as though my neighbour being in cahoots with my mother was normal. Maybe it was. I'd lost track of who was doing what to whom.

Helena called Bim inside, and I realised why when I looked at the envelope. "Bim and Sam", it said.

I showed it to the little boy. "I think we're sharing a present."

He looked dubious, and if it hadn't been from Helena and Mr Rudiger, I would have agreed. Apart from cake and James Bond films, we don't have many tastes in common.

"You open it," I said, and he did, carefully reading out the lettering inside the card. "In the garden," it said.

Bim and I looked at each other. We looked at Helena and Mr Rudiger. And then we looked into the garden. There was nothing there that resembled a present.

"Come on," I said, taking his hand. They might tease me, but they wouldn't tease him. We went out, and I moved over to the boxes and glasses and plates Kay had put out the night before. It was then that I noticed they were piled on a long box. "Maybe this?" I said to Bim.

I moved the plates and he set to work, ripping off the cardboard. Inside the box was a garden bench made of delicate silvered wood, long and low, with a box seat. It was very beautiful, but while I was thrilled to have it, I couldn't see Bim's share in it. Neither could he, and his lip trembled.

Mr Rudiger stepped nearer. "Lift the lid," he said gently.

Bim's face cleared and his small fingers quickly found the catches in the seat. He pulled, and with some help from Anthony, up rose the lid. And under it was magic. In any other garden bench, the underseat area might have served as storage space. Nothing so dull here. A miniature ladder unfolded, attached to the bench. Bim went headfirst back into the box, and next came a plastic "O" which, when extended, created a tunnel. The bench was like the clown car at the circus, with more and more spilling out than could possibly fit

326

into such a small interior: the tunnel, the ladder, which clicked out into a climbing frame, complete with miniature tyre to swing from. It was an entire playground in a box.

"And," Helena stressed, looking firmly at Bim, "it folds up just as easily, and can be put away in minutes." She turned to me. "Pavel designed it, and I had the prototype made."

"Prototype?" I asked absently, unable to take my eyes off the transformation Anthony and Bim were producing out of a one and a half metre bench.

"Of course, darling. We thought you and Bim would enjoy it, but we planned it for the shelters, for the children."

I remembered their discussion on the terrace. "Of course," I repeated meekly. Then I thought about it. "How did you get it here? When did you do this?"

Mr Rudiger joined in. "I thought of it earlier this summer, when I saw Kay carrying Bim's toys back and forth. I wondered if I could design something that made it easier for parents who didn't have enough space to dedicate entirely to children." He waved his hand as if brushing away a wasp — it was the kind of idea anyone might have, the wave said. "When Helena asked me to look at the shelter plans, I thought it would be perfect for their garden. So I designed it, Helena had it built, and a few weeks ago, when we knew you would be at Helena's party, we tried it out, to see if it would fit."

Throughout his explanation my eyes had been glued to Bim's ecstatic response as each new piece unfolded.

But now I swung around, my mouth open in an "O" as wide as the tunnel on the grass. Jake did too, and we spoke in unison: "When we were at Helena's party?"

Mr Rudiger and Helena looked at each other, and then us. Helena took the lead: "Yes, why? What's the matter with that?"

Jake pre-empted me, which was sensible, since he was more diplomatic than I would have been. "Whoever brought the bench left mud on the floor, and the bench must have hit the door jamb. We thought there had been an intruder." He was reproachful. "You frightened Sam."

Helena wasn't accepting responsibility for my fear. "Why didn't you say something?"

I leapt in. "Like what? *Mother, did someone carry a bench I don't know exists in and out?* Anyway, if I didn't say anything, the police did. The police who came *because I thought there had been a break-in.*" I wasn't shouting, but I was awfully close. I turned to Mr Rudiger. "Didn't someone come up and see you the next day? He was supposed to."

For the first time, I saw my neighbour look anything other than pleasantly entertained. He was abashed. "I'm so sorry," he said. "He did come up, but he just asked if anyone had borrowed my key, and I said no, because no one had: the men who brought the bench had Helena's keys. He didn't say that the question related to the day before, or a possible break-in." He repeated, "I'm so sorry."

I nodded acceptance that it was an honest mistake, and looked over at Jake. "So there were only two break-ins, if you don't count Winslow." How had I reached a place where "only" two people breaking into my flat was an improvement?

He began to agree, then frowned. "There were only two, including Winslow."

"The one when Steve's papers went," I reminded him.

Jake got the same look on his face that Mr Rudiger's had. "You thought someone came in and took Steve's papers?"

"Someone *did* come in and take Steve's papers. He left them on the kitchen table, and when I looked for them later, they were gone. I searched the whole place."

He sounded like Mr Rudiger, too. "I'm so sorry."

Birthday bench or no birthday bench, this was not a good morning. "What are you sorry for?" I folded my arms and let an unspoken *this time* dangle off the end of the question.

"I didn't like Steve working here. You knew that. So I took them. They didn't disappear: I took them to run a check on him."

I closed my eyes and told myself, *Do not mention that that is an illegal use of police resources. Or that he scared you out of your mind. Do not mention it.* So I didn't. But I couldn't manage more than that. I couldn't manage a carefree, *Oh, it doesn't matter.* "Why didn't you say something when I told the policeman who came about the break-in that they were missing?"

He thought back to that morning. "If you told him, I wasn't in the room. I left him to take your statement.

I was with the crime-scene tech and the locksmith, remember?"

I grudgingly moved on to my next anxiety. "How did Steve know about what I grew in the back garden, then, if he was never out there?"

Jake smiled gently and turned me around. "The morning he came to talk to us, where was he sitting?"

Oh. I stared out through the garden door, outside of which all my herb pots could be seen.

I was saved from having to admit I was an idiot by the doorbell ringing again. This time it was the outside bell, to the house. My turn, and I marched down the hall. It was Sam. Because I'd been staying at Jake's, I'd only seen him when we got together to look at photos of potential thugs. Today he looked different, older. He was wearing a button-down shirt instead of a T-shirt, and he was carrying a bunch of flowers, and a bottle of wine. Life was now just too confusing, so I didn't ask any questions, just headed back to the cast of thousands standing in my kitchen. I assumed someone knew why he was there.

Or not. Sam stopped in the doorway, as startled to see everyone as they were to see him. His glance skittered around the room. "Um. That is. I just —" Then, in a rush, he pushed the flowers at me and the bottle at Jake. "I came to say thanks. Thanks a lot." By the time I had a grip on the flowers, he had turned and fled back down the hall.

Helena went after him, so in as calm a voice as I could manage, I said, "Does anyone know what's going on? About Sam, and why he is thanking us, would be a good place to start, but I'm not proud. If anyone wants to fill me in about anything, feel free."

Jake cleared his throat. He knew the answer to this too. "You told me Sam wanted to be an electrician, but he couldn't get enough hours to qualify."

I stared at the bottle of wine in his hand. "And you certified him?" I wasn't cross anymore, just confused. Should I remind Jake he was a detective, not a National Vocational Qualifications certification officer, if such a post existed?

No need. Jake was looking casual. "After the fire, I got in touch with Mike. He's an electrician," he informed me, as if that were news.

No shit, Sherlock, would be vulgar, but nothing else sprang to mind. Fortunately, Jake continued without waiting for a reply. "Mike told me that Arthur Winslow had hired him and Steve to take over from his son."

For the past weeks I had refused to talk about Winslow, apart from asking if he'd been charged. Now I was ashamed. Arthur Winslow and I had been on nodding terms for years, I'd been on more than that with the squatters, and I hadn't asked what had happened to any of them.

"Arthur hired them?"

"He hired them to look after his properties — to supervise their upkeep and maintenance. And since his upstairs tenants had just moved out, he moved Mike and Steve and Mo and Dan and their kids in until the empty house is rebuilt. The plan is that Mike and Steve will stay on there afterwards, and Mo and Dan and the kids will get the empty house."

I smiled hugely. Then I saw movement in the hall. Quickly, before Helena could return, I asked, "And how does Sam come into it?"

Jake shrugged. "I heard about it, and suggested to Mike that if he was looking for people to work with in his new job, Sam was a good kid. So he took him on as an apprentice, and as well as earning, Sam will get the hours he needs to get his certification."

First he'd tried to dissuade me from hiring Steve, and had frightened me by taking his papers; then he got Mike to help Sam. I didn't know whether I should throw something at him or kiss him. One after the other might be the way to go.

But I had to postpone those plans, because Helena was back, bringing Sam with her — and for some reason Victor was with them. I hadn't been aware of plans for a breakfast party, but someone had: I should have noticed that Mr Rudiger had brought over a dozen croissants.

I didn't say anything, just waggled the coffee-pot questioningly in Victor's direction. In return, he waggled an envelope in my direction. "For me?" I asked. I'd only met Victor once — a birthday present would be embarrassing.

"At Helena's request," he said, handing over the envelope over in exchange for coffee.

I opened it. My passport application, countersigned by one Victor Walker, university professor.

I looked around the room again. Bim was running underfoot, yanking everyone's hands, whether he knew them or not, shrieking, "Look!" as he dragged us out in turn to admire the glories of his new playground. My mother, my partner, my neighbours and friends. I poured myself another cup of coffee and took a croissant. If I were editing this novel, I'd tell the author that this was exactly where I wanted it to end.

THE CIRCUS TRAIN CONSPIRACY

Edward Marston

1860: Following a string of successful performances, the Moscardi Circus is travelling by train to Newcastle for their next show. Amongst the usual railway hubbub, the animals have been loaded, the clowns — now incognito — are aboard, and Mauro Moscardi himself is comfortable in a first-class compartment with a cigar. Yet a collision on the track with a couple of sleepers causes pandemonium: passengers are thrown about, animals escape into the night, and the future of the circus looks uncertain. When the body of a woman is discovered in woodland next to the derailment, Inspector Colbeck is despatched to lend assistance, believing the two incidents might be connected. It is up to Colbeck to put the pieces together to discover the identity of the nameless woman and unmask who is targeting Moscardi's Magnificent Circus.

THE BOWNESS BEQUEST

Rebecca Tope

Winter has arrived in the town of Windermere, and has brought with it the death of Frances Henderson, the best friend of Simmy Brown's mother. Having known the Hendersons all of her life, Simmy must cope with the loss of an important figure from her childhood — as well as surprise at being bequeathed something in Frances's will. Then, when Frances's husband Kit is violently murdered in his home, Simmy must face the fact that this family she was once so close to as a child holds some dark and sinister secrets. How will Simmy react to seeing their son Christopher, her childhood sweetheart, after so long — and could the rumours of Kit's infidelity provide a clue as to who killed him?

THE COMPLETE BOOK OF

DRIED-

FLOWER

TOPIARIES

THE COMPLETE BOOK OF

DRIED- FLOWER TOPIARIES

A STEP-BY-STEP GUIDE TO CREATING 25 STUNNING ARRANGEMENTS

CAROL ENDLER STERBENZ
PHOTOGRAPHY BY RICHARD FELBER

A FRIEDMAN GROUP BOOK

This edition first published in Great Britain in 1995 by Michael O'Mara Books Limited,
9 Lion Yard, Tremadoc Road, London SW4 7NQ

A CIP catalogue record for this book is available from the British Library.

ISBN 1-85479-670-4

THE COMPLETE BOOK OF DRIED-FLOWER TOPIARIES
A Step-by-Step Guide to Creating 25 Stunning Arrangements
was prepared and produced by
Michael Friedman Publishing Group, Inc.
15 West 26th Street
New York, New York 10010

Editor: Elizabeth Viscott Sullivan
Directions Editor: Kathleen Berlew
Art Director: Jeff Batzli
Designer: Susan E. Livingston
Photography Director: Christopher C. Bain
Props and Styling: Sylvia Lachter
Photography © Richard Felber

Colour separations by Bright Arts (Singapore) Pte. Ltd.
Printed in China by Leefung-Asco Printers Ltd.

For George, Bert, and Gus

CONTENTS

INTRODUCTION
8

PART I
TOPIARY-MAKING BASICS

PART II
THE TOPIARY COLLECTION

APPENDICES

INTRODUCTION

Making a dried-flower topiary is one of the most satisfying ways to work with dried flowers and foliage. Whether shaped into domes in pretty pots, globes with stems, patchwork patterns in low boxes, or any one of the vast number of variations possible, dried-flower topiaries are easily produced by experienced and novice crafters alike. All of the necessary tools and materials are readily available, and you probably own many of them already. Best of all, the construction techniques are simple to learn and can be used to make topiaries of any size, complexity, or design.

Of course, using dried flowers and foliage to create decorative accents is nothing new. Dried flowers have always been fashionable, most notably since the Victorian era, when small bouquets, known as tussie-mussies, graced side tables, providing rooms with attractive visual accents.

Dried flowers are popular choices for floral decoration for several reasons: they extend the decorative life of certain flowers; they emphasize the intrinsic beauty of flowers in their dried form; and they can be displayed year-round.

Today, dried flowers are arranged into virtually every shape and placed in every decorative vessel imaginable, from circular wreaths of velvety cockscomb to Lalique vases filled with majestic spires of larkspur and pussy willows. Add to design possibilities the noble topiary, historically related to the aristocratic hedge gardens so popular in the sixteenth and seventeenth centuries, and you have a unique and striking application of dried-flower arranging that produces fabulous, eye-catching results.

The Complete Book of Dried-Flower Topiaries was written to make the art of topiary making accessible. All the techniques are demonstrated here, and these techniques form the basis for the collection of projects included in the chapters that follow. Once you have mastered the basic styles—the dome, the globe, and the standard—you will be able to make virtually any topiary. Look at this book as your handbook to dried-flower topiaries; its step-by-step instructions will lead you through the whole process. In no time at all, you will begin to understand the capabilities of dried flowers, and hopefully, you will be inspired to use your favorite flowers in innovative topiaries of your own design.

Part One

TOPIARY-MAKING BASICS

AIR-DRYING IN AN UPRIGHT POSITION

Some flowers and foliage can be dried upright in a vase. In this method, plants such as hydrangea, eucalyptus, gypsophila, and acanthus gradually absorb water from a vase; the unabsorbed water is allowed to evaporate. Pampa grass and bulrush can be dried in an empty vase. Each stem will take on the contours of the original arrangement as it dries.

Drying Hydrangea in an Upright Position

You Will Need:

5-7 stems of mop-headed hydrangea

Vase

2.

Line up 8 to 10 stems, staggering the rose heads so they don't bump against one another.

3.

Lift the bunch by the stems, realigning any rose heads that are touching. Wrap a rubber band around the bottom of the stems to secure. (The rubber band will contract as the stems dry and reduce in diameter.)

1.

Place the stems of the hydrangea in a vase with 1 inch (2.5cm) of water. Separate any flower heads that bump against one another so they won't flatten as they dry.

2.

When the water in the vase has evaporated and the flower heads feel like paper and are no longer pliable, the hydrangea are ready for use.

4.

Invert the bunch and hang it up to dry (as shown above) using string or wire on a clothesline or dowel. Repeat the process for the remaining stems.

Note: For natural-looking curled leaves, gather 4 to 5 leaves by their stems and bind them together using sewing thread; hang them upside down until dry.

Drying Grasses and Pods in an Upright Position

Ornamental grasses, weeds, and pods can also be dried upright in a vase. The surfaces of some weeds should be sealed to prevent them from bursting into feathery wands.

You Will Need:

Bouquet of grasses, weeds, and pods

Newspaper

Pump hair spray

Vase

1.

Lay the fresh plant material on the newspaper and apply 3 light coats of hair spray.

2.

Arrange the plant material in a vase ⅛ full of water.

3.

Allow the water to evaporate.

AIR-DRYING IN A FLAT POSITION

Most foliage can be dried flat on a layer of newspaper or tissue placed in the bottom of a cardboard box or on an old window screen. Lightweight foliage often curls somewhat as it dries, but in most cases this natural curling is attractive. Some heavier plant materials, such as heavy leaves or large-petaled flowers, should be supported with wadded-up newspaper as they dry to maintain their natural shape.

Flat-drying is a good alternative when drying space is at a premium. The material can be laid in boxes, stacked, and stored until needed. Boxes should be long enough to allow the stems to fit without bending or breaking.

Drying Grasses, Twigs, Seed Heads, and Pods on Flat Newspaper

You Will Need:

Cardboard box

Newspaper

Selection of grasses
(or chosen plant material)

1.

Line the bottom of a cardboard box with several sheets of newspaper.

2.

Lay the leaves on the bottom of the box in a row, allowing room around each stem for air circulation.

Drying Heavy Plant Material on Flat Chicken-Wire Screens

Heavier vegetation, foliage, and flowers can be dried individually on a framed screen made by stretching a length of chicken wire between two strips of wood and nailing it into place. The screen can be laid across two stacks of cinder blocks.

Chicken wire provides support for material while allowing air to circulate freely, preventing mold and rot from developing. Stems can also be inserted through the mesh for stability.

You Will Need:

Selection of heavy plant material, such as artichokes

Chicken wire frame or a length of chicken wire stretched across an open space and secured with heavy weights such as cinder blocks

1.

Insert the stem of each artichoke into one mesh of the chicken wire.

2.

Check the leaves of the artichokes every day or so. Artichokes may take up to 3 weeks to dry, depending upon humidity.

DRYING WITH DESICCANTS

The desiccants used for drying plant material are granular, moisture-absorbing agents such as silica gel and fine white sand. Both desiccants are effective and readily available.

When plant material is placed in a desiccant, the moisture in the plant is drawn into the desiccant crystals, leaving the material dry and ready for use as decoration. Two types of silica gel are available: one white, another with blue crystals that turn pink when they absorb moisture (and the plant material is dry).

There are several advantages to using desiccants for drying. Since desiccant crystals "embrace" the plant material entirely, the natural contour and color of the material is more accurately preserved. Desiccants have a high moisture-absorption rate that promotes the quick drying of plant material. In addition, both silica gel and sand can be reused: pour the used desiccant in a metal container, then place the container in a preheated (250°F [120°C]) oven to redry. The redried desiccant can be stored in an airtight container until it is needed.

Plastic containers with tightly sealed lids are most suitable for desiccant drying. Large, shallow food-storage containers can accommodate a generous amount of plant material without requiring too much desiccant. Flowers should be placed in the desiccant so they won't bump against one another. Because the number of blooms you can dry in a household container at one time is limited, you may want to set up several containers.

You need to take care with desiccants, though, as they can overdry your plant material. You should check the crystals every 2 days. If the colored crystals have turned pink or if the plant material is firm to the touch, gently brush away any desiccant and remove the specimen.

Because the plant material must fit a relatively shallow container, desiccant drying is usually used for flowers and foliage with short or nonexistent stems. (False stems can be added later by following the directions on page 31.) Flowers that have fragile petals (roses, peonies, camelias, and pansies) and leaves (rose leaves, oak, ferns, and ivy) are best suited to this method.

Drying Roses with Chemical Desiccants

You Will Need:

Plastic container with lid

1 pound (454g) of
silica gel crystals

Roses (or selection of
chosen plant material)

Soft artist's paintbrush

Teaspoon

Masking tape

1.

Fill the container to ½ inch (1.3cm) with silica gel crystals.

2.

Place the head of a rose faceup on the surface of the silica gel. Use the paintbrush to gently move the silica gel against the flower, filling all the spaces between the petals and leaves with crystals.

3.

Referring to the photograph, use the teaspoon to scoop up some silica gel and sprinkle it over the entire rose head. Repeat with the remaining roses.

4.

Place the lid on the container and seal it with masking tape. Store the container in a dry, dimly lit area.

5.

When the roses are dry, gently remove each flower head by its stem, pouring off the silica crystals as you lift it up. Use the paintbrush to clean off the petals.

DRYING WITH FINE WHITE SAND

Fine white sand does not have colored crystals to signal drying. But with a little care and vigilance, the sand can serve the purpose just as well. The method is the same as for silica gel, but the plant material must be checked every day so it doesn't overdry. Handle the plant material carefully; it becomes very fragile when dry.

STORING PLANT MATERIAL

Dried plant material may be stored for a year or so before using. The material must be packed carefully so it keeps its shape and color and does not rot. To prevent insect infestation, place a few mothballs in the storage box.

Storing Large-Headed Plant Material

Some large, heavy floral varieties such as mop-headed hydrangea, and vegetable varieties such as artichoke, should be wrapped separately when you store them.

You Will Need:

1 sheet of white tissue paper

Artichoke or hydrangea

One 6-inch (15.2cm) long medium-gauge stub wire

Cardboard box

1.

Crumple a sheet of tissue paper, then open it up. Place it on a flat worktable.

2.

Gather the paper along one side to form a cone.

3.

Hold the cone in your hand at the gathers and lay the stem of the plant material in the gather with the head pointing up.

4.

Wrap the plant material with the tissue, securing it at its stem with a wire.

5.

Store the plant material in a cardboard box.

Storing Dried Flowers

Flowers should be arranged loosely in a storage box to allow air circulation. Do not pack flowers on top of one another; moisture can collect and cause the material to develop mold or rot.

You Will Need:

Cardboard box

Newspaper

Dried flowers

Masking tape

1.

Line the bottom of the cardboard box with several sheets of newspaper. Place the dried flowers in a row on the bottom of the box.

2.

Place a length of masking tape across the stems just under their heads to hold the flowers in place.

3.

Lay a second row of dried stems just below the first row, allowing the heads of the second row to overlap the stems of the first row.

4.

Repeat Step 2 to secure the second row of dried floral material.

5.

Lightly cover the rows of dried material with several sheets of newspaper and cover the box. Store the box in a dry, dimly lit place.

Chapter 3

PREPARING PLANT MATERIAL

Most plant material needs some preparation before it can be used to decorate a topiary. Preparation techniques include four procedures: wiring and wrapping stems in order to reinforce weak or fragile stems, or to lengthen short stems; creating false stems for stemless flower heads and foliage; wiring single-headed stemless material, such as pinecones and pods; and wiring bunches of material together.

WIRING AND WRAPPING STEMS

By wiring and wrapping dried material you can create a strong stem that can stand independently or be inserted into the head of a topiary. The wire provides support for the original weaker stem; a wound layer of stem wrap secures the wire to the stem and conceals both.

A precut length of medium-gauge wire, also called stub wire, is usually used for reinforcing or lengthening stems. All types of stub wire—painted, unpainted, or cotton-wrapped—work well and can be used interchangeably for our purposes. Spool wire can also be used to wire a stem, but it must first be straightened. To do so, simply pull and stretch the desired length of wire with your hands.

When wiring flowers, choose a stub wire that is flexible, strong, and long enough to support the chosen stemmed material and a compatibly colored stem wrap. A false stem is usually attached to the stem, then trimmed to the final desired length when the topiary is being decorated. Therefore, you should choose a wire length that is the desired finished length of the stem (or a bit longer, if necessary). Fine-gauge wire is suited to fragile stems, while stronger, lower-gauge wire is suited to thicker stems.

WIRING FRAGILE-STEMMED FLOWERS

Many flowers, such as strawflowers, have thin stems that cannot support the weight of their own dried flower heads. Fine-gauge wire should be used to reinforce such delicate stems.

Wiring and Wrapping a Strawflower

You Will Need:

Rose wire

Teacup

One 6-inch (15.2cm) long
fine-gauge stub wire

1 dried strawflower

Wire cutters

Stem wrap

Florist's scissors

1.
Place the spool of rose wire in a teacup and allow the wire to unreel. Place the stub wire against the stem, with the end of the wire gently resting on the underside of the flower head.

2.
Carefully draw the rose wire from its spool (without removing it from the teacup) and hold it against the stem/stub wire with the end of the rose wire pointing downward.

3.
Wind the rose wire around the stem/stub wire, overlapping all materials and trapping the loose end of rose wire.

4.
Bind the full length of the stem/stub wire; cut the end of the rose wire when finished.

5.
Hold the end of the stem wrap against the top section of the stem/stub wire with one hand, and the stem wrap with the other. Turn the stem/stub wire, wrapping the stem wrap at an angle around the full length of the stem. Cut the stem wrap and press the loose end to the end of the stem.

WIRING MEDIUM-STEMMED FLOWERS

Of all the medium-stemmed flowers used in topiary making, the dried rose is the most popular. The directions that follow can be applied to other medium-stemmed flowers or to any long- or short-stemmed flowers that need reinforcement or lengthening.

Wiring and Wrapping a Rose

You Will Need:

One 6-inch (15.2cm) long
medium-gauge stub wire

1 dried rose

Wire cutters

Green stem wrap

Florist's scissors

1.

Place the stub wire against the stem, with the end of the wire pushing gently on the underside of the rose head. Use the wire cutters to trim the stub wire, if necessary.

2.

Hold the end of the stem wrap against the top section of the stem/stub wire with one hand, and the stem wrap in the other.

3.

Pull on the stem wrap with one hand while turning the stem/stub wire with the other; angle the tape so it spirals down the entire length of the stem.

4.

Cut the stem wrap and squeeze the loose end against the stem to secure.

CREATING A FALSE STEM ON A FLOWER HEAD

Single-headed stemless flowers can be attached directly to a topiary with glue. But adding a false stem to a stemless flower head (or one with a very short stem) expands its possible design uses.

Wiring a False Stem on a Rose

Dried roses are beautiful but their heads often break off. You can easily create a false stem for rose heads using the method below.

You Will Need:

Pliers

One 6-inch (15.2cm) long
medium-gauge stub wire

1 dried rose

Wire cutters

Stem wrap

1.

Using the pliers, bend a small, narrow loop at one end of the stub wire, as shown in photograph A.

A

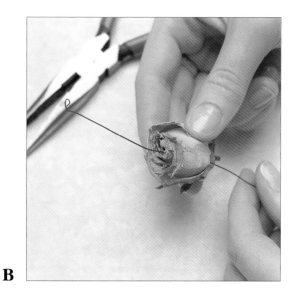

B

D

2.

Insert the other end of the wire down through the center of the rose head, exiting as close as possible to the center underside of the flower (see photograph B). Pull the wire down and draw the narrow loop into the flower head, parting any petals that might obstruct its path. Stop pulling when the loop is concealed in the flower head, as shown in photograph C, being careful not to pull the loop all the way through and out of the flower head. Wrap the wire around the stem two to three times to secure.

3.

Conceal the stub wire (photograph D) by wrapping the stem with stem wrap.

WIRING A FALSE STEM ON HARD, BRITTLE, OR SOFT MATERIAL

Natural dried materials that are stemless and particularly hard, brittle, or soft present special problems. Items in this category include pinecones, which resist piercing; poppyheads, which are very brittle; and fresh fruits and vegetables, which are soft and tear easily. These materials can add interesting texture and natural color to seasonal topiaries, but each requires a different method for adding a false stem.

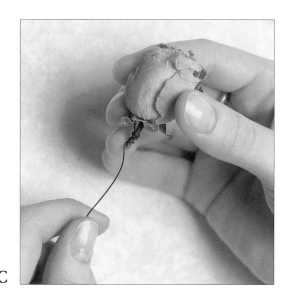

C

WIRING FRESH FRUITS AND VEGETABLES AND A POPPY POD

The method for creating a false stem on fresh fruits vegetables and poppy pods and is the same: the wire is inserted through the item itself. Lightweight pods, which are often brittle and require gentle handling, can be wired with fine-gauge wire and displayed in almost any position. Stems for heavier fruits and vegetables should be made from heavier-gauge wire. These items must be displayed with some type of support so that the wired stem does not rip out under its own weight. This can be done by positioning them so that the Styrofoam helps support their weight. You can also insert a toothpick or a section cut from a wooden skewer underneath any of these heavier decorations to provide additional support.

Wiring Fruits and Vegetables

You Will Need:

1 piece of fruit or vegetable
(lady apple, brussels sprouts, or
lemons work well)

One 8-inch (20.3cm) long
medium-gauge stub wire

1.

Holding the fruit or vegetable in one hand and the stub wire in the other, pierce the skin of the fruit or vegetable at its lower 1/3 with the wire. Push the wire through and out the other side.

2.

Bend the two free ends of the wire down and under the item, twisting them together to secure.

Wiring a Pod

You Will Need:

Rose wire

Teacup

Wire cutters

Sewing needle

1 stemless poppyhead

White or brown stem wrap

1 florist's pick (optional)

1.

Place the spool of rose wire in the teacup and allow the wire to unreel. Draw the wire from the spool (without removing it from the teacup) and use the wire cutters to cut a 6-inch (15.2cm) length.

2.

Use the sewing needle to poke a tiny hole on opposite sides of the lower portion of the pod.

3.

Insert one end of the wire into one hole, gently guiding the wire across and through the other hole until 3 inches (7.6cm) of the wire protrudes.

4.

Gently bend the wire ends beneath the pod head, twisting them to secure.

5.

Conceal the wire ends with stem wrap. If necessary, attach the false stem to a florist's pick if the item is to be inserted in resistant material.

Wiring a Pinecone

The pinecone is sturdy and easy to handle. Its collar of scales makes a good anchor for a false stem.

You Will Need:

1 pinecone

One 6-inch (15.2cm) long
medium-gauge stub wire

Pliers

Wire cutters

General-purpose scissors

Brown stem wrap

1.

Holding the pinecone in your hand, center the stub wire against the back of the bottom row of scales (see photograph A). Bend the free lengths of wire around to the front, fitting the lengths of wire carefully between the scales.

A

B

2.

Twist the ends of the wire tightly in front, making certain that the pinecone does not twist freely within the wire collar.

3.

Use the pliers to bend the ends of the wire down and press them against the underside of the base of the pinecone (see photograph B). Use the wire cutters to trim the stub wire, if necessary.

4.

Conceal the wire with stem wrap.

WIRING BUNCHES

Wiring several stems of plant material together has several advantages. It allows you to attach a bunch of flowers or foliage to the base material at once and achieve broad, quick coverage of the topiary. Also, because a bunch of stems is added with a single stub wire or florist's pick, the base material is less likely to weaken and crumble over time.

Wiring bunches means exactly that: gathering stems of plant material, wiring them into a small bouquet, and using the wire as a false stem. The bunch can also be wired to a florist's pick.

Wiring a Bunch with Stub Wire

Because the technique for wiring bunches with stub wire is the same for most thin and medium-thick stems of plant material, the following directions can be used to prepare the stems of a single variety (such as statice or baby's breath), or a mixed variety (such as roses, statice, and cockscomb). Stub wire allows you to gather a large number of stems (up to 1½-inch [3.8cm] diameter) in one bouquet.

You Will Need:

1 bunch of dried flowers
(4–6 stems with a ¾-inch
[1.9cm] diameter)

Florist's scissors

Stem wrap

One 8-inch (20.3cm) long
medium-gauge stub wire

Wire cutters (optional)

1.

Align the heads of all flowers on a flat work surface. Using the florist's scissors, trim all the stems even to 2½ inches (6.4cm) to create a small bouquet.

2.

Hold the bouquet by the stems and wrap the stems with stem wrap (see photograph A). Place the stub wire against the stems, leaving 1 inch (2.5cm) extend-

B

ing below the trimmed ends and the opposite end of the wire extending into the flowers or foliage (see photograph B).

3.

Referring to photograph C, bend the top wire down and wind it around the stub wire and stems for the full length of the stems.

4.

Twist together the ends of the wire extending below the stem ends.

5.

Use the wire cutters to trim the stub wire neatly, if necessary.

A

C

Wiring a Bunch with a Florist's Pick

A florist's pick—a length of fine-gauge wire attached to a slender wooden pick—can also be used to affix a small bouquet of dried material to a topiary head. Because the picks are relatively long and thick, take care not to insert too many in a small area, as this could cause the foam base to crumble.

You Will Need:

6 slender stems
of dried material

Florist's scissors

Stem wrap

1 florist's pick

1.

Lay the dried material on a flat work surface and trim the stems even using florist's scissors.

2.

Hold the dried heads of the floral material in one hand and wrap the stems with stem wrap (see photograph A on page 35). Carefully wind the wire attached to the florist's pick around the bound stems just under the floral heads. Twist the wire ends to secure.

3.

Position and insert the florist's pick into the foam base material.

Making Your Own Florist's Picks

If florist's picks are not available, you can easily make your own by using lengths of wooden skewer and fine-gauge wire.

You Will Need:

General-purpose scissors

1 wooden skewer

One 4-inch (10.2cm) long
fine-gauge wire

1.

Use the scissors to cut a 2½-inch (6.4cm) length of skewer from one pointed end.

2.

Center and wrap the wire around the blunt end of the cut skewer.

3.

Use the pick to bind and attach the chosen floral material as described in the directions given in the previous column.

Wiring a Bunch with a Florist's Staple

Florist's staples—purchased or those you make yourself—can be used to attach several stems of dried material onto a topiary head.

You Will Need:

4–6 slender (or 3 thick) stems of dried material

Florist's scissors

Stem wrap

1 commercially made florist's staple

1.

Lay the stems of the dried material on a flat work surface and trim them to 2½ inches (6.4cm) with the florist's scissors.

2.

Bind the stems together with stem wrap.

3.

To decorate a topiary using bunches of dried flowers and florist's staples, position the bunch on the surface of the foam, then straddle the florist's staple across the stems near the flower heads. Push the wire legs into the foam until only the staple crossbar shows. Conceal the staple crossbar with the heads of the next bunch of dried material.

Making Your Own Florist's Staples

Because purchased florist's staples are relatively large, they could crumble the foam base of a small topiary. For small projects that use fragile-stemmed flowers you can make florist's staples of any size from medium-gauge wire.

You Will Need:

Wire cutters

One 6-inch (15.2cm) long medium-gauge stub wire or one 6-inch (15.2cm) long medium-gauge spool wire

Pliers

1.

Use the wire cutters to cut the stub wire into two 3-inch (7.6cm) lengths; or unroll and cut two 3-inch (7.6cm) lengths of medium-gauge spool wire.

2.

Bend one length of wire into a horseshoe shape using pliers; repeat with the second wire length.

3.

Use the staples to attach chosen floral material to a topiary head as described in the directions given in the previous column.

Chapter 4

CONSTRUCTION METHODS AND DESIGN PRINCIPLES

There are three basic methods of constructing a topiary: the dome, the globe, and the standard. These methods are the foundations for all the topiary variations featured in this book.

The components of the topiary include the head, the container, and, in some cases, the stem. By manipulating certain variables—the size of each component, proportion among components, and the choice of decorative materials—you can create different effects. The color and texture of the decorative material, the kinds of plant material you choose, and the manner in which you place it on the topiary are all important elements of communicating a particular style or feeling, or suggesting a season or holiday.

This chapter will offer guidance in understanding the principles of good topiary design. Once you have mastered the basic construction techniques, you can go on to create your own designs using any materials or combinations you wish.

The Dome Topiary

The dome topiary comprises two basic components: the head and the container. The head, often made from dry foam (Oasis), is usually shaped like a mound. It rises up from the opening of the container and is decorated with plant material. The proportion of the topiary head to container is very much a question of personal taste, but the container must be heavy enough to support the decorated head.

The Globe Topiary

Similar to the dome topiary, the globe topiary contains an additional component—a trunk or stem. The trunk is usually a straight column representing the trunk of a tree; it connects the head of the topiary with the container. The proportion among the three components is usually ½ head, ¼ trunk, and ¼ container. However, there is no hard and fast rule for determining the size of each component. The head of the topiary is the focal point and usually of some weight; the trunk must visually support the size of the decorated head, balance it visually with the container, and anchor any top weight.

To prevent a topiary from tipping over, you can weight any container with florist's clay, or you can use an inexpensive terra-cotta pot filled with plaster of paris as the primary container, which can later be placed into a decorative container (see page 42).

Decorating the Dome and Globe Topiary

After it is constructed, a dome or globe topiary requires some type of decorative covering. Decorating a topiary can be as simple as applying sheet moss to the entire surface of the head, or as relatively complex as attaching bouquets of flowers and foliage in a particular pattern. Again, personal taste rules: when you have mastered the basic construction techniques, you can substitute one color flower or type of leaf for another and choose the decorative materials that are most appealing to you.

The Standard Topiary

The standard may appear to be the simplest topiary to make. But a well-designed standard topiary depends on the manipulation and balance of a complex set of variables.

The standard is the only topiary that is constructed and decorated in the same procedure. Completely different in construction from the other two topiary types, the standard requires that the plant material stand up straight, either in a loose bouquet bound with string, raffia, or ribbon, or in small bunches in a flat-bottomed container. The foam in the container is usually concealed with moss that has been hot-glued, put in place with florist's staples, or tucked into the sides of the container. Designs for the standard topiary vary from a simple bouquet of wheat to more studied combinations of plant material, such as a patchwork pattern of flower heads. In the single bouquet using one kind of material, the contour and texture become the focus; in the studied design approach, it is the pattern of neat rows and sections that draw the focus.

Design possibilities are limited only by the character of the dried materials and the container into which they are placed. The color, type, and texture of the plant materials as well as the height, width, and pattern they create when placed in the base all affect the appearance of the standard topiary—and almost any combination works technically.

BASIC CONSTRUCTION TECHNIQUES

In the pages that follow: you will find instructions for creating the topiary styles featured in this book.

Constructing the Basic Dome Topiary

The dome topiary has two components: the head and the container. A lightweight dome topiary does not require a weighted container. But if the planned decoration makes the topiary top-heavy, you can place florist's clay in the bottom of the container to counterbalance the weight of the head.

You Will Need:

Container with a round opening

Adhesive clay
(florist's clay tape)*

1 dry-foam sphere with a
diameter slightly larger than the
opening of the container

*Option: substitute low-melt glue
gun and glue sticks, if desired.

A

1.

Place the container on a flat work surface.

2.

Press a length of adhesive clay onto the full circumference of the inner top rim of the pot (see photograph A). (You could also use the low-melt glue gun to apply a stream of glue on the inner top rim.)

3.

Push the sphere into the container so that the clay (or glue) forms a tight bond between the sphere and the inner edge of the container's opening (see photograph B).

B

Constructing the Basic Globe Topiary

The basic components of the globe topiary are the head, the stem, and the container. If the head is heavy when decorated, or rises up too high over the container, shifting the center of gravity, the container must be weighted (see the directions that follow in the next column).

You Will Need:

Serrated knife

Dry-foam block, 9 inches (22.9cm) long × 4 inches (10.2cm) wide × 3 inches (7.6cm) high

Terra-cotta pot, 3½ inches (8.9cm) in diameter, 3 inches (7.6cm) high

Dry-foam sphere, 3 inches (7.6cm) in diameter

8-inch (20.3cm) long dowel, ¼ inch (0.6cm) in diameter

Adhesive clay (florist's clay tape)

1.

Use the serrated knife to sculpt the foam block to fit the container snugly. Insert the foam into the container and trim it even with the rim of the pot.

2.

Center and impale the foam sphere on the dowel, but do not allow the dowel to poke through the top of the sphere. Apply a narrow collar of adhesive clay around the dowel to secure the sphere.

3.

Making sure that the dowel is perpendicular to the pot, center and insert the other end of the dowel into the foam in the container.

Constructing the Basic Globe Topiary with a Weighted Container

In this method, plaster of paris is used to weight the container to counterbalance the topiary's heavy head and stabilize the construction. Never pour plaster directly into a fine pot made of china. Plaster expands as it hardens and will cause the china to crack. Instead, follow the directions below and place the weighted terra-cotta pot into the more valuable container afterward.

You Will Need:

Saber saw

Dowel

Dry-foam wedges

Terra-cotta pot

Adhesive clay (florist's clay tape)

Plaster of paris

Plastic mixing container

Wooden paint stirrer

Dry-foam sphere

Packing tape, ¾ inch (1.9cm) wide

1.

Following a ratio of head to stem to container of 2:1:1, use the saber saw to cut the dowel the length of the overall height of the topiary; set it aside.

2.

Place wedges of dry foam on the bottom of the container, then place foam wedges at even intervals all around the interior of the container (see photograph A; the number of wedges necessary is in direct proportion to the size of your container.) The dry-foam wedges will act as a cushion to prevent the container

A

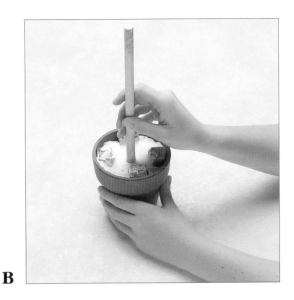

B

from cracking as the plaster of paris hardens. If necessary, you can use a bit of adhesive clay to secure the foam.

3.

Prepare the plaster of paris following the package directions. Fill the container with the wet plaster, to about ½ inch (1.3cm) below the rim.

4.

Insert the cut dowel into the center of the wet plaster, making certain that the dowel is straight when viewed from all angles (see photograph B).

5.

Hold the dowel in place until it is secure (this will take about 3 to 4 minutes). The plaster will continue to harden for an hour or so. Let the plaster harden completely before proceeding to step 6.

6.

Impale the dry-foam sphere on the dowel, pushing with even pressure in a vertical direction until the top of the sphere just meets the top of the dowel. (Do not wiggle the sphere as you push down; it will make the channel too wide and cause the head to wobble on its trunk.) Add a narrow collar of adhesive clay to secure the sphere to the dowel. (When making globe topiaries of substantial weight, cut a length of packing tape in half lengthwise, then crisscross the two tape lengths over the top of the sphere. Wrap the loose ends around the dowel just beneath the sphere to secure it.)

7.

Insert or glue dried flowers to decorate the head of the stem. Conceal the plaster with moss or other suitable plant material.

Constructing the Basic Standard Topiary

In this method, upright stems of plant material are inserted one at a time into a foam base.

You Will Need:

Dried plant material
(14 rose stems and a 4-inch
[10.2cm] square of sheet moss)

Florist's scissors

1 dry-foam sphere with a
diameter slightly larger than the
opening of the container

Container with a 4-inch
(10.2cm) round opening

Serrated knife or saber saw

Florist's staples

½ yard (45.7cm) of
ribbon or raffia

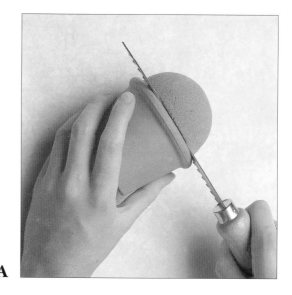

A

1.

Lay the stems of the plant material on a flat work surface, heads even. Use florist's scissors to trim the bottom of the stems even.

2.

Push the sphere into the pot. With the knife or saber saw, slice away the extra foam, making sure that the remaining foam is even with the rim of the pot (see photograph A).

B

3.

One by one, insert the stems of the plant material, making sure that the flower heads are even (see photograph B).

4.

Conceal the foam by stapling sheet moss, torn to size, to its surface. Gently tie the ribbon or raffia around the flower stems to secure the arrangement (see photograph C).

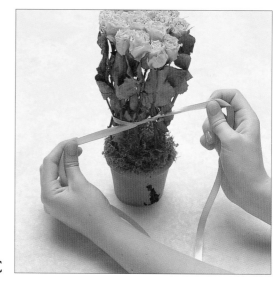

C

Constructing the Patchwork Standard Topiary

The patchwork standard topiary utilizes the same techniques used to create a basic standard. But in this case, several kinds of plant material, chosen primarily for their color, are inserted into a base of foam in a preconceived pattern. The design is often called patchwork because it resembles the geometry of pieced quilts. For the purpose of illustration, four types of material were used.

You Will Need:

Serrated knife

1 to 2 blocks of dry foam (equal
to the area of the container)

Flat-bottomed container

Spool wire

Florist's scissors

Dried plant material
in 4 different colors

1.

Use the serrated knife to trim the dry foam so that it fits snugly into the container. Trim the foam even with the top rim.

2.

Mark 4 triangular sections in the foam: stretch a length of spool wire diagonally over the foam and press the wire into the foam to create an indentation. Repeat on the other diagonal.

3.

Use the florist's scissors to cut the stems of all plant material: for a low standard, cut all stems to the height of the container plus 1½ inches (3.8cm); for a high standard, cut the stems 6 to 10 inches (15.2 to 25.4cm) above the rim of the container.

4.

Insert the stems of one color of plant material perpendicular to the foam, densely filling one triangular section.

5.

Insert the second color plant material into the opposite triangular section, followed by the third and fourth colors. The entire top of the foam should be filled with plant material.

CREATING VARIATIONS ON THE PATCHWORK STANDARD TOPIARY

The technical principle of standing up dried material in marked patterns is the underpinning of all possible variations on the standard topiary. However, each variation usually highlights one feature—for instance, the different heights of material in a tiered standard, the contrast between bands of single-color varieties, or the textured effect created by mixing varieties of same-color dried materials.

To create the variations described here, refer to the materials list in "Constructing the Patchwork Standard Topiary" on this page. Then follow the directions on this page and the next for preparing and inserting the dried flowers.

THE TIERED STANDARD

Raise the stems of one color of plant material in marked sections opposite one another. Or create tiers by inserting the dried material in descending heights working toward the front of the container.

THE MONOCHROMATIC STANDARD

Use 4 shades of one color to create subtle contrast in color among marked sections.

THE CONTRASTING COLOR STANDARD

Use 4 contrasting colors, such as orange and purple, light green and burgundy, to create bold sections of contrasting color.

The Bouquet Standard

The bouquet standard is the purest example of the standard topiaries. Dried material is simply gathered in a bouquet with the stems in a vertical position. It is displayed upright or upside down.

You Will Need:

6 to 10 bunches of long-stemmed plant material

Florist's scissors

Nylon string

Ribbon or raffia

1.

Lay the stems of the plant material on a flat work surface, heads even. Use florist's scissors to trim the bottom of the stems even.

2.

Gather the stems and hold them upright; tap the bottom edge of the stems gently on the work surface to even them.

3.

Tie the string around the middle of the plant material to secure it.

4.

Conceal the string with a ribbon bow or a rope-width thickness of raffia.

DESIGN PRINCIPLES

The attraction of topiary making is that it is not only easy—it is easy to achieve a pleasing design. When an overall design is appealing, it is usually the result of balancing several variables: the overall size and shape of the topiary, and the colors and textures of the basic components.

SIZE AND SHAPE

Topiaries can range in height from 5 inches (12.7cm) to over 3 feet (91.4cm), and from an overall width of just 3½ inches (8.9cm) to over 1½ feet (45.7cm). In general, the height and width are planned in proportion to one another so that the topiary is physically and visually balanced. If you look at the topiaries in this book as if they were silhouettes, you will begin to understand this relationship and be able to design your own topiaries accordingly.

The dome topiary, with its head seated on a container, is designed to present solidity. The globe topiary is slightly more refined and generally more poetic in feel. The stem that separates the base container from the topiary head allows the eye to move more freely, resulting in a lighter, less compact effect. The standard topiary is a hybrid of sorts in that the dried material itself can create a subtle or strong impact, depending on the combinations used and the patterns those combinations form. Standard topiaries can be majestic—for instance, tall stalks of dried material standing in straight rows—or whimsical—crisscrossed bands of dried material in a shallow box.

Size and shape must serve to balance the topiary physically. But size and shape also combine in an overall visual configuration that communicates style and attitude—and it is in this aspect that you have immense creative freedom. Choose the overall silhouette you prefer and manipulate the proportions according to the setting in which it will be placed.

Consider using a square container in combination with a conical head; use a cylindrical container and a cylindrical head; or stack several spheres on a central stem and anchor them to an urn-shaped container. There are no rules for manipulating the geometry of the basic components. Plan your own design: sketch it on a piece of paper first, changing the components until you are satisfied. Then gather your materials and let the fun begin.

COLOR AND TEXTURE

Your choice of dried material will also convey the message of design and style. Whether purchased or home grown, flowers and foliage are available in an endless variety of colors and textures. It is sometimes difficult to know which combinations will work well together. Before beginning a project, it is a good idea to collect many samples of dried material and place them together in different combinations. This way you can be more sure of being satisfied with the color and textural relationships.

Of course, your decorating style will influence your choices, too. If your home has a traditional English interior, you may gravitate toward soft shades of rose and blue, selecting roses and strawflowers to further carry the theme. In a Southwest-style interior, you may choose peaches and sea foam greens, painted pods, and broad-leaved foliage. You might even wish to borrow the palette from an upholstery or drapery swatch so that your topiary design coordinates with your living space.

Consider your dried materials as an artist might regard paint. The principles of coordinating colors to achieve a design with impact relate clearly to the principles of the color wheel. When the primary colors—red, blue, and yellow—are used in combination or alone, they make a strong statement. (Imagine an arrangement of red roses, blue larkspur, and golden yarrow.) Primary colors suggest the warmer months, when reds, blues, and yellows abound in nature.

When the primary colors are mixed a second level of colors results. These secondary colors—orange, purple, and green—also create a strong look. You'll find them in a wide range of hues in nature such as purple statice, orange safflower, and green leaves of every description. If you approach dried floral varieties with these basic understandings you will be able to plan designs that please you. For inspiration, you might want to keep a file of illustrations taken from magazines, botanical drawings, postcards of favorite paintings, and the like. There are also many books on color harmony and theory; check your local library, bookstore, or art supply store.

Texture, intrinsic to dried floral material, is a design element that carries great impact when used in arrangements where the plant material is of one color or color family. Presented in feathery grasses and pods, sensuously curved stems, or staccato dots of miniature daisies, texture adds visual interest without introducing a new color. To emphasize texture, combine dramatically different materials—velvety cockscomb and spiky strawflowers, for example. As you become familiar with the variety of dried material available, you can use texture to amplify the drama of your designs.

Part Two

THE
TOPIARY
COLLECTION

Chapter 5

THE DOME TOPIARY

MINIATURE ROSEBUDS IN A TERRA-COTTA POT

The rosebud topiary is perhaps one of the most popular dried-flower arrangements, and it is also very easy to make: rows of miniature rosebuds are simply hot-glued to a dome of dry foam.

This design is as practical as it is beautiful, as any flower heads can be used as decoration. Miniature strawflowers and globe amaranth are attractive alternatives to the roses, and because the heads of these flowers are somewhat larger, you will need less material to cover the dome.

A simple terra-cotta pot was chosen as the container for this arrangement because of its straightforward shape and subtle color, but other small containers would work just as well. A china teacup or a small bandbox covered in a small-print wallpaper, for example, would be a pretty substitute.

Finished Size: 4½ inches (11.4cm) high, 4 inches (10.2cm) wide

You Will Need:

Terra-cotta pot, 3 inches (7.6cm) high, with a 3¼-inch (8.3cm) diameter opening

Adhesive clay (florist's clay tape)

Dry-foam sphere, 4 inches (10.2cm) in diameter

Hot glue gun and glue sticks

75 pink miniature rosebuds

1.

Place the terra-cotta pot on a flat work surface.

2.

Press a length of adhesive clay onto the inner top rim of the pot, creating a clay collar around the entire circumference.

3.

Push the sphere into the opening of the pot, squeezing the clay between the foam sphere and the inner edge of the pot opening to create a tight seal.

4.

To decorate the dome, hot-glue rosebuds around the lower perimeter of the foam in a tight ring with the buds touching the pot rim and radiating outward.

5.

Continue hot-gluing buds in even rings, working from bottom to top, until the dry foam is concealed.

GOLD NUTS AND PODS IN A TERRA-COTTA POT

Small dome topiaries can be put together quickly, which makes them ideal gifts. You can combine a wide variety of small items, including dried and silk flowers with small heads, foliage, nuts, pods, beads, and even Christmas tree ornaments.

For the holidays, pinecones and holly make a fanciful arrangement, as shown here. Simply choose your material, arrange it on the dome, and secure it either with hot glue or by inserting it directly into the foam, then accent the arrangement with a ribbon.

Finished Size: 5 inches (12.7cm) high, 5½ inches (14cm) wide

You Will Need:

Terra-cotta pot, 3 inches (7.6cm) high, with a 4-inch (10.2cm) diameter opening

Adhesive clay (florist's clay tape)

Dry-foam sphere, 4½ inches (11.4cm) in diameter

1 pinecone

3 miniature lotus pods

3 poppyheads

4 nutmeg nuts

6 small holly leaves

4 heads of silk Queen Anne's lace

Newspaper

Gold spray paint

Wire cutters or general-purpose scissors

Hot glue gun and glue sticks

½ yard (45.7cm) of green wire-edged ribbon with gold borders, 1 inch (2.5cm) wide

1.

Prepare the pot following Steps 1–3 of Miniature Rosebuds in a Terra-Cotta Pot on page 50.

2.

Lay the decorative material on the newspaper and spray paint it gold, following the manufacturer's directions. (Be sure to work in a well-ventilated room.) Let the material dry.

3.

Use the wire cutters or scissors to trim the silk floral stems to 2 inches (5.1cm).

4.

Hot-glue the gold decorative elements, one at a time, in a pleasing arrangement on top of the dome of dry foam (refer to the photograph as a guide for placement).

5.

Tie the ribbon in a bow around the pot.

GOLD AND RUST FLOWERS IN A CHINA POT

Instead of using only one type of flower, this topiary combines a variety of flowers and foliage of one colorway. The appeal of this topiary is that the head has a subtle box shape, made possible by using an uncut block of dry foam in the container instead of the traditional sphere.

Using one colorway is an effective way to communicate the feeling of a particular season. For spring, pastel blooms make for a very pretty combination, while red roses, burgundy and green-dyed cockscomb, and holly leaves sprayed gold are nice for the winter or Christmas. Tying a cord and tassel around the outside of a decorative pot or wrapping pretty gift wrap around a simple terra-cotta planter makes the arrangement a perfect gift.

Finished Size: 14 inches (35.6cm) high, 12 inches (30.5cm) wide

You Will Need:

Dry-foam block, 9 inches (22.9cm) long × 4 inches (10.2cm) wide × 3 inches (7.6cm) high

Painted and glazed china pot, 5½ inches (14cm) high with a 5-inch (12.7cm) diameter opening

Adhesive clay (florist's clay tape)

Packing tape

Florist's scissors

30 rust safflower blossoms and buds

20 yellow strawflowers

12 orange strawflowers

16 sunflowers

12 yellow tea roses

1.

Center and attach the dry-foam block over the pot opening: press small strips of adhesive clay over contact points and crisscross strips of packing tape over the top center of the dry foam, attaching the loose ends to the sides of the pot to secure.

2.

Use the florist's scissors to trim the stems of all dried flowers to 4½ inches (11.4cm).

3.

Insert the safflower stems evenly around the foam, making sure they radiate outward.

4.

Continue inserting flowers, one variety at a time, all around the block, distributing them evenly.

5.

Cover the entire block with dried material, filling in any bare spots with extra flowers.

MIXED FLOWERS IN AN URN

Perhaps the easiest of all topiaries to make, this particular arrangement is made by placing a large foam sphere in the opening of a low urn, then decorating it. This arrangement can be densely and lushly decorated, as its heavy container and attendant low center of gravity make it very stable. Because of this, you can insert dried material with long stems to create a sweeping, overgrown look. This topiary is large enough to place in an entrance foyer, or next to a fireplace during the warmer months.

Finished Size: 18 inches (45.7cm) high, 16 inches (40.6cm) wide

You Will Need:

Iron urn painted white, 8 inches (20.3cm) high, with a 10-inch (25.4cm) diameter opening

Newspaper

Dry-foam sphere, 12 inches (30.5cm) in diameter

Packing tape

Florist's scissors

20 branches of melaleuca foliage

8-10 stems of yellow tansy

10 stems of yellow craspedia

40 stems of red phalaris

20 branches of oregano

1.

Fill the bottom cavity of the urn with crumpled newspaper; then place the dry-foam sphere on top, crisscrossing the packing tape over the top center of the foam and attaching the tape ends to the sides of the urn to secure.

2.

Use the florist's scissors to cut the stems of the foliage, tansy, craspedia, and phalaris to 5 inches (12.7cm); cut the stems of the oregano to 3 inches (7.6cm).

3.

Insert the stems of the oregano into the foam, making sure they radiate outward and are distributed evenly around the dome.

4.

Continue inserting floral material, one variety at a time, distributing it evenly and fully. Alternate the heights of adjacent flowers for an airy effect by pushing some stems deeper into the foam than others.

5.

Finish by inserting the stems of melaleuca foliage.

Boxwood in an Urn

Simple, classic, and elegant, this dome topiary is a favorite. Made from only one type of foliage, boxwood painted hunter green, the decorated head of this topiary rests in the opening of a majestic urn. Here, too, the urn serves to anchor the large head of the topiary, while its rich, boot-black color adds a nice contrast to the shiny green leaves. A rope and tassel can be added for a dramatic touch.

Painted boxwood, however, tends to be expensive, particularly if purchased from a florist or craft store. Fortunately, one stem of boxwood goes far because it is very branchy, that is, many short sections can be snipped from one stem.

If you have a boxwood bush, you can bleach the stems yourself for a different look. To do this, you need to construct the topiary first, using the freshly cut stems of fresh boxwood to decorate the head of the topiary (if you bleached out the boxwood first, the stems would become fragile and the leaves would drop off). When the topiary is finished, it should be moved in front of a sunny window and turned often to insure that it bleaches evenly. A full bleaching should occur in 2 to 3 weeks, depending on the season and the intensity of the sun's rays.

Finished Size: 34 inches (86.4cm) high, 24 inches (61cm) wide

You Will Need:

Adhesive clay (florist's clay tape)

Urn, 21 inches (53.3cm) high, with a 10-inch (25.4cm) diameter opening

Premolded foam sphere, 12 inches (30.5cm) in diameter

Packing tape

Pruning shears

160 branches of boxwood, painted or dyed dark green

Rope and tassel (optional)

1.

Press adhesive clay onto the inner rim of the urn, then press the sphere firmly onto the rim, creating a secure seal.

2.

Crisscross 2 lengths of packing tape over the top center of the sphere and attach the ends to the sides of the urn.

3.

Use the pruning shears to trim the boxwood branches into 5-inch (12.7cm) stems. Beginning at the top center of the sphere, insert the boxwood in the foam, placing the stems close together with the foliage radiating outward.

4.

Continue inserting the boxwood stems in the foam until the sphere is covered.

5.

If desired, loosely tie a rope and tassel around the urn as shown.

ROSES AND MOSS ON A CANDLESTICK

Candlesticks made from virtually any material, such as glass or metal, offer elegant contrast to the rounded colorful contour of a topiary head by providing a slender base for the arrangement. In this particular case, the sophisticated lines and traditional shape of a brass candlestick inspired the choice of the dried plant material. Romantic pale pink roses were selected because their color complements the brass; also, the stems are strong and easily pierce the dry-foam sphere. The moss was chosen for its subtle green color and for the ease with which it can fill in the rows between the roses.

Finished Size: 14 inches (35.6cm) high

You Will Need:

10 lemon leaves or salal

Newspaper

Gold spray paint

Adhesive clay (florist's clay tape)

Candlestick, 4 inches (10.2cm) high

Premolded foam sphere, 6 inches (15.2cm) in diameter

Packing tape

Hot glue gun and glue sticks

Florist's scissors

72 pink tea roses

12 ounces (336g) of reindeer moss

1.

Lay the leaves on newspaper and spray paint them gold, following the manufacturer's directions. Let them dry.

2.

Press pieces of adhesive clay onto the rim of the candle cup, then press the foam sphere onto the clay. Secure the sphere by crisscrossing 2 lengths of packing tape on the top center of the sphere; attach the loose ends around the neck of the candle cup.

3.

Hot-glue the gold leaves around the bottom of the sphere in a radiating pattern.

4.

Using the scissors, trim the stems of the roses to $3\frac{1}{2}$ inches (8.9cm); insert them in rings around the sphere as shown.

5.

Hot-glue bunches of moss in the remaining spaces between the rows of roses.

Chapter 6

THE
GLOBE
TOPIARY

TEA ROSES ON A
GOLDEN STEM

Sweet and romantic, this globe topiary combines three basic elements: a head of tea roses, a stem made from a painted gold dowel, and a whitewashed terra-cotta container. The simplicity of its construction makes this arrangement an especially appealing first globe topiary. Virtually any flower heads can be substituted for the roses.

This globe topiary can be made in a larger scale; just keep the proportions the same. Make certain, though, that the dried material does not become top-heavy, as this will cause the topiary to topple over. Weighting the bottom of the pot with florist's clay will help prevent this from happening.

Finished Size: 10½ inches (26.7cm) high, 5½ inches (14cm) wide

You Will Need:

10-inch (25.4cm) long dowel or stick, ¼ inch (0.6cm) in diameter

Newspaper

Gold spray paint

Serrated knife

2 dry-foam spheres, each 3 inches (7.6cm) in diameter

Whitewashed terra-cotta container, 2 inches (5.1cm) high, with a 3-inch (7.6cm) diameter opening

Adhesive clay (florist's clay tape)

Florist's scissors

48–72 tea rose heads

3-inch (7.6cm) disk of sheet moss

1.

Lay the dowel on a sheet of newspaper. Following the manufacturer's directions, spray paint the dowel gold; let it dry.

2.

Use the serrated knife to sculpt one foam sphere to fit the container snugly.

3.

Insert the dowel into the second sphere. Press a narrow collar of adhesive clay underneath the sphere to secure.

4.

Insert the opposite end of the dowel into foam in the container.

5.

Use the florist's scissors to trim the stems of the tea roses to 1 inch (2.5cm); then insert the stems, one at a time, into the foam sphere to cover it completely.

6.

Conceal the foam in the container with the sheet moss.

SHEET MOSS
IN AN ANTIQUED POT

Sheet moss, with its rich texture and mottled green color, makes a wonderful decorative cover for the head of a topiary or base of a container. As shown here, sheet moss doesn't need to be accented with flowers or other decoration; it can easily stand alone.

Moss comes live in the form of folded sheets with some of the soil still attached. When making a large topiary, the soil does not affect the application process. But with a small topiary like this, it is necessary to shake off some of the soil so that the remaining sheet is thin enough to adhere to the contours of the small sphere without bunching up or adding weight to the topiary head.

A variation on the previous topiary, this design requires only sheet moss for decoration and an easy sponging technique to lend the terra-cotta pot a weathered look.

1.

Squeeze or pour a small amount of white acrylic paint onto a piece of waxed paper. Dab the sponge into the paint, then lightly blot the outside of the terra-cotta pot to create an antiqued look; let the pot dry completely.

2.

Use the serrated knife to sculpt one foam sphere to fit the pot snugly.

3.

Impale the second foam sphere on the stick, pressing a narrow collar of adhesive clay underneath the foam sphere to secure it.

4.

Use the paintbrush to lightly coat the outside of the sphere with white glue. Cover the sphere with sheet moss. Gently squeeze the sphere with both hands to secure the moss. Let the sphere dry thoroughly.

5.

To make small florist's staples, use the wire cutters to cut 1-inch (2.5cm) lengths of medium-gauge wire; then bend them into horseshoe-shaped staples (see "Making Your Own Florist's Staples" on page 37). Use the florist's staples to tack the sheet moss to the sphere where necessary.

6.

Use the scissors to cut a disk of sheet moss to cover the foam in the base of the container. Tuck in any raw edges between the pot and foam.

Finished Size: 8½ inches (21.6cm) high, 3½ inches (8.9cm) wide

You Will Need:

White acrylic paint

Waxed paper

Household sponge

Terra-cotta pot, 3 inches (7.6cm) high, with a 3-inch (7.6cm) diameter opening

Serrated knife

2 dry-foam spheres, each 3 inches (7.6cm) in diameter

8-inch (20.3cm) long natural stick or dowel, ¼ inch (0.6cm) in diameter

Adhesive clay (florist's clay tape)

Small paintbrush

All-purpose white glue

Two 8½-inch (21.6cm) × 11-inch (27.9cm) sheets of sheet moss

Wire cutters

Medium-gauge wire

Pliers

General-purpose scissors

GOLDEN FLOWER
GLOBE WITH
A MOSS STEM

Instead of the roses used in Tea Roses on a Golden Stem on page 64, this topiary uses safflowers, strawflowers, and statice. The stem is played up by decorating it with moss, another design idea that can be taken in many other directions. Instead of covering the stem with moss, ribbon can be wound around the stem for a more festive look, while silk cord or braid could be used to attain an elegant effect. The stem could also be painted to coordinate with or offset the color of the flowers.

Finished Size: 19 inches (48.3cm) high, 10 inches (25.4cm) wide

You Will Need:

Dry-foam block, 9 inches (22.9cm) long × 4 inches (10.2cm) wide × 3 inches (7.6cm) high

Glazed terra-cotta pot, 4 inches (10.2cm) high, with a 4½-inch (11.4cm) diameter opening

Serrated knife

Dry-foam sphere, 6 inches (15.2cm) in diameter

18-inch (45.7cm) long dowel, ½ inch (1.3cm) in diameter

Adhesive clay (florist's clay tape)

Florist's scissors

32 stems of yellow statice

24 yellow strawflowers

12 gold strawflowers

8 orange safflowers

12 small rust silk leaves

5 ounces (140g) of reindeer moss

1.

Press one side of the foam block onto the rim of the pot to make an indentation in the foam.

2.

Using the indentation mark as a guide, use the serrated knife to sculpt the foam block to fit snugly inside the pot.

3.

Impale the foam sphere on the dowel, pressing a collar of adhesive clay around the dowel just under the foam to secure it.

4.

Use the florist's scissors to trim the stems of all dried material to 3 inches (7.6cm).

5.

Beginning with the largest varieties and working down to the smallest, insert the flowers into the foam, making sure that the flower heads radiate outward and are distributed evenly around the sphere.

6.

To finish, insert the stems of the silk leaves as an accent.

7.

Conceal the dowel and foam in the container with moss, securing it with strips of adhesive clay.

SEA LAVENDER WITH TEA ROSES

Sea lavender is a frothy flower that grows in arched sprays with multiple buds. It makes an excellent filler material, but its rough, sharp stems and flowers necessitate wearing gloves when working with it. The main stems also contain so many flowering branches that it is often necessary to cut smaller sections from the main stem in order to work more easily with the plant.

The design featured here appears airy and light, but is actually quite top-heavy due to the abundance of dried material inserted into the topiary head. In order to counterbalance the weight of the topiary head, it is necessary to prepare a weighted container using plaster of paris.

Finished Size: 22 inches (55.9cm) high, 14 inches (35.6cm) wide

You Will Need:

Saber saw

17-inch (43.2cm) long dowel, ½ inch (1.3cm) in diameter

6–8 wedges of dry foam, each approximately 4 inches (10.2cm) long × 1 inch (2.5cm) wide

2 terra-cotta pots: one outer pot, 4 inches (10.2cm) high, with a 6-inch (15.2cm) diameter opening; one inner pot, 4 inches (10.2cm) high, with a 4½-inch (11.4cm) diameter opening

Plaster of paris

Plastic mixing bowl

Wooden paint stirrer

Dry-foam sphere, 6 inches (15.2cm) in diameter

Adhesive clay (florist's clay tape)

General-purpose scissors

Packing tape

Florist's scissors

32 branches of sea lavender

48 pink tea roses

12 ounces (336g) of reindeer moss

1.

Prepare the smaller terra-cotta pot following directions for "Constructing the Basic Globe Topiary with a Weighted Container" on page 42.

2.

Use the florist's scissors to trim the stems of sea lavender to approximately 5 inches (12.7cm). (Because sea lavender grows in cascading arches, your cutting will be uneven. The effect will add beauty to the arrangement.)

3.

Insert the stems of sea lavender all over the sphere, making certain that the flowers radiate outward. Pierce taped areas with the point of the scissors before inserting the dried material. (You will have to brace the back of the topiary head with one hand as you work around the sphere inserting the dried material with the other hand.)

4.

Trim the rose stems to 6 inches (15.2cm), then insert them throughout the arrangement as shown.

5.

To display, place the finished topiary into the larger pot. Conceal the foam in the container with mounds of reindeer moss.

SEA LAVENDER WITH A MULTISTEM TRUNK

Concealing a stem made from a dowel not only makes this topiary more attractive, but also creates textural interest. Precut lengths of grapevine (chosen for its undulating nature) were bound to the supporting dowel stem with wire. Other materials, such as sphagnum or sheet moss, or wheat, can also be used to conceal the supporting dowel and enhance the impact of the topiary.

Another reason to decorate the stem is that you can use it to highlight other components of the topiary. If a topiary contains roses, for example, you can wrap the stem with rose stems (with or without the flowers). Another option is to arrange lengths of leafy branches around the supporting dowel, tying them in place with raffia. Each of these coverings presents a distinct decorating style: the roses might go with a more formal topiary, while the leafy branches might be compatible with a more rustic topiary.

Finished Size: 22 inches (55.9cm) high, 14 inches (35.6cm) wide

You Will Need:

Metal urn with a flared top, 6½ inches (16.5cm) high, with a 5-inch (12.7cm) square opening

1 pound (454g) of florist's clay

17-inch (43.2cm) long dowel, ¼ inch (0.6cm) in diameter

Four 6-inch (15.2cm) to 7-inch (17.8cm) lengths of straight grapevine or curly willow

Brass spool wire

Wire cutters

Styrofoam sphere, 6 inches (15.2cm) in diameter

Adhesive clay (florist's clay tape)

Packing tape

General-purpose scissors

Florist's scissors

30 stems of sea lavender

5 ounces (140g) of reindeer moss

1.

Fill the urn with florist's clay. Insert the dowel into the center of the clay, pushing it straight down until it touches the bottom of the urn.

2.

Conceal the dowel with lengths of straight grapevine or curly willow, leaving the top 5½ inches (14cm) of the dowel undecorated to accommodate the foam sphere. Cut lengths of brass spool wire and use the wire to secure the grapevine or willow at the top and bottom of the dowel.

3.

Center and impale the foam sphere on the dowel, pushing straight down until the sphere touches the vine wrapping. Secure the sphere with a collar of adhesive clay. Crisscross two lengths of packing tape over the top of the sphere; wind the loose ends around the dowel, just beneath the sphere.

4.

Use the florist's scissors to cut the sea lavender into 3-inch (7.6cm) stems. Insert the stems of sea lavender all over the sphere, making certain that the flowers radiate outward. Pierce taped areas with the point of the scissors before inserting the dried material. You will have to brace the back of the topiary head with one hand as you work around the sphere inserting the dried material with the other hand.

5.

Conceal the clay in the container with buns of reindeer moss.

BOXWOOD
AND STATICE GLOBES

This design uses two foam spheres instead of one. Although shown here in a relatively small scale, this same construction principle can be applied to larger arrangements for a more formal statement. Instead of decorating each of the spheres with foliage and then adding floral accents, you could try decorating the spheres with flowers only; the impact is lovely. Purple statice on both spheres is pretty, as are white strawflowers accented by bands of deep red roses.

Finished Size: 18 inches (45.7cm) high, 6 inches (15.2cm) wide

You Will Need:

Glazed china teapot, 5½ inches (14cm) high with a 3½-inch (8.9cm) diameter opening (Do not use a valuable pot. Florist's clay is difficult to remove without the risk of breaking the pot.)

1 pound (454g) of florist's clay

16-inch (40.6cm) long dowel, ¼ inch (0.6cm) in diameter

Two dry-foam spheres, 4 inches (10.2cm) in diameter

Adhesive clay (florist's clay tape)

Pruning shears

16 branches of boxwood, painted green

Florist's scissors

16 stems of white statice

1.

To weight the teapot, fill the pot with wads of florist's clay to just below the rim.

2.

Center and insert the dowel into the clay.

3.

Impale one foam sphere on the dowel and push it down to 4 inches (10.2cm) above the rim of the pot. Secure it with a collar of adhesive clay.

4.

Use the pruning shears to trim the boxwood branches to 2½-inch (6.4cm) lengths.

5.

Insert the boxwood in the foam sphere with the branches radiating outward; cover the sphere completely.

6.

Impale the second foam sphere on the dowel and push it down to 4 inches (10.2cm) above the decorated sphere.

7.

Cover the top sphere completely with boxwood as described in Step 5.

8.

Push the top sphere down to abut the bottom decorated sphere.

9.

Use the florist's scissors to trim the statice to 3-inch (7.6cm) lengths. Referring to the photograph, insert the stems in an even pattern among the boxwood on both spheres.

Chapter 7

THE STANDARD TOPIARY

LAVENDER IN AN ANTIQUED POT

Lavender is a good material for a first standard topiary, as it is very easy to work with: its stems are straight and strong, and its buds are uniform and sturdy. With such cooperative elements, good results are practically guaranteed.

Finished Size: 15 inches (38.1cm) high, 4½ inches (11.4cm) wide

You Will Need:

White acrylic paint

Waxed paper

Household sponge

Terra-cotta pot, 3 inches (7.6cm) high, with a 3½-inch (8.9cm) diameter opening

Serrated knife

Dry-foam block, 9 inches (22.8cm) long × 4 inches (10cm) wide × 3 inches (7.6cm) high

80 stems of lavender

General-purpose scissors

Nylon string

Cotton ball

Vial of lavender oil

½ yard (45.7cm) of copper wire-edged ribbon, ½ inch (1.3cm) wide

4-inch (10.2cm) square of sheet moss

1.

Squeeze or pour the white acrylic paint onto a piece of waxed paper. Dab the sponge into the paint, then lightly blot the outside of the terra-cotta pot to create an antiqued look; let it dry completely.

2.

Use the serrated knife to sculpt the dry foam to fit snugly inside the pot.

3.

Lay the stems of the lavender on a flat work surface and trim the ends even with scissors.

4.

Gather the stems together, aligning the lavender heads in a spray; bind the bouquet 1 inch (2.5cm) below the lavender heads with the string.

5.

To add fragrance to the arrangement, dab a cotton ball in the lavender oil. Tuck the cotton ball inside the stem bunch, then use the string to bind the stems together approximately 2½ inches (6.4cm) above the ends.

6.

Hold the bouquet in two hands and push the stems into the foam in the container using steady, even pressure until the bouquet can stand alone (approximately 2 inches [5.1cm] deep).

7.

Conceal the string with a length of ribbon twisted and tied in a neat knot at the back of the arrangement. Conceal the foam with a piece of sheet moss trimmed to size.

DRIED VEGETABLES IN A WOODEN TRUG

There is no "order" to speak of in this arrangement, for it is simply based upon creating a pleasing juxtaposition of color and texture. The design, however, is unified by the muted palette, one that calls the viewer in to get a closer look at the curly edged cabbage leaves tinged with purple and green, and to discover the soft pink rose-buds nestled between the spiky safflowers.

This particular design is easy to make up, and its principle of construction, to create a sense of lush abundance, is applicable to any small box or basket. Wood or cardboard Shaker-style boxes, metal tins, china bowls with colorful patterns, old wooden draw-ers, and trays with low sides are just a few of the possible options.

Finished Size: 11 inches (27.9cm) high × 13½ inches (34.3cm) wide × 6 inches (15.2cm) deep

You Will Need:

2 dry-foam blocks, 9 inches (22.9cm) long × 4 inches (10.2cm) wide × 3 inches (7.6cm) high

Wooden trug stained white, 5½ inches (14cm) high × 13½ inches (34.3cm) wide × 6 inches (15.2cm) deep

Adhesive clay (florist's clay tape)

Serrated knife

4 artichokes

3 commercially dried purple and green cabbages

Hot glue gun and glue sticks

2 sunflower heads

12 bleached poppyheads

10 cream tea roses with peach-edged petals

10 pink tea roses

10 safflower buds

8 stems of love-lies-bleeding, dyed light green

12 sprigs of light green silk berries

½ yard (45.7cm) of dark green wire-edged ribbon, ½ inch (1.3cm) wide

Florist's pick

1.

Insert one block of dry foam inside the trug, securing it at the bottom with a strip of adhesive clay.

2.

Press the second block of dry foam in its intended position to create an indentation mark. Using this mark as a guide, sculpt the foam with a serrated knife so that it fits snugly inside the container next to the first laid section of foam. Make certain that the foam blocks cover the trug bottom and are even with the rim of the container.

3.

Insert the stems of the artichokes in the top center of the foam. Surround the artichokes with the cabbages, securing them with hot glue if the stems are not long enough to anchor the material.

4.

Use the photograph as a guide to adding other materials, inserting stems or hot-gluing elements in a spray radiating outward.

5.

Accent the arrangement with a ribbon tied in a bow and secured with a florist's pick.

RYE WITH BERRIES

Grasses such as rye or wheat are well suited to dried-flower topiaries. Like lavender, rye and wheat are easy to work with because of their sturdy stalks and grainy heads.

As you work with rye, you'll notice that adding stalks to the bouquet causes the rye to flare. Flaring is a desirable effect since it creates an attractive contour and adds textural interest to what would otherwise be a plain arrangement.

For variations, you could use other straight-stemmed plant material such as lavender, German statice, or phalaris. You could also make a topiary with shorter lengths of grass for a different look. Should you do this, you'll want to use a smaller pot in order to keep the design in proportion.

Finished Size: 24 inches (61cm) high, 5½ inches (14cm) wide

You Will Need:

Serrated knife

Dry-foam block, 9 inches (22.9cm) long × 4 inches (10.2cm) wide × 3 inches (7.6cm) high

Metal urn with a flared top, 6½ inches (16.5cm) high, with a 5-inch (12.7cm) square opening

100 stems of rye

Florist's scissors

Nylon string

Silk berries on wire

5-inch (12.7cm) square of sheet moss

1.

Use the knife to sculpt the dry foam to fit snugly inside the urn.

2.

Lay the stems of rye on a flat work surface and trim the ends even with scissors.

3.

Gather the stems together, aligning the rye heads in a spray; bind the bouquet 1 inch (2.5cm) below the rye heads with the string.

4.

Hold the bouquet in two hands and push the stems into the foam in the container using steady, even pressure until the bouquet can stand alone (approximately 2 inches [5.1cm] deep).

5.

Wind silk berries around the bouquet to conceal the string.

6.

Conceal the foam with sheet moss.

WALL BOUQUET

The standard topiary is typically associated with orderly rows of material, but this particular arrangement breaks the rules—with beautiful results. Wild grass and flowers are gathered into a bouquet, tied with raffia, then displayed on the wall. The stems of the flowers are cut to accommodate the design of the bouquet; then the flowers are laid down. Textural variety is an important consideration as it adds visual interest: mix spiky flowers with rounder blooms, smooth textures with rough ones.

Because this bouquet is so easy to make and can be composed quickly, you can readily make small arrangements as studies for larger works.

Finished Size: 25 inches (63.5cm) high, 16 inches (40.6cm) wide

You will need:

8 branches of melaleuca foliage (or eucalyptus)

30 blades of isoplexis (or any long-blade grass)

24 stems of larkspur

60-70 stems of red phalaris

40 stems of chamomile, dyed blue

40 stems of chamomile, dyed red

Nylon string

Hank of raffia strands, ¾ inch (1.9cm) in diameter

Display hook

1.

On a flat worktable, lay a bed of foliage and grass so that the stems line up evenly.

2.

Layer one type of flower on top of the foliage, so that the heads are slightly lower than the tallest foliage.

3.

Continue adding layers of flowers in this manner until all the flowers have been used.

4.

Gather the foliage and flowers in a bouquet, covering the front stems with more foliage. Bind the bouquet together with string.

5.

Tie a rope of raffia around the bouquet to conceal the string, twisting the raffia slightly to prevent the short ends from sticking out. Tie the raffia in a large double knot; trim the ends even as shown.

6.

Tie a string in a long loop at the back of the bouquet. To display, hang the bouquet from a hook.

BANDS OF FLOWERS IN A PAINTED TRUG

The impact of this standard-style arrangement is intensified by strong color contrasts, such as the purple phalaris and the golden yarrow, and the blue trug and the deep rose cockscomb. You can readily adapt this design to any flowers you wish to use: try more subtle mixes, such as pastels, or mono-chromatic arrangements, such as a blend of flowers, pods, and leaves in natural tones.

Finished Size: 8½ inches (21.6cm) high × 12½ inches (31.8cm) wide × 6½ inches (16.5cm) deep

You Will Need:

2 dry-foam blocks, 9 inches (22.9cm) long × 4 inches (10.2cm) wide × 3 inches (7.6cm) high

Trug painted blue, 6 inches (15.2cm) high × 12 inches (30.5cm) wide × 6 inches (15.2cm) deep

Adhesive clay (florist's clay tape)

Serrated knife

Florist's scissors

24 stalks of deep rose cockscomb

74 purple phalaris

24 stalks of cream cockscomb

34 magenta tea roses

24 stems of golden yarrow

Ruler and pencil

1.
To prepare the trug, follow Steps 1 and 2 of Dried Vegetables in a Wooden Trug on page 87.

2.
Use the florist's scissors to trim all the stems to 5 inches (12.7cm).

3.
Use the ruler and pencil to mark off 7 equal bands in the foam.

4.
Referring to the photograph, decorate the arrangement as follows: insert a row of deep rose cockscomb in the center band, followed by two even and adjacent bands of purple phalaris. Add cream cockscomb, then magenta tea roses in equal bands. Finish with bands of golden yarrow.

5.
Fill in any bare spots in the bands with like flowers.

THREE-TIERED WHEAT AND ROSES STANDARD

This topiary is a simple variation on Rye with Berries on page 88. A collar of roses and a collar of wheat are added to the central stand of wheat. The result is a sophisticated topiary—without a lot of work.

Finished Size: 22 inches (55.9cm) high, 8 inches (20.3cm) wide

You Will Need:

Serrated knife

Dry-foam block, 9 inches (22.9cm) long × 4 inches (10.2cm) wide × 3 inches (7.6cm) high

Container, 5 inches (12.7cm) high, with a 5½-inch (14cm) diameter opening

100 stems of triticum wheat

Florist's scissors

Nylon string

Silk berries on wire

24 pink tea roses with 12-inch (30.5cm) stems

8-strand raffia hank, 18 inches (45.7cm) long

6 stems of golden yarrow

1.

Follow Steps 1–5 for Rye with Berries on page 88; substitute 60 stems of wheat for the rye.

2.

Trim the rose stems to 11 inches (27.9cm) and insert them around the central standard of wheat.

3.

Trim the remaining 40 stems of wheat to 8 inches (20.3cm) and insert the stems in a collar around the rose stems.

4.

Tie the raffia rope around the standard.

5.

Trim the stems of the yarrow to 2 inches (5.1cm). Insert the yarrow in a collar around the base of the standard.

Chapter 8

TOPIARY VARIATIONS

MOSS CONE IN A CHINA POT

Simple to make, this topiary is a moss-covered cone around which is glued a rope made of the same moss. A variation on the globe topiary, the arrangement was inspired by the hedge sculptures of sixteenth- and seventeenth-century gardens. Conical shapes were popular at this time, as were the diamond, oval, and combinations thereof. Each topiary was scrupulously maintained, and resident gardeners spent much time shaping the unruly branches into ornamental forms including beasts, crests, arches, and gates, in addition to geometrically based structures.

Finished Size: 8½ inches (21.6cm) high, 4½-inch (11.4cm) diameter at base

You Will Need:

Serrated knife

Dry-foam block, 9 inches (22.9cm) long × 4 inches (10.2cm) wide × 3 inches (7.6cm) high

Glazed china pot, 3 inches (7.6cm) high with a 3½-inch (8.9cm) diameter opening

6-inch (15.2cm) long dowel, ¼ inch (0.6cm) in diameter

Small paintbrush

White glue

12 ounces (336g) of reindeer moss

Dry-foam cone, 4½ inches (11.4cm) high, 4-inch (10.2cm) diameter at base

Florist's staples with 1½-inch (3.8cm) legs (See page 39 for "Making Your Own Florist's Staples.")

Green thread

1.

Use the serrated knife to sculpt the dry-foam block to fit snugly inside the pot.

2.

Center and insert the dowel in the foam in the container.

3.

Use the paintbrush to cover the cone lightly with white glue. Wind the reindeer moss into small buns; then cover the entire outer surface of the cone (excluding the underside) with the moss buns. Bind the moss in place with florist's staples.

4.

Make a 28-inch (71.1cm) rope of moss: overlap sections of moss and bind them together at each joint with thread.

5.

Center and impale the moss-covered cone on the dowel.

6.

Working from top to bottom, wind the moss rope around the cone; secure it with florist's staples.

FINIAL OF GREEN AND GOLD LEAVES

In this arrangement, a variation on the dome topiary, a simple dry-foam cone is layered with green and gold leaves, but it would be equally attractive to attach the tiers of leaves to other shapes such as orbs, obelisks, and cubes. The simple flat leaves make the layering process neat and easy.

Finished Size: 10 inches (25.4cm) high, 5½-inch (14cm) diameter at base

You Will Need:

20 lemon leaves or salal painted gold (or follow Step 1 to paint your own leaves)

Newspaper

Gold spray paint

Dry-foam cone, 10 inches (25.4cm) high, 5½-inch (14cm) diameter at base

40 white mallee eucalyptus leaves

Florist's staples

½ yard (45.7cm) of dark green wire-edged ribbon, 1 inch (2.5cm) wide

1.

Prepare gold leaves if necessary: lay the lemon leaves or salal on newspaper and spray paint one side gold. When they are dry, turn the leaves over and spray paint the other side. Let the leaves dry completely.

2.

Working from top to bottom, decorate the cone with leaves: position 1 eucalyptus leaf near the top of the cone and secure it with 2 florist's staples at the bottom of the leaf (the staples will be concealed by the next layer of leaves). Place the next leaf so that it slightly overlaps a side of the first leaf; then secure it with 2 florist's staples.

3.

Working in rounds, position and staple the eucalyptus leaves in place to cover the top ⅔ of the cone. Be sure to conceal the leaf bottoms of each row with the leaf tips of the new row.

4.

Cover the bottom ⅓ of the cone with 2 rounds of gold leaves.

5.

Tie a ribbon bow around the base of the finial for an accent.

Moss Cone and Sphere

A simple variation of Sheet Moss in an Antiqued Pot on page 67, this topiary design puts together a moss-covered cone and sphere to re-create the look of an early English hedge garden.

Finished Size: 16 inches (40.6cm) high, 6 inches (15.2cm) wide

You Will Need:

Terra-cotta pot, 5 inches (12.7cm) high with a 5-inch (12.7cm) diameter opening

1 pound (454g) of florist's clay

17-inch (43.2cm) long dowel, ¼ inch (0.6cm) in diameter

Small paintbrush

White glue

White Styrofoam sphere, 4 inches (10.2cm) in diameter

White Styrofoam cone, 4-inch (10.2cm) diameter at base

Three 8½-inch (21.6cm) × 11-inch (27.9cm) sheets of sheet moss

Florist's staples

Skewer

Green thread

Florist's scissors

24 stems of red chamomile

1.

To weight the pot, fill it with wads of florist's clay to just below the rim.

2.

Center and insert the dowel into the clay.

3.

Use the paintbrush to apply a thin coat of white glue on each foam shape. Cover the foam sphere and cone with sheet moss, securing the foam with florist's staples.

4.

Use the skewer to poke a "starter" hole through the moss-covered sphere; then impale the sphere on the dowel, pushing straight down with even pressure.

5.

Repeat Step 3 for the cone, pushing it down on the dowel until the base of the cone touches the sphere. Wrap the cone and sphere at even intervals with green thread to secure the moss.

6.

Use the florist's scissors to trim the chamomile stems to 2 inches (5.1cm). Referring to the photograph, insert the chamomile into the sphere and cone, using even pressure to push the stems through the outer covering of moss. (If a stem breaks, glue the flower head in place.)

7.

Conceal the florist's clay with sheet moss trimmed to size.

HERB CONE WITH A MINIATURE ROSE BASE

A pretty, decorative accent, this topiary uses culinary herbs. Oregano is featured here, but other herbs, such as sage or bay leaf, could be substituted for an equally attractive result. A larger cone-shaped head would enable you to decorate the topiary with dried chili peppers, garlic, and the like; all you need is a larger container to maintain the correct proportions.

Finished Size: 10½ inches (26.7cm) high, 4-inch (10.2cm) diameter at base

You Will Need:

Terra-cotta pot, 3 inches (7.6cm) high, with a 3¼-inch (8.3cm) diameter opening

Adhesive clay (florist's clay tape)

Dry-foam sphere, 3 inches (7.6cm) in diameter

Hot glue gun and glue sticks

100 miniature pink rosebuds

8-inch (20.3cm) long dowel, ¼ inch (0.6cm) in diameter

Florist's scissors

6–8 rose stems (without flowers)

Dry-foam cone, 4 inches (10.2cm) high, 3½-inch (8.9cm) diameter at base

12 stems of oregano

Brass spool wire

Wire cutters

1.

Follow the directions for making Miniature Rosebuds in a Terra-Cotta Pot on page 50, but do not finish gluing rosebuds in the top center of the dome. Instead, center and insert the dowel in the top center of the dome.

2.

Use the florist's scissors to trim the rose stems to approximately 2 inches (5.1cm) and hot-glue them around the dowel.

3.

Continue hot-gluing rosebuds in a tight row or two to form a collar around the stems at the center of the dome.

4.

Center and impale the foam cone on the dowel, pushing it down to meet the stem-wrapped trunk.

5.

Trim the oregano stems to 2½ inches (6.4cm). Use the wire cutters to cut the brass spool wire; then wire bunches consisting of 4 to 6 stems of oregano.

6.

Hot-glue the oregano bunches to the foam cone in order to cover it completely.

Fruit and Flowers with Rose Stems

A variation on Sea Lavender with a Multistem Trunk on page 76, this topiary style utilizes rose stems that were not used in another topiary, but here serve to conceal the plain wood of the supporting dowel. The large globe head is decorated with an abundance of dried flowers to create a contrast of textures and colors. Silk berries and grapes and dried orange slices add interesting accents.

Finished Size: 20 inches (50.8cm) high, 13 inches (33cm) in diameter

You Will Need:

Saber saw

18-inch (45.7cm) long dowel, $\frac{1}{2}$ inch (1.3cm) in diameter

8 wedges of dry foam, approximately 5 inches (12.7cm) long

Terra-cotta pot, $5\frac{1}{2}$ inches (14cm) high, with a 6-inch (15.2cm) diameter opening

Plaster of paris

Plastic mixing bowl

Wooden paint stirrer

Styrofoam sphere, 6 inches (15.2cm) in diameter

Adhesive clay (florist's clay tape)

General-purpose scissors

Packing tape

Medium-gauge wire

Florist's scissors

8 pink tea roses with 10-inch (25.4cm) stems

Wire cutters

Brass spool wire

10 stems of sea lavender

4 stalks of deep pink cockscomb

4 stalks of cream cockscomb

10 blue mop-headed hydrangea

3 yellow tansy

6 golden yarrow

6 white strawflowers

6 yellow strawflowers

4 gold strawflowers

10 blue salvia

4 orange slices (purchase commercially dried orange slices, or dry your own on chicken wire; see the directions on page 25)

4 small silk grape clusters

6 clusters of gold silk berries

6-inch (15.2cm) disk of sheet moss

1.

Follow the directions for "Constructing the Basic Globe Topiary with a Weighted Container" on page 42. Wire any elements without stems or in need of reinforcement following the directions in Chapter 3, "Preparing Plant Material."

2.

Use the florist's scissors to cut the rose heads from their stems $4\frac{1}{2}$ inches (11.4cm) below the head. Set the rose heads aside.

3.

Conceal the dowel with rose stems. Use the wire cutters to cut lengths of brass wire; then secure the rose stems to the base and midpoint of the dowel.

4.

Trim the stems of the sea lavender to $4\frac{1}{2}$ inches (11.4cm) and insert them in the foam in a soft spray pattern.

5.

Insert the remaining dried materials: beginning with the largest pieces and working down to the smallest, insert one type of material at a time, distributing the stems evenly on the topiary head.

6.

Fill in any bare areas with hydrangea florets.

7.

Conceal the plaster with sheet moss trimmed to size.

HEART-SHAPED TOPIARY

This heart-shaped topiary puts to use a great variety of dried material and is a terrific way to utilize broken flower heads and sprigs left over from other projects. The mix of delicate pastel blooms along with the open heart-shaped topiary head lends the arrangement a very romantic touch. If you prefer, an open circle, or any free-form shape, could take the place of the heart. The only technical difference would be substituting an appropriately shaped metal frame for the one used here.

Finished Size: 14 inches (35.6cm) high, 8 inches (20.3cm) wide

You Will Need:

Saber saw

5-inch (12.7cm) long dowel, ½ inch (1.3cm) in diameter

4–5 dry-foam wedges, 4 inches (10.2cm) long × 1 inch (2.5cm) wide

Terra-cotta pot, 5 inches (12.7cm) high, with a 5½-inch (14cm) diameter opening

Plaster of paris

Plastic mixing bowl

Wooden paint stirrer

Wire cutters

Wire clothes hanger

Pliers

Medium-gauge spool wire

Heart-shaped wire frame, 8 inches (20.3cm) high

Green thread

2 to 3 ounces (56–85g) of sphagnum moss

Hot glue gun and glue sticks

48 pink tea roses

60 miniature rosebuds

20 pink strawflowers

20 white strawflowers

Sprigs of sea lavender, larkspur, golden yarrow, purple statice, yellow statice, and boxwood

Two 8½-inch (21.6cm) × 11-inch (27.9cm) sheets of sheet moss

1.

Follow Steps 1–5 in the directions for "Constructing the Basic Globe Topiary with a Weighted Container" on pages 42–43.

2.

Use the wire cutters to cut the crossbar off the wire hanger so that the hook and two arms remain; use the pliers to bend the hook straight.

3.

Use the spool wire to bind the straightened hook to the center of the dowel.

4.

Bend the arms in a V and attach them to the V of the heart frame using spool wire; make certain that the heart frame is secure.

5.

Use thread to bind wads of sphagnum moss to the heart frame.

6.

Hot-glue flowers in a colorful variety to all surfaces of the moss-covered heart; finish with sprig accents.

7.

Conceal the plaster in the pot with sheet moss trimmed to size.

Maypole Wreath

This variation on the globe topiary, because of the use of a dowel, was also inspired by the open nature of the Heart-Shaped Topiary on page 109. Suspended from the stem with white ribbons, this innovative topiary head features delicate blossoms in white and blue. White ribbon streamers top the stem in maypole fashion to complete the design's airy spring look.

Finished Size: 22 inches (55.9cm) high, 18 inches (45.7cm) wide

You Will Need:

Saber saw

22-inch (55.9cm) long dowel, ¾ inch (1.9cm) in diameter

6–8 dry-foam wedges, approximately 4 inches (10.2cm) long × 1 inch (2.5cm) wide

Terra-cotta pot, 5 inches (12.7cm) high, 5½ inches (14cm) in diameter

Container, 12 inches (30.5cm) high, with a 12-inch (30.5cm) outer diameter

Plaster of paris

Wooden paint stirrer

Plastic mixing bowl

Straw wreath, 16 inches (40.6cm) in diameter

8 ounces (227g) of sphagnum moss

Green heavyweight thread

Florist's scissors

24 white strawflowers

10 white silk roses

16 stems of purple larkspur

12 stems of light green love-lies-bleeding

40 stems of chamomile, dyed blue

6 stems of purple statice

6 stems of golden yarrow

Hot glue gun and glue sticks

4 yards (43.8m) of white satin ribbon, ¾ inch (1.9cm) wide

Wire cutters

Brass spool wire

Container, 12 inches (30.5cm) high, with a 12-inch (30.5cm) outer diameter

Two 8½-inch (21.6cm) × 11-inch (27.9cm) sheets of sheet moss

1.

Follow Steps 1–5 in the directions for "Constructing the Basic Globe Topiary with a Weighted Container" on pages 42–43 for the terra-cotta pot.

2.

Prepare the wreath for decoration by binding overlapping wads of sphagnum moss on all surfaces of the wreath using heavy-weight thread.

3.

Use the florist's scissors to trim all stems to 4 inches (10.2cm).

4.

Hot-glue the dried and silk floral materials around the wreath, starting with the largest pieces and working down to the small-est. Work with one type of floral material at a time and distribute it evenly. Alternate heights of adjacent flowers and foliage to create an airy effect.

5.

Wind the ribbon around the center dowel, securing it with dabs of hot glue; cut the ribbon when the dowel is covered.

6.

Lay a 1-yard (91.4cm) length of ribbon horizontally across the center of the wreath; wrap the loose ends around the wreath and tie them in a knot at each side to secure. Repeat with another 1-yard (91.4cm) length of ribbon, laying it over the wreath vertically.

7.

Cut an 8-inch (20.3cm) length of ribbon and tie it at the intersection of the ribbons to secure.

8.

Referring to the photograph, balance the intersection of ribbons on the dowel and bind it tightly in place with wire.

9.

Place the arrangement in a larger decorative container. Finish by adding streamers and bows as desired.

10.

Conceal the plaster in the pot with sheet moss trimmed to size.

APPENDICES

CARING FOR DRIED-FLOWER TOPIARIES

Do not move topiaries frequently or vigorously. Dried-flower topiaries should be handled gently, as their dried petals and leaves are intrinsically fragile. Moving the topiary frequently from one location to another increases the risk of its being bumped and broken, so try to select a safer, more permanent setting for display, such as a mantel, shelf, table, or cold hearth. If you must move a topiary, hold the container from underneath and keep the weight of the head equally distributed as you carry the arrangement to its new location.

Do not expose topiaries to direct sunlight. Subject to fading, dried materials should be kept out of direct sunlight. A room with northern or southern exposure is best, as it gets indirect light. If direct light is unavoidable, a curtain or shade can help to retard bleaching. Never display a topiary outside in the sun or leave it outdoors.

Keep topiaries in a cool, dry environment. Excessive humidity will cause petals and leaves to soften and droop. This is why you should avoid displaying or storing dried-flower arrangements in a bathroom or kitchen.

If humidity is a real problem where you live, you may wish to use a dehumidifier or store your topiary in an airtight container, such as a plastic garbage can or large biscuit tin, and display it in drier months. To prepare an airtight container, simply place a few inches of silica gel on the bottom of the container that is large enough to hold the entire construction and place the topiary inside. Close the container lid and secure it with masking tape. Store the container in a cool, dry, dimly lit place until you are ready to display the topiary again.

Cleaning and Repairing Dried-Flower Topiaries

It is natural for a topiary to suffer some breakage and fading, but here are a few suggestions for keeping arrangements in top condition.

To remove dust from flowers and foliage, gently brush the bristles of a soft artist's paintbrush over the surface of each element. To remove dust on very delicate elements, dampen a cotton swab with a little water and dab gently.

The three most common topiary repairs are: replacing a flower head or leaf, creating a false stem or reinforcing a weak one, and rejuvenating the color of a faded arrangement.

You can reaffix or replace a broken flower head or leaf as follows. Gently grasp the stem with a pair of tweezers; then place a dab of hot glue on the blunt end of the stem underneath the flower or leaf stub. Hold everything in place until the glue sets up (this takes only a few seconds).

To create a false stem or to reinforce a weak one, refer to "Wiring and Wrapping Stems" on page 30.

Sometimes faded flowers and foliage are pretty in themselves, or make a nice contrasting backdrop for added material. To freshen a faded arrangement, add more vibrantly colored flowers by inserting the new plant material between the faded blooms or in specific patterns. You can also spray paint the entire construction with acrylic paint.

Finally, a dried-flower topiary may be too unattractive to display any longer. Simply remove the dried blooms from the container, keeping any salvageable materials. To reuse the container, clean it with a damp cloth. Pots that have been weighted with plaster of paris are reusable: just remove the head of the old topiary, snipping away any tape that held the foam in place. You can then position a new head on the dowel and redecorate it.

Most dry foam that has been pierced with stems or other sharp items is not reusable, as in the example of a globe topiary head that has broken off its stem. In this case, the foam head will need to be replaced, as the channel in the foam will no longer be snug enough to hug the dowel. It is possible, however, to reuse the foam topiary head for decorative material that doesn't need to be inserted. Simply wrap the foam with a cover material, such as sheet moss, and use hot glue to adhere the new decoration.

DRIED FLOWERS AND FOLIAGE USED IN THIS BOOK

LATIN NAME	COMMON NAME
Achillea sp.	Yarrow
Amaranthus caudatus	Love-lies-bleeding
Anthemis nobilis	Chamomile
Buxus sp.	Boxwood
Carthamus tinctorius	Safflower
Celosia cristata	Cockscomb
Cladonia rangiferina	Reindeer moss
Craspedia globosa	Craspedia
Cynara Scolymus	Globe artichoke
Delphinium Consolida	Larkspur
Eucalyptus sp.	Eucalyptus
Gaultheria Shallon	Salal, Lemon leaves
Helianthus sp.	Sunflower
Helichrysum bracteatum	Strawflower
Hydrangea macrophylla	French hydrangea
Ilex sp.	Holly
Isoplexis sp.	Isoplexis
Lavandula sp.	Lavender
Limonium sp.	Sea lavender
Limonium sinuatum	Statice
Melaleuca sp.	Melaleuca
Mnium sp.	Sheet moss
Myristica fragrans	Nutmeg
Nelumbo nucifera	Lotus pod
Origanum vulgare	Oregano
Papaver sp.	Poppy
Phalaris arundinacea	Phalaris
Pinus sp.	Pine (cones)
Rosa sp.	Rose
Salix Matsudana 'Tortuosa'	Curly willow, Corkscrew
Salvia azurea	Blue salvia
Secale sp.	Rye
Sphagnum sp.	Sphagnum moss
Tanacetum vulgare	Tansy
Triticum sp.	Wheat
Vitis sp.	Grapevine

SOURCES

The great appeal of making your own topiaries is that most of the necessary tools and materials are readily available from your local florist, hardware store, and craft store—not to mention your kitchen utensil drawer and toolbox. But here are some ideas of where to find the tools of the trade.

TOOLS AND MATERIALS

Pliers, wire cutters, saber saws, dowels, plaster of paris, nylon string, and spool wire can be found at your local hardware store. An inexpensive version of the saber saw designed for cutting dry foam is available at craft stores.

Pruning shears and florist's scissors can be found at most garden supply stores.

Chances are, you already own skewers, general-purpose and serrated knives, and general-purpose scissors. If not, these items can be found in the housewares section of most department stores and in some hardware stores.

Styrofoam, dry-foam (Oasis) blocks, planks, adhesive clay (florist's clay tape), cones, spheres, hot glue guns and glue sticks, florist's clay, stem wrap, and florist's staples and picks can be found at most craft stores and florist's supply shops.

Dried flowers, florist's scissors, spool wire, and stub wire are available in a wide variety at craft stores, at florist shops, and at some garden supply stores. Of course, dried flowers and foliage can be found in your own garden or can be "recycled" from fresh cut flowers that have peaked.

Containers can be found at department stores, at garden supply stores, and in gift and stationery shops. Check also for interesting finds at flea markets, garage sales, antique stores, and thrift shops.

RECOMMENDED READING

Hillier, Malcolm, ed. *Flower Arranging*. New York: The Reader's Digest Association, Inc., 1990.

_____, and Colin Hilton. *The Book of Dried Flowers*. New York: Simon and Schuster, 1986.

Packer, Jane. *Jane Packer's New Flower Arranging*. London: Trafalgar Square Publishing, 1994.

Tolley, Emelie, and Chris Meade. *Gifts From the Herb Garden*. New York: Clarkson Potter Publishers, 1991.

Turner, Kenneth. *Flower Style*. New York: Weidenfeld & Nicholson, 1989.

_____. *The Floral Decorator*. New York: Random House, 1993.

INDEX